FOR ME
FATE
WOVE THIS

ALSO BY OCTAVIA RANDOLPH

Sidroc the Dane

The Circle of Ceridwen

Ceridwen of Kilton

The Claiming

The Hall of Tyr

Tindr

Silver Hammer, Golden Cross

Wildswept

The Circle of Ceridwen Cookery Book(let)

Light, Descending

The Tale of Melkorka: A Novella

Ride: A Novella

BOOK EIGHT

THE CIRCLE OF CERIDWEN SAGA

FOR ME FATE WOVE THIS

OCTAVIA RANDOLPH

PYEWACKET PRESS

For Me Fate Wove This is the eighth book in
The Circle of Ceridwen Saga by Octavia Randolph
Copyright 2021 Octavia Randolph

ISBN Softcover: 978-1-942044-30-7
ISBN Hardcover: 978-1-942044-31-4

Book cover design by DesignforBooks.com. Maps by Michael Rohani. Photo credits: Image creation, textures and graphics by Michael Rohani; Raven in flight © Erik Mandre/Shutterstock; Long exposure of Milky Way © Anakin Fox/Shutterstock; String © xpixel/Shutterstock.

Pyewacket Press
The Circle of Ceridwen Saga employs British spellings, alternate spellings, archaic words, and oftentimes unusual verb to subject placement. This is intentional. A Glossary of Terms will be found at the end of the novel.

LIST OF CHARACTERS

Hrald, son of Ælfwyn and Sidroc, Jarl of the
Danish keep of Four Stones in Lindisse

Asberg, uncle to Hrald, brother-in-law to Ælfwyn,
in command at the fortress of Turcesig

Jari, a warrior of Four Stones, chief body-guard to Hrald

Haward, a young Danish war-chief

Dagmar, a young woman of the Danes

Inkera, a young woman of the Danes

Siggerith, a child, daughter of the
late Thorfast, killed by Hrald

Ælfwyn, mother to Ashild and Hrald, widowed
of Yrling; marriage dissolved with Sidroc

Burginde, companion and nurse to Ælfwyn

Ashild, daughter of Ælfwyn and the late
Yrling, Hrald's older half-sister

Ealhswith, daughter to Ælfwyn

Kjeld, a body-guard to Hrald

Sigewif, Abbess of Oundle

Bova, consecrated nun and brewster at Oundle

Æthelthryth, sister to Ælfwyn, wed to Asberg

Bork, an orphan boy, taken in by Hrald

v

Wilgot, the priest of Four Stones

Styrbjörn, second in command at Turcesig

Onund, a warrior, formerly of Four Stones

Ceric, son of Ceridwen and Gyric,
grandson of Godwulf of Kilton

Worr, the horse-thegn of Kilton, pledged man of Ceric

Eadward, Prince of Wessex, son of Ælfred

Ælfred, King of Wessex

Raedwulf, Bailiff of Defenas in Wessex

Modwynn, Lady of Kilton, widow of Godwulf

Edgyth, Lady of Kilton, widow of Godwin,
mother by adoption to Edwin

Edwin, Ceric's younger brother, Lord of Kilton in Wessex

Eorconbeald, Captain of Edwin's body-
guard, and **Alwin**, his second

Cadmar, a warrior-monk of Kilton

Dunnere, the priest of Kilton

Begu, a woman of Kilton

Aszur, ship master and captain

Rannveig, a brewster on Gotland, mother of Tindr

Ceridwen, Mistress of the hall Tyrsborg on
the island of Gotland, wife to Sidroc

Sidroc the Dane, formerly Jarl of South Lindisse

Eirian and **Yrling**, twin children of Ceridwen and Sidroc; **Rodiaud**, their little sister

Tindr, a bow hunter, and **Šeará**, his Sámi wife

Juoksa, their son, and **Jaské**, their daughter

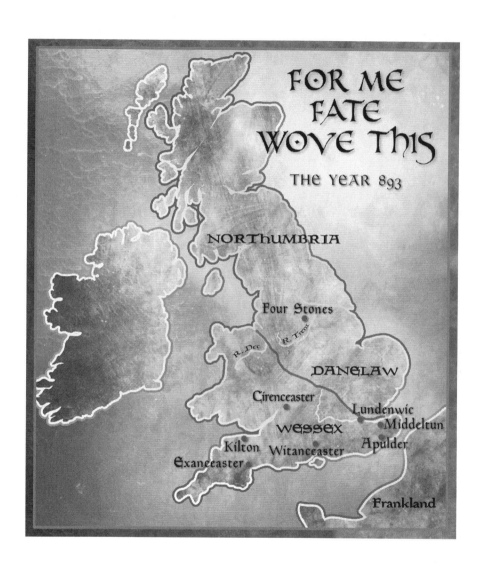

FOR ME
FATE
WOVE THIS

THE YEAR 893

NORTHUMBRIA

Four Stones

R. Dee

R. Tren

DANELAW

Cirenceaster

Lundenwic
Middeltun

WESSEX

Kilton Witanceaster
Apulder

Exanceaster

Frankland

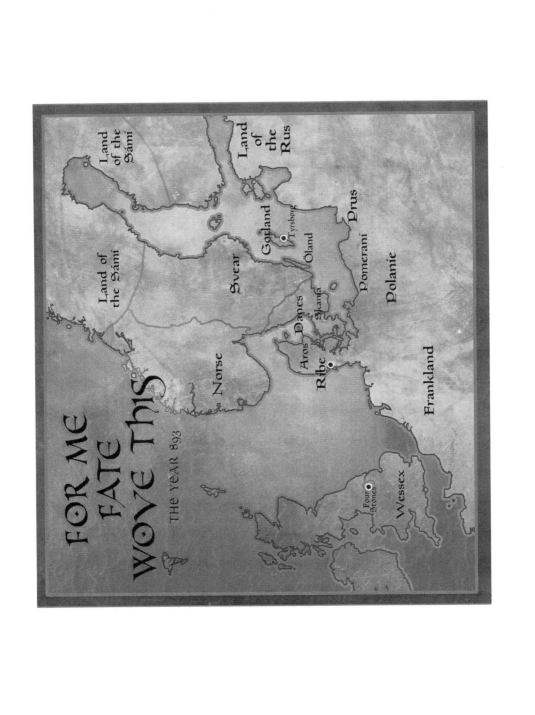

FOR ME
FATE
WOVE THIS

THE YEAR 893

Land of the Sámi

Land of
the Sámi

Land of the Rus

Norse

Svear

Gotland
Tyrsborg
Öland

Prus

Pomerani

Polanie

Aros
Danes
Skania
Ribe

Frankland

Four
Stones
Wessex

CONTENTS

FOR ME
FATE
WOVE THIS

You have given yourself to something, know it or not. A deeper pledge, a sacred claim, dwells in the heart of all. Whether gold-crowned King or wretched slave, you must go into the vault of your own soul, and see what lies enshrined there.

A KING'S DAUGHTER

Four Stones, South Lindisse, Angle-land

Summer, The Year 893

HRALD turned in his saddle to look at the ranks of men behind him. The ruddy clay road was dry and well-worn, and with twenty horses they had kicked up considerable dust this morning. Hrald and his troop were close unto the gates of their neighbour Haward's hall, and his men who had been fronting him had all shifted to the rear. Whenever he travelled past the reaches of Four Stones' lands, his chief body-guard Jari insisted that Hrald stay in the middle of the files of men riding with them, so they might quickly close up around him in case of attack. As ever, Jari was fast on his left, where his broad shield, held in Jari's right hand, would supply added cover for Hrald.

Now that the gates of their destination were in view, Hrald could approach as was his due, fronting his men.

The young Jarl's anticipation had only grown during the ride. He was come to escort Dagmar, daughter of Guthrum, the late King of the Danes in Anglia, to Four Stones, and thence on to view the religious foundation at Oundle. When he had escorted her back after her first visit to his hall, he had asked her to extend her stay with her cousin Haward a few more days, so he might take her to see the famed stone church at Oundle, and be presented to the esteemed Abbess Sigewif. This would not only allow Hrald more time in the young woman's company, but permit his mother, Ælfwyn, Lady of Four Stones to know her more. There was a third reason he had sought this visit. Hrald had great respect for the Abbess' opinion. After Dagmar had voiced her interest in seeing Oundle, he knew this outing would provide both chance and setting for Dagmar to win her approval, as well.

Yet Dagmar had hesitated. She was travelling with her half sister, Inkera, to whom she also had an obligation. Inkera's uncle expected them at Cruland, had undoubtedly made preparation for their reception. But perhaps the Cruland visit might be made rather shorter, and then the sisters return to Haward's hall. So it was that two weeks after Hrald had first seen the elder daughter of Guthrum, he rode once more to bring Dagmar to Four Stones.

Hrald's uncle, Asberg, also rode with him this morning, flanking his nephew. Hrald had placed him in command of the lately-won garrison of Turcesig, but on hearing of Hrald's plan to again see Dagmar, Asberg would take advantage of a call on the maid's cousin, Haward.

The guards on the palisade ramparts had already whistled their arrival, and the double wooden gates were swung open to admit Hrald's party. Haward was just within, at the door of his hall, and next to him stood his young cousin Inkera, beaming at the newcomers. On Haward's other side stood Dagmar. Her smile was modest, her fine teeth covered by her full and well-formed lips, but her interest real, for her deep blue eyes found Hrald's and held them for a moment in welcome.

Once off their horses, the beasts were led to water, and the men into the hall. They wiped the dust from their clothes, washed their hands in the offered basins, and all took up ale with their host and his cousins. Further refreshment was brought from the kitchen yard, in the form of small oaten cakes. Fast behind this platter was the person of Siggerith, Haward's little niece. She took a cake in each small hand and with a shy smile ran out of the side door of the hall. The brilliant Sun which had shone all during the ride was still shining, and most of the young people followed the child out into the work yard.

It was their host Haward who stayed behind, with Asberg. Haward, though not much older than Hrald, felt sure that the older man wished to speak to him. Haward nodded dismissal to the serving woman who remained by the table. Whatever Asberg wished to say should be heard only by him.

Once she left, Asberg would brook no delay. He tilted his head toward the door through which his nephew had passed.

"Dagmar," he began. "Is there anything a man who would wed her should know?"

Asberg's abruptness was so great that Haward might have grinned but for the seriousness of his guest's tone.

"You speak as though Hrald has made up his mind about her," Haward answered.

Just now his cousin and Hrald were walking toward the paddock together, and could be seen through the open door. They were laughing about something, and no one looking on could have faulted them as a couple. Strikingly tall, both dark-haired, they suited one another.

"He may have," Asberg allowed. "And the times push men to action." He did not need to say more, with war so near at hand. He gave Haward a searching look.

Asberg's clear blue eyes demanded answer. Haward broke that look by glancing again at the couple as they walked in the sunlight. He recalled a rumour, some re-pressed scandal concerning one of her father Guthrum's body-guards, but knew nothing factual of it. And whatever it had been was over, over and done. If Dagmar had caught the eye of the young Jarl of South Lindisse, his would not be the staying hand. He would not destroy his cousin's chance at this marriage, which would benefit him as well.

After a pause he gave his answer. "I know of nothing."

Asberg did not respond at once. The younger man's hesitation had been enough. Had it been caused by a thoughtful searching of Haward's memory, or by a deci-sion to conceal, Asberg wondered. At any rate, Hrald's uncle would not now broach the topic of bride-price. Haward had been more than candid about the girl, admit-ting to Asberg that her late father, despite his Kingship, had left Dagmar and her sisters nothing. Asberg would wait. The girl was still to spend more time with Hrald's mother Ælfwyn, and meet the Abbess Sigewif. No dis-cussion could be begun this soon, despite Hrald's grow-ing interest.

The horses having been watered, the party made ready to leave for Four Stones. Hrald saw that two saddle horses awaited Dagmar and Inkera. He was more than glad that Dagmar could thus ride at his side, but wondered about their serving woman.

He looked about, expecting to see a waggon or cart readied, which would carry such a woman, and the sisters' necessaries for their stay. Leathern packs had been fastened to the saddle rings of the sisters' mounts, but he saw no more than this.

"Your serving woman," he asked, glancing about for such a one.

Dagmar gave the slightest pause. Then she smiled at him, a frank and open smile.

"I travel with none," she admitted.

Hrald nodded. Of course, he thought, once you are in the halls of your kin there is no need; there will be many women there to serve you. Yet, given the travelling the sisters had been doing, it puzzled him, too. All ladies of estate had at least one serving maid or woman with them to care for their clothes and person. Her not requiring one surprised him, and added to his admiration. It was another proof of the self-sufficiency of her nature, that when travelling she could live almost as simply as a man.

She was dressed just as he had recalled her when they met, in a green long-sleeved shift, over which a gown of midnight blue was fastened at the shoulders with large oval bronze brooches. These brooches Dagmar bore were unlike any Hrald had ever seen before their first meeting, for they were studded with pearls set in silver mounts, four pearls to each brooch. Between those brooches were strung strands of fine silver chain, and one doubled strand of rare rock crystal beads, spaced by pierced beads of silver. It was these roundels of crystal that the long fingers of her hands often returned to, when she was thoughtful. Attired thus, and with her height, her abundant dark and glossy brown hair, and the dark and strongly arched eyebrows, she was arresting in every way. And Dagmar had something rare in a woman her age, presence. She lent a kind of maturity to Hrald's youthfulness. Dagmar made him feel older, more assured, as she was. Her assurance gave him confidence in himself.

Hrald helped first Inkera and then Dagmar to their horses, giving them his hand as they stepped upon the mounting block, and holding steady the animals' heads as they mounted. Inkera was also just as he recalled, smiling and laughing. He smiled back, remembering he had met her first, and wondering how he ever found her mere prettiness attractive, even for a moment. Charming as she was, Inkera's airling and girlish charms now seemed trivial.

Dagmar had wanted her half sister to accompany her on this outing. Inkera was the only chaperone she had, and would make her visit to the Jarl more seemly, even though Hrald's mother be with them the whole time. Inkera was glad at the prospect of returning to Four Stones, a hall in which she had found much to admire, not the least being the appreciative eyes of the young men housed there.

Of the trip to Oundle she was less certain, for as she laughed to her sister, "It is nought but nuns and monks."

The sisters would spend two nights at Four Stones; the first so that they might get an early start on their way to Oundle, and so return to Four Stones on the same day; the second to set out at leisure back to their cousin Haward's hall.

When the party arrived at Four Stones they were greeted by Ælfwyn and both of Hrald's sisters, his older

sister Ashild, and his younger, Ealhswith. The importance of this visit was reflected in the care with which
these three were dressed. As Lady of Four Stones, Hrald's
mother was attired each day in a gown and head wrap
appropriate to her station. Her gown today was of an
almost moss green, the veil-like wrap upon her head of
ivory hue, and fastened into her hair with straight pins
with golden heads. She had been the possessor of rare
and costly jewellery in her life, much of which she had
granted to the Benedictine foundation of Oundle for
its growth and endowment. Yet today she had added
to the richness of her garb by pinning on a golden pin
which she had owned since girlhood. It was one her own
mother had given her, she who was now a nun at Oundle.
Although Ælfleda had left the world to live as a clois-
tered sister, it was important to Ælfwyn that she meet
the young woman who had quickly come to dominate
her grandson's thoughts.

For Ashild's part, she had consented to wear one
of her mother's fine linen head wraps rather than those
of far sturdier weave she typically tied about her head.
Unlike her mother, who had never forsaken the Saxon
style of long-sleeved gown, Ashild had early adopted the
Danish way of dressing. She was thus dressed as Dagmar
and Inkera were, in a long-sleeved shift, over which was
pulled a sleeveless over-gown, fastened at its shoulder
straps with bronze brooches. Ashild possessed two pairs
of these brooches, both large and oval. She had selected
the more cleanly wrought pair, her better set, to wear
for their visit, and these held the long straps of her deep
yellow gown. Her young sister Ealhswith dressed as did
their mother, and this morning in a light blue gown

looked as lovely as any maid nearing fourteen years could be. About her slender wrist she wore a silver bracelet she favoured, one brought her by Ceric of Kilton the same day he had given Ashild a gown of golden silk.

After the welcome ale taken in the hall, the sisters were shown to the timber house of Asberg and Æthelthryth, where they would sleep. Since Hrald had won the garrison keep of Turcesig his aunt and uncle had moved there to run it. Ashild, who lived with them here at Four Stones, had gone with them at first, to aid her aunt in the setting up of Turcesig's hall, but had returned home to Four Stones. She surrendered the small house now to their guests, to sleep in the bower house with her mother and her mother's nurse-companion, Burginde.

That night both Dagmar and Inkera would sit with Ashild at the women's table. This was the table where the unmarried girls and women of the hall sat, and was presided over by Burginde. Ashild sat always by her right side, and Ealhswith at the nurse's left. As she waited for their guests to arrive Ashild looked about her.

Ashild had never travelled to Headleage, where Guthrum had kept his main hall, but she doubted that any having seen that royal residence would find Four Stones wanting. She was herself often late to the evening meal, hurrying in from where she had been at the valley of horses or at some other activity which absorbed her. Tonight she well knew she must be there at table to welcome Dagmar and Inkera when they arrived, and had not needed her mother's reminder as she combed her hair in the bower house. Being there early as the hall filled allowed Ashild to take in its sights and sounds, and as the procession of serving folk began massing in the kitchen passageway, the smells of approaching food as well. The dark red and creamy white blocks of the stone floor had rippled in waves away from her as she entered from the side door. The lower portion of the walls were stone, giving the hall its name. Upon this foundation thick oak planks made up the rest of the walls. Her mother had them lime-washed years ago, and the whitened boards reflected much light as a result. Ashild had no memory of them being dark. The alcoves pocketed about the long sides of the hall were draped with thick woollen curtains, and the fire-pit ran along the centre, warming all during Winter's cold. Tonight in Summer's warmth the smallest of fires burnt there at either end, to lend more light to the oil cressets upon the tables and the iron torches angled out from the walls. At the far end from the front door stood the high table, which was left up day and night, unlike those of trestle make which were knocked down after supping. Behind this, affixed to the wall, was a length of linen fabric which her mother and Burginde had worked years ago, to replace a drawing done in charcoal upon the bare wood boards. It was a raven in flight the two women had worked, laid down in coloured thread, the emblem of the Danes. Also upon that wall, hanging in honour, was a round red and black shield, a deep crack in one of its alder boards. It had hung there but a few months, and was that which Hrald had used in his single contest with Thorfast. Ashild's eye, falling on it now, thought how strange it was that Hrald now courted the cousin of a man he had killed.

She would not let her thoughts linger there; they touched too close to her own tangled circumstances. But as she looked upon her brother's shield the door to the treasure room opened and he stepped out. Their eyes met at once; the first place he would look was to where he might find Dagmar, who had yet to arrive. But he smiled at his sister, and she, seeing his gladness, was forced to smile back. Her smile deepened as she became aware he had spent no little time at his own dressing. Their mother and Burginde made all of Hrald's clothes, and lavished the attention on his tunics and leggings which might be expected. Tonight he wore a tunic of a warm brown, nearly that shade of his hair. At collar and cuffs Ælfwyn had worked interlocking chains of golden yellow wool, set off with a small curling spiral design in bright blue within each link. On his right arm he wore a broad band of hammered gold encircling his wrist. It was one of the great treasures of the hall, something his father had been awarded by Guthrum. His wearing it now for the daughter of the man who had given it had an aptness that again reminded Ashild how tight was the circuit within which their lives revolved.

Her mother appeared, with Wilgot the priest, and took their places at the high table, and Burginde, who had entered with her mistress, took her own place next to Ashild, Ealhswith at her side. The hall was loud now with the voices of the massed men and their wives and families, and the serving folk who carried the ale had begun moving amongst the tables. Then the side door was opened again, to admit Dagmar and Inkera. Ashild stood up from her bench and extended her hand to them in greeting. The eyes of most at the high table were turned to the new arrivals, and the pinkness of Dagmar's cheek as she held her skirts in her hands and made her way to the table was both becoming and unexpected.

Everyone would be watching her, Ashild knew, and even as a King's daughter such scrutiny could not be pleasant. Inkera on the other hand, moved with raised head, her smile as she gazed upon the ranks of tables one of almost childish delight.

Ashild would do what she could to place both sisters at ease, yet was grateful that the eating of a meal demanded its own time and attention. She herself would eat well tonight; she must. On the morrow upon awakening she would feel sick enough, and be able to take no food.

As Dagmar took her place on the bench at the woman's table, Ælfwyn performed the task she did every night at the high table. She took ewer in hand and poured out ale for those who sat in honour with her. First was her son, Jarl of Four Stones, next Wilgot the priest, then Jari her son's chief body-guard, then the rest of the men who had won the right by prowess of arms to claim a seat at that table. Lastly she filled her own cup. Hrald was not able to sit with Dagmar, but as he raised his cup he looked at her, and she raised hers in return.

That night after the hall had quieted, the silver cups locked away, and the bronze cups numbered and returned to their own chests, Ælfwyn retreated to her bower house. Burginde had ever slept there in an alcove, and since Ashild's return from Turcesig a second bed had been carried in as well. Ælfwyn was tired and would welcome sleep, and one look at her daughter's face told her Ashild would as well. Tomorrow would bring the ride to Oundle and the presentation of Dagmar to the

Abbess Sigewif. It would be a long and full day, one of importance, as the Lady of Four Stones placed great stock in the wisdom and judgement of the Abbess. But before Ælfwyn kissed Ashild goodnight, she must return to a topic that she and her daughter had earlier discussed.

"I will not go to Oundle," Ashild had told her before their guests had arrived. "I will welcome the time alone."

"That may be," her mother returned, "but both for my own sake and for Hrald's I would welcome your presence there." Her mother smiled then, and spoke what she knew was a truth. "And you know the Abbess takes special delight in you."

Ashild had ready answer for this, and gave the slightest toss of her head as she spoke it.

"The Abbess will have her mind occupied with Dagmar and Hrald. I will stay here."

Rather than press the point, Ælfwyn let it drop. Yet when alone she took up a quill and wrote a short message to the Abbess, entrusting it to one of Hrald's picked men.

"Kjeld," she told him, "I bid you take this letter to the Abbess Sigewif. Place it in her own hand, and await her answer. Do so in all haste."

Ælfwyn had days earlier sent a letter to the Abbess, telling her of Dagmar, and alerting her that she and Hrald would be bringing that maiden to Oundle to present her. Now she found herself sending a second, far shorter missive, telling of Ashild's reluctance to come to this meeting.

Kjeld had arrived back at Four Stones just before the evening meal, and given her the response from the Abbess. It was written on the back of Ælfwyn's own short letter, proof of the decisive haste of that Reverend Mother's answer. Ælfwyn now handed the letter to Ashild, who read the single line.

"It is my express desire that Ashild be present."

The bold signature at the bottom fully conveyed the command.

"Sigewif," Ashild repeated.

Ælfwyn would ride in a light waggon to Oundle, and offered her daughter the chance to do the same. Skilled horse-woman as she was Ashild had always scorned travelling by waggon, and did so today. Yet she checked the impatient motion of her head, and murmured, "I will ride, as long as I am able," an admission which made her mother bestow a kiss on her daughter's brow. "I know you will take care," her mother whispered back.

Ashild chose her bay mare for the trip; it was her favourite mare, and she had no wish to ride the white stallion Thorfast had given her, nor could imagine doing so now, before Dagmar. Hrald was on his bay stallion, and Dagmar and Inkera on the horses they had been lent from Haward. They were decent animals, but Ashild could guess that her brother secretly wished to give Dagmar one of his own fine mares or geldings for the trip.

Burginde sat with Ælfwyn in the waggon, the reins held by one of the hall's trusted drovers. Another thirty men surrounded them, riding in ranks of four, with Hrald, Dagmar, Inkera, and Ashild making up the riders just before the waggon, and the thirty picked men taking up position at the head and rear of this column. Asberg was not amongst this party; he had returned to Turcesig to resume his duties there. Jari rode alone, just in front of the line in which Hrald did. Two men acting as scouts rode ahead a short distance. To travel thus on Four Stones' own lands was unheard of in Hrald's experience, yet when he had suggested these numbers Jari had nodded in agreement. No less could be expected with the warriors of the renegade Dane Haesten ravening throughout Anglia and Wessex. All of Hrald's men were almost as heavily armed as if they rode to war, with spears, swords, knives, and those who owned them, ring-shirts and helmets. The presence of the Jarl's mother, sister, and he himself demanded such precaution. Add to this the two daughters of Guthrum and the numbers of their guard were fully justified.

Ashild was riding at the end of her row. Inkera, who was next her, turned often to speak with Dagmar and Hrald, allowing Ashild to fall into an almost meditative silence of her own. The stretch of pounded clay road from Four Stones to Oundle passed amongst the most pleasant of her home's landscapes. This road, slightly arched in its middle from long wear by waggon wheels, looked like the spine it was, connecting the two places. It wended through a rolling procession of stands of oaks and beeches which rose from grasslands dotted with wildflowers. It rolled past ash trees hoary with age. These stood solitary, nodding their great boughs over bare and loamy soil they had long ago cast into shade. The passage was lightened on its way by the lithe brightness of slender birches whose leaves looked nothing so much like cut gems as the Sun hit them. Only the valley of horses gave more to pleasure the eye, thought Ashild as she took this in.

As they turned off the main road to approach Oundle, they came to the final woods they must pass, one which lined both sides of the clay they trod. It was mostly of elms, and a few ash. The trees were of good size, their canopies outspread, branches intertwining. Two of the ash trees had been singled out for a special duty, one which Ashild herself had a share in. After the attempted assault on Oundle by a troop of Danes, she had ridden here with her step father Sidroc and uncle, Asberg. The horses they led bore the corpses of those attackers, and she had watched as those bodies were flung upon the ground and then strung up into the two ashes nearest the road. After so many months little could be left of those ghastly remains, and they were now, in Summer's fullness, hidden by dense foliage. Yet the rotted corpses could not be cut down. They were left not only in punishment but as a kind of Offering to Odin, whose sacred tree was the ash.

She glanced to Hrald, to see if he paused to look up, but his head was turned, speaking to Dagmar on his right. Ashild was glad the ugliness was so disguised, and would draw neither Hrald's nor Dagmar's attention to what they passed beneath. Glancing at the two trees and then away, Ashild was strongly aware that the man she had killed was also hanging there.

As it happened Hrald was now relating a story appropriate to Ashild's thoughts, for in answer to a question from Dagmar, he began to tell her more of the Abbess Sigewif.

"She is like no other woman I have ever met," he began, inclining his head to where the buildings of Oundle still lay hidden by the trees. "But she has cause to be so. Her older brother was Edmund, King of Anglia."

This was the kingdom lately ruled by Dagmar's father, one wrenched earlier and by other hands from Edmund.

It was where both Hrald and Dagmar had been born, and where Hrald knew he would spend his life.

Hrald and Ashild had heard this story recounted since childhood. Ashild listened to her brother as he shared it now with Dagmar. A large force of Danes had invaded Anglia, and after pitched battle they put the King to flight. Edmund barely escaped with his life, and was in hiding by a stream bank when he was discovered. The Danes, in celebration, got drunk on wine. They tied the King up, shot him full of arrows, then severed his head from his body. As the wine wore off, the Danes abandoned the body in shame.

Hrald was drawing to the end of the tale, the most thrilling part.

"A wolf appeared, which spent all night guarding the head of the King, sitting with the head between his front paws. In the morning the beast was found by the brothers of a nearby monastery, who had been brought the news of the King's capture and death. The wolf would allow none but the monks to claim the head of the monarch. The brothers carried Edmund's remains back to their monastery.

"Shortly thereafter the King came to be regarded as not only a hero, but a saint."

The story had many qualities to spark the imaginings of young minds. The valiant King, the ignorant viciousness of his killers, the fierce and wild wolf who recognized the noble head and would relinquish it to none but holy men. They knew as well that many of those who venerated Edmund as saint were the sons and daughters of the Danes who had killed him. These had taken the Cross, become confirmed in their devotion to Christ, and saw in Edmund a worthy model of Kingship. So brutal an end had been answered by veneration, even adoration, and eventual supplication to the powers of this lost hero. Edmund's callous murder had become a martyrdom.

Dagmar had listened with care to Hrald's telling. "I had heard something of the King, and knew he was held in high regard after death," she said. "But not this – not that he was now a saint." She pondered a moment. "And the Abbess is his sister?"

This connection seemed to heighten her apprehension of meeting Sigewif, it was clear in her tone. Even the name of the Abbess was off-putting, as Sigewif meant "Victory-woman."

"She was a child when it happened," Hrald confirmed, "but yes. She is Edmund's sister."

All four of the young people were silent. They were Danes, and half-Danes, and being born as they had two and even three generations after the first predations of Angle-land, dwelt in a kind of after-land that warriors such as those who killed Edmund perhaps never dreamt of. All four of them had been christened. There was confusion, and wonder both, in such stories.

Ashild, who thought of herself as more Dane than not, and echoed this even in her clothing, had at times thought on this. Hers, like Hrald's, was a blurred ancestry. The Danes may have killed a King and conquered his lands, but their own children went on to pray to him. She was aware of the twining process of absorption and accommodation by the conquerors; even at Four Stones it was not the folk of Lindisse who learnt to speak the Norse of Dane-mark, but the conquerors who had learnt the tongue of Lindisse. In fact, approaching this symbol of Christianity, they spoke that tongue now.

Edmund, once King and now saint, was weighing heavily on her mind as they passed into sight of the foundation ruled by his sister. Her thoughts returned to a much more recent event. There were the closed gates, before her. Here was the spot she must have reached, many horse lengths out but directly before those gates, where that spear hit her shield. She could gauge without looking back where the Dane who had thrown it stood, the Dane at whom she then flung her own spear, finding home in his young breast. The Dane whose tattered corpse now hung in that ash tree behind her.

She turned her head to the other side, where the small burial ground of Oundle lay. It was bordered by yews, as such places ever were, and she had never given it more than a glance. Today she wondered what nuns and brothers, yard and kitchen workers slept there.

The ward-men upon Oundle's parapet needed no horn-blast nor whistled signal to recognise who neared, but they whistled out their approach nonetheless so those within the palisade might know. The great gates were slowly swung open to admit the Jarl and family of Four Stones.

The forecourt of Oundle was a large one, and as they passed through the gates, the grey stone church with its belltower stood before them. The foundation was divided into two spheres, to accommodate both its female and male inmates. The larger of the timber halls, that in which the nuns ate and slept, was to the left of the church, and to the right, the smaller hall of the monks and lay brothers. Attached to the nuns' hall was another timber building, where the Abbess and prioress and elderly sisters kept their own small cells. The two priests who served at daily Mass had their own house, on the men's side. A full range of outbuildings and the kitchen yard were clustered within the shelter of the palisade walls, as was the timber barn. Behind the church sat the expansive garden of herbs, flowers, fruit, and vegetables, for which Oundle was known almost as well as for its stone sanctuary. This garden was in fact two, for down its centre ran a tall wooden wall, allowing both nuns and monks privacy as they worked, prayed, or wandered within these verdant confines.

The prioress of the place, Mildgyth, was now approaching from the nuns' hall, her hands outstretched in welcome. The escort dismounted, leading their horses to the paddock area by the barn. The men themselves, headed by Jari, would spend their time in the kitchen and work yards, and both they and their beasts would be fed and allowed to rest as the family of Four Stones went about their affairs here. Hrald gestured to the mounting blocks standing by the barn wall. He swung off his own horse and was quick to offer his hand to Dagmar and then Inkera so they might step down upon the block as he held their horses' heads. As he did so Ashild claimed one of the blocks for her own. She was on her feet and leading her mare to the paddock when one of Oundle's stable men approached her to take the reins. With a smile she shrugged him off; she would take her mare in herself, as did Hrald's men.

She joined her brother and Dagmar and Inkera. Mildgyth was standing at the waggon wherein sat the Lady of Four Stones, and Dagmar's look to Hrald seemed to ask if this was the Abbess.

"No," he told her, with a shake of his head.

"What more can you tell me of her," Dagmar asked. Her smooth and white brow was furrowed, and her quiet question carried a note of uncertainty.

Ashild looked at her, and recalling how the Abbess always made her feel, could not repress a slight smile. "She knows your thoughts."

Dagmar's lips opened. Ashild, seeing her concern, lifted her hand, and laughed at herself. "At least she seems to know mine."

THE RICHES
OF OUNDLE

PRIORESS Mildgyth led the party within the hall. At one end the slight figure of a lone nun stood by the side of a long table set with basins for the washing of hands. A side door to an inner chamber opened, and the large and imposing figure of Abbess Sigewif stepped into the hall. The Abbess wore a dark habit and sweeping white veil on her head, reaching almost to her knees in back. The cross of pale walrus ivory on her breast stood out in sharp relief from the charcoal coloured wool of her gown. The other nun, gowned in a dark habit and short veil of light grey, was quick to join her. This was Bova, lately become a consecrated nun. This young woman, whether as novice or now nun, was always present to welcome the Lady of Four Stones on her visits to Oundle. Ceridwen's gold piece had dowered Bova, but Ælfwyn was ever her special patron here.

As they moved towards the Abbess, Dagmar hoped she had made the right decision in how she had attired herself for this meeting. She knew Sigewif was a noble-woman, and had as well attained the highest position any churchwoman could, that of Abbess, ruling over not only many nuns but the monks and brothers of this dou-bled foundation. Dagmar was a King's daughter, yet knew that before such a woman as Sigewif a certain reserve in dress and manner was not only becoming but required. She had but one set of bronze shoulder brooches, those given her by her father, and set with pearls as they were, they proclaimed opulent, even undue wealth. Strung between these brooches she typically hung another gift from her father, the doubled strand of slightly smoky beads cut from rock crystal, both strands interspersed with silver beads. She had other silver to hang from her brooches as well, chains and narrow twisted rope. This morning Inkera had urged her to wear all her gems, to impress the Abbess, who was herself sister to a King. Yet Dagmar had hesitated. Any crystals were costly, and served to proclaim the wealth of she or he who sported them. Sigewif would be well apprised as to Dagmar's lineage, and she was not certain that an overt show of riches, especially of ornaments as eye-catching as were hers, was what she wished to convey before so august a personage as the Abbess.

She had decided for modesty and indirectness, pin-ning instead a far simpler chain of twisted silver between her pearl-set brooches. She felt the rightness of this reserve as soon as the steel-grey eyes of the Abbess met her own.

Dagmar had been in the presence of a number of per-sons of importance in her short life. With many of them, one might be impressed by their treasures or achieve-ments, but rarely were they themselves impressive. She had seen herself that few had about them a commanding air, one that drew eyes towards them, and made others stop and listen. Her father Guthrum, late King of the Danes in Anglia, possessed such command. This woman was another.

Dagmar found herself standing even straighter before Sigewif, and hoping her face did not betray the strain she was feeling.

Sigewif looked at all before her, from the Lady of Four Stones and her nurse Burginde to Inkera, with a quick yet penetrating glance. Lastly she looked to Guthrum's elder daughter. Dagmar felt she had been taken up, and decided upon, in a moment by the Abbess. Ashild's words, "She knows your thoughts," were still sounding in her ear.

All bowed before Sigewif, and Dagmar, lifting her lowered head, saw true reverence in Hrald's eyes as he raised his own. It was the Abbess herself who made intro-duction, in greeting all, and welcoming Dagmar and her sister by name. This formality complete, Dagmar watched as the Abbess opened her arms to Hrald's mother. The two women kissed.

Sigewif now turned to Ashild, who stepped forward. The Abbess placed her hands on Ashild's shoulders, and kissed her brow. She held her long enough to make this gesture more benediction than mere greeting. As she let go of Ashild, the Abbess looked to Dagmar and Inkera.

"She is our Judith," she said, with no little pride.

The allusion was unknown to the two sisters; that was clear to all from the slight puzzlement which briefly shadowed their faces. Inkera smiled and nodded, content in her innocence. Dagmar regained the same interested expression as before, but no light shown in her eyes in acknowledgment of the reference, nor affirming word fell from her lips. Instead her face took on a heightened state of attention. Sigewif, watching her, read at once that she was not familiar with the Old Testament tale of the great Hebrew beauty. It was a Bible story which Hrald and Ashild had been raised hearing. The resourceful Judith had saved her people from siege by slaying the savage and lustful general Holofernes in his tent.

Ashild felt the awkwardness of it for Dagmar, witnessing the warm, quietly fulsome greeting bestowed by the Abbess on her own head. This was a world from which as a newcomer Dagmar was naturally excluded, one which she seemed very much to wish a part in. The unintended exclusion ran even deeper, as Dagmar did not understand the praise lavished on Ashild by the Abbess.

Sigewif would not embarrass their young visitor by making any more of it, and shifted the mood in a moment. A slight gesture of the Abbess' hand granted permission for Bova to make her own greeting. She stepped forward, and with a shy smile made a deep and reverential bow to Ælfwyn, followed by one almost as deep to Hrald. Then her eyes turned to Ashild. She took another step forward, her eyes shining, her face aglow. Bova extended her gently cupped hands to Ashild, then placed them on her own breast, over her heart. She stood there, her slight figure gently swaying as she looked at Ashild.

In the young nun's mind, the preservation of Oundle had been inextricably linked to the presence of Ashild. Her courage in riding out to face the attackers and her words of encouragement to Bova before she did so had made deep and lasting impress. Furthermore, Bova had had her own vital role to play in that rout, for she had flung herself at the rope of the church bell, forcing the bronze it tethered into voice. Its loud pealing gave cue to the forces within Oundle to attack. Bova had fainted from fear and the strain of her efforts, yet upon awakening had been both warmly commended for her own efforts and told of Ashild's valour. In Bova's heart and mind, she and the daughter of the hall of Four Stones were thus linked. Together they were as sisters in the fight for the salvation of the sacred property and persons of the foundation.

Hands were rinsed and dried, and the ale poured out by the brewster herself, Bova. The young nun herself took no refreshment, but the praise the others offered as they took a draught coloured her pale cheek. Then Sigewif turned to her.

"Sister Bova, will you await us at the church? We will not be long."

With another bow Bova left them. The Abbess raised her large and well formed hand to the door behind her, which she had left ajar. She smiled at the daughters of Guthrum.

"I should like you to see my writing chamber, in which Hrald and Ashild perfected their hand."

They filed inside, to find an elderly nun standing within.

"Mother!" This warm salutation was from Ælfwyn, as she hastened to her mother's side, and into her arms. Ashild was then gestured into the old woman's arms, and finally Hrald.

Sigewif lifted her hand to the nun, and looked at her young visitors. "This is Sister Ælfleda, who in the world was mother to the Lady of Four Stones." The sister so named gave a bow to the Reverend Mother, before allowing her eyes to rest on the young women before her.

Hrald spoke now. "Grandmother, this is Dagmar, daughter of Guthrum. She and her sister Inkera are visiting us at Four Stones, and wanted to see Oundle."

She looked kindly upon them, her eyes crinkling. "I am happy to meet you, my dear girls."

Ælfwyn's mother had lived as first novice and then nun at Oundle most of Ashild and Hrald's lives. Ælfwyn was of her flesh, but Ælfleda was no longer of the world. Perhaps due to her own reawakening to the potential pleasures of the world, Ælfwyn now looked upon her mother with fresh eyes. Seeing her son present Dagmar, a young woman she knew Hrald hoped to wed, to his grandmother spurred Ælfwyn's thoughts. Her children had given her the greatest and most lasting satisfactions of her life. She desired their happiness with an ardent longing, and would do everything she could to support them in their path towards it. This respect for the desires and inclinations of her offspring did not stop at her son, marked almost from birth to great power, even the Jarlship should he prove able. It extended to Ashild and Ealhswith as well.

Her mother Ælfleda had an innate mildness, a suppleness of nature about her. She had not been able to keep Ælfwyn's father from sending their eldest daughter off to a captured keep as part of a private and ultimately fruitless quest for peace. There was no room in Ælfwyn's breast for harboured resentment over this; her father and grandsire both were men of such firm purpose that no tears nor pleading from either she or her mother had moved them once they had come to decision.

None could know what strife may lie ahead for the young of Four Stones, but Ælfwyn felt an almost fierce conviction that never would she force her daughters to the kind of marriage she herself had been sold to. This knowledge filled her breast as a single taper lit a small room. It was enough; gift enough for her girls, and source of strength for her. And she would do all in her power to help her son to a happy match.

Dagmar looked about her. Entering this private chamber of the Abbess was, she knew, honour akin to entering the treasure room of a great keep. The precious goods were of an entirely different sort. A slanted reading table by one of the two casements held an array of bound volumes, lying flat, the leathern faces of their cover boards worked in scrolls and intertwined spirals. A few even bore gemstones, held in mounts of silver, studding the covers with flashes of glinting colour as the Sun glanced over them. A table near these clearly acted as work-desk for the Abbess. It bore shallow basins, several mortar and pestle sets, tiny mixing bowls, and baskets of tree bark and galls, all telling of the preparation of ink. Another broader table must be Sigewif's own writing desk. Upon it lay a lining rule, scraper, tiny pots of what Dagmar guessed to be the finished ink, and a pottery tray of long grey-feathered goose quills, with a knife and wooden slicing board to open up the nib of the cut quill.

The largest item in the room was a long and plain table of deal, up to which two benches were drawn. The surface of this table was darkened from years of ink blots, and as if ready for one of them to sit down at it, a few pieces of squared parchment were stacked at one end.

Dagmar raised her eyes to see Sigewif looking at her. "This is where Hrald and Ashild practised their hand. But they had a fine start; their mother writes beautifully."

"Through diligent effort," murmured Ælfwyn with a smile. "I take no credit for any gift."

"It is application which counts, always, in life," answered Sigewif, with a smile of her own.

Of a sudden Dagmar feared being asked to show a sample of her own hand. She could read a few words, but could scarcely write out more than her own name. She knew she should speak now about her own lack of skill, and express her wish that she lived closer to Oundle, where she might receive tutelage from one of the learned sisters there. But she kept silent, abashed to admit her own lack, and the need for its correction. And as a wish, it was almost a request to be granted a privilege which she had not yet proven she deserved. Unwilling to speak the truth, she ended up saying nothing. She must let them think what they might.

It was Ashild who spoke. She had seen Dagmar's growing discomfort, and understood it.

"Hrald's hand is far better than mine," Ashild told her. "My scrawl is no better than it was as a child."

Her mother began to protest this self-judgement, but Ashild smiled and shook it off.

Dagmar was aware of the kindness of Ashild's words, yet her own thoughts had leaped ahead. Hrald writes well, she told herself. And his mother writes beautifully, the Abbess said so. Ashild may make light of her own skill, but I can do little more than write my name. I will be expected to teach my children . . .

It was not only Ashild who sensed the unexpected lack of self-assurance in Dagmar. Ashild's mother and Sigewif too were aware of it. This young woman had an almost preternaturally mature bearing for a maid, a bearing that told either of exacting schooling or a long and close observation of her elders. Dagmar's face was composed and placid, but the dropped lids over her dark blue eyes could not hide their darting movement. Sigewif, looking on her with her own eyes of steel grey, thought of nothing so much as a beautiful but threatened animal.

The Abbess now asked a question of both girls, one which seemed to turn the thoughts of all away from the less than happy topic of facility with quill and ink.

"When were you baptised, Dagmar, Inkera?"

The two sisters turned to each other. "Together," Dagmar remembered. She studied Inkera's pretty face for help, but the girl's lips were pursed in thought. "I was perhaps eight or ten, and Inkera, half that."

Sigewif went on. "Let us think back. Your father Æthelstan received Christ as part of the Peace of Wedmore." The Abbess here used the baptismal name of Dagmar's father, that which he was given at that event. The name was sometimes used in his official dealings, but all Danes still knew him as Guthrum.

The Abbess' quick mind worked the needed calculation. Guthrum had not received the Cross until after the defeat of Danish troops at Ethandun, in the Year of Our Lord 878. His doing so was part of the Peace he and Ælfred had agreed. This maid looked to be of twenty years or so. She must have been five or more years of age then. And Guthrum was not likely to be scrupulous in the speed in which he shared his new faith with his several wives and offspring. It made sense Dagmar would have eight or ten years, perhaps more, until she had received the sacrament. It was no wonder that she was ignorant of Judith. She was fathered by a man forced to become Christian. Her schooling in the faith, unless she had shown unusual interest, would have been indifferent, even at the hands of the best priest. Her birth decreed her Fate lay elsewhere. Dagmar looked as though she had been formed to be every inch a heathen King's consort. Considering her, the Abbess could fault none of this, no just woman could.

Sigewif smiled at the sisters, and gave a nod of her head. "You were both, I should say, of the perfect age when Christ came into your hearts," the Abbess ended.

Sigewif led the way out of the hall and to the single broad step of the grey stone church. Bova stood at its closed door, and bowed as she pulled it open for Sigewif and her party. The door was a heavy one, and showed the same care with which the entire church had been erected. The portal was built of upright planks of oak, embellished with strap hinges whose beaten iron work extended across the face of the wood like metal tendrils. The iron box lock on its front was as massive as on any treasure-bearing hall. Passing its protective heft gave added importance to the act of processing into a sacred edifice.

The Abbess entered first, and Ælfwyn, who was just behind her, paused for a moment on the threshold. It was not the beauty of the church which stayed her motion, though the church was an unusually fine one, but rather a natural respect she felt for the Abbess, that she should enter, first and alone, into this sanctuary. Indeed, all of the small party found themselves looking at the white veil trailing down the back of the Abbess as she progressed up the aisle, stopped to genuflect, and then continued toward the altar. Reaching there, she turned and opened her arms to her guests.

Dagmar and Inkera had entered within but one stone church, that dedicated to St Mary at Headleage, where they had been given the sacrament of baptism, and where their father had been buried. This edifice at Oundle was no larger, yet was in every way possessed of a greater beauty, and somehow of greater comfort. The day was warm; the interior held a soothing coolness. The dome-topped windows admitted abundant sunlight through panes of pale glass, whose entrapped bubbles gave a sense of airy lightness and even movement. The massive altar was a block of white stone, draped with pure and snowy linen. Upon that cloth was set two branched candle hold-ers of gleaming silver, reaching with tall tapers of yellow beeswax toward the lead-topped timber roof. A crucifix of wonderfully wrought silver stood between them, glint-ing down upon all who approached the altar. It was a larger version of what the Abbess wore upon her breast, for the figure of the Christ upon this was carved in walrus ivory. The pale figure was as long as a man's hand. As she neared the altar Ashild found her own eyes rising to it. She had ever found it her favourite depiction of Christ, for the artisan had so sculpted that warm material that no anguish shown on the Saviour's face or body. He looked, with his outstretched arms, as if he were almost dancing, not hanging in his death agony.

Three statues of saints, carved of wood and painted in vivid hues, sat on three columns, two to the right of the altar, and one to the left. They were all three skillfully carved, but of noticeable age, the mazing of the paint telling of multiple

layers, and in some places only emphasizing the cracking of the old wood. The one on the left was the largest,
and was of blue-gowned Mary, the Mother of God. Inkera
went to it at once, and Dagmar found herself following her
younger sister. It was impossible not to, as about the statue's
neck and wrists hung three marvellously worked chains of
gold. They were made up of golden disks, linked together,
each with a different coloured gemstone in its centre. The
bracelets, made for a human woman, were far too large
for the wooden wrists of the statue, and hung down, glittering, from the figure's outstretched hands. Inkera found
her own hand reaching towards one of them, and had
to check her motion, so great was her desire to touch it.

Ashild had come up beside the two and now spoke. The
expression of wonder on both their faces made her explain.

"Those are the gifts my father Yrling gave my mother,
the day of their hand-fast."

Both Dagmar and Inkera looked at her, but it was
Dagmar who spoke. "And she gave them . . . here?"

Ashild nodded her head and went on. She was aware
of something close to awe in Dagmar's voice, but there
was none in her own, just a quiet retelling of fact. "This
church and much of Oundle was built with Yrling's
treasure."

Dagmar knew Ashild and Hrald had different fathers,
and that it had been Ashild's father who had won, and first
ruled Four Stones. She found her eyes lifting to where
Ashild's mother stood with the Abbess. The gift of such
gems said as much about she who had given them as it
did of the prowess of he who had won them.

Sigewif, seeing the raised eyes of Dagmar, now spoke
aloud, and to all.

"We will leave you now. The Lady Ælfwyn and I have the affairs of the abbey to discuss. Sister Bova will attend you. Enjoy the church, and gardens. We shall meet later for a meal in the hall."

She turned, and with Ælfwyn at her side and Burginde just behind, passed through the still opened door and out into the day.

Bova had been standing near to Ashild, off to her left, watching all she said and did. Hers was a gentle presence, but her hovering about the daughter of Four Stones made Ashild all too aware of the young nun's admiration. They had seen most of what the church held, and Ashild yearned to be again out in the open air. She moved to the door, Inkera at her side, Bova just behind her, and Dagmar and her brother last. As Bova carefully pulled closed the door, the rest of them paused on the wide stone step, and looked out over the fanning expanse of the nuns' garden arrayed before them in the fullness of its Summer blossoming.

Though fruit and flowers grew there, the heart of the plot was a large herb garden, for the leafy things therein were used not only to lend savour to food. The base material for easing the ills of body and mind sprang from that well tended soil. From its scented confines the nuns plucked and dried single plants, known as Simples, and from an array of many, compounded their healing remedies. Abbess Sigewif knew the properties of each and every plant, root to stem to blossom. The young of Four Stones could recall being at her side as she cut or pulled herbs to take to her writing chamber so she might draw with her fine hand those best for relieving chest pains or soreness of the throat.

Ashild could guess that Hrald would value a few minutes wandering its paths alone with Dagmar. It was in her power to grant this, and she did. At the furthest end of the garden sat the brewing house, giving Ashild perfect reason to absent herself.

She turned to the young nun. "Bova, will you please show Inkera and me your brewing garden?"

Bova's hands rose to her throat in happy surprise. A few moments later nun, Ashild, and Inkera were far from earshot.

Dagmar smiled at them as they moved off, then turned and looked back at the church. Hrald felt that it, and all of Oundle, had a strong and positive effect on his guest. She gave a small sigh, one which to him signalled contentment. When she turned back to him the smile was still there upon her lips. Despite her regal bearing, and her beauty, he felt at ease with her. He had to fight the urge to say, "We will be wed on this stone step, and then all who have gathered to witness will come in to celebrate Mass together."

He could not say this, despite her earlier prompting at Four Stones when she had jested about how tall their offspring would be; but he was thinking it. Because he could not say this, he did not know what to say.

Dagmar smoothed the way. "It is all more wonderful than I had guessed."

"Do you think so?" was his hopeful and happy response.

"Yes. Inkera would say the same. St Mary's is not so beautiful." She again turned her eyes to the church. "And the treasure therein . . ."

For answer Hrald only nodded. As proud as he was of his mother's many benefactions to Oundle, he knew boasting of them was unseemly. But some acknowledgment of Dagmar's praise was needed. At last he said, "My mother was glad to give it."

She nodded herself, and went on, sharing her thoughts with him. "The gemstone necklace and bracelets . . . Ashild is Yrling's daughter. Would not she have wanted them?"

At this Hrald must smile. His sister enjoyed wearing her circlet of gold on her brow, on those occasions on which she had donned it, but the glittering multi-coloured gems on that golden set were not things he could picture Ashild wearing.

"Or perhaps she favours ornaments of a more simple nature," she offered.

"Yes, that is it," he agreed. Once again he thought how easy she made it to speak with her. She could almost give voice to his thoughts.

Her eyes now travelled past the tended beds of herbs and flowers, bordered by neatly trimmed hedges of box, or edged by freer lines of waving lavenders. Leeks and onions, cabbages, turnips, beets, carrots, skirrets and other vegetables were also there. These were backed by the timber wall dividing the garden, against which apple, pear, cherry and damson trees had been trained to grow. This divider was nearly the height of the palisade wall protecting Oundle. As a barrier it served to block the sight only, and did not wrap around to enclose either space. When monks and brothers crossed to the church they could glance into the nuns' garden, yet did not. Dagmar realised it was more symbol of separation than separation itself. Yet as a physical barrier it hid the comings and the goings of the respective halls. She had seen the brothers' hall when they rode in, and now asked Hrald about it.

"Have you been to the other side, the hall of the men?"

He nodded. "Many times. As a boy when I visited and we passed the night, I would stay with my mother on the nuns' side, but when I grew older I would stay with the brothers." He paused a moment. "Once I spent several days living there amongst them."

"As an act of devotion?" she wanted to know. Sincere interest was in her voice, and her eyes.

Hrald did not wish to say that it had been more an act of contrition. The cause for his riding here then, and the painful confusion he had felt, was too readily recalled. Gunnulf's attempt at seduction had been followed by his own sordid coupling with a kitchen woman. The former incident had deeply dismayed him, the latter greatly shamed him.

As he paused, Dagmar supplied an answer. Her voice, low and even, carried in it no note of prodding, but of real attention.

"Or perhaps curiosity, to see what their lives were like?"

He was grateful. "Yes," he told her. It was not strictly true, but he had in fact absorbed what he could from those few days spent in almost silent contemplation. "It was strange, and at the same time much like Four Stones. Men living together, focused on one goal, but needing to contribute to the daily life of the hall, as well."

She seemed pleased with the thoughtfulness of this response, for her smile broadened, and she nodded her head in understanding.

I can tell her things, he thought. Even things I could not share with any, I will be able to share with her . . .

He thought of Ceric, and his sister. He did not know if this was one of the things Ceric felt for Ashild, a sense of openness which somehow led to inner safety. But the ease at which Dagmar had put him, almost at once, grew steadily. The attraction he had felt on first seeing her led now to a blossoming certainty. This is the woman I care for, and who will care for me.

⁂⁂⁂⁂⁂⁂⁂⁂⁂⁂

Sigewif had not dissembled in saying she and the Lady of Four Stones had the affairs of the abbey to discuss. Ælfwyn's benefices extended to the welfare of elderly nuns and monks, the care of the lay folk of Oundle who served the foundation, and even the freeing and establishing in farm work or trade of the last of Oundle's slaves, accomplished several years ago. Though the Abbess, prioress, and the two priests administered these many benefactions, silver was needed to carry out their execution. Oundle, as isolated as it was, was far from self-sufficient, and though it occasionally received gifts from other sources, had of necessity relied on the generosity of first the Lady, and now also the young Jarl of Four Stones for its growth and continuance.

As Ælfwyn had walked with the Abbess past the garden, she found her eyes falling to a bed of blossoming bushes. Which was the rose from which Raedwulf plucked that single bud, she wondered. Where was that bud now, where was the man . . . her thoughts could stray thus only as long as her feet trod the garden paths. Then she and Burginde and the Abbess were within the latter's writing chamber.

Sigewif did not today belabour the description of accounts nor condition of the treasury. On this visit a cursory report would suffice; the young people would be awaiting them.

The Abbess had been reviewing a parchment with her guest, one on which she had charted the various bequests and gifts received in this half year, and how these had been brought to bear for the benefit of the poor and aged. She now set this aside.

Sigewif folded her hands, fixed her eyes on her guest, and uttered a single word.

"Dagmar."

Ælfwyn smiled, and nodded her head. She was unable to prevent a soft sigh from escaping as she did so.

The Abbess was known for a habitual firmness of manner. Her tone now was more of exploration, than decision. "We can not help but be sympathetic to her circumstances, even as we remain unsure about her character."

Ælfwyn was in full agreement with this statement, and full of admiration for the concision with which it had been delivered. In her first letter to the Abbess, written shortly after Guthrum's elder daughter had entered their ken, she had detailed all Asberg had learnt about the girl, and some of what she herself felt.

"She is lovely, I cannot gainsay it," Ælfwyn began. "But Hrald . . . he is so young."

"There is a tenderness to him, one which I hope he possesses always," Sigewif agreed.

Burginde was sitting off to one side, and now her mistress glanced to her. The two of them had often discussed the advent of Guthrum's daughter in Hrald's life, and Burginde had used just that term to describe him. Ælfwyn's look now granted speech to the nurse.

"Tender, he is," Burginde summed, with a respectful bob of her head to the Abbess, "and though he be a Jarl, no weapon can protect a tender heart." She added something, almost as an afterthought. "Ashild be the hardy one."

Sigewif took the final comment as seriously as the first. "Yes. Just as Judith was." The Hebrew heroine, undeterred by her tribe's despair under attack, would allow no interference in her secret plan for victory.

This unexpected mention of Ashild gave her mother a pang. Here, in the quiet of the Abbess' chamber, she wished to unburden herself to Sigewif concerning her daughter's condition. She would not; it was not her story to tell. It must be Ashild's choice as to when and to whom she would share it.

The Abbess' thoughts continued. Under her nun's veil Sigewif had the mind of a military strategist. It forced her to ask herself who or what could hurt this girl, where was the weakness here, who could compromise her. She wrestled with such thoughts, deeming them unworthy, for at the same time her higher self believed that one's inner nature was always above such assault. God made all new, expunged all flaws and faults, and we struggling mortals must support each other on our paths to perfection. Yet here, on the Earthly plane, and most of all in the marriage contract of a powerful man, caution was warranted. As unjust as it was, a woman's repute was too easily damaged, her virtue disparaged. Should Hrald wed amiss, mayhem could result.

"There is something about Dagmar," she said at last. If she allowed herself pride in anything, it was fairness, and she wished to be fair to Guthrum's daughter. The girl's self-assurance seemed to be all on the surface, with no well-spring as its source. In her scant time with her she felt the girl was far from candid.

"It is hard to say just what," Sigewif admitted. "She lacks forthrightness, though Ashild's own self-possession and openness may be colouring my judgement. But there is something guarded about Dagmar."

"Or something she is guarding," mused Ælfwyn.

NOTHING
TO BRING HIM

BY the time they reached Four Stones in early evening, Hrald had succeeded in persuading Dagmar to remain a few further days. Why need she and Inkera head back to Haward's hall on the morrow, when there was so much more to see and do at Four Stones, he posed. He wished to take her hawking, and with a meaningful look at Ashild, proposed they also visit the valley of horses so that the sisters might see the fine bloodstock of the place.

Dagmar paused long enough considering this offer that he feared he had overstepped. Yet he had reason to believe her seeming interest in him was well founded; she had accepted his invitation to go to Oundle and had even cut short her trip to Inkera's uncle in Cruland, so she might return to Four Stones the sooner. Now she had further strengthened his hopes by accepting his offer of an extended stay.

That night, sitting next Dagmar at the women's table, Ashild could not but note Dagmar looking at the high table, and at Hrald. Does she picture herself there, at his side, she wondered. Yet she must admit Dagmar's eyes were no bolder. If anything there was a wistfulness in the young woman's gaze, a look she blinked away with a smile when she grew aware of Ashild's own eyes upon her.

As they rose at the end of the meal Dagmar asked Ashild if she might speak to her mother. Before the hall quieted each evening every bronze cup was numbered and locked away in chests lining the kitchen hall passage, just as those of silver were secured in the treasure room. Ælfwyn and Burginde themselves oversaw this counting, and as Dagmar indicated her willingness to help, both she and Ashild joined in, laying the rinsed and wiped cups in the straw layers filling the chests as their numbers were checked against the notches on a tally stick.

Dagmar's joining in on this simple yet vital domestic chore was lost on none of them. Indeed, in the torch light of the passage, with serving folk still moving behind them, it was impossible not to imagine a future in which the keys unlocking these chests hung at Dagmar's waist. The fact that Hrald lingered at the hall end of the passage, smiling upon the tall young woman as she bent to nestle yet another bronze cup in the waiting straw, coloured Dagmar's cheek, making her glad for the dimness of the place. She glanced in his direction, the serene smile she often wore deepening for a moment. Her sister Inkera stood not far from Hrald, chattering away and comparing necklaces with two girls who also sat at the women's table.

When Ælfwyn twisted the key in the final chest, she turned to Dagmar with her thanks. The Lady of Four Stones had been told on the road home that Guthrum's daughters would extend their stay by a day or two; her son had turned his horse back to her waggon with gladsome eyes to tell her so. And it was of this Dagmar must ask further favour.

"If your Lady would be so kind," she began, "I have only two shifts with me. And this one I have muddied the hem of in Oundle's garden."

She said no more; her words carried their own hesitation, and hope. Dagmar owned only two good gowns, and had them both with her. Few women owned more than a handful of gowns, and none were expected to have many. For the women of the Danes, the mixing of shift and contrasting over-gown could result in many pleasing and fresh combinations, expanding the life of a few pieces. Yet she wished she had a third over-gown or shift, to help vary her look, as would be expected from a woman of her estate.

Ælfwyn glanced a moment to the hem of Dagmar's skirts. There was too little light to see any soiling, but she smiled anyway.

"Burginde will wash it for you," came the ready response. She did not trust her own gowns with the washing women and their wooden bats, and would extend this courtesy to her guest. Ælfwyn was further aware that she could lend her one of her own gowns. She had one of yellow which might well suit. It would be short on Dagmar, but with an over-gown upon it as addition, would be fine. "I will give you a gown to serve as shift; it will be brought to you early tomorrow," she promised.

Dagmar appeared next morning at the hawk cote attired in the borrowed gown, over which she had layered a sleeveless over-gown of rusty red. It was a happy pairing, bringing out the tiny flecks of golden brown in her blue eyes. She was alone in meeting Ashild and Hrald there. Inkera was not sporting, and was instead spending time amongst a few of the thegns' daughters with whom she had already made fast acquaintance.

With six birds, two keepers were needed for their training and care, and the men handed the three young hawkers each a leathern gauntlet for the right wrist. Hrald was glad to see Dagmar pull on the protective sleeve with familiar ease. The hawk cote housed four falcons; the two goshawks were in their own separate cote, and he went in to fetch them himself. Dagmar followed Ashild into the larger hawk cote, remaining just inside the door as she watched Ashild approach the birds. The cote was round, of wattle and daub, lime-washed inside and out for brightness. Small as it was, the pierced openings beneath the conical roof kept a free flow of air, and the straw upon the earthen floor was raked out and changed daily, giving the place a freshness far beyond that of a fowl house. Four falcons perched upon branched upright wooden supports, and Ashild went to the largest of them. Ashild cooed to the bird. Its head swiveled and the bright yellow eyes fastened on her. She ran the back of her hand along its brown speckled back, then slipped the tiny leathern hood the hawk keeper had given her upon the sleek head. The bird well knew her, and hopped from its perch with little more than a click of Ashild's teeth, and the touch of her leather-guarded wrist against the falcon's clawed feet.

Outside again Hrald emerged from the smaller goshawk cote. The bird on his wrist was a dappled silvery grey. Even hooded it seemed alert, and he brought it to Dagmar with a grin.

"You will fly the female, as my sister does," he told her, inclining his head to his sister with her female falcon. He gave a short laugh. "Even without a brood to feed, they are often the better hunters."

As he passed the bird to Dagmar's wrist he kept smiling. What would my father think of her, he could not help but ask himself. I would he knew that I court a daughter of Guthrum, and go hawking with her, carrying the birds he brought me . . .

Hrald went back for the male. He had flown only these two birds since their arrival at Four Stones, and sharing them now with Dagmar made the day the more singular.

Mul the stableman had arrived, leading Hrald's bay stallion and Ashild's mare. At his side was a thin boy leading the horse Dagmar had ridden from her cousin's hall. The boy bowed his head at Hrald, the look on his face so solemn and respectful that even Hrald's returning nod and smile could not soften the child's searching countenance.

He and his sister and Dagmar passed the birds to the hawk keepers so that they might mount, and then again took the birds upon their wrists for the short ride to the tall grasses beyond the orchard groves.

Ashild, with her favourite falcon on her wrist, the young brown female, thought of using that same bird when she and Hrald went out hawking with Ceric. It felt half a lifetime ago. She could not let her thoughts stray there; she was here to act as chaperone. A brief and wry smile passed her lips, remembering that Hrald had done the same for her on that faraway day.

It was fine being out, the morning sky a brilliant blue, the grasses they rode through nodding their ripening seed heads in the breeze. The very fineness of the day and growing warmth of it may have doomed the hawking, for few birds were to be found. They flushed a hare which

Ashild's bird was after at once, but the creature, with vast bounds, vanished into a thicket of brambles before the falcon, talons foremost, could reach it. Likewise both goshawks had a single chance to capture a bird on the wing, Hrald's a blackbird which speedily joined a circling mob of them, confusing his raptor, and Dagmar's, making rush at a songbird which found shelter amongst the heavy hanging pears in the orchard.

"Just watching them fly is thrill enough," Dagmar remarked. They had slipped their birds' hoods back on, and were now turning back to the hall. She rode side by side with Hrald, while Ashild took the chance to ride ahead of them, giving them time alone.

He smiled at her words, the smile deepening as he kept looking at her. It prompted her to ask him why.

"My father. I thought of him. These goshawks we fly were his gifts."

"A kingly gift," she answered, smiling back at him. "Your father," she went on. "Haward told me what he could about him. He has been gone a long time."

He nodded. "More than half my lifetime. When I was a boy he went to Saltfleet. There he was captured by the tribe called Idrisids. They live hundreds of leagues to the South, near a place called Fes. They have their own Gods, and are rich slavers. But he escaped, and made a life for himself, a good one, in the Baltic.

"I spent nearly a year with him on Gotland, with his wife, and twinned children."

She could read how meaningful this time had been to Hrald. Her hours alone with her own father had been scant enough. She dared asking the next, aware of the boldness of her query.

"Why did he come back?"

Haward had told her that Sidroc had appeared in time to witness the duel in which Hrald killed her cousin Thorfast, but she knew his being there for this was but an act of Fate. Something pressing must have drawn him here, to make such a journey.

Hrald drew a long and slow breath before he answered.

"He had heard, even on Gotland, about the arrival of Haesten. He came to see . . . " He paused, not knowing how to go on. "He came to see if I could truly serve as Jarl."

He let his eyes rest upon her face as he said this, and she took a moment, looking back into his own eyes of dark blue.

"And he saw that you could, and were," she confirmed. She spoke with earnest warmth, as if she herself attested to his fitness to lead. From her lips it was neither flattery nor praise, but a show of quiet confidence in his ability.

He was taken by it. She seemed to have the same faith in him his father did. Thanking her did not seem right, but as he nodded he hoped she read his gratitude.

※※※※※※※※※

Next day was the Sabbath. On each such day the family of Four Stones attended private devotion at the house of Wilgot the priest, then followed him to the stone preaching cross outside the palisade walls. All of hall and village would assemble there, standing before the carved face of the cross, and Wilgot would repeat the Mass, offer the sacrament of communion through the breaking of bread, and deliver the homily he felt most beneficial to the souls of his listeners.

This morning, as was their custom, the family of the hall gathered on one side of the preaching cross, standing in respectful silence as did the rest of their folk. Today they were joined by the daughters of Guthrum, who stood between Ashild and the Lady of Four Stones. Dagmar and Inkera had never been regular in attendance at the Church of St Mary at Headleage, going only when their father did during his lifetime, and after his burial ceremony, not at all. Dagmar had felt awkward and uncertain within the priest Wilgot's small house, carefully watching for cues as to when she should begin to kneel, or bless herself in a gesture she felt she performed ineptly. The tongue of Rome was near to utterly foreign to her; she had heard it in the droning Masses offered by the priest at St Marys, and in his mumbled blessings, but other than a few words she was ignorant of its meaning. Seeing with what promptitude Hrald and his sisters and mother responded to every line of Wilgot's maundering preaching was a strain almost greater than her fear that she be asked by the Abbess of Oundle to write something on a parchment and so exhibit her hand. Now the exercise was extended in this second service, in which the eyes of all of Four Stones were upon her. To address the assembled folk Wilgot used both the tongue of Rome and that of Lindisse. Dagmar could attend more, and nod her head when warranted, but could not control her thoughts.

She feared she had been found wanting in front of Sigewif. Now by the preaching cross she had openly admired on her first visit here, she regretted prolonging this second one. It was a growing sense that the longer she was with the family of Four Stones, the poorer she fared. She fastened her eyes on the pale grey stone of the cross, carved on both sides with interlacing spirals. On the front face of it was also carved the likeness of Christ, hands and feet pinned, the mouth opened as if in surprise of his own crucifixion. The eyes were sorrowful enough, deeply incised, and larger than any man's ever were. Some master carver had wrought this; such work could only issue from the hand of an artisan of both ability and faith. The material was as noble as his conviction. It was new work, no older than the Lady of Four Stones' own presence here. The incised lines were still sharp, fresh, and unmarred. The solid substance of this stone cross was like Four Stones, or even Hrald himself. It contrasted sharply with the wooden statues she had seen at Oundle, which she knew had been old before they were carried there by the Abbess. She felt herself like one of those painted saints, which should be admired from afar. One did not wish to come too close and see the flaws, the cracks in the wood.

As the service drew to a close she let her eyes shift to those standing directly opposite. She recognized some folk of the hall yards, the serving woman she and Inkera had been granted, and the stableman Mul, she thought he was called. He was there with his wife, as lean and spritely looking as was he, and their sons. Another boy unlike the others stood with them, the one Mul had brought their horses with to the hawk cote yesterday. The child was staring at Hrald with a look of mingled awe and hope on his thin face. Then she saw the boy's gaze move to Hrald's mother. As Wilgot gave the final benediction, the boy broke from where he stood by Mul's sons. He ran to

Ælfwyn, stopped short before her, and pulled something from his belt, which he extended in his hand. It was a single blue windflower. The Lady of Four Stones smiled as she took it.

"Bork. I thank you," she murmured. She had asked Wilgot to baptise the boy the day after his arrival at the hall, and with his new family's help, he was learning Christian ritual. As she held the proffered blossom, Ælfwyn looked past the child to Mul and his wife. Her action made the boy turn his head as well, to see Mul gesture him back with a lift of his hand. Mul's smile for the boy was almost one of reassurance, yet the stableman bobbed his head at the Lady of Four Stones as if asking her indulgence.

"That child," Dagmar asked Hrald, as they began walking through the gate. Mul and his family had gone on ahead, as it was the custom for Ælfwyn and Hrald to remain after the dismissal, should any of their village folk wish to speak with them.

Hrald's first answer was a deep exhalation of breath. "His father was killed by my men, after he attacked us on the way to Haward's hall. I lost one man, a good one. It was the day I met you."

Dagmar's own surprise was sounded in her low gasp. After a moment of reflection she spoke again. "Now he can scarce keep his eyes from you, and your mother."

Hrald shook his head. "He feared I would kill him." He turned his eyes away a moment, far above the palisade wall. "As if I would kill a boy."

He had not mentioned this incident before, and with reason; it had been a blot on a day that had otherwise been marked with success, for he had gone on to Turcesig and fairly won the warriors of that place over.

"He lives with Mul now, and works with the horses alongside his boys," Hrald went on. "For the first time in a long time he has enough food."

Shortly after Bork's arrival Mul's wife had told Hrald that when she had first taken the boy to the kitchen yard, he began wolfing down his food in such haste that she took it from him lest he retch it up. She fed him smaller portions, but the boy had already too much inside his shrunken belly, and it came up again. She gave him broth after this, and then warm browis, a spoon at a time, until he fell asleep leaning against her on the bench.

They were nearing the stable now, and young Bork stood in the dimness of its opening, looking out at them, his eyes large as he watched Hrald pass.

"You have made him part of the place, given him a family," Dagmar summed. "He will do anything for you, now, and when he is grown," she predicted. "And for your mother."

That afternoon the young people rode up to the valley of horses. Inkera stayed behind, but Ealhswith begged to go, and Ashild rode side by side with her little sister, ahead of Hrald and Dagmar. Jari and another warrior trailed behind. Even given the short distance from the hall, and riding deep within the borders of Four Stones, Jari would take no chances on this passage. Since Guthrum's death and the arrival of the war-chief Haesten to these shores the watch along the well-worn road had been doubled. Hrald's whistled warning of their approach was met with a shrill response from those secreted in the trees.

The great timber longhouse came into view first, where the unmarried men assigned here lived. Its thatched roof was even then being replenished, and upon one end of the gable a gang of young men worked side by side beating in handfuls of dried rye straw so that they might sleep dry through the Winter. For the first few years of the Danes' occupation of Four Stones this longhouse had been the only feature of the valley, save for the horses pastured here, but over the years a hamlet of crofts had sprung up around it. When ships bearing the wives and sweethearts of Yrling's men began arriving, a number of his warriors settled here, planting vegetables, herding sheep and cows, raising pigs and fowl. Some of these men who had served under Yrling and then Sidroc were no longer in active duty to Hrald now that he was Jarl. Their sons had taken their places, and might be now living within the barracks of the longhouse, or serving within the palisade. There were never fewer than forty men barracked within the longhouse, a number augmented by those who lived in their own crofts dotting the former greensward surrounding it. All these were set here to secure the great treasure of Four Stones, its horses.

The small valley, well watered with its own broad stream, served as a natural paddock for the beasts kept there. The lush grassland supported well over two hundred head. A dense wood ringing three sides allowed the animals to roam within its cool confines and browse on forest growth without straying far. An open-staved fence kept the horses from the road, and spared from their trampling the blue-flowered flax plants blanketing either side of it.

They reined up, and just stood their horses, looking. A few choice stallions had small paddocks of their own, as did mares close to their foaling time. But the bulk of the mares and geldings mingled freely in the vast open grassland.

Hrald never came here without a small thrill of pride arising in his breast at the number and quality of the animals. His father had told him that Yrling was skilled with horses, and had set about almost from the first to raise the best he could. Hrald knew he looked at over twenty years of careful breeding and culling. The rest was the result of the blessing of Fate and the richness of the soil. He glanced at Dagmar, who seemed transfixed at the sight. She became aware of his looking at her, and turned to him.

"Sometimes my father would speak of the days before I was born, the desperate search for horses, stealing all they could," she began. "What he would think of yours . . ."

She began to ask a question, then realised she must already know the answer. "He had seen these, of yours," she mused.

"Yes. Guthrum's first visit was when Ashild's father still ruled here; my father told me. He must have come many times after that, as well as those visits I recall."

Dagmar looked to where Ashild and Ealhswith had reined up. The look of satisfaction in Ashild's eyes as she scanned the herd could be read by anyone. Dagmar and Hrald watched as she turned her horse and led her sister on her pony to a separate paddock where some of the other ponies and smaller horses stood browsing with lowered necks amongst the lush grasses.

"She will be ready for a larger horse, soon," Hrald thought aloud. "Ashild will help her choose one."

This placed him in mind of the dowry he had once promised for Ashild's hand. There was something he must ask Dagmar, something which they had not directly spoken of. It was not a topic easy to broach.

"Your cousin Thorfast. Were you close to him?"

An old image and its attendant sensations flooded her mind, unbidden and unwelcome. When she was seventeen, not long after Thorfast had lost his wife, she almost let him kiss her. She had scarce known his wife, but sorrowed for her loss for his sake. Thorfast had been a frequent enough visitor at her father's hall at Headleage, and she saw how well disposed her father was to him. Yet she stopped Thorfast in his action. Another young man in her father's train had already claimed her attention, as he was soon to claim the rest of her.

It was only after the one she loved had been lost to her that her thoughts returned to her cousin. By now her father was ailing and many men both young and old were wrangling openly to be considered as heir to the Kingship of East Anglia. Thorfast made several trips to her weakening father, occasions on which she tried to place herself in her cousin's way. He was cordial, nothing more. She was left wondering what they had spoken of behind that closed door in the weapons room of her father's hall. And what, if anything, had Thorfast heard of her . . .

She gave a short sigh, rousing herself from these thoughts. Hrald was looking at her, awaiting her response.

"Not close, no," she said, forcing a steadiness into her tone which she did not feel. "I saw him at Headleage of course. He was – useful to my father, who always liked him."

"And who gave him a holding as rich as Turcesig."

She nodded. And she had been left with nothing. She was more than certain Hrald knew this.

She felt now distracted by her own thoughts. She realised she was tired as well, the kind of weariness that arises from the strain of scrutiny. And she felt something rare for her, frightened. She had had to be strong for years, and now she found herself almost mired in a sudden rush of confused fear. All was moving too quickly, placing too much in danger. She had come into Hrald's life from nowhere, and had nothing to bring him, save for her father's blood in her veins. Yet she had his regard for her, warm, and she knew, growing. Before she went further she must ascertain what she could, and now.

She composed herself, and with a slight smile at Hrald gave a nudge to her horse's barrel, turning him to ride at an amble alongside the stave fencing. Hrald followed. "Having asked a question of me," she posed, "may I ask one for myself?" Her smile grew. "Or rather, for my sister, Inkera."

A smile of bewilderment formed on his lips. The girl was not even with them, but then that perhaps gave her sister the greater freedom to inquire for her sake. He nodded assent.

"She is pretty, and lively," she began. "I should like to see her make the best match." She took a breath and reframed this. "The best match possible for her." These last few words were added in a lowered tone, as if Dagmar referred to future concessions which might be necessary.

Hrald was about to say that he felt such a spritely creature should have little problem amongst the men of estate here in Anglia. Almost as if she anticipated this, she went on.

"I speak not of her prospects here, amongst Danes who knew our father, but further afield." She slowed her words a moment, then went forward, with a note of near-apology in her voice. "You are Jarl here, and were raised to be so, and thus must have heard much of other Kingdoms. We as girls heard little. Could Inkera find a suitable match in Mercia, of which our father conquered half, or perhaps amongst the Welsh? Or best of all, in the Kingdom of Wessex, as that King has been our most able opponent?"

Hrald's mouth was open, in wonder, she felt, but she must go on.

"They will be seeking well-born women of the Danes to wed," she offered.

But Hrald was shaking his head. She looked down, her fine teeth clamped on her lower lip for a moment in discomfiture.

"I . . . I do not know," he began, in a voice which showed how seriously he had taken her question. "I wish I did. I have never left Lindisse, save for my journey to Gotland.

"Mercia . . . Wales . . . " He shook his head. "The one place I know something of is Wessex, though seen it I have not. But my friend – my best friend – is Ceric of Kilton. It is a rich fortress there, and he is the godson of King Ælfred himself."

"And he is not yet wed?"

She watched Hrald lift his eyes to the sky. She had seen him do this before, while collecting his thoughts.

"He is not wed."

His pause was long enough to tell her he would not go on.

"And how did you come to meet him?"

At this he gave a short laugh, and ran his hand through his hair. "When we were boys he travelled with me to Gotland, and before that we had spent a whole Summer together here. Our mothers were friends. His mother is now the wife of my father."

Dagmar had from her childhood been exposed to enough labyrinthine relations that she took this in with a simple nod.

"Would he wed such a maid as Inkera?"

Hrald almost could not answer. At last he forced a few words out. "No. As charming as she is."

"Perhaps he has a brother?"

"He does, his younger brother, who through adoption by his uncle is now Lord of Kilton."

"And he is yet unwed?"

Hrald nodded. "As far as I know, yes. But he is young, no older than Inkera herself."

She took a breath. This younger brother was the lord of a great hall. He would be able to command a treasure-bearing princess as his bride.

"Inkera would have little attraction to such a man." Her voice was soft, even thoughtful, but the bluntness of her next words seemed to startle even herself.

"The daughter of a dead king, regardless how great, would not be enough for such a lord."

Hrald was forced to consider this. The thought of Ceric marrying a maid such as Inkera seemed beyond the realm of any possibility, and given what Asberg had said about the sisters' straitened circumstances he could scarce imagine young Edwin choosing such a maid, however winsome she be. All he could do was share his own thoughts.

"Everything . . . everything is in disarray now, both here in Anglia and in Wessex. Their King Ælfred still lives, we would have heard if he had fallen, but with so much war, anything can change. War-chiefs, Lords, and Jarls who today command many warriors and hold great treasure could fall tomorrow. They might lose everything, their lives and wealth be swept away . . . "

Hrald knew the peril faced by brides who wed into enemy camps in hope of serving as peace-weavers. If war nonetheless ensued these women could be taken captive by either side, to be used as ransom or debased in retribution as slaves. It was not a danger to be wished upon the heedless and carefree Inkera.

He said the next with renewed energy. "I only hope . . . I hope Ælfred will not fall."

Her searching look in answer to his words made him go on.

"He was our greatest enemy," he admitted. "My father fought against him. But Ælfred and your father Guthrum made the great Peace which allowed this –" he lifted his hand to the sweep of the valley and its horses. He ended with a firm pronouncement.

"Ælfred is a good man. And a great king."

Dagmar was unused to any man who was an effective leader being called good, and was watching Hrald's face carefully.

"I met him," he said next.

Her startle showed in her question. "I thought you had not travelled thence, to Wessex?"

He must go on, having committed the first breach. "I did not. He came here. Or rather to Saltfleet, to speak to me. It was . . . just after Thorfast's death. My father was there too, on his way back to Gotland."

"Ælfred came, to speak to you," she repeated. "A great honour," she murmured.

She was aware of the awkwardness he felt; he had let words escape which he had not meant to utter. Perhaps his embarrassment hid her own; she felt abashed at her clumsy questioning, fearful he had seen the baldness of her goals. At any rate, she would end giving what comfort she could.

"Thank you for your counsel," she said. Her voice, always low, carried with it an unexpected warmth. "I think Inkera's prospects the better here, in Anglia."

Hrald felt he had imparted almost nothing of value to Dagmar's concerns for her sister. Yet the confidence she placed in him by asking meant more than he could easily express.

That night, lying in the alcove given her in the house of Asberg and Æthelthryth, Dagmar struggled for sleep. On the morrow they would set out to return to her cousin Haward's hall. She did not know what might come after that. Haward had made it clear she and Inkera were welcome to remain as long as they wished. He had not intimated that he soon expected a formal call from Hrald and his uncle Asberg, but Dagmar suspected that he held this as a desired end. The Jarl of Four Stones had permitted Haward to hold on to his small ancestral hall, when with Thorfast's death the huge garrison of Turcesig had fallen to Hrald. Her wedding the Jarl would benefit her cousin; she knew this. Hrald and his uncle would be dealing with Haward for her bride-price and dowry, elevating Haward, who was only two or three years older than Hrald, to a position of at least temporary authority over them both. She also knew that Haward was no schemer; and before she had herself met Hrald he had let drop that he counted himself fortunate that he had not in fact been swept from his hall, or one of Hrald's own men be sent there to oversee it and its defence. Haward wanted this union, she was certain.

She was grateful for whatever trust she could place in Haward, for she had no one else to turn to, save her young cousin. She had but slight acquaintance with her oldest half brother Agmund, who must be nearing forty Summers in age. Despite this she would risk trying to travel to him and ask his advice, if he had not already declared himself for Haesten. In doing so he became in her eyes a traitor to their shared father, and she would not seek out such a one to guide her at this critical juncture in her life. Yet he must know so much more than Hrald could offer, concerning her prospects for a favourable marriage in another Kingdom. She had dissembled in asking on behalf of Inkera; it was her own prospects she wished to ascertain, but she could scarcely ask on her own account, not when she felt certain Hrald wanted her as wife. And she profited nothing, for he could tell her little.

Agmund would know more, but by refusing to appeal to him she placed herself at odds with her own potential gain, and interests. She feared Anglia would fall by Haesten's hand and those of his confederates, and yet would not ally herself with her one blood relation who could establish her as a war-lord's wife when the kingdom was parcelled out. She would spare herself a debasing audience before him, pleading to be made a part of his future plans should he and Haesten triumph. Nor could she even expect Agmund's help. He had not reached out to either her or Inkera, despite their distress. He knew the terms of the will as well as they did; better as it had been read out to him by the priest of St Mary's; whereas she and her sister, excluded from this reading, had heard at second hand of its terms.

Her talk with Hrald today had only confirmed what she herself had long suspected, but she had needed to speak it aloud to accept it. Her greatest value – Inkera's too – would be here in Anglia, where at least their blood carried with it the distinction of their great, lost father. A man desiring robust and war-like sons should prize a bride whose own sire had been the uniter of so many Danish war-lords, and been named King over them all. She must count upon that.

Her argument began and ended there. There was nothing else she could offer. Hrald wanted her, and was in fact the best match she could make. As welcoming as his mother had been, Dagmar felt her doubts about her ran deep. His sister Ashild had spared Dagmar several awkward moments, and seemed despite her brisk manner to understand, even commiserate with her. But she had felt woefully inadequate with the Abbess of Oundle. Ashild was right about that august woman – she did seem to know your thoughts.

Tomorrow when Hrald returned from escorting her back to her cousin's she felt the young Jarl would face nearly as much scrutiny from his family as she had. What if, under their pressure, his interest began to wane?

She pressed her hands upon her face in the dark, needing to quell her doubts. She had thought several times during her stay at Four Stones that this had been a keep her father had known, that he had walked and ridden much the same paths here as she now did. It brought no comfort.

She felt instead a flash of anger at the dead Guthrum. It confused the loyalty and respect she also felt for he who had been both father and King.

Her thoughts of her father could never travel in any straight line. He had been indulgent and sometimes even playful with her. Yet before his death he cost her the greatest pain her young life had known, occasioned a loss she knew could never be compensated.

He had cast a young man from his hall and from his service – cast him out, and far worse, passed the decree of outlaw upon him. Everything Vigmund owned was forfeit, and though he was allowed to escape with his life, that was as good as forfeit as well, for if found he could be slain by any without penalty. Further, the decree of outlaw meant that any aiding him could themselves be slain, and their goods confiscated. And it was Vigmund whom Dagmar loved.

He was banished so swiftly and silently that it took her days to learn the truth. Her father would tell her nothing beyond the fact of the judgement, and even puzzled over why she should care. He knew nothing of her and Vigmund. She knew only that his life was forfeit should he ever return.

At this point Vigmund was dead, or beyond recovery. She had lived with this knowledge for three years.

She forced her thoughts away from her past, and back to the pressing need of today. Being her father's daughter was the one thing that distinguished her from any other dower-less maid, and she must cling to that. Guthrum would sometimes jest that women were his sole weakness. After his death she had seen how his surprise gifts of jewellery or trifling sums of silver hid the real neglect in his dealings with his daughters. She and Inkera were thrust upon their own slight resources, left dependent on male relations who rightly felt burdened by these dower-less girls. Why had not her father looked to these matters, why had all his thoughts been to his sons and nephews?

Tonight, admitting her father's pridefully careless indifference, and her own faulty efforts toward a union with Four Stones, she felt herself wanting on nearly every front. She must be more than she was; more modest, more devout, more learned and able, possessed of more riches. She wished these things, but she could only live the truth of her life as she knew it now, and hope that was enough.

Next morning after all had broken their fast Dagmar and Inkera prepared to return to their cousin's hall. Hrald and twenty men, fronted by Jari, would escort them. There was no especial rush, and Hrald, though eager for the ride with Dagmar, was not looking forward to surrendering her to her cousin's care. There was still much he wished to show her, and one particular desire prompted him to seek out his mother and speak to her alone in the kitchen passageway of the hall. The sisters were at that moment gathering their belongings in Asberg's house.

"Mother," he began, and then after a breath went on. "Dagmar. I would like her to see the treasure room."

Ælfwyn straightened up from where she bent over the chest holding the bronze serving platters. She looked at her son's face, reading his hopefulness even in the dimness of the passage. She took in his words. True, the treasure room was an armoury, and vault too for all the treasures of the hall, but it was also the most intimate of spaces as well, that where its Jarl slept. And after having spent time within the palisade, and then seen the foundation at Oundle, Dagmar needed no more proofs of the riches of Four Stones. There was no need to attempt to impress upon her the life that would await the bride of the young Jarl.

He did not expect his mother's look of surprise. Her tone was gentle, but decided.

"Hrald. Your bed is there."

He paused at her words. The room had always a dual nature. It was where the most trusted of his men, Asberg and Jari, would meet and talk with him, where his mother and sister and Burginde too had discussed the workings of the hall. It was where he and Asberg had treated with Thorfast for Ashild's hand, and where she had met alone with him, attended only by Burginde, as he made his suit. And it was bed-chamber too, there, amidst the bound chests laden with swords and other weaponry and casks filled with silver. That broad bed in which he spent increasingly restless nights alone was no small feature of the room.

His uncertainty was there upon his face. He would do nothing to offend Dagmar, and saw now that his mother felt that admitting a young woman to his sleeping chamber was tantamount to such an offence.

"When she returns, she will see it then," he decided. All Ælfwyn could do was smile and nod.

On the ride back to Four Stones Hrald fell into thought. He had returned the sisters to their cousin's keeping. Haward's respectful compliance to the will of Four Stones in all martial issues was gradually being replaced by a warm cordiality between the two young men. It placed Hrald in mind of the far greater number of men at Turcesig, a garrison he now both owned and commanded.

Hrald's first trip to Turcesig as its war-chief had showed surprisingly little treasure there. On the day of the duel Styrbjörn had taken the key to the massive box lock of its weapons room from the inert body of Thorfast, and presented it in silent solemnity to he who had felled him. When Hrald arrived a few days after this, Styrbjörn had been at his side as he turned the key for the first time. Turcesig had been built by Guthrum and kept as a garrison by him, but any silver or precious goods he had amassed while there had been earlier transported to Headleage, or one of the Danish King's other holdings. Its value was in its landmass and the trained men living there, the productive village which had grown up around it in the past five and twenty years, and now most vital of all, its position as a northern buttress to Four Stones, adding to its protection. For this alone Turcesig added great worth to Hrald's holdings.

The chief men of that place had agreed to abide by Hrald's rule the day he had struck down Thorfast. Yet four of these ten who had witnessed the conflict had deserted, fled to try their luck with Haesten. An additional score or two had followed. When he had gone to address the garrison, the massed folk of Turcesig, those of its warriors and hall and village, had listened well to Hrald's appeal for loyalty. Yet he must do more to win it.

He turned to Jari, riding just at his left. "If I am able to wed Dagmar, it will bring Haward closer to Four Stones, as she will serve as peace-weaver between our halls. And as Guthrum's daughter this would extend to Turcesig as well."

Jari gave a grunt. "Haward will give you little trouble, wed her or not. With his brother Thorfast dead he is all too glad to stay in your shadow."

Hrald must admit this view; Haward seemed to possess little of the war-like spirit of his older brother.

"But wedding her will only help," Jari conceded. "If you wed his kin, the temptation to throw in with Haesten or any other must be weighed against the great gain to him in alliance with you. He and his sixty men will be glad to stand behind the shields of our almost two hundred."

Hrald nodded. "I must bring the men of Turcesig that close to us."

Styrbjörn, second in command at Turcesig, had adhered to his oath made there at the duel in which he watched his war-lord Thorfast die. Hrald remembered how Styrbjörn had placed himself at his right when he went to Turcesig to address the warriors thereof. He must build on this good will.

Hrald spoke his plan. "Let us send three score of our men there, to live and work amongst them, and they do the same, that they might know each other the more, and share the partnership of defending both keeps."

Though Asberg had taken a number of warriors with him when he took over the running of Turcesig, neither he nor Hrald had considered such an exchange of men before.

"Já," considered Jari, with a decided nod of his shaggy head. "Those who are young and unwed. They are those you must win, those looking for gain and to make their marks. Asberg will choose at Turcesig, and I will help you pick those from Four Stones."

At this Hrald must smile. "Já, the hot-heads, as you like to call them."

"A man with a wife and babes causes less trouble, that is the truth," Jari confirmed with a laugh of his own. "You will soon be one such," he ribbed.

Hrald grinned, but said nothing. Yet he silently uttered a prayer that his long time body-guard was right.

※※※※※※※※※※

At Haward's hall that night Inkera climbed into Dagmar's alcove. All was quieting. It was late enough that only a few of the serving folk still moved about, but the younger sister's curiosity would allow her no sleep. The banked fire in the middle of the floor glowed iron-red from behind flaking chunks of charcoal. It threw just enough light to move from alcove to alcove. Dagmar edged over to make room for her sister, and curtain pulled, they lay side by side in the dark.

Inkera asked, "So. Will you wed him?"

Dagmar paused just long enough that Inkera answered, for herself.

"I would. But he is such a sober-sides. Does he never laugh?"

Dagmar turned her head to Inkera. In the low light she could barely make out the line of the girl's pert nose. "He does laugh," she defended. "You have seen him do so."

"Já," the younger girl grumbled, "but not as if he meant it."

Dagmar pushed herself up on one elbow to face her younger sister. "What has he to laugh about? We are on the verge of war. There is war, now. We have just had luck enough to be out of its way, so far. What do any of us have to laugh about?"

"Oh, Dagmar, do not scold."

"I am not scolding, silly. And I think as you do. Hrald is my best hope for a good match."

A long moment passed, and when Inkera spoke again her voice was soft, her words almost hesitant. "Do you . . . care for him?"

Even young and sometimes thoughtless as she was, Inkera would not pain her older sister by the mention of her earlier attachment.

Dagmar spent a moment considering. She had not asked herself this question. Now perhaps she had the right to. Her answer was voiced in a low and thoughtful tone.

"I think I do." She added two reasons why she should. "I find Hrald well-favoured, and I believe he is kind."

"He is good-looking," Inkera offered. "But he is young. Three years younger than you."

Dagmar dropped down upon her back again, and squeezed her eyes shut.

"And he is Christian. You will be his only wife," Inkera added. She hoped the same for herself, when she wed.

Inkera's thoughts had gone on. "At least here you are far from Bodil."

Dagmar stared up into the dimness of the roof rafters far overhead. The light from the fire-pit made a slanted webbing of their shadows against the broad wooden planks of the roof. Like a spider who was drunk on mead, she thought.

"Já," she answered. "This travelling we have been doing . . . the best part of it has been being away from Headleage, and my mother."

"The best part is the hope of finding husbands," Inkera corrected, with the return of a merry lilt in her tone.

Dagmar now had a question for Inkera. "If I wed Hrald, what will you do? Would you live there at Four Stones, with me?"

Inkera gave thought. "Hrald's uncle, Asberg, at Turcesig, has two sons. But they are younger than I. And the family is not likely to want us both. I would like to make a match as good as yours, and here . . . it would be hard."

"Já," admitted Dagmar. "And you have time yet. I do not." Her thoughts passed on to the future. "Perhaps it is better that you do not stay with me. Who knows what will happen in the next year or two, if Haesten is not driven off or killed?"

Inkera's answer was uncharacteristically sombre. "Or if Ælfred is," she suggested.

QUICK, AND CERTAIN

HRALD had only lifted his spear when one of the watch-men upon the parapet whistled out warning. It was not yet noon and the Jarl of Four Stones was about to begin sparring with several of his men in the practice yard. At the shrill sound Jari lowered his own spear, but with them still held in their fists, led the way with Hrald to the opening palisade gates.

The whistle was four short blows, a sign that some from Saltfleet approached. Hrald expected this; five men had ridden out two days ago to relieve five who had been stationed at that landing place. They should expect five to return. What made them all go to greet them was the final whistle appended, two sharp and short calls, signalling something untoward.

The condition of the horses and the speed at which their riders drove them made the two extra whistles warranted. Five men rode in on lathered horses, the stressed beasts tossing their heads as the men upon their backs reined them to a stop and leapt down. Tied to the saddle rings of two of them were two additional horses, saddled but riderless. Both horses were spare, their ribs showing from too little feeding and likely hard usage. Mul and his boys and little Bork gathered up reins from over all the beasts' heads and led them to cool in the paddock.

"We had reached the jagged oak when these two horses trotted toward us, coming from the path leading from Snotingaham," explained the lead man, Orri, raising his hand to the horses now being walked by Mul's boys. The jagged oak was a landmark along the way, a venerable but still living tree which through age and perhaps a lightning bolt had split in two.

"We caught the horses and rode back on the path they had come until we saw where they had joined it. With tracks so fresh they were easy to follow. Finally we came upon an encampment, empty of men but active."

"Where?" Hrald questioned. "On Four Stones' land, or beyond?"

Orri shook his head. "There are few markers there; we saw no cairns, but I think we were beyond our borders."

Hrald nodded. Even with double the number of ward-men upon the roads and along the borders such distances could not be perfectly patrolled.

"We kept going, following the tracks of many horses and more men, on foot. Then we came to a field of battle.

"We heard them first, some three score men –" here Orri turned to one of his fellows, who corrected, "More. With those already on the ground, say four score."

Hrald looked up into the sky for a moment. Eighty men fighting, either on his lands or at his border.

"Who," he asked. "Who are they? Could you see?"

"We saw no banners, no ravens nor dragons."

When Danes fought, if they used war-flags, it was often one picturing the raven.

"All Danes, we think, in a battle they were not pre-pared for," ended Orri. "Those at the camp may have had a scout discover the second troop, and they made haste to meet them before they reached their encampment."

Hrald blew out a breath. A conflict so near their borders could not be ignored. He made his decision and turned to Jari. "We must go, now, and find who they are."

"And why they fought," Jari agreed.

The palisade gates were still open and Hrald found his eyes drawn to the village. Beyond the limit of the huts some of the folk stood in ranks in the common fields scything the last of the rye harvest. Others were out amongst their flocks, or with their pigs in the forest, but many were about their own crofts, hoeing weeds from their patches of cabbages, plucking beans, tending to fowl, or wringing washing. Should he order them within the palisade walls, their beasts as well, for safekeeping?

Jari must have read his thoughts, for he spoke. "Nej. Let us wait. We will take an extra horse, so one of us can ride back at speed, if needed, with that order."

Hrald wished no needless fear nor disorder on his folk, and nodded. An extra horse would still be fresh enough to carry one of his men swiftly back and give the alarm.

"But we must send to Haward, and to Turcesig, that they know," Hrald said. He chose two men to ride to each hall, with the scant knowledge that he had of this action so near his own domain. He thought of Dagmar, there at Haward's, and how he wished she were here in the greater safety of his own walls.

He turned to see Ashild moving towards him across the stable yard. She had been out by the Place of Offering, and come through the kitchen yard. Two of the bakers had told her of the arriving men, and of the warning whistle which had also been sounded. The tight cluster of men around her brother and the look on his face told her the alert had been real.

She recognized the men from Saltfleet, knew they were due to return, and a glance at the horses being walked to coolness in the paddock told of the speed at which they had been ridden. That, and the fact that two of the beasts were unknown to her, was preparation for Hrald's greeting to her.

"There is a pitched battle to the west of the jagged oak. The two horses came from there. They saw no war-flags." Hrald gave thought of his response. "I will ride out with twelve men, that we might see who they are. We will not engage."

Her jaw had tightened at his words, and the bile she fought against each morning rose again in her throat. Twelve men, with Jari, to protect Hrald seemed far too few to Ashild, but a small number of observers made discovery the harder. If he were going only to discern who these interlopers were, fewer men were safer.

Her brother's face was not free from alarm, she could see it by the tenseness about his eyes. Yet he spoke with calm decision. The rush of fear she felt was met and overcome by her pride in his voice and manner. Asberg was not with her, to wield authority over Four Stones in Hrald's absence, and Jari must ever be at his side. Hrald's next words proclaimed who must bear the burden of command.

"I leave Kjeld with you," he told her, and inclined his head to this warrior who was one of his most trusted. The import of Hrald's directive was lost on none gathered about him. With this wording, it was almost as if either could be in the other's keeping. He did not say, "Kjeld will command," but rather paired him with Ashild, and her role here.

He named was a frequent sparring partner, and accompanied Hrald and Jari on most of their excursions from the hall. Kjeld was an able warrior upwards of five and twenty years, quick-witted and savvy, and one free from needless anger or viciousness. It was for these last qualities that Hrald had asked him to bring the child Bork back to Four Stones after the boy's father had been killed. Kjeld had also been one of those fifty who had ridden to the defence of Oundle with Ashild, and there had made two kills.

Kjeld, singled out in this way, had taken a step forward. He glanced at the daughter of the hall, and then, in a gesture as quiet as it was striking, moved to stand at her right. The flare of pride Ashild now felt in her breast was on her own account. This act of a trusted and older warrior placed them nearly as co-commanders in Hrald's absence. And Kjeld had been with her before the gates of Oundle; they had shared that action together, giving them almost a warriors' bond.

The Lady of Four Stones now came towards them. Ælfwyn had been within the weaving room up in the hall. She had heard the whistles signaling an arrival, but such were not unusual. It was the added blasts that told of alarm. In such cases she was used to herself appearing, ready to react to any need that arose from the news so carried.

A few words from her son made clear the necessity of his now riding out. Ælfwyn's light blue eyes now travelled to Ashild, standing shoulder to shoulder with Kjeld.

Her mother's lips gently parted, and Ashild stood looking back at her. Ashild's mouth did not smile, but somehow her eyes in that resolute face did.

Ælfwyn found herself mutely nodding, to both Ashild and Kjeld, and then to her son.

⁂

The Lady of the place stood at the gates of Four Stones with Ashild and Kjeld, seeing Hrald off. The air was fresh but the sky slightly over-clouded. A light rain at dawn had dampened the clay road enough that little dust arose from the hooves of the men's horses, even at the canter. The troop headed up the road which had ever divided the village into two, and all working at croft or field noted their Jarl on his bay stallion, and gave a nod in his direction.

To the Jarl's mother standing in the gateway, such acknowledgment held more meaning than Hrald himself could know. He had no memory of Four Stones when the village folk looked up in fear at those who ruled them. Her first husband Yrling had conquered this place through destroying the lives and livelihoods of its family and folk. During her marriage to Sidroc, and then in the long years alone, she had worked tirelessly to restore it, and had in great measure made it as just and pleasant a place as any burh in Wessex or Mercia. It was still a fortress filled with warriors, but these did not ride out on rapacious forays, despoiling neighbouring lands and depriving simple cottars of the grain they needed to survive. Four Stones' fields and flocks now provided plenty in good years, and enough in poorer ones, to keep all within its boundaries fed and clothed. Its horses were movable treasure. Four

Stones sold its beasts throughout South Lindisse, to all who could afford a fine animal, warriors and merchants alike. And this hoofed treasure meant every warrior of Four Stones could be mounted. For an inland fortress without ready access to ships the ability to move swiftly when needed gave its fighting force rare advantage.

Ælfwyn knew she should turn away. The doubled file of men was nearly out of sight. Upon her lips was a silent prayer for her son. Now she must return to the hall and the manifold tasks awaiting her. She had been stitching up new linen sheets in the weaving room, hemming the narrow panels which she and Burginde had jointly woven. No one but her nurse knew whose bed these new sheets would grace. They were destined for Hrald's bed; his bridal bed if the truth be known. They were meant to be one of the many wedding gifts she had planned for him, gifts that she felt certain would be needed soon. Just now she also was at work on other linens, those meant for swaddling a babe, that of her daughter. This too was secret. The panels Ælfwyn wove and hemmed might serve many purposes, and even when Ashild was in the room with her, her working on them did not elicit her daughter's curiosity. No bridal-cup had yet been raised, no babe yet born, and to Ælfwyn it was better that she keep the fruits of her labour a secret until she was certain these woven and sewn offerings, so fraught with meaning, were actually called for.

Still at the Lady of Four Stones' side were Ashild and Kjeld, keeping silent watch as she had. She nodded to them, much as she had before her son, in acquiescence of their role in his absence. Then she started across the forecourt to the hall door.

The two she left spent another moment there, then
turned to face the hall. The interest prompted by the
departure of Hrald and his party had dissipated, and
those involved in preparing the horses or who had stood
watching were returning to their own duties. The sawyers
straddling wood in their saw-pit returned to smoothing
their planks. Mul and his boys about the stable, the men
working in the side sheds at bending soaked staves to
form casks, the boys pumping the bellows for the weap-
onsmith and ironsmith who stood beating red metal, the
kitchen yard workers nearer the hall trundling sacks of
flour – all had resumed their everyday tasks.

Those in temporary command found it hard to con-
template any such return to usual duties. Kjeld, having
over the last two years won a coveted role as a member
of Hrald's body-guard, would normally be amongst those
riding with him. Ashild, having done no spinning nor
weaving yet this day, ought to be following her mother.
Yet she could not. In the past when Hrald had been away,
Asberg had been there, and commanded in his stead.
Ashild had been there with him, a shadow commander, as
she thought herself, acknowledged by no one but valued
by herself. During those times she could indeed return to
her needful everyday tasks, though with an ear cocked to
any whistled warning which might ring out. Today was
different. After her brother's dictum, investing her as an
equal with Kjeld, she could not do this. Marked by his
trust and his words, she felt unable to climb the wooden
stair to the weaving room to work alongside her sister
and aunt, listening to Burginde's cheerful chaffing about
the unevenness of her spun thread. She must stay here
about the work yards, the stable forecourt, any place near

to the watch-men on the parapet. She must stay upon the ready.

Kjeld, looking over the work yards, found his hand rising in some slight gesture, almost as if in question. If there was distinction, even honour in his temporary role, it was also one tinged with tedium. His brothers in arms were out with his Jarl, not him. He must stay here, waiting and watching. He was not used to being bound by restrictions.

Ashild saw the movement of his hand, and guessed at its meaning. This warrior, so accustomed to action, must be feeling the same check on his natural impulses she, as a girl, had ever known. There were those who rode out, those who acted, and those others who were forced to wait.

Almost at the same moment they turned to face each other. Their eyes met, his a warm brown, hers a stormy grey-blue. Her mouth softened, and so did his. Then they both began to laugh.

It was late in the afternoon that Hrald's party reached the jagged oak and turned from there up the westward track. Orri led them with much greater speed than he and the others from Saltfleet had earlier approached, and when they neared the clearing where the encampment was, he rode on alone. A short time later his whistle summoned them all forward.

"Some of the tents have been struck, several are missing from this morning," he told Hrald.

Jari gave a grunt. "Survivors, making it back, and quitting the place," he judged. Indeed, the churned soil said as much, showing the hoofprints of horses ridden next to holes where tent posts had been hastily yanked.

They rode about the abandoned camp, dismounting long enough to peer into the remaining tents. Clothing, bedding, and cooking gear could be found, but no weaponry nor war-flags from which they could discern allegiance.

They rode on at a brisk walk. The path leading to the battle ground was more marked for the horses which had been ridden back to the camp, and breaks in the trees admitted light. A movement to one side was followed by the whicker of a horse. A dark chestnut gelding, saddled and bridled, moved out of the green shadows of the shrubby growth. Orri, still in the lead, was quick to urge his horse toward the animal, which came without hesitation.

"And another," Jari nodded. At least they were gaining in beasts for their trouble. Any horse was a boon, but one complete with trappings was a prize indeed. With some rest and feeding in the valley of horses this gelding, like those brought in earlier in the day, would put on needed flesh and soon be fully fit for use.

"Blood." This word came from Orri, standing by the found horse's head. He lifted his hand from where he had been running it along the chestnut's neck. It was red from it. Orri moved both hands along the gelding's neck, from poll to withers. "It is not his; he is unhurt."

Orri tied the new animal to his saddle ring and was about to swing up upon his own mount. He stopped; they all did, at the sound of a human groan.

Hrald and Jari pressed their horses forward toward the sound. There, behind the clump of elders the gelding had moved from lay a man, face down where he had fallen from the animal's back.

They got off their horses. Jari moved first to the downed man, knife drawn, should this be a ruse and the man be ready to attack. The size of the spreading red blotch on the fallen man's tunic rendered this possibility remote. Still, Jari used his booted foot to prod the man, slipping it under his belly and with the use of his free hand flipping him over upon his back. The deeper groan the man gave at this, and the pallor of his face, told of ebbing life.

"Who do you fight for?" asked Hrald. His low and urgent demand sounded almost choked in his own ears.

The warrior Hrald questioned was of thirty years or more; lean and weather-beaten. His face, contorted by his grimace, sported a reddish beard, clotted with deeper red from a cut through the right eyebrow. The eyes were closed, and mayhap the one beneath the torn eyebrow could not open. No sword was at his waist, but a knife was there, one the man was beyond reaching for. It was not easy to stand over such a man, harshly demanding answer of one who had perhaps mere moments to live. Hrald had his own sword in his hand for defence, but was aware he was clenching his left hand as well.

The dying man breathed out his answer. "Haesten."

"And who did you fight?"

The man's grimace drew the deeper, but he did not speak.

"Men of Wessex? Or Mercia?"

The mouth moved.

"Agmund."

Agmund. Guthrum's eldest son, who had declared himself for the invader from Frankland. Now Agmund had turned against Haesten.

Hrald lifted his eyes to meet those of Jari. "What . . . what does this mean?"

Jari shook his shaggy head. "A splinter group, perhaps, followers of each who deserted, looking for better offers. Or . . . a true fracture between Agmund and Haesten." His eyes dropped to the man before them. "If he was one of Haesten's on some unknown mission, he was trying to head back to their camp." Jari tilted his head toward the abandoned encampment they had passed. He looked about them into the deep green of the surrounding trees as he considered this, then down at the figure at their feet. "One thing, dying men rarely lie."

The man had sounded again, more rasping wheeze than groan. He had taken a hit in the chest, and his lungs must be failing.

"Asgard awaits you," Jari now said.

The nod the dying man gave was acquiescence and welcome both. As Jari bent over with his knife, the man forced his eyes open, ready to meet the death blow Jari's sure hand delivered to the hollow of the throat.

Hrald watched with narrowed eyes. Jari was Christian in name and in practice, but this Dane's comfort could come only from the Old Gods. Hrald had sometimes mused on the dictum that no Christian should take another's life as an act of mercy, only as an act of war. But he was glad that Jari ended this Dane's suffering, enemy and renegade though he be.

A shake of Jari's head at Orri told him Jari wanted none of what might be found upon the dead Dane. Jari

was second in riches only to Asberg amongst the men of
the hall, and the younger Orri, lately stationed at Saltfleet,
had scant chance to win battle-gain. But Orri must wait to
collect it, for first they must reach the plain upon which
he had seen the fighting.

They had brought archers with them, six of them, to
provide cover from a distance should any of them need
to creep near to the field of combat. The hours that had
passed since discovery and return rendered such cover
unneeded. The fighting ground opened up before them at
the end of the trail they followed, a tract of no great size
running to oozing marsh along a stream bank. No man
stood upright upon that field, and no remaining horse
wandered the trampled ground, or skirted the trees,
bereft of its rider.

None upon the ground lived. Their bodies had been
so thoroughly plundered to tell at once of the need of the
victors. Weapons, purses, jewellery, any protective gear
these men may have donned, all was gone. Some of them
were stripped naked; even their boots had been taken.
Those still clothed bore huge rents in their tunics, ren-
dering the blood-soaked items beyond use. The forsaken
state of the shattered bodies and the desperation of their
looting was underscored by the ceaseless buzzing of flies,
circling above the dead, landing upon open wounds from
which blood pooled.

Hrald looked upon this in fascinated horror. He had
seen men, freshly killed, when he had fought Thorfast
and his men. Thorfast had fallen by his own hand, and
Jari had killed both Thorfast's body-guards. Gunnulf,
Jari's brother and Hrald's friend, had fallen first. These
had been men Hrald had known, and in Gunnulf's case,

grown up with. More recently his men had felled Bork's father and another man, in self-defence. This grisly spectacle before him was of far greater scope, and looking on the toll, it took every power of his inner command to keep his gorge from rising.

They counted the bodies of thirty-four men, considerable slaughter if eighty had engaged. The broken stream banks opposite showed where men and horses had fled, splashing in and climbing out of the water to bolt towards the forest beyond.

"No pennons, no flags," muttered Jari, returning to where Hrald sat his horse. No golden dragon of Wessex, no green serpent of Mercia had been left behind, but then any such was a prize piece of booty. From what they could see it was true, what the dying man had told them. This was Dane against Dane.

Without war pennons or distinct battle cries it was ever hard to discern who might be facing which enemy on the field of battle. It was true that Saxon swords differed in subtle ways from those of the Danes, and that the Saxons most often bore as their knives the distinctive angled-bladed seax, hung lengthwise across the belly, instead of the straight-backed knives Danes carried at their hips. But many warriors adopted the weaponry of those they had vanquished. The several fractured shields remaining gave little clue as to who these men had been. Few were ever painted in such a way to directly signify that Saxon or Dane held them, and no war-chief asked that his men carry similar shields. One might see a rune carved or painted within the protective inside of a shield, where the bearer might see it and take heart, or a depiction of the Christian cross. Indeed, some men inscribed both. From the little left they could discern almost nothing, save the likely truth of the dead Dane's final words.

The dissension in Haesten's troops had grown so extensive that the followers of the greatest of these who had thrown in with him, Guthrum's own son Agmund, were now openly hostile towards the men of their erstwhile leader. None could tell what had occasioned this deadly engagement. Had both set their sights on a common target, one they gauged they could conquer with two or three score trained men, such as Oundle, or Haward's hall? Was it a squabble turned deadly over their limited resources? Warriors who have seen little success and less feeding will swiftly move to block any in their path to food and silver.

Hrald remembered the words of his father at Saltfleet, the day they had ridden there to meet Ælfred. Sidroc had reminded them all that Haesten's men were hungry, and had followed their war-chief a long way, and with too little reward. How much hungrier would these men be now, Hrald thought, how much more desperate. Even with the destructive raids they had carried out, food so won was quickly consumed, and men could not live long on promises.

They turned their horses back the way they had come. Orri took the little he could from the man they had found alive, and Hrald awarded the man's horse to him as well. The rest of the men rode through the encampment, taking anything of use. These were mainly articles of clothing and cooking implements, but one man found a bridle, and another a small store of silver in a worn purse stashed beneath bedding. Anything of real worth they would offer to Hrald, but those who had ridden to fight had taken all they had with them, and some of that must now be in the hands of Agmund's men.

Hrald sat his horse as his men combed through the scant offerings. Several crows had alighted in a nearby tree, as if watching, and then flew off toward where the dead lay. The carrion-eating beasts of sky and woodland would have their fill.

Jari was also still horsed, and with Hrald watched the flight of the crows.

"If the Gods smile Haesten and Agmund will kill each other," Jari offered.

※※※※※※※※※

On his return to Four Stones at dusk that day Hrald again sent riders to both Turcesig and to Haward. They carried the news of what they found, Danes who had fought and killed each other on the border of Hrald's lands. That those retreating had taken a southwesterly track was all he could append. Still, the fact that the intruders had not driven northeast, with the abbey of Oundle or either Hrald's or Haward's hall as immediate target provided some relief.

He took the further step of sending thirty men to Oundle, as precaution. His mother had as much as asked for this, and he could not deny the abbey greater succour. He must grow used to the fact that a standing force of warriors need be left there. This was disruptive to the abbey and likely distasteful to its Abbess, but it must be done. Yet it left Four Stones with thirty fewer men for its immediate defence. With the doubled patrols along his borders and the fifty men always at the valley of horses to protect the animals he had fewer than ninety warriors within his gates. Those lately come from Turcesig he shared out amongst these duties.

Hrald's thoughts turned to Dagmar. Indeed, his mind was never far from that young woman. He wanted her to return to Four Stones; the battle ground he had just surveyed was too near her for his comfort. She remained at Haward's hall, but her half sister Inkera had returned under her cousin's escort to her home at Headleage. Dagmar's remaining behind was enough of a prompt to Hrald to encourage him to invite her again.

His mother knew Dagmar was there, and perhaps was not surprised when Hrald came to her with his request. He had awakened early considering it, and appeared at the gate of her bower garden as she was leaving for the hall. He had ever been respectful of his mother's private enclave, and her inviting Dagmar and Inkera to dine with her there on their first visit had seemed a mark of her favour toward the young women. Since his boyhood he himself had been a rare visitor within that enclosure. He felt sure no man had ever ventured within; he had never seen his father do so.

His mother came toward him with the loving smile she almost always met him with, the slight crinkle about her eyes showing her interest.

"I would have Dagmar back," he told her.

His mother paused before responding. "I should like to know her more," she said, and then smiled again. "And for you to know her more, as well."

Later that morning Hrald shared this with his sister. He would send word to Dagmar that he would arrive in two days to escort her to Four Stones.

"If she will come," he ended. The small laugh he added was one at his own expense, and his briefly lowered chin did not hide the slight colouring of his cheek.

Ashild kept her eyes upon him, taking him in. There was a ringing hopefulness in those four words. She felt of a sudden filled with a rush of love, and pity both, for her younger brother. She tried to master this sensation, squeezing her hands into fists, so that her fingernails bit into the flesh of her palms. She felt outside of her own control, and in these past few weeks grown a stranger to herself. The weepiness she disdained in weak women was something she fought against almost every day. And she never knew what would bring it on – the sight of the men sparring together, a glimpse of the baker's daughter with leathern mitts braving the heat of the oven to pluck steaming loaves from its glowing mouth, or a foal frisking joyfully alongside its dam. Almost anything could make her cry. She found it impossible to marshal her thoughts as to imagine the life ahead for her and her child. She had made two quick and momentous decisions – her love-making with Ceric, and the second, not to rid herself of its produce. Both had transformed her, but the second, surrender to the coming babe, was altering the course of her life.

Add to this the changes to her body, the morning retching which met her when she awakened, the ever-tender breasts, that sense of constant bloat presaging the swelling of her waist – and she was utterly unsettled in her own skin. And it was all made the worse by the fact that only her mother and Burginde knew. Hrald, with whom she had shared so many secrets, with whom she had a deep understanding – he was outside the knowledge of this great change wrought in her. And she yearned to tell him. Right now she could not. She must respond to his appeal for support.

She always knew her brother must wed, just as she once thought she must, as well. But she had never been able to picture the helpmeet Hrald would choose. Now, faced with a woman as impressive as Dagmar, Ashild grappled with her own mixed feelings. She wanted Hrald's happiness as much as she wanted her own; more she understood now, as she felt she could not realise her own happiness.

He must wed a woman worthy of him, and one who would be worthy of her new estate. None could know if Dagmar might be such; perhaps she was. All that was certain was Hrald's wife would become the Lady of Four Stones. On her management and judgement would depend the future welfare of hall and village. Their mother would be there to guide her, but such guidance could be ignored. A new Lady of Four Stones would impose her own standards, could dismiss or reassign any or all of the kitchen and hall folk who had faithfully performed their duties under their mother. And Ælfwyn herself would no longer be essential; she would become a relic of a past Dagmar had no part in. The current Lady of Four Stones might choose to re-order her life at Oundle, as her own mother had . . .

Ashild took a breath. "Oh, she will come," she answered.

Hrald sent Kjeld with his invitation. He rode back with the news that Haward would bring Dagmar himself; Hrald need not come for her. Hrald was struck by this. It seemed significant to him, as if her cousin were delivering her, handing her over as a true guardian might, to her new home. It implied his consent.

Haward did not linger after the welcome-cup, taken two days later at the high table. He gave his thanks to the Lady of the hall, and parted from his cousin with affectionate words. Yet he seemed to move with new ease and comfort amongst them, regarding all he looked upon within the hall with a familiarity not before noted. It was Hrald's mother and sister who noticed this, and the snapping dark eyes of Burginde, which rarely missed anything. Hrald's attention was taken up by his guest. Dagmar looked as well as she always did, her long and rich brown hair cascading from the new linen head wrap she had completed, much adorned with coloured thread work in blue and green.

Once her cousin left, Dagmar was again shown to the empty house of Asberg and Æthelthryth. She had not slept here without her sister, but was told by the same serving maid who had attended to her on prior visits that she would sleep within as well, should she be fearful of being alone in a strange place.

"I have not felt so safe anywhere, as I do here," her stately visitor confessed.

The weather had turned unusually warm, with a kind of crackling dryness to the air almost unknown in Lindisse with its abundant rain. The rye had already been gathered, the threshing floor deep with it as the men flailed in the slight breeze blowing in the open doorways of the common granary. In the fields barley heads trembled in the heat on their golden stalks, and tender lettuces in the vegetable plots of village and hall went from leaf to tough and bolted stalk in a single day.

Such weather did not favour riding out nor hawking, though Hrald was eager to again do both with his guest. Instead they walked out the palisade gates together, pausing before the preaching cross, its stone warm to their touch. Not much presented itself before them, save for the villagers' huts with their roofs of thatch, sitting snug within woven wattle fences. But off to the left lay the burial ground, where the village folk had long been buried. It was rimmed by a score of yews, their sober yet evergreen boughs serving as reminder of death and immortality. These yews proclaimed by their height and girth they had been planted long before the memory of any who yet lived. Their scaly-barked and ruddy trunks supported growth that shot Heaven-ward, green arms lifting and interlocking far over their young Jarl's head. The burial ground they encircled was by nature a solitary place, but one not devoid of its own attraction, and they made for it now. The yews were dense enough that no paling was needed to keep a loose cow or sheep from straying in. A low and rough gate was there as the only opening, and they stood at it as they looked in.

It was a grassy place within, its growth scythed down twice during Summer. Markers for those who lay resting there were few, and of uncarved rounded stones chosen for their shape or colour. Fragments of planed wood showed where crosses had once been pounded upright, and now as was fitting were allowed to return to the earth, just as those whose brief passage here had. Roses were also within, a tangle of them in red and pink and white. The bees that flew drowsily amongst their blossoms made one forget this was a place of death; to those tireless workers it was one more garden.

Dagmar was quiet looking on this, and when she spoke did so with a musing thoughtfulness.

"There is a loveliness here," she offered, with a slight smile at Hrald. "One even in a place like this."

He took her remark to mean Four Stones as a whole. While he knew his home to be a worthy bulwark, he was glad she found beauty here as well, and not only within his mother's bower garden.

Her eyes had returned to the heaped roses rising amongst the green tips of the grass.

Her nearness, the softness of her voice, the gentle melancholy of where they stood, pressed him onward. He would risk speaking to her.

First he craned his neck over his shoulder. Their backs were to the village, and though they were far from earshot he knew the eyes of some of his folk must be upon them. Sure enough, a few old women, standing at their scrub basins, had turned in their work towards them. Sure enough, they ducked their heads and scrubbed with greater industry when he looked in their direction.

He knew that his guest should not be left strictly alone with him. Neither of their sisters were near to serve as chaperone. But when they had set off it seemed to Hrald that the village itself acted as such; they would be within sight of many as they worked about their crofts. Now he would have a few words alone with Dagmar, and would hazard his next action. With a lifted hand he invited her to walk with him along the line of yews surrounding the burial ground. Hidden behind their shelter they would soon be outside the sight of any but the few sheep they might encounter in the far pasturage.

They moved off together, walking side by side, with only the slight soughing of the yew boughs and the chirping of an orange-beaked blackbird as company. Hrald had in mind a question. Dagmar had spent weeks at her cousin's hall, broken only by her trip to Cruland and her visits here to Four Stones. Hrald wanted to know about another destination she had mentioned.

"You spoke of going to Dane-mark, on your first visit here," he began. It had been at the first meal they had shared together, there in his mother's bower garden, when Dagmar of a sudden proclaimed her interest in travelling to the land of both their fathers.

He could hear the uncertainty in his own voice, as if he feared her response. Yet he must ask.

She answered, in mild tone, with a question of her own.

"Do you never desire to see Dane-mark? It is your true home," she said in way of return.

He gave thought. His father had rarely spoken of his life in Dane-mark, and never with regret. He had made it clear that seeing Angle-land, with its endless forests and fertile soil, dearth of folk and ready riches to be found in its keeps and holy houses, put Dane-mark out of his mind forever. And Hrald was not only of Dane-mark. His mother was a woman of Wessex.

"All I own is here," he answered. He lifted his hands as he said this, as if to include the whole of Four Stones, and even beyond. His next words were offered with lowered voice, and a look at her from under his dropped eyelids. "All I care for is here."

She did not answer, prompting him to speak. "And you – do you still wish to go there, to Dane-mark?"

She looked down as well, the dark lashes veiling her eyes, and then up at him. His eyes met hers fully.

"No, I no longer have that desire."

This admission signalled a shift, one that could only benefit him. Before he could speak she went on.

"Your hall and men, your family and lands," she numbered. "You have much to remain for."

She continued, with a smile. "And you have a friend in the King of Wessex." This was said almost teasingly, and he laughed as well. "And your good friend of Wessex, Ceric, I think you named him."

"Yes. Ceric of Kilton. As I mentioned, he is the King's godson. But he fights with the King's son, Prince Eadward."

She seemed to reflect on this. "Hard for friends to be parted such great distances," she offered.

"One day I hope he will be more than a friend, kin in fact."

She looked her question, which he readily supplied.

"Ashild. Ceric has pursued her a long while. They have known each other as long as Ceric and I have, and he is set upon her. Next to the King's burh at Witanceaster, I think his at Kilton must be amongst the richest in all Wessex."

"And yet she hesitates?"

"Yes. I think if there were peace . . . it would be easier for her to accept."

Her full lips barely bowed into a smile, and her response was so softly spoken that he leant closer to her.

"Sometimes those who follow their hearts cannot wait for peace."

He felt a catch in his chest, as if her words and tone forced him to hold his breath. After a moment he spoke.

"I would take your hand," he asked. She offered it by lifting it to him, and he held it in his own, then laid his left hand over it. His heart, thumping in his chest, felt as though it was pounding in his ears as he went on.

"Fate is too uncertain to wait. Will you be my wife, Dagmar, and join your father's blood with mine, of both Anglia and Wessex?"

He had spoken to her first, and on his own account, giving his uncle no notice. He felt certain Asberg was expecting him to consult with him before doing so. Yet the knowledge that Dagmar's bride-price would not be high and thus could be easily met freed him from the absolute need to speak to his uncle before declaring his intentions to her. Just as Hrald knew his mother expected his suit of Guthrum's daughter, so must Asberg.

And Hrald did not wish to dwell on the fact that the woman he desired would come cheaply. Dagmar was of natural regal bearing, possessed of a kind of beauty which deeply attracted him, and had a signal distinction in being a King's daughter. If her father still lived and had made suitable allowance for her, her bride-price would be a sum which might stretch the limits of Four Stones' treasure room. She would be worth every ounce of it, and the fact that he could not demonstrate this to her kin bothered him not a little. Her value was apart from what he would have been demanded to pay for her, but as proof of his commitment he almost wished he was forced to dig deep into his store of treasures so he might make her his own.

Her gaze was cast down, where his two hands clasped her own. She lifted her eyes to him and gave her answer.

"I will wed you," she whispered. This was spoken with enough gravity to imbue a sacred vow, and indeed he saw her blue eyes were filling.

He gave a squeeze to her hand, and brought his head nearer hers. Their lips met, a gentle brushing, but the first kiss Hrald had known.

When he pulled back he saw she was truly smiling. The tiny drops of salt water on her lashes only added to the lustre of her eyes.

He wished to press her to him, and began to pull her close when he stopped himself. That would be wrong, a liberty he could not yet take. This single kiss, this and her words, was the bond.

A sense of lightheadedness replaced the deep pounding he had felt. He almost began to laugh, in relief and in joy both. He lifted her hand in his and kissed the back of it, pressing it to his lips as he wanted to press his own to hers.

She gave a small laugh as well, as if she shared in his relief and happiness.

"We will wed, as soon as my uncle and your cousin come to terms." He looked about him, eyes raking the blue sky and then coming back to rest on her. "Wed, in this fine and warm weather."

He still held her hand, and she gave it a returning squeeze of assent. He thought of something more.

"Headleage," he said. "You must return there, to get your things. And bring your mother to witness our being wed."

Her faced changed, a shift from her smile to a look of true concern.

She took a breath. "I have little there. Anything of worth I have with me." Another breath followed, with a hushed admission. "That is the truth of the narrowness of my life there, Hrald."

This speech was striking on two accounts. The first was the modest honesty of her straitened condition, and how she had braved to tell him of it. The second was the utterance of his name. Never before had she used it in direct address.

He was moved, deeply so, by both, and in response again allowed himself to touch his lips to hers.

Her words carried with them something more, something near an appeal. It was reflected in the soberness of her face, an almost pained expression that shadowed her loveliness for a moment.

"You need not go," he assured her. "And I would rather you not, for the risk of travel. We will send word, and gifts as well, to your mother, bidding her come under my escort."

She did not answer, but his mind was wheeling with plans. He must go first to his mother, and now; then soon ride to Turcesig and get Asberg so they might deal with Haward.

They had paused in their walking, at the furthest point from the gate of the burial ground. They still traced the line of the thick greenery of the yews, while beyond them in the open pasture not even a single sheep had witnessed Hrald's profession. This moment had been granted them alone, as hallowed as it had been solitary. Now they continued on, rounding the final corner of the hedging, and coming back to the front of the ground. One of the old women who had been watching them was still there at her wash-tub, and gave a toothless grin in their direction. Hrald had to keep himself from letting loose a hoot of joy in salutation.

Nearing the burial ground gate the new couple looked in a final time. There along this edge of yews lay a freshly dug grave, before unnoticed by them. They both paused a moment, looking on the still-dark clods of soil. Hrald recalled his mother telling him that a woman and newborn babe of the village had died, not two days ago. This must be their double grave. The young mother left three small children and a husband so numbed by grief that when the Lady of Four Stones appeared, bringing foodstuff from the kitchen yard to his croft, he could do no more than bow his head to her in thanks.

How short life is, Hrald told himself. But the woman soon to be his wife was now walking at his shoulder.

⁂

When Hrald and Dagmar returned to the hall, he went out in search of his mother. He found her on the village road, Burginde at her side, each bearing a now-empty hand basket. In addition to visits she made to those recently bereaved, it was her custom to call upon the ill or aged fortnightly or when pressing need arose, and carry to them some small delicacies of the hall kitchen yard, cheeses or small crocks of nourishing broths. Ælfwyn had expected to hear such news from her son, and took it with calm acquiesce. Hrald's own joy was enough to bring a smile to her lips, as she listened.

"I will go to Turcesig, get Asberg, and we will see Haward," he went on. "We will be wed as soon as we may, on the step of Oundle."

She nodded, smiling still. She must not formally welcome Dagmar to the family until the deal had been struck; to do so was to invite Fate to look askance at the union. When Hrald returned, having won her cousin's consent and come to terms would be soon enough.

He began walking back with them, but his jangling stride betrayed his eagerness to return in haste to the hall, where he had left his betrothed. His mother urged him to go on.

Burginde had remained silent throughout the brief telling of Hrald's report. Now her mistress murmured aloud her thoughts. "I must write to Sigewif, and tell her."

"Aye," nodded Burginde. "Though there be not much to tell. 'Twas as quick as it was certain." She gave her head a shake. Dagmar had been a willing worker, and she must admit the girl had in every way treated her with marked respect, as if she were no servant, but an aunt to the Lady of Four Stones. She is either quick, or kind, Burginde had sometimes thought; perhaps both.

Burginde was not one to dwell on the past, but now, having lately visited the croft of an old man dandling a toddling grandson on his withered lap, found herself thinking of how hard had been Hrald's teething. An image arose of her holding the little Hrald, trying to comfort him with a crust of bread as he cried from pain.

LEAVE ROOM
TO BE SURPRISED

"WEAPONRY."

That single word was Haward's answer to the question posed by Asberg as to what would be Dagmar's bride-price.

The directness with which her cousin announced it said as much as the price itself.

Haward had shown Asberg and Hrald into his hall, and from thence into the small room that served as armoury. The three men stood facing each other, Hrald and Asberg on one side, their host on the other. They had taken a cup of ale in the hall proper, after which Haward had invited them within, where Asberg had cleared his throat, and stating his nephew's desire to wed Dagmar, asked what might be the terms.

Haward had given thought before this visit as to what he would request in exchange for Dagmar's hand. Four Stones was famed for its horses, but Haward had only sixty men, most of whom, due to his late uncle's generosity, were already horsed. His interest did not lie in more animals. What he asked for, steel, coupled with the tone of his voice, was slightly unsettling in its baldness. Yet each father or guardian would ask for that which would be of greatest benefit to their own hall and holdings.

Asberg answered with a soft but rumbling, "Já." He had told Hrald to say as little as possible during this dealing, and Hrald remained silent as they both absorbed the solitary word of Haward's demand.

"And in return?" Asberg wished to know.

Haward gave a quick smile. "Dagmar herself, a maid of considerable charm, and more than this, daughter to Guthrum, King of the Danes of East Anglia."

The King named was dead, the Kingdom he had united in tatters. Yet blood was blood. Dagmar was the daughter of a King, who himself had been nephew to the King of Dane-mark. For a Danish Jarl in Angle-land seeking a wife on whom he could sire sons to fight at his side, this lineage was second to none.

It remained that Dagmar had been left dower-less, though, and her cousin's next words addressed this unhappy fact.

"Also, this."

Haward had crossed behind them to a table covered by a length of linen which he now drew off.

Upon it, arranged with some care, was a small pile of hack silver, a footed silver bowl of a handspan's width, four silver mantle pins of varying sizes, and two necklets, sized for a man, of twisted silver.

Haward watched his guests as their eyes fell upon this offering. The older man's eyes, well practised in assessing booty, flicked over it without widening or narrowing as he gauged the value before them. Hrald's expression was even harder to assess.

Asberg gave a glance to his nephew before returning his gaze to the metal upon the table. No gold. Hrald's mother had brought cloth of purple, bronze basins and ewers, silver salvers and cups, gemmed arm bands and buckles of silver, and amongst coins and other ornaments of the rare metal, an entire plate of pure red gold. Asberg would never forget the day of the revealing of that treasure, pulled by Yrling piece by piece from the waggons to the acclaim of all his men. But given Dagmar's circumstances they must not expect gold.

Asberg was ready with his own offer. He looked to Haward and named it.

"Five good swords. Twenty spear heads."

Haward stood silent. Other than gold outright, weaponry was the most valuable of all goods he could hope for, and Hrald's uncle was meeting his request head on. But Haward, sister-less as he was, had never bargained thus, with the hand of a kinswoman at stake. He would be glad for five more good blades, but took thought that the first offer was rarely the best.

He wanted this match, and though she had not said so directly to him, felt that Dagmar did as well. She had certainly gone willingly with him to Four Stones. Still, Haward gave his head a slight shake.

While he was waiting for Haward's response, Asberg had picked up the silver bowl. It was a well-worked piece, the silver walls thick and undented, with curving arms projecting from either side giving the whole balance. Holding it in his hands, Asberg saw it had served as a chalice, for a flared-armed cross was engraved within, where the priest, tipping the bowl up to his mouth, might see it during the performance of the sacrament. Wilgot will be happy with this, he thought, thinking of how that priest might share in the bounty of the coming nuptials.

But at that moment Haward shook his head. His host's rejection of his offer made Asberg return the bowl to the table with an almost careless indifference.

"Ten swords," Hrald countered. They were the first words he had uttered since entering the armoury, and were spoken with crisp decision. "Chosen from the chest which holds those reserved for me." His eyes were fastened on Haward, and they shifted for a moment to his uncle before returning to Haward. "And twenty spear heads."

Haward knew what this meant. The swords would not only be good. They would be of the best, pattern-welded, and worthy to be borne by the Jarl himself. He could assume that Hrald's pride would assure that the twenty spear heads would be similarly fine; new, their edges unchipped, their deep sockets ready to be fitted to spear shafts of ash. Haward could not gainsay that it was a great deal more than what Dagmar would be bringing with her.

Asberg had not allowed his face to change at his nephew's interjection. He wished the boy had kept his silence, which was ever the most powerful response in any dealings. Yet he understood why he could not.

His thoughts turned back through the years, to when he had gone to Sidroc, asking for the hand of his young sister in law, Æthelthryth. Sidroc would not let her go lightly; as comely as Æthelthryth was, and sister as she be to the Lady of Four Stones, any of the men within his hall would eagerly wed her, even if it meant putting away their current wives to do so. And in fact the young woman had refused him. It had set Asberg back on his heels; he was second in command at Four Stones and had confidence his suit would be welcomed. It was not just him; after the abuse she had suffered at the hands of her captors during the fall of Cirenceaster she was inclined to no man. Yet Æthelthryth, possessed of both natural cheerfulness and deep practically, was blest also with handiness and thrift. The many ways in which she worked alongside her older sister in righting Four Stones made her all the more attractive to Asberg. He grew the more smitten, so much so that as she steadily warmed he readily agreed to every condition thrown before him. Æthelthryth, though young, was of decided mind, and did not hesitate in providing them. He must build a house of his own for their shared use, keep his beard trimmed, and foreswear any other woman. She held out until Asberg was half mad with desire. She ordered him to be shriven by Wilgot for all past sins, and catechized in the faith of Rome. As a final condition she insisted he swear before the priest that even should she die young their offspring would be raised within the Church. All this he readily agreed to. Reviewing this in his mind, Asberg decided he could not chide his nephew for failing to hold firm at the five swords.

Dagmar's cousin stood looking at both his guests. He knew nothing of Asberg's courting of Æthelthryth, but he shared the same desire Asberg had then, to bind himself closer to the man who was his war-chief. That war-chief stood before him, and Haward was glad to speak his next words.

"Ten good swords," he agreed, looking up at Hrald, "from your own reserve. And twenty spear heads."

Ashild was sitting in the bower house garden. Her morning queasiness and resultant retching meant that she seldom made an appearance within the hall before noon. The dizzying heat from her head had abated, and just to sit still surrounded by her mother's blue cornflowers and the deep green of the beech hedge lent her coolness. Burginde had this morning carried to her the news that her brother had ridden off to bargain with Haward for Dagmar's hand. Now the nurse sat down next to her at the small table, in a silence that was as thoughtful as it was companionable.

"Do you like her," Ashild finally asked.

The nurse made a clicking sound with her teeth. "Matters not if I do or do not," she answered, with that briskness she often used to sum up her position. But now, looking at Ashild's slightly downcast face, she added something in a brighter tone.

"Your own father – the Dane – I did not like him, not one bit. And he turned out to be a far better man than I had judged."

Ashild had to smile. She envied Burginde every moment she had spent about her father, even those in which the old nurse had disparaged him. It was harder to place herself in her mother's role, that of wife and bedmate to a war-chief as formidable as Yrling had been. And her mother had been years younger than she was when she entered into that union. How would she have reacted, under that strain, she must ask herself.

Burginde reached over and patted Ashild's hand. "Leave room to be surprised, that taught me. Leave room."

Ashild nodded. She had spent weeks berating herself over her reluctance about Dagmar. Was it Dagmar herself, or would she feel the same toward any woman Hrald had determined to wed? She questioned her own motives, unable to untangle the threads of her response to Guthrum's daughter. She could not envy Dagmar her stately bearing nor abundant beauty; those things were given by Fate or God or the Gods, all powers far beyond the command of those here on Midgard. What Ashild hated was in herself, the sense of jealousy she felt creeping into her heart around this woman who had captured Hrald's imagination and attention. She loved her brother with a kind of fiery protectiveness that granted her leave to question Dagmar's intentions and Hrald's discernment. It placed her in a role she despised, and Dagmar into a role she had feared for herself should she go to Kilton, of being crushed under expectations unattainably high. But here she was not being judged and found wanting; she was become a judge, of her own making. It placed her outside the love she bore for her brother.

Her lips twisted into a wry smile, thinking on the endless loop of her ruminations. The fact that she had found herself with child the very day that Hrald had found the woman he would wed was irony too great not to smile. Two beginnings, on one and the same day. Yet her beginning had also signalled an ending.

She picked up the cup of well water which Burginde had earlier brought her and took a final sip. The acidic taste of her vomit in the back of her throat had receded. The larger issue remained. She could hide her morning retching easily enough, living in the bower house as she did, with her mother and Burginde to care for her. Burginde made up any number of soothing herbal possets for her unsettled belly, and by night she was able to eat well, even heartily, in the hall. But soon her waist would thicken, and even given the looseness of her gowns, her truth proclaim itself to all.

"I must let the hall know," Ashild told her, setting down her empty cup. "I will not have them whispering and wondering, grinning behind my back as they guess."

Burginde was clear-seeing in these matters. "Then we will make of it no secret, my girl. For after all, 'tis no secret. The whole hall, and village too, knows Ceric of Kilton has been courting you, and for years. We will make of it their secret, by making it open. They might as well believe a secret wedding, as not."

Ashild's eyes opened the wider as Burginde went on.

"'Tis a simple thing for me to bear the news. A word or two to those in the kitchen yard will reach the ears of all in hall and village. Every good gossip will spread it for us. You need say nothing."

"What will you say?"

Burginde leant forward in eagerness, her dark eyes snapping with glee.

"Only the truth, my girl. How the hall rejoices that Ashild will soon bear the child of Ceric of Kilton. All knew of his recent visit."

Ashild had set her elbows on the table, and with folded hands and furrowed brow looked over at the nurse as she went on.

"Wilgot may not have muttered his prayers over you, but you are man and wife, for you gave freely of yourself, and he to you." Burginde's firmness in this made it its own proclamation.

Ashild was forced to consider her words. Indeed, Ceric had named her wife several times. Amongst the

Danes, two need only to agree they were man and wife for their hand-fast to be upheld in law. Even in Wessex a union need not be blest by a priest or even witnessed by others. It was enough for a man and woman to both consider themselves wed to the other.

Burginde was watching Ashild's face, and went on with renewed strength. "So what if the wedding be a secret one? 'Tis as good a one as if you had stood on the step of Oundle, and the priests there, and the Abbess herself, had blest your union."

Tears of clarifying gratitude wet Ashild's eyes. Burginde had lived a life of such uprightness that none could doubt that which she pronounced was true, or even hinted was so, to be anything but.

"Burginde, from your mouth it is all so . . . simple."

Burginde crooned her approval, stroking Ashild's hair in reassurance. "Aye, and 'tis simple, my girl, 'tis.

"All will know this now. When you begin showing, you will be met with nought but smiles."

To seal this promise, Burginde leant in and kissed her cheek.

Ashild nodded her head, wanting to believe all this. "But . . . I must tell Hrald first. And soon." She was chewing on her lip, thinking on this.

Burginde gave a decided nod of her rounded chin. "Aye. He is brother, and Lord, both, and must know of it. 'Twill gladden him, truly it will."

Ashild had opened her mouth in silent protest. But the nurse ploughed ahead.

"You be the daughter of the hall, destined for a fine match. And Ceric be his fast friend. This be what Hrald most wants for you both."

The nurse let her eyes scan the garden, a sanctuary of flowering beauty which gave respite to those privileged to be invited within. She nodded her head in satisfaction and then went on.

"All works round in its own time, that is what I can say. Look at me. I loved a village boy at Cirenceaster, and was got with his child. He was slow to wed me, even when my own father gave him a shake. After that, riled as I was, even if he had asked I would not wed either him or the baker's boy, who had been following after me for months. The first was now unworthy, and took hands with the smith's daughter, and the second I would not settle for. I wanted the babe though, and prideful as can be went ahead and had her. She was born blue, and died the second day of her sweet life. I wept as I had never before, cried my eyes out. Then the cook from the hall knocks on our door. The Lady there had just given birth, was weak as a kitten and could give little milk. Could I come up and suckle the babe? And she was no less than your own dear mother, that babe. I had never been within the hall before, and now could care for both babe and mother."

Burginde paused in her telling of this tale, one Ashild had never before heard in its entirety. She gave Ashild's hand another pat.

"Something bigger came to me when I thought all was lost. Something bigger is coming to you, Ashild. Mark my words."

Hrald rode back to Four Stones with Jari and the rest of his body-guard, having parted with his uncle at the turning to Turcesig. The young Jarl approached in a state of elation as he neared the gates of his keep, and urged his horse into a canter as he heard the whistled signal ring out that he was returned.

The first member of his family he saw was his sister Ashild, who came towards him wiping her hands on the apron panel of her gown. She had been in the paddock, performing a task that always gave her pleasure, that of brushing down her horses. She had two at the hall just now, her bay mare, and the white stallion, and each knew the firm touch of her hands and the skillful wielding of brush and comb upon their coats, manes, and tails.

Hrald was returned from his riding to see Haward, and one look at his jubilant face told her he had known success. He caught her up in his arms and hugged her.

"She is mine," he told her. He broke from their embrace to look at her, his grin making him even more boyish to her eyes.

"I am glad," she managed. She answered him in Norse, which led him to switch to it as well.

"I will go and tell her," he said, twisting his head back in the direction where Asberg's house lay. "We will be wed at Oundle, and soon." It was custom that the maid be told by her own kin that her marriage was assured. Dagmar had none with her, and it left the bridegroom to deliver this news himself.

But Ashild would stay him for a short while. All the action of the hall work yards swirled about them as they stood there. His body-guard were relieving their mounts of saddles and bridles and releasing them into the paddock from which Ashild had just come. Young Bork had taken Hrald's horse and yet stood staring at the Jarl from the threshold of the stable doorway. Two of the kitchen boys were hauling water lately pulled up from the well, a wooden bucket in each of their hands. A cowherd was leading the hall's own cows back in for their afternoon milking, while one of the goose girls ran after three goslings which had waddled, wings flapping, to challenge the lead cow in her progress across the yard.

"Could we go to the treasure room," she asked. "There is another matter to speak of, as well."

She wondered if she looked as wan as she felt. But her brother, after searching her face for a moment, gave a nod of his head, and led the way. The interior of the hall was dim, even in the strong afternoon light, and being sunken into the ground a few steps gave it a reviving coolness. A few toddling children were about, playing at the feet of the women who clustered near the light of the door, chatting as they teased out wool thread from masses of fluffy roving to fill their ever-whirling spindles.

They reached the high table and the length of linen which sported the raven embroidery hanging on the wall behind it. By it was Hrald's old shield, its red and black swirls curling toward the domed iron boss fronting the hand grip. The crack in its alder face was broad enough to show the lime-washed wood of the wall it hung upon. Now Hrald was at the door just to the left of the shield, and drew forth the key to the box lock from his belt. The door was oak, almost black from age, its upright planks as thick as Hrald's strong wrist and their height enough so he need only bob his head as he crossed the threshold with his sister.

Shutting that door sealed off one world and admitted those who passed through it to another. Weapons room it was, the range of painted shields stacked in ranks against one wall, and a deep cluster of throwing spears ready to be grasped told of this. The number of wooden and iron bound chests, trunks, strong boxes and casks stacked as to size and what they held was beyond easy counting. More weaponry was within some of these, swords, knives, the war axes called the skeggox, and spear-points not yet fitted to shafts. Others held treasures Merewala and Merewala's father, the latter of whom had founded Four Stones, had amassed. This had been added to by Ashild's father, Yrling, who had wrenched this keep away from Merewala, and then expanded threefold by Hrald's father, Sidroc. And Hrald himself had added to it. He had left most of the armaments in Turcesig there, to serve its men, and though that fortress had not been rich in treasure beyond this, had brought hack silver, coins, and a few silver ornaments from that which Thorfast inherited from Guthrum.

The table and chairs within that room were not large, but had been carved with care, and their comfort seen to by the Lady of Four Stones, who had provided plush cushions of dark blue wool upon their seats. Even Ashild had contributed handiwork to this room and he who owned it, for against one wall near the hooped spears was set the war-flag she had woven and worked for her brother. The raven thereupon, spread-winged like a raptor, beak agape, hung in folds, ready to be brought to life by some young man who would wave it upon the field of battle to signal to Hrald's men that their war-chief still lived. Ashild had seen it live before, furling out from the cantle of her saddle as she charged from the gates of Oundle. Hrald had fixed it there before she rode to the abbey's defence.

The single window, high upon the wall, faced west, a piercing beam of sunlight striking the planked floor, and making tiny motes of dust look golden as the Sun.

He was looking at her, looking quizzically as he waited for her to speak. He was eager to find Dagmar, she knew, and she herself must go and welcome her.

"I am happy for you, Hrald," she repeated, and forced more heartiness into her voice.

He smiled, and was about to speak when she went on.

"Do you love her?"

She thought it a strange question to hear, but she must ask it, as she wondered, young as he was, if it was mere want that drove him.

He nodded, grinning, a little abashed at this directness. "Já, já."

Ashild's next question went deeper.

"Do you feel loved?"

His hesitation gave Ashild an answer for herself. She felt Ceric's love, even though she also felt she could not spend her life with him.

He moved his head, for a moment confused. All he could feel was his own love and desire for Dagmar, his sense of fitness that she should be his wife. He had not thought to examine if his heart was warmed by the corresponding emotion from his intended.

"I feel her regard . . . I believe she welcomes me."

It was her turn to pause as she considered this. She studied his face, and thought he was reaching for further words to express these new sensations. Nothing came, yet the earnestness of his face spurred her on. She must tell him, and now.

She kept her tone light, despite the directness of her next question.

"Did Ceric tell you of his time at Turcesig?"

"A few words, only." The surprise of what Ceric had told him rose again, yet he tempered his voice, not wanting to betray his friend. "That you would not go to Kilton."

"Anything more?"

He gave a slow and single nod. "That you did not . . . reject him."

She drew breath, grateful that he knew. "I will have his babe, in the Spring."

His lips parted. He blinked his eyes, and she thought she watched an entire spectrum of emotion move in her brother's face: surprise, confirmation, awe, urgency, everything.

His first words were of happiness.

"Nothing could bring Ceric more joy, than this." He shook his head, his wonder at her news uppermost. "We must send you to him," he began. "He will – "

"I cannot go to Kilton."

He tried to take this in. Of course, she was right. She could not travel such a distance, not with Anglia in turmoil, Wessex under sporadic attack, and certainly not with her being with child as she was now. It could not be risked. And the escort she would need would deplete his forces at a time when every man counted.

"Já," he nodded. "Not now. Not until it is safe."

She gave her head a shake to correct him.

"I will not go to Kilton. It will not end well if I do."

Her words jarred him. They brought to mind his father's words at Saltfleet, when Ælfred, King, was urging him to stay in Anglia. His father had answered that disaster would follow if he remained. And it was Hrald who believed his father, and released him to go, without regrets, he hoped.

In dealing with his sister Hrald had need of deeper resources, and summoned the words of Raedwulf, the Bailiff of Defenas. He had in this same room told both Ceric and him that Ashild perhaps preferred a peacetime rather than a wartime alliance, and that once peace was again attained she might indeed go to Ceric. He must believe the bailiff.

"When there is peace," Hrald said, recalling the words of Raedwulf, "when there is peace, then you will go."

"It will not end well for me if I do," she answered, but quietly.

What voice was she listening to, her brother wondered, that made her speak so? It was nearly the same words used by his father, there at Saltfleet.

She had not heard that speech, and had moved on with her own thoughts. These were of practical nature, for she knew the importance of her role in enriching his holdings.

"Hrald, I know I should bring as my bride-price a treasure to fill more chests in this room." She dropped her voice to say the next. "It is all the more pressing, as Dagmar can bring you so little. Yet I would have you keep the fifty head of horses, or any sum of silver and gold you would send me off with. So I do not think I have left Four Stones the poorer.

"I have no shame in this child," she ended. "But I will live my life here at Four Stones."

He stood listening to her, shaking his head at her words, the decision of which he could not accept. "Then you leave Ceric with nothing. You know he loves you, but he can have neither you, nor the coming child."

The starkness of his words struck her. Her brother was right.

She saw the naked justness of this, but had answer for it. "I did not wish for this. But I accept it. Welcome it, even. I could have rid this child and did not."

Hrald winced. It forced her to touch his arm.

"I do not see the end of this, Hrald. Only what I must do now."

"But all that you forgo, all that you will lose . . . "

She felt her selfishness, and her confusion. Yet she saw what she had won, in accepting Ceric that night, and now this babe. She could not know why this happened on her first night of love, but felt there was greater reason for it. She would have a woman's joy in her child, but like a man, be able to stay at the home she was raised in and felt sworn, by her very presence, to protect. That was what mattered to her. Yet the strain of standing there before her brother, with his shocked and almost wounded face, had her near tears.

Hrald's eyes shifted from her face to the roof rafters above their heads. Ashild's news, all of it, was proving hard to compass.

"Ceric considers you his wife," he told her.

"I know, I know," she murmured.

"And you are wed in the eyes of nature," he went on.

"Já. That is true as well," she admitted, "having given ourselves freely, as we did."

"If the babe is born here . . . " he wondered aloud. For the first time it struck him how this would be received, not only by his men and folk, but by Wilgot the priest. "I should tell all here that you are wed to him."

Her lips curved in a quick smile, the first in a long time. "No need. Burginde is at work already, in the kitchen yard. She says all will expect a secret wedding had taken place, owing to Ceric's long courtship of me."

Hrald's relief allowed for the smoothing of his brow. "Good." It did not cover what came after this, but it was a start.

He thought now of Dagmar. He, or Ashild herself, or perhaps their mother, would need to tell her of this. Dagmar must hear it from them, not from the prattle of the yard. Would she be shocked, he wondered, and think less of her new sister-in-law. He gave his head a shake to clear it, and forced a smile at his sister. She would relent and go to Kilton, he told himself. When it was safe for her, her babe, and the treasure she brought Ceric to travel, she would go to Kilton.

Hrald had just put his foot on the first step of the wooden stairway leading to his mother's weaving room when he heard the door above open. The Lady of Four Stones appeared on the upper landing. She smiled down at him, and his initial elation at his betrothal resurfaced. She came down to meet him, Burginde just behind her.

His mother gave his cheek a kiss, and he nodded at her, unable to keep from smiling.

"We are agreed," he said. "Ten swords, twenty spears. Dagmar will bring silver with her." He remembered the lot upon the table which her cousin had revealed. "Nothing of great value, but there is a cup, a chalice, of good size amongst it."

Another chalice, his mother silently marvelled, from the store house of a Dane. Ælfwyn at times wondered how any church or monastery had yet any sacred silver; so much had been swept off like this. At least once in their keeping it could be restored to its former use. Perhaps Hrald would present it to Oundle as his marriage gift.

She had placed her hand over his. "I take happiness in your own," she told him, with warm truthfulness. Burginde, off at her shoulder, pressed her lips together, but gave her head a firm nod just the same.

His next words were more uncertain. "I want to see her now, but first . . . I saw Ashild when I rode in, and she spoke to me."

His mother's sudden intake of breath said much. He looked about them. They were still at the foot of the stairs. Both his aunt and little sister would likely be up at work in the weaving room. They needed privacy. He lifted his hand to the treasure room which he had just quitted, and a moment later unlocked the door again.

After he closed the door he spoke.

"She told me. About her coming child. Ceric's child," he felt need to add.

"She also said she will remain here."

Burginde had clicked her teeth, and did not attempt to stifle her sigh. "She be a mule, that girl." She tilted her round chin a moment, as if thinking on her own words. "Prances like that big white beast of hers, but she be a mule, at heart."

Hrald had let his eyes roll upward at this. Burginde was abetting Ashild's behaviour by devising stories around the coming child. The look he gave her prompted the tartness of the nurse's next words. "I need not agree with all she says and does, to want to aid and protect her."

He could not gainsay this. Ashild's natural forthrightness made it hard not to help her, even when he disagreed with her. Mention of the stallion Thorfast had presented his sister with pushed Hrald to consider the dead man's cousin whom he was about to wed.

"I will see Dagmar now, and tell her that Haward and I have come to terms." He glanced down a moment. "The other matter . . . it can wait."

"As well it must, Hrald," his mother said. Her earnestness was gentle, but real. "It is Ashild's life, and her child. She will tell Dagmar in her own time."

Ælfwyn had another thought. It was hardly seemly that the bridegroom brought word that his suit had been accepted; this was news told by the prospective bride's parents or guardian. She herself fulfilled that role while Dagmar was under her roof and yet unwed. She wanted to spare both young people any awkwardness over this.

"Let me tell her your gladsome news," Ælfwyn proposed.

Approaching the house which Dagmar now inhabited, Ælfwyn gave thought to something Ceridwen had told her years earlier. When she had arrived at the burh of Kilton, bringing Gyric seemingly back from the dead with her, his mother had greeted her in singular fashion, naming her at once "daughter." No such woman awaited Ælfwyn at Four Stones when she entered its gates as a bride. But she could offer that same heartfelt welcome to the maid her son chose as his wife.

The door to the small house opened at once to her knock. Dagmar stood there, a look of hopeful expectation on her face, which changed but little when she saw who stood there.

"My daughter," Ælfwyn said in greeting. She opened her arms to embrace her.

Dagmar gave a small gasp, but readily returned the embrace. The generosity of these words surprised her. "My Lady," she answered.

Ælfwyn smiled and lifted her hand as if to wave this off. "We shall be much closer than that, Dagmar. Hrald has just returned with the happy tidings that your cousin and he have agreed on bride-price and dowry."

The Lady of Four Stones gave a mirthful laugh, which allowed Dagmar to do the same. Ælfwyn took her hand and led her to the bench at the little table set before the sleeping alcoves.

"Hrald wishes the ceremony to be held as soon as Oundle can prepare for it," she went on. "I will write to Sigewif today, asking her to make ready."

Ælfwyn had already given thought on this. A Summer hand-fast was greatly to be desired. Women made mothers then had the benefit of harvest abundance, giving their Spring-born babes a strong start. No woman of Four Stones' hall nor village lacked grain or other essentials, but fresh fruit and vegetables, eggs and butter and cheese in plenty could only be enjoyed before the onset of the cold.

Dagmar nodded, half afraid that Hrald's mother would ask her to append her own note to the letter she would write. She did not. As a mother herself, Ælfwyn's thoughts were travelling in quite another direction.

"We must tell your mother," she said next, "and though your bride-price has been settled between your cousin and this hall, I will send her a gift of silver. Hrald will send escort to bring her to witness."

Dagmar's sudden intake of breath was matched by the look of dismay on her face.

"Nej," she answered quickly. She took a breath in attempt to calm herself, and went on. "No."

"Your mother must come," Ælfwyn prompted. Her tone was low, but not without a note of surprise at Dagmar's reaction.

"My Lady, my mother – she . . . I fear her meeting you."

"Dagmar, why?"

She named stared at Ælfwyn. Dagmar felt her eyes begin to fill. She must say it. Only the truth would suffice, as ugly as it was.

"She did not take well to being set aside by my father. She spends much of each day with a mead cup in her hand. I am fearful that if Hrald sees her, the shame I feel will rob us of our happiness." The tears she tried to blink back were now escaping down her cheeks. "I do not want her here, either for my hand-fast, or ever."

Ælfwyn felt true pity. Her own parents had been praiseworthy in their habits, and to be shamed by the behaviour of your mother would be a burden difficult for a young bride to bear.

"I understand," she murmured, and again took Dagmar's hand. Guthrum had put away Dagmar's mother when she was yet young, and moved on to the mother of Inkera. There had been other wives, both before and after. And Guthrum had left nothing to his daughters, and likely nothing to a discarded wife. She would be in need of silver. But she understood and honoured Dagmar's request that she not be present.

"We will suggest the dangers of travel are too great," Ælfwyn posed. "And send her gifts," she promised.

Dagmar did not like to deny the open-heartedness of this feeling, but could not stop her next words.

"Please to keep your gifts," she breathed.

"We must at least send her silver," Ælfwyn said, "so she may share our joy in your union."

"She will drink up your silver, just as she drinks up my own."

How terrible an admission for a daughter to make of her own mother, thought Ælfwyn.

Ælfwyn nodded her head, but her sense of justice propelled her forward. "Yet she must have a share in your bride-price, widowed as she is."

Dagmar shook her head, almost helplessly. "Anything you send she will change to drink." She wiped her tears away with her hands, and took a breath. "I pray do not make it much, for it will end up in her cup."

Ælfwyn took thought. It was clear Dagmar had told Hrald nothing of this, else she would not have reacted in such fear of discovery. Yet the shame was not Dagmar's, but her mother's. Ælfwyn found herself sighing inwardly. Dagmar seemed at more disadvantage than either she or Hrald knew. Fatherless, dower-less, and with a burdensome mother.

She could not in good conscience deny sending the woman something in acknowledgement of the upcoming nuptials; every mother, flawed as she might be, had the right to know her daughter would be well taken care of. Ælfwyn need not tell Dagmar of this, but her daughter-in-law must allow her own mother to know of her changed estate.

"I will send word to her, telling her of your wedding, but offering no escort," she assured her.

Dagmar's head had dropped, and her hand went to her brow. This offer, kind as it was, was not enough. She looked at Ælfwyn, a direct, even piercing look of entreaty. "My Lady," she asked, "could you not wait until I am already wed?" Her eyes moved about the small house, seeking answers. "Perhaps there will be less reason for her to try to come, if you wait until then."

Ælfwyn's heart moved in pity for the girl's desperation. What dreadful scenes had the drunken woman subjected her daughter to, that she fear her arrival like this.

"Very well," Ælfwyn agreed. "I will wait to send word until you are wed." She would send the woman a small sum; she must. She thought of what more she could say to reassure Dagmar.

"Also offer our regrets that travel from Headleage was too dangerous to undertake."

⁂

That same day Ashild went to visit Dagmar as the latter was preparing for the evening meal. Dagmar invited her in, and Ashild stepped inside the same small timber house in which for years she had lived with her aunt and uncle. She took it in once more. Æthelthryth and Asberg were bound to stay at Turcesig, and run it. Perhaps I will live here, with my child, Ashild thought. She looked at Dagmar, whose sleeping chamber would soon be the treasure room.

"Hrald told me," she began, and then tried to temper the clumsy abruptness of this. "I am happy for you. Both."

She leant forward and gave her future sister-in-law a kiss on her cheek, as Dagmar murmured her thanks.

"I have news as well," Ashild went on.

Dagmar was ready for the hall, a fresh apron panel pinned to her pearl-studded brooches, her thick and glossy hair neatly combed and falling from beneath the head-wrap she had lavished such fine thread-work upon. But Ashild must stay her, and got it out all at once.

"I will have a child in Spring. The father is of Wessex."

The sudden movement of Dagmar's head showed her startle. Hrald told her Ashild had been courted a long time, but had not added this result.

"Ceric, he of Kilton," Dagmar supplied.

The moment she said it she saw by Ashild's face that a confidence had been breached. Dagmar knew of this man who pursued Hrald's sister. She smiled as warmly as she could and said the next.

"Hrald told me of his courtship of you, that Ceric is a great friend of his." She thought what more she could say of these unforeseen tidings. "Hand-fast and babe both. There is much for which to congratulate you."

Ashild nodded. She could scarce be angry at Hrald for mentioning Ceric to his future bride, not when he wanted the union between them. But the sense of having been talked about stung. At least her coming babe was a surprise.

Dagmar felt off balance enough to inwardly confront her need for frankness. Ashild lacked beauty or grace, yet possessed an attraction through the force of her character that intimidated her. She was not used to any woman making her feel such, and as different as they were, both Ashild and Abbess Sigewif sparked this emotion within her. It was uncomfortable, and made her feel at a loss. It led to her next, heartfelt words.

"I want to be your friend," she hoped aloud.

Ashild gave thought to this statement. Friendship, in Ashild's ken, was a privilege allowed a few, and proximity and even relationship could not impose it. It was always earned, not granted. Still, she must then earn it herself, in return.

"As I hope to be yours," Ashild answered.

"We have much in common, you and I," Dagmar now offered.

"Já. Hrald, and Four Stones."

Ashild's switch to Norse seemed to confirm this, yet the bluntness of her reply forced Dagmar's lips into a brief smile.

"More than that," Dagmar went on. "I meant . . . we are like each other. You dress as a Dane."

"My father was Yrling." Ashild's words were low pitched, and voiced in the same solemn tone Dagmar might use to report that her sire had been Guthrum, King. It was a received dignity that affirmed its own authority.

Dagmar, her eyes fixed on Ashild's face, nodded. This woman before her had every right to her pride, more so perhaps than Dagmar herself, as Ashild's self-esteem was seated not only in her rich war-lord father, but in her own heroic action defending one of the fruits of his treasure, Oundle.

Dagmar asked the next question with the gravity it deserved.

"He died in battle?"

Ashild gave a single nod of her head. "At my mother's home of Cirenceaster. Other Danes tried to lay claim to it."

Dagmar took a moment to reflect on this. "May he who struck him down be denied a place in Asgard."

It forced a rueful smile from Ashild. "He was Christian, who slew my father." She could see Dagmar's puzzlement, attempting to compass a Christ-believing Dane who had been at that battle.

"A Saxon, of Wessex," Ashild said next, relieving Dagmar of her wonderment. There was no need to say more than this, to name him or his burh.

Dagmar paused a moment. The death of such a war-lord as Yrling would have ready avengers.

"He who avenged him won the regard of many," she offered.

It was Ashild's turn to reflect. "It was Hrald's father, Sidroc, who did so."

It was meet that vengeance should be wrought by kin, and Dagmar's next words conveyed this. "All the more honour upon your hall," she murmured.

Ashild's eyes traced the lines of Dagmar's face. Her brother loved this woman, one possessed of notable beauty. Hrald's joy in winning her could not help but touch her own heart, one which she knew she sometimes willfully held closed. The change wrought in her from her coming babe, that softening and blossoming which she could not fight, swelled within her now. It gave Ashild the chance to extend her hand to Guthrum's daughter, and more than her hand.

"Our hall," she answered, taking Dagmar's hand in her own.

THE NEW LADY
OF FOUR STONES

THE date of the joining of hands of Hrald, Jarl of Four Stones and Dagmar, daughter of Guthrum had yet to be announced. As Oundle was to be the site of the wedding, Abbess Sigewif was the determiner of when the liturgical calendar and the foundation's harvest needs could best accommodate this event. The ceremony was to be small, given the bride's lack of kin and the difficulty of travel, and quiet as well, so that none outside those immediately concerned knew that Hrald and his chosen would be that day at the more lightly defended Oundle rather than the stronghold of Four Stones. Hrald only hoped it might be upon the Feast of St Matthew. That Feast, marking equal day and night, lay at the apex of the final harvest, and seemed in every way of good omen.

Dagmar had remained at Four Stones. She wished her sister Inkera might be with her, but his reluctance when she asked her cousin Haward if he could send for her forced her to forgo this hope. Such a distance would require him to send at least four men to fetch her, and he would not expose either his own men nor Inkera to the hazards of the journey.

Yet unbeknownst to Dagmar riders had been sent.

"My men will be returning from Headleage soon," Hrald told her one wet morning after the hall had broken its fast. Dagmar was sitting at the women's table, and he had come over to her. Ashild was rarely there in the morning, and Burginde had risen to attend to her own duties before ascending the stair to the weaving room. Of late Dagmar had joined her future mother-in-law and kin there, happy to sit amongst them with her own hand work, or to aid Ælfwyn in the finishing of the new linens for the treasure room.

"Headleage?" she repeated. Her heart had almost missed a beat at the mention.

"My mother and I sent silver, to your own mother. Also they will tell Inkera that you will soon be my wife."

"Word was sent now, before our wedding," she said. It was neither question nor answer, and was uttered more to herself than to him. She did not wish to believe this.

"Yes. My mother bid me not to bring your own here; I hope you will forgive her that. Even with my escort she felt the trip too dangerous. But she wanted to send silver to her there at Headleage. As I did. She wished to wait until after we were wed, but I would give my men the benefit of the longer days so they might travel the faster. So I sent them three days ago, instead."

Dagmar nodded mutely. Hrald's blithe reporting of his actions made clear that he knew nothing of her fears about her mother's untoward appearance. And the Lady of Four Stones had not betrayed her confidence, not in that. If Ælfwyn was to insist upon a gift for her own mother, she could hardly resent such open-handedness, though Dagmar feared its result.

Dagmar was staring straight ahead, seeing nothing. She was still sitting, and now rose.

"I would we could wed now. Today," she said.

Early that afternoon Dagmar came down from the weaving room into the hall. She had been working the morning amongst the women there, rehemming a linen shift of hers. She had not spoken to Ælfwyn about the men Hrald had sent to Headleage, and indeed was not even sure she knew he had sent them early. But the strain of anticipation was great. Hrald's men may have found Bodil in a drunken stupor, or a fit of rage, or collapsed in tears. She may have received them as haughtily as a queen from the Sagas, or been as coquettish as a milk maid. Her mother had many moods, and Dagmar never knew which she might find her in. She feared what the returning couriers might tell her husband-to-be, and her fear was even greater that perhaps Bodil had persuaded them to take her with them to Four Stones. Thinking on all this made it hard to focus on her sewing, and even harder to be good company. At last she told Ælfwyn her head ached from the close work, and asking her pardon, excused herself to go to her small house and lie down.

The rain had only increased, but she had a length of boiled wool Burginde had handed her. Held above her head it would serve as proof against the wet as she crossed the hall yard.

She walked down the wooden stair, noting the creak of the third tread, and came into the hall proper. All the trestle tables were away, and the place quite empty, save for some movement in the dim kitchen passage, where two women who had finished sweeping the stone floor were now hanging their birch brooms.

As Dagmar began to cross the floor, the door of the treasure room opened. Hrald stepped out, and looking down as he was, was yet unaware of Dagmar's presence. He placed the key in the lock to secure it and it clicked in response. He turned, key in hand, to see her there.

The smile on his face spread from his mouth to his eyes. She was forced to smile back, to take pleasure in his own at seeing her. He made a slight motion, enough that she read it as a gesture to approach. She went to him.

She was wearing the yellow gown his mother had given her, with an over-gown of deep blue. Her long dark hair was held back by the white kerchief she had been working on the day they had met. The coloured thread work she had embellished it with had grown over the weeks, so that the border was a riot of blue and green interlacing. Her hair fell over her breast, at times obscuring the gleaming brooches at her shoulders, other times parting enough so that the metal glinted through the dark strands.

This is my wife, Hrald told himself. All his young life, ever since he had been old enough to care, he had been chaffed by older men about the pick he would have of beautiful women. He had not quite imagined one so desirable as Dagmar, and now she would be his.

She was now before him, and an idea struck him, one he voiced in almost hushed tones.

"I would like you to see the treasure room," he told her.

Her lips parted. She knew it served not only as treasury, but as bed chamber.

"It shall be our room," he said.

She placed the wool Burginde had given her on the table, as Hrald turned back to the door.

He returned the key to the iron lock and twisted it. He pushed open the door and led the way inside. It was dim within, and the dullness of the rain outside made it the dimmer. She could smell the linen wick he must have just snuffed out, and his first act was to move to the table in the middle of the room, and strike out sparks from flint and iron to light the still-warm cresset sitting there. Once lit, he moved and closed the door behind them.

She stood by the table, taking in the room. It was not large, but the height of the walls and the number of chests and casks, neatly arranged, gave the air of a vast storeroom. Like the timber walls of the hall proper, the wood planks had been lime-washed, making the most of the light from the lone window, and that cast by the flickering yellow flame of the cresset. Hrald felt no small measure of pride as her eyes rose and fell as he pointed out which chests held weaponry and of what kinds, which held silver in coin, which hack, and where the ornaments of that precious metal were stored. Almost every chest had its own separate key, kept ready on a black iron ring hanging on one wall, and Hrald moved to it to open a few.

He opened one large chest, built of wood, covered over in deep brown leather, and strapped with brass. It was filled to the brim with what looked like sheep's fleece. He lifted the one on the top, which rested flat, fleece side down. The deep volume of the chest was almost filled with swords.

"These are the best of my store," he told her. "Won by my father, and by his uncle, Ashild's father. It is this from which I chose my own sword." He tilted his head to that weapon, hanging in its scabbard upon the wall.

His smile deepened. "And it was from this chest I selected the blades to go to Haward."

Dagmar had not been told the exact terms of her bride-price, but knew the worth of a fine sword. Looking down at the workmanship of those within, she felt a ripple of satisfaction that her value had been gauged in these noblest of weapons.

He replaced fleece and lid, and seeing her gaze shift to the war-flag which stood hanging from a shaft by the massed spears, spoke of it.

"Ashild made that," he told her, and went and picked it up, and swung it about over their heads so she might see the raven fly.

"It is fine work," she praised.

"I have not yet fought under it," he said, setting it back against the wall. He gave a short laugh. "Ashild has. At least her horse carried it behind her, when she rode to defend Oundle."

From there they both turned. Hooks and shelves hung from the wall by the bed. A polished silver disc hung there, so smooth and flat as to throw a true reflection of those who gazed into it. There was one of copper in Asberg's house, which made the viewer look golden, but Hrald's returned a truer vision. The shelves held more of a personal nature, his comb of carved apple wood, leathern belts, a bronze basin, a rolled stack of linen towels. The broad bed itself was also there, against one wall, and they faced it now. It was laid with an extravagant fur throw of some kind, long fur of white and grey and near-black.

She moved to it, and then reached out her hand to touch its surface.

"Is it wolfskin?" she asked.

"Yes," he answered, and with a slight laugh added, "and like a wolf it sometimes sheds." He came to it as well. "It is very old. My mother's mother made it for her bridal night, when she came here."

"It is still beautiful," she murmured. It was coarse under the hand, not soft like fox, but its sturdiness must have helped preserve its warmth over the years.

Her eyes followed the pattern of pelts where they had been pieced together, admiring the skill in which they had been joined, and her hand turned a corner over, to see the loomed backing of soft grey wool. The bed was plush, with several featherbeds, she guessed, and the pillows sheathed in linen cases at the head looked equally soft.

This will be my bed, she thought.

Another thought followed, that of the men returning to Four Stones. What if they tell Hrald things which make him change his mind . . .

She turned, and took a step back, so that the backs of her knees were against the edge of the bed. He was right there, and it took a mere look from her to make him close the slight distance between them.

She lifted her chin and brought her mouth to his. Their lips touched, not the grazing caresses they had exchanged since the day of their betrothal, but a meeting, firm and with intent.

His hands rose up around her, and he clasped her to him. Their mouths clung with the kind of passion Hrald had only guessed at, and when she opened her lips and slid her tongue into his mouth he clutched at her, at once on fire with urgency. He moved his hands down her back to rest in the hollow at her waist, and pressed his hips to hers.

She did not flinch, did not pull away, and his mounting excitement as they kissed and kissed again was such that if he did not open the distance between their bodies he feared losing control of his own.

He pulled himself back enough to breathe her name. She kept her own hands wrapped about his shoulders, but enough space was there that his eye fell upon the door.

His mother or Burginde could walk in, at any moment. His mother had the second door key and Burginde oftentimes took it to perform some errand here.

"We must stop," he murmured. He could scarce speak, but looked to the door. Her eyes followed his.

"There is a bar," she whispered. Her eyes had fastened on the length of iron which could be shot across the oaken planks. No key could overcome that. "All you need do is slide it."

He felt stunned, and exhilarated, all at once. It forced him to study her face, which looked as fetchingly lovely as it had a moment earlier. But he must ask. "Do you mean it?"

"I do mean it," she breathed, her lips forming the slightest of smiles. She moved to go deeper into his arms again.

But he had not closed his eyes, and was looking over her shoulder at the door. The woman he would wed was ready to give herself to him. The hot thrill of his bodily yearning for her was almost too much to overcome, but he tilted his chin up and away, looking at the roof timbers. He did not want it like this. Dagmar was a maid of noble blood. He was proud to have won her, and wanted all to be proud as well. He wanted to stand on the step of the church of Oundle before his mother, and Abbess Sigewif, and the two priests thereof, and have them witness their union. Even should he bar the door, they would be discovered if his mother or Burginde tried to enter. Their first act of love must not be done hastily, and in fear of discovery. The sordidness of his frantic encounter with the kitchen woman rose in memory, and he beat it back.

He wanted no ugliness attached to this woman he loved, and no shame cast upon his desire for her. They had overcome the limitations of her lack of dowry, and he wanted no taint on her moving forward. He wanted them to be blest in the eyes of the Church, and in the eyes of those who loved him. He wanted the hand-fast ale, and the feast which would follow here at Four Stones, and wanted to enter this room with his bride awaiting him, that they might discover each other in the glow of honour and deserved ceremony.

He stepped away from her, with real regret.

"Hrald," she whispered. She did not care if they were discovered. She remembered the wool she had left upon the high table. If either his mother or Burginde came down into the hall and saw that wool, it would as good as tell them she must be inside with Hrald. And she did not care. She only knew that if she gave herself to him now, this hour, he would not cast her aside, regardless of any tales her mother might tell in a drunken rage. Her giving of herself would mean his utter commitment to her, and she need not fear he retract his offer of marriage.

"I love you, which is why I stop," he answered. "I love you, Dagmar."

It shook her out of her self-absorption, and out of her fear. She looked at his face a long while before she could speak. She lowered her eyes before him, her heart more open than it had been in years. May I be worthy of you, she told herself.

***

The day of the union of Hrald and Dagmar drew nigh. His riders had returned from Headleage with no ill report; they had found Bodil, mother of Dagmar easily enough, and though she evinced surprise at he who her daughter would wed, accepted the small box crowded with silver with little remark. Kjeld, who had been entrusted with speaking to the Lady, thought her almost too eager to dismiss him, for she held the carved wooden box to her bosom as she gave thanks, and then with a rapid movement of her chin reminded him of the door he had entered to deliver it.

This he did not convey to Hrald, nor the disordered state of the house, the floor wanting sweeping, the alcove hangings left parted so that the tumbled bedding and cushions were open to his view. She was in every way a surprise to Kjeld, and not a pleasant one, for given Dagmar's beauty he had imagined a handsome woman as her mother. This haggard beldame, gaunt yet with a puffy face, stale of breath and with stringy hair falling down from a head wrap tied askew, bore little apparent relation to she who would soon be the Lady of Four Stones. Kjeld had not expected Hrald to question him about her, and was caught off guard when he did, only repeating that as ordered he had placed the gift into her own hands, and that she expressed gratitude in receiving it.

Hrald, grasping for more, asked, "Is she tall?"

This was at least a fact Kjeld could confirm; she was indeed tall.

Hrald knew Guthrum had not been himself tall, and so Dagmar's height must have come from her mother. When Hrald went and found his mother and Dagmar, these were the two things he could repeat, their gift had been welcomed, and Kjeld had remarked that Bodil was also tall.

Ælfwyn had not known that her son had sent to Headleage earlier than she had asked, and her eyes were upon Dagmar as Hrald conveyed the news. They had both heard the whistled notice of returning men, but busy as they were in the weaving room had not gone down to see whose arrival it heralded. Dagmar's eyes grew wider as Hrald began to tell of Kjeld's return, but his easy manner allayed her concerns. Indeed, Ælfwyn had placed her hand over Dagmar's in reassurance, as Hrald turned and with a smile, left them to their stitching.

The Feast of St Matthew dawned, that harvest day of equal day and night. A fog which had been gathering over the reaped fields the day before thickened into a mist which bedewed every russet stalk. The warmth of the brown soil made the mist roll and drift like steam above a rusted cauldron, and the silver grey fingers of the sky slipped and shifted above it. The nuptial party would set out early to Oundle, with the goal of the bridal pair's vows being said under a noon Sun. One waggon would suffice to convey Hrald's mother, sisters, and bride. Burginde of course would witness as well, but Hrald's aunt Eanflad was happiest left at Four Stones. Asberg and Æthelthryth would come directly from Turcesig to Oundle, just as Haward, Dagmar's sole kin, would from his own hall.

Wilgot too was there, astride the quietest horse which could be found for one as unskilled at riding as he. The priest had no slight reasons to envy Oundle, and had hoped Hrald would exchange vows at the hall's stone preaching cross, or at the door of the near-chapel his own small house served as. Yet he understood the high moment of the occasion, and was unwilling to miss being there at Oundle to witness. Their sojourn there would be brief; ceremony, the said Mass, a cup of ale taken, and the return to Four Stones, where the kitchen yard had been in preparation for three days for a feast not seen in many a year.

The same thirty men who had served as body-guard upon the first foray to Oundle rode with them. Hrald on his bay stallion rode next Jari, on his prized chest-nut. Both men were attired in their finest clothing, and indeed every man of them had taken care in dressing this day. The deep blue linen tunic Hrald wore was one woven and sewn by his mother, and of the finest thread that Burginde, still the best spinner amongst them, could roll from her plump fingers. His dark leggings were set off by leg wrappings of brown leather, and his low boots were new, of walnut-dyed leather, fastened with toggles of silver. About his right wrist was his wide cuff of pure gold, a gleaming treasure of the precious stuff.

His bride, sitting between Ælfwyn and Ashild, wore a new gown of dove grey, upon which lay an over-gown, also newly sewn, of muted blue. The subdued shades lent a chasteness to her garb, one made the more flattering by the fine cream-coloured veil of silk Ælfwyn had presented her with, as head wrap. Never had her pearl-set bronze brooches had better accompaniment, and the doubled strands of crystal and silver beads hanging from them lent a dazzling yet quiet richness.

Ashild wore her best gown, save that one of golden silk given by Ceric which lay within the chest in her mother's bower house. She had worn that silk gown but twice; the night Ceric had presented it, and the night of the battle for Oundle, when her brother had rewarded her with a circlet of gold for her brow. This morning, sitting in the jostling waggon in a gown of pale yellow and over-gown of deep green, she briefly wondered when she might wear that golden gown, one fit for her own wedding, again. She could not help but feel the weight of irony that the second time she had donned it was in celebration of the death of Dagmar's cousin Thorfast.

For her part Ælfwyn had selected a gown of rose pink, one whose linen had been dipped so briefly in the dye pot that it took but a blush of colour into its warp and weft. Her hand had gone to it within her chest of gowns almost without thinking; it was one she rarely wore, and one she knew, reaching for it, brought to mind the Bailiff of Defenas, for whom she had never had the chance to wear it. The budded rose he had plucked for her in Oundle's garden may have been just this shade, she thought, smoothing her hand over her lap.

Though the day did not brighten as they reached Oundle, the rain held off. Once within the gates the party was welcomed by the Abbess and prioress into the hall. Asberg and Æthelthryth were already there, as was Haward, and after a welcome-cup, those assembled took a few moments of rest before being called to the church. The natural division between men and women during worship took form even here, for Hrald sat on one bench with his uncle and Jari, with the rest of his men ranged behind them on benches near the door, while his mother sat with his sisters and Burginde and Dagmar on a single bench by the portal to the Abbess' writing chamber.

Hrald, sitting between Asberg and Jari, found it hard to speak to either of them, and equally hard to look over at Dagmar, whose hand was being held by his mother. Of a sudden his uncle cleared his throat, just loud enough to make Hrald turn his head to him.

"Hrald," he muttered. The following pause was such that Hrald moved his head closer to his uncle, lest he miss what he said. At last Asberg went on. "Do you know how to treat a woman?"

Jari gave a muffled chortle, planted his hands firmly on his knees, and looked away. Hrald as much as felt his own cheek colour, for his face warmed. It was true they were now little together, but when they had met over the past weeks his uncle had said nothing to him about this topic. To do so now, moments before he was wed, and within sight of she who would be his bride, seemed a waggish drollery. He looked at his uncle, unable to hide his surprise. Yet he could see the man was serious, and thinking hard.

Asberg, having broached the subject and seen his nephew's open-mouthed reaction, was thrown into his own confusion as to what to say. He settled on a comparison which while indirect, was yet clear.

He could only liken a bride to that most valuable of creatures, a fine horse.

"Think of a filly you aim to become a good saddle horse," he instructed. "Just . . . be gentle. Easy hands."

Hrald listened, and understanding that these few words were the sum of the directive, finally nodded.

Asberg, having delivered this message, stood up, as if restless. His eyes fell upon the bench where the women sat, and regarding the bride he now wondered if he need say anything. He had his doubts about Dagmar. Despite her showiness, her mouth might be harder than it looked.

⊱⊰⊱⊰⊱⊰⊱⊰⊱⊰

While Hrald was sitting with his uncle, Ashild rose from the bench. Abbess Sigewif had retreated to her writing chamber, and Ashild now tapped upon the door. The Abbess' resonant voice granted entry. Ashild closed the door behind her, to find Sigewif standing at her writing table. She gestured Ashild over with a smile. The parchment thereupon was already inked.

"The record of your brother's wedding," the Abbess told Ashild. "It will make the first page in the register I will build, of his union and offspring, to bind within the volume I began years ago when your mother re-founded Oundle."

Ashild scanned the lines of small, well-rounded writing, that of the Abbess' own hand, giving the name and title of Hrald of Four Stones, Jarl of South Lindisse, and that of Dagmar, daughter of Æthelstan, King of East Anglia, born Guthrum.

"They need only sign, following their pledging," Sigewif ended. She placed her hand upon Ashild's, and through its warm pressure conveyed her pleasure at this.

Ashild almost bit back the words she had come to utter. Yet there might be no better time. She was alone now with Sigewif, a rare enough occurrence. The Abbess never left Oundle, which compassed her entire mortal world; she was in some ways a mountain unto herself. One must go to her, and here Ashild was.

"Reverend Mother," she began, "I have news of my own changed estate."

At once Sigewif's countenance altered, the smile creasing her eyes softening to an alert openness, the hand which had rested upon Ashild's now lifting it in her own.

"Tell me, my child," she invited.

"When Ceric journeyed here . . . we knew each other."

The expression the Abbess bore had not shifted, making it almost more difficult for Ashild to go on.

"I will have his babe in Spring."

A slight parting of the firm lips was the only sign Sigewif gave of any surprise. Her arms opened, sweeping Ashild into an embrace. Ashild, her cheek against the softness of the nun's white veil, was for a long moment enveloped in that scent of camphorwood and resinous incense that Sigewif carried about her person.

Now the Abbess stepped back, and using her distinctive gesture with Ashild, placed her hands on the girl's shoulders.

"Did you declare yourselves wed?"

Ashild drew breath before making answer.

"We did not." This was stated without shame, or any trace of boast. What she would say next was of high import, and it was also the truth. "Ceric named me wife more than once during the night, and the next day as well. And my mother and brother now know, and take joy in both fact . . . and result."

With any other young woman Sigewif would have asked a second question, to ascertain if she considered herself wife to the man to whom she had given herself. It was not caution which stopped the Abbess from doing so with Ashild, but respect for the girl's own self-contained character. Sigewif kept her eyes upon Ashild's face as she considered her.

"I think you fully wed in the eyes of God, and the law," the Abbess answered. "The Church is man's making, a symbol of His actions here on Earth. And its blessing an extra boon, which can be conferred when next you and Ceric meet."

The Abbess had more to add, and did so with a returning smile. "Ælfred will take joy in this pairing," she predicted.

Sigewif thought of another monarch, long dead, one who had once ruled Anglia. Edmund had been felled by Danes. To now have a union between Saxon and Dane at such a high level as was the joining hands of Ceric of Kilton and Ashild of Four Stones might have been beyond his ken after the years of bitter conflict he had known. Yet she could guess how welcome it would have been.

"As would my brother," she ended, planting a kiss on Ashild's brow.

The bronze bell in the church tower rang, signaling the first chime of twelve, and calling the party to the door of the sanctuary. As they rode here the mist had settled, almost gem-like, as the finest of droplets on the tunics of men and the horses' coats, and mantled like dew the oiled tarpaulin covering the waggon. It now thickened to a drizzle. Ælfwyn and Burginde, having gazed out upon the dull skies from the weaving room before they left, were prepared, and had laid by a light-weight woollen cloak to shield the couple as they made their pledging. As the party walked to the broad stone step of the church, the drizzle hardened. Hrald and Dagmar were in the lead, and as they reached the step and turned to face those assembled their chagrin at the worsening weather could be read in both their faces. Hrald had imagined exchanging vows with Dagmar under the brilliant Sun which had graced his first visit to Oundle with her, not a pelting rain.

Burginde grinned at Hrald, and looking at his face made merry answer.

"Nay, 'tis good luck," she assured them both with a hearty laugh. "Rain on the heads of those clasping hands brings many babes to come."

Good luck or ill, before the couple got too wet, Jari and Asberg, along with Kjeld and Haward, unfurled the woollen length over their heads and held it taut as makeshift shelter.

Hrald had given thought to what he would say. No couple need utter more than the words, "I marry you," one to the other, to make their union binding. The young Jarl wished for more than this. He looked out at the faces of his mother and sisters, of Burginde and the Abbess, and at Asberg and Jari and Kjeld and Haward shielding him from the rain, then let his eyes flick back at the rest of his escort, gathered behind his family. Then he turned to face his bride.

"Here at Oundle on St Matthew's Day, I, Hrald of Four Stones, take you to wife, Dagmar, daughter of Guthrum. I will protect your body with my own, and preserve ever the bond we create today."

He lifted his left hand now, and took her own in his.

"I choose you above all women. And before my friends, I marry you."

He felt her hand tremble in his own, and indeed, her dark blue eyes were all the more lustrous with welling tears.

He watched her steady herself with a breath, and gave her hand the slightest pressure in support.

"I, Dagmar, daughter of Guthrum . . . " She almost faltered here, under the force of his eyes which were fastened on her own. She dropped her eyelids and said the next. "I marry you, Hrald of Four Stones."

She could not equal in grace what he had said to her, nor even echo it; his words had already slipped away from her, leaving only the impress of their beauty.

It mattered not to Hrald. He placed his right hand over those already joined. He smiled at her, a smile which found root deep in the recess of his heart, and beamed forth over his young face.

He turned to those watching, and lifted in salute the clasped hand of his wife in his own.

A cry went up, of gladness from the women, and bellowing good cheer from the men.

The door was pulled open, and all filed within. The church was already brim-full, for nearly all the community of nuns and monks awaited them, lacking only those too infirm to attend. Hrald's grandmother Ælfleda stood in front with the oldest of the consecrated sisters, and her daughter and granddaughters processed to her side, where she warmly took their hands. The rite of Mass was chanted by Oundle's two priests, and the sacrament offered and received the first time by Hrald and Dagmar as a married couple.

Ashild, standing there next her mother and Ealhswith, felt a strange wash of sensation. Her hair and gown were damp, and though her hands were almost cold she felt as if her body might be steaming. It was the smoking incense, she knew, being swung with vigour by the younger of the two priests in its brass censer, filling the crowded sanctuary with a smell that evoked burning heartwood and the rare oils that sometimes were brought from the trading centre of Jorvik for her mother.

She glanced at her mother from the tail of her eye. What was she thinking, standing there, looking upon her son who had just wed and truly would enter a man's estate. Did she shed thought for Hrald's father? Ashild looked to Hrald, standing on the men's side. His eyes were cast down, but he looked as though he attended fully to the words of the priest. She guessed only his father's presence could make this day the better for him.

Sidroc. He and her mother had no fine hand-fast such as Hrald had; Oundle was still mostly a ruin when they made pledge. The fact of her own coming child made her remember that Sidroc had wed her mother knowing she would bear Yrling's babe. Just as her own father perhaps never learnt of her, the father of her own babe did not know of its coming. She and Ceric had no true hand-fast, no secret marriage, despite the assurances of Burginde and Sigewif. Ceric had called her wife, but she had not been able to call him husband.

She had been struck by her brother's words as he pledged to Dagmar. He could give himself utterly, and he had. Here she stood at his hand-fast, where he and his new wife were attended with honour, witnessed by the chief men of three halls, and hosted by an Abbess, sister to a King.

Such was not to be hers. She had turned her back upon it. She had never craved the honour and acclaim of being a powerful noble's bride; it was easy to set that aside. Yet she had tipped the scale all in her favour, and the injustice of it pricked her like a spur. Hrald's words returned, more plea than accusation, "Then you leave Ceric with nothing. He can have neither you, nor the child."

※※※※※※※※※※

The Mass ended, the elder priest giving his benediction in the tongue of Rome. Bova was there in the back of the church, nearest the door, standing with the younger nuns on one side, while the most junior of the brothers stood on the other. She beamed at Hrald and his bride, bowed her head to a smiling Ælfwyn, and when she saw Ashild, again pressed her hands to her heart.

Nuns and brothers returned to their daily offices, while the men and family of Four Stones, Asberg and Æthelthryth, and Haward gathered in Sigewif's hall. First the couple must be ushered, with their nearest of kin, into the Abbess' writing chamber, to sign their names upon the parchment registering their union. A narrow tray of freshly-cut goose quills awaited their selection, and the Abbess' quill knife, sharp as any razor, awaited he or she who wished to make a custom cut to form the nib. The tiny pot of brown-black ink was waiting, and Hrald took up a feathered quill, dipped it in the pot, gave it a tap against the rim to shake off any excess, and then in his finest hand recorded *Hrald of Four Stones*. He looked down at his work, and then with a smile passed the quill to Dagmar.

Few could write, and the union of couples was only recorded if they were of special parentage, and connected in some way to a foundation such as Oundle, where men and women learned in reading and writing had need to document issues of inheritance and property. If bride or groom could not sign themselves, they might make a simple mark by their name, written out by one possessing the scribal art.

Dagmar, taking the quill in her fingers before the eyes of those surrounding the writing table, paused. Her eyes rested on Hrald's signature, bold and firm letters nearly as well formed as those of the Abbess herself.

She dipped the nib into the tiny pot, gave it a slight tap, then lowered it to the creamy parchment. *Dagmar*, she pressed. She lifted the quill over the sprawling word. As it hovered, a droplet of ink rolled from the nib, splashing down upon the end of her name. A blot.

Dagmar could not stop the whispered, "Nej!" that sounded under her breath.

Hrald, watching her cheek colour, gave a small laugh, one dismissing the flaw. When the ink dried, Sigewif could use her scraper to amend the blotch, flicking away tiny shavings of the excess ink. He took the quill from his wife's hand, returned it to the tray, and then again lifted Dagmar's hand in his own. They led the way to the body of the hall.

It was time for the bridal-cup. It was Bova's ale they lifted, regarded by most who had tasted it as the best brew in South Lindisse. She was not there to hear them praise it anew, but to Hrald the fact that the young brewster was a link to his father Sidroc and the island of Gotland brought an added pleasure as he raised its foaming creaminess to his mouth.

The ride back to Four Stones was slowed by rain and attendant mud, but even this could scarce dampen the spirits of those who looked forward to the awaiting feast. Hrald, riding steadily on between his uncle and Jari, was not thinking of the waiting food, though he was aware of his hunger, nor of the gaming that would follow, but of the night's end, when he would step into the treasure room for the first time with his wife awaiting him.

The whistled calls which greeted the party from the ramparts of Four Stones were made raucous by the hooting of many men who had joined them upon the parapet, and their bantering jests raining down on the head of the bridegroom.

By the time all assembled in the hall, a keen expectation for the coming food and drink had reached a fevered pitch. It was fully dusk, and every torch projecting from the timber columns had been lit, every table laid with oil-filled cressets. With all in their best clothing, and adorned with silver and some with gold, the flickering light danced over knife hilt and necklace, brooch and arm-ring. At every table serving women held jugs of ale, and upon the high table was set the silver bird ewer the Lady of Four Stones ever poured from. In the kitchen passageway, kitchen folk were lined up, bearing their laden platters. All was in readiness, all present, save for the Jarl, his mother, and his bride. Burginde too was absent from her customary seat at the women's table, and when she came bustling in from the side door, she went not to it, but the door of the treasure room, on which she gave a sharp knock. Hrald stepped out and moved to the great carved chair which was his. Burginde sat down next Ashild, and as she did, the side door again was opened, and Ælfwyn walked in, with Dagmar at her side.

They walked with measured step to the high table, the hall quieting as they did so. They reached a grinning Hrald where he stood. Ælfwyn's slender hands went to the silver ewer. With deliberate action she picked it up, and turning to her daughter-in-law, placed it in her hands. Dagmar nodded, and turning to Hrald, filled his gold-trimmed cup, A shout went up, an exulting cheer. Dagmar blushed; all near could see this, even in the low light, but her lips formed a smile. She next poured out for Ælfwyn, then for Wilgot the priest, then Asberg and his wife Æthelthryth, rare visitors these days to this board, then Jari and her cousin Haward, and after this the rest of Hrald's picked men who sat at this high table.

She made circuit of its length, then returning to her husband's side, filled her own cup. It was one new to her, a gift from Ælfwyn, silver, with her name inscribed on its rim. As she did this first act as the new Lady of Four Stones, the serving folk had been filling the proffered cups of all. Hrald raised his cup. He lifted it first to his new wife, and drank deep, and then to all gathered in his hall.

The food appeared, in brimming bowls and still-warm wheaten loaves and platters both shallow and deep. Some held scores of boiled eggs seethed in butter and rolled in ground and toasted nutmeats. Cheeses of both sheep's milk and cow had been cured in the cool spring house in the yard, then smoked over beechwood chips, and were offered up with the loaves. So many fowl were roasted that each might have half a bird to glisten on their salvers. The minced meat of two oxen was spooned into eager mouths, stewed up with barley and apples, the fruit giving the whole a sweet tang. Forest mushrooms, fried in butter, gave earthy richness to the firm oaten biscuits they were spooned over. The abundance of eggs and milk allowed puddings, some baked with stoned plums and others with dried cherries made plump by soaking in wine.

Up to this night Hrald had, as all single men did, eaten from a single salver. Now he shared his food from a doubled one, as did all blest with living spouse.

Ashild, sitting at the women's table, had in honour of the night placed upon her brow the circlet of gold her brother had awarded her. She looked across at him. Last night Dagmar had sat here next Ashild; tonight, as was fitting, she was at her husband's side. Hrald had a chair made for his wife, similar to the one his mother sat in. It was of walnut, with carved back and arms, and his mother had woven and stuffed a cushion for it of the same dark blue wool which adorned the treasure room chairs. Ashild was taken by Dagmar's handsomeness, how well she looked sitting there at the high table, wife of a Jarl.

The bride was smiling, sometimes laughing, as she talked with Hrald and her mother-in-law. Ashild had to force her eyes away. It struck her almost with a pang, their happiness, though she begrudged them not one moment of it. Rather, she wished the night would go on forever, so that this first blush of joy might see no end.

After the meal, mead was passed, swirling golden and slightly sweet into their cups. Ashild had eaten enough, and had no thirst left; she wished to rise and go to the bower house. She could not, she must stay until the bride be seen safely within the bridal chamber. First there must be the merriment of games, as dice and counting pieces were brought forth, and men made ready to arm-wrestle. Ashild settled on her bench and gave an unwitting sigh, one heard, for she felt Burginde's plump and strong arm wrap her shoulders and squeeze her in support.

"This will be yours, when you go to Ceric," she promised of the celebration. "This, and more, for Kilton outshines all in riches."

Ashild would not rob Burginde of this belief, and only smiled her response.

As the evening went on, Ælfwyn fell into her own musing. Her own hand-fast with Yrling rose in memory. She recalled coming down the creaking wooden stair, Ceridwen before her, the gown of red silk she had donned, and that of green wool Ceridwen wore. The face of the grizzled and wandering brother who had uttered a prayer over her head was still clear. She remembered that Sidroc, sitting next Ceridwen, wore a tunic of blue, and that when Toki took up his harp and sang she must grudgingly admit the quality of both. There had been men who juggled, and dice games which Yrling left her side to play. Most of all she remembered the walk to the treasure room door, and Ceridwen and Burginde readying her for her wedding night, and the first time she would know a man's caress.

Tonight the hand-fast revelry would not overly extend the evening. After a surfeit of ale and two cups of mead, the older men were glad to begin breaking down the tables and climbing into their alcoves with their wives to make way for sleep. The younger men lodged in the second hall just across the work yard, and were sent away by their Jarl with a cask of mead to be tapped there.

Ashild rose too, and went with Burginde to where Dagmar sat. She kissed her new sister-in-law and her brother too, and bid them good night. Lacking female kin, her mother and Burginde would lead the bride to her new chamber. Ashild smiled on all, grateful she could leave. The noise of the hall was muffled as soon as the side door closed behind her. Stepping into the cooler air of the stable yard, she drew a deep breath. Her white stallion was there in the paddock by the rail, ghost-like in the dark. She went to him, and reached up her hand to pull at the forelock from behind his furred ear, as she knew he liked. He nickered in response, the big head bobbing. She did not wish to think of how he had come to be hers. She did not wish to think of anything just now, and only hoped she would be granted sleep as soon as she laid her head on her pillow.

Within the hall, Ælfwyn made gesture to the door behind them. Dagmar nodded, and with Burginde and her mother-in-law slipped quietly from the table. Ælfwyn picked out the treasure room door key from those at her waist, and let the three of them in. Once shut, the heavy door muffled the dying sounds of revelry, as if it all were far away. In near darkness Burginde went to the small table where iron and flint were always kept, struck out sparks into the pottery dish of waiting tinder, and lit the cresset. The room, suffused with sudden light, revealed itself.

Mindful of her own becoming Lady, Ælfwyn's first act was to untie the ring of keys from her waist.

"Your keys," she said, and passed them into Dagmar's hand. As she did so she planted a kiss upon the young woman's cheek. Besides keys to the doors of the hall and those of certain kitchen storehouses always kept locked, there were small keys to the chests in the kitchen-yard passageway which stored the bronze platters and cups and other valuables in everyday use. Most precious of all was the big key she had just turned to allow them entrance to the treasure room proper. With a smile she promised, "Tomorrow I will show you what each opens."

"I thank you, my Lady," Dagmar murmured.

Ælfwyn had not been given the keys from Yrling until she had been his wife for three days. She had never learnt if this was purposeful or mere forgetfulness on his part, but she would not allow any such affront to her son's wife.

Burginde was grinning like a cat who had drunk purloined cream. "This be your bed," she crowed, pointing to that expanse of wolfskin-covered softness. But she was disappointed at the bride's reaction, which to the nurse did not seem to register fitting awe.

"My Lady's sire took these very wolves, and her mother, she who now resides at Oundle under a veil, pieced the skins, and sewed the backing."

At this further news Dagmar took on the desired countenance.

"And – " Burginde went on, pulling some herbal green from underneath her apron, "'Tis valerian, for sweetness."

She reached beneath wolf spread, sheets, and feather-beds, and thrust the sprig upon the wooden frame work.

Ælfwyn, recalling these same words from her nurse from more than twenty years ago, felt her eyes grow moist.

Early that morning a new chest had been hauled into the treasure room, and it was opened now. Over these past weeks Ælfwyn, Burginde, Eanflad, and then even Dagmar had worked at the provision of fitting linens for a bridal chamber. Under ordinary circumstances a bride of high rank would arrive at her new home with a store of household linens: sheets, towels, lengths of fabric ready to be sewn into shifts and tunics, woollens in the form of blankets and alcove curtains, throws of soft stuffs, perhaps even fur, for her bed. Her mother would have made up pillows and cushions for her daughter's bridal bed. After what Dagmar had told Ælfwyn, she knew Guthrum's daughter would be possessed of none of this. Rather than a fine gown or piece of jewellery she thought the best and most welcoming gift she could provide for her daughter-in-law was to make up for this want, and supply the girl with ample linens to call her own.

There seemed little more to do. Basin and water for washing sat ready, here; a stack of rolled towels of linen upon the shelf, there; and a disc of pure silver to show one's reflection awaited upon the wall. All the goods Dagmar owned had been carried in before they left for Oundle; everything lay at hand. All was pointed out to the bride. Another kiss from Ælfwyn, a final cheering word from Burginde, and Dagmar was left alone.

As Ælfwyn crossed the threshold into the hall proper she felt how light was her waist without that ring of keys. There was her son, across the hall, standing by the side door and bidding goodnight to Asberg and her sister Æthelthryth, who for this one night would again sleep in the house Asberg had built for them.

Serving folk, fire-blackened pottery cups in hand, were snuffing out the guttering torches. Most alcove curtains had been pulled tight, and given the quantity of ale swallowed, it was no surprise that the snores of more than a few issued from behind their woollen draperies. Ælfwyn, Burginde at her side, walked to her son, and granted him a final goodnight kiss.

Within the treasure room Dagmar slid between the nubby linen of the thick sheets. She had removed her gown, over-gown, and stockings, and left them folded on the lid of the chest holding the linens. The veil of silk her mother-in-law had presented her with also lay there, in a neat roll. Her brooches and crystal strands she had set upon a shelf near the polished silver looking-disc. She placed them there by Hrald's comb, something he reached for every day, and this small act seemed almost an intrusion into his male realm. Once in bed she pulled the wolfskin spread up to her shoulders, then freed one arm to run her hand down its furred face. She had not reacted as she should when Burginde had showed her this spread, and had need to feign surprise so neither she nor the Lady of Four Stones guessed that she had seen it before.

She caught herself at this second thought; she herself was now Lady of the place, and Ælfwyn its dowager. She squeezed her eyes closed for a moment, wishing for the dark. She knew the cresset upon the table would burn for a long while, and soon he whom she had wed would enter this room and consummate his union with her.

She felt a thrill of fear. She was not a maid, for she had given herself wholly to the man she had loved. Despite her mother's anger, they would have wed. His name rose from her breast to her lips now, and she whispered it aloud: Vigmund. Having been driven away from Anglia by his outlawing, he was likely dead; the dulled centre of her heart could sense no trace of his living presence.

When her father had told her of his outlawing the pain of dire loss was outstripped only by a fervent desire that he somehow live and be safe. Few survived being outlawed; there was too much ease in killing a man whose death could not by law be avenged. It was akin to having a price upon one's head. Bring the aggrieved parties, they who demanded and decreed outlaw, proof that he so marked was dead, and a reward might follow. She could not know if Vigmund lived or died, only that unwelcome as he was in this land, he could never return.

The fear she felt now was not for the marriage-debt, that act of bodily possession of man over his wife. It was the pain of yielding up, and willingly too, that part of her which she had already given. She had shared a joy with a man, and now she must be willing bed-mate to another, one other than he whom she loved. This was compounded tenfold by the pressure of need and the shame of duplicity, which clung about her like a mantle.

She heard the key in the lock. The door opened, admitting almost no light; the greater part of the hall was nearly pitch. Hrald was a tall and dark figure crossing the threshold. He spoke aloud her name as he shut the door, and she heard him slide the iron bar across it, as she had tempted him to do that rainy day. Both days had been marked by rain, she realised; the day she had offered herself and he had, out of a greater rectitude than she herself possessed, refused; and this hand-fast day, in which she must not refuse him.

He came to the bed side. The wolfskin spread was drawn up to her bare shoulders, and she had not yet plaited her hair, which streamed out upon the pillow. He pulled the cresset to the end of the table that it might cast the more light on her. His smile, looking down on her, was one of such joy that she found herself smiling back. She lifted her hand to him. He took it, and bending low, kissed the open palm of it. Then he bent the lower, and kissed her face.

She let the hand he released reach up to his shoulder. Her touch felt a beckoning, and led him to break away. He pulled off his cuff of gold, that which his father had won. His arms went round his waist and took hold of the hem of his tunic. His feet were bare and his leggings in a pile on the floor before many more moments had passed. He stood there, naked for the first time in his adult life before a woman.

He felt no shame, not even in the all too apparent eagerness of his body as it yearned towards her. With his eyes on the loveliness of her face, he reached for the wolfskin spread, and lifted it away from her waiting body. Since the day he had first seen her, he had imagined doing just this, entering his bed with her welcoming him. Now it was real.

For a moment all he could do was look at she who was now his wife. The unbound dark hair flowing across both pillows was alone a thing exceptional. The comeliness of her face, with her downcast eyes, drew his own gaze to her breasts. The nipples were deep enough in shade to give striking contrast with her blush-tinted ivory skin. Her slender waist swelled to hips where his eyes must pause at the triangle of dark curls where her thighs met. His gaze lingered there. But he must, at this first sight of her, drink all in, and he followed the long and gracefully formed legs to her feet. He wanted almost to shout in wonder, and was at the same time nearly struck dumb by her beauty.

He let himself slide in next her, hearing a voice in his head saying, This is what you wanted, and what you waited for, now she is truly yours. His earlier self-restraint was rewarded by coming bliss.

He took her in his arms, pulled her towards him, seeking her mouth with his own. Their lips met, a long and steady pressure. He waited for her to kiss him as she had when they had first entered this room together.

Now, wed to the man who wanted her, Dagmar felt none of the desperate compulsion of that first deep kiss, when she was ready to do or say anything to ensure Hrald would accept her. She felt measured in her actions, careful and deeply conscious of every motion, every gesture and response. Mindful she must not betray her past experience, she responded to his caresses with a hesitant openness, which he read as innocence of the act of love.

Of course he expected Dagmar to be a maid; a King's daughter would not lightly dispense of her favour. Yet there was a lack of ardour which, considering the passion with which she had then kissed him and her willingness to give herself before their witnessed hand-fast, almost confused him.

She took the lead in nothing yet seemed to welcome all his actions. Perhaps some new shyness took hold of her, for she kept her eyes closed the entire time, a surprising show of modesty in such a self-assured maid. He felt awkward, knew he must seem awkward, yet tried to touch her with gentleness despite his mounting desire.

As thrilling as was the feel of her flesh under his hands, he could not for long stroke her breasts and thighs. His own urgency to know her as wife compelled him to lift himself over her, and with his legs part her own. Looking down at her, his knees between her own, was its own culmination of his imaginings. The sensation as he lowered his hips, and his body sought and found her woman's hollow made him close his own eyes for a long moment in near-sacred savouring.

"I make you my wife, Dagmar," he breathed.

Her arms reached round him, and when their lips met, she opened her own and kissed him. Her tongue gently touched his own, so that he responded with a forceful thrust of his own tongue. This action, coupled with the fire in his loins, suffused him with a keenness of sense outstripping all imaginings. Its purity was such that his entire being was engulfed in the unique rapture of this moment, one which could never come again. As he moved above her, he felt a fervour both singularly distinct, and wholly connected to another.

At Hrald's whispered words, Dagmar had one thought: If this be so, I am already wed. For an instant her body clenched, a response she could not control, as he entered her. A name rose again from the depths of her, one ingrained in her heart, summoned by what felt a violation of her self. Vigmund.

Hrald's euphoric climax to this congress was a surrender as powerful as it was exquisite. Cradling the head of his beautiful wife in the moments afterward, kissing her face, he uttered a prayer to God that she had been delivered into his keeping. His only experience with carnal passion had been with a wanton kitchen woman, an act devoid of tenderness or affection. His new wife's kindness and welcoming of his caresses was the revelation Burginde had promised it would be.

He pulled back and kissed her once more, and she smiled up at him. The light of the cresset fell upon her face, and he saw tears on her lashes. He thought it due to the pain of her maidenhead breaking.

It was not, only what was left of her heart.

MUCH TO PROTECT

DAGMAR proved in every way an asset to Four Stones. As its young Lady she looked to Ælfwyn for direction and advice, consulted her on every action, gratefully accepted help when offered, and yet worked hard to assume her rightful duties, and show husband and mother-in-law that she was up to the task of running such a large keep.

She made no changes, sought no alteration in how hall or kitchen yard was run. Indeed, she was all too grateful at her good fortune, that Four Stones under the hands of she who had preceded her had been brought to such a height of functioning that no amendment was needed. Her own domestic arrangement at Headleage was the small timber house shared with her mother. It had given her almost no preparation for the running of a hall feeding and housing so many, beyond that growing need for thrift which shadowed every month following her father's death. His royal hall there had not, she thought, been run as ably as her new home, nor were its folk as content as those she now lived amongst. Her first Sabbath at the preaching cross as Hrald's wife she had the pleasure of seeing all smile upon her in welcome, and when later that week she accompanied Ælfwyn on her rounds in the giving of alms and in comforting the sick she felt for the first time the satisfaction of bringing some larger good to lives she could make the easier.

Ælfwyn, walking with Dagmar and Burginde on their charitable circuit, took silent pride in how her daughter-in-law responded to being shown to the neediest of her new folk. Aged men and women, their eyes filmy with years reached forth their hands, wishing to touch their new Lady, and Dagmar, nothing dismayed, took the knobby hands into her own, and bestowed greeting.

Watching this, Ælfwyn remembered after her own arrival here sending to every despoiled croft a silver coin, and how, when they next saw her, the village women in their hunger and desolation had thrust their hands to her so they might touch she who had begun to relieve their want. That hard work of restoration had been her own; she had achieved it, and now had the gladsome task of turning a well-fed, productive, and happy folk into the care of she entrusted with its continuance.

Nor did Dagmar disappoint in the private sphere within the hall. Her initial reserve was replaced by a growing warmth and openness to the women of Four Stones, one which Ælfwyn thought already blossoming into true affection. She quickly befriended Ealhswith and made much of the girl, showing her new ways in which to plait her hair, allowing her to attempt the plaiting of her own far longer and thicker locks, and patiently answering her ceaseless questions about life in the royal hall of her father.

During those daily hours when Ælfwyn, her sister, and two daughters stood at loom or spinning, or sat cutting and sewing the cloth they had made, Dagmar worked alongside them, eager to improve her skills. Demand for cloth was ever great, for from the weaving room on the partial second floor of the hall issued not only all the cloth which the family of Four Stones required, but some of that needed for the men yet unmarried. Beyond the giving of arms and silver as reward for service, part of Hrald's charge was to feed, and if needed, clothe those warriors who fought for him. Those without wife or mother to spin, weave, and sew must be supplied by the hall. And the need for bedding and linens such as sheets, towels, blankets, alcove curtains and other everyday items was constant. Thankfully Ælfwyn had help in this, as certain women of the village returned to her, spun and woven, the carded fleece and flax delivered to them.

Re-hemming a tunic of Hrald's where the stiches had unravelled, Dagmar one afternoon confided to her mother-in-law that she could not make so fine a shirt herself. Indeed, even her new hemming was inferior to the tiny stiches laid down by his mother, who had sewn it. Ælfwyn was quick to take issue with this, assuring her that her skills were far advanced to those she had possessed when she became Lady of Four Stones.

"Starts with spinning, everything does," interjected Burginde, without stopping in her drawing of thread from her fast whirling spindle. She was standing in the middle of the floor, between Ashild at a loom, and Dagmar seated at the table with Ælfwyn. "Fine thread works up to fine cloth, and deserves steady hands and patience with shears and needle."

No one's spinning was as good as Burginde's, nor could it ever be. Ashild craned her head to see the nurse move to Dagmar and in an unasked-for lesson, place the spindle in her hands. Dagmar caught Ashild casting her eyes up to the ceiling as the nurse instructed Hrald's bride how to roll a finer thread. Both young women found themselves smiling.

As for Hrald, his happiness in his wife grew unabated. When they awoke after their bridal night, Hrald had ready his morgen-gyfu, his morning-gift, that gift a new husband presents to his bride after their first night. It became her property alone for the remainder of her days, and one she could leave in her will to anyone she wished. Hrald's gift to Dagmar was a ring of twisted yellow gold for her finger. He wished to give her something she would wear every day, as reminder of their union. The ring was from a small store of gold housed in one of the treasure room chests, and he had selected it not only for its bright colour, but because it was unmarred. He took her left hand and began to slip it along her fourth finger.

It did not fit; it was too small.

Four Stones had no worker in precious metal. Hrald looked at the pretty thing, stopped there above her knuckle. "I will send it to Jorvik," he told her. "The gold-workers there will fix it." He felt abashed, yet she only smiled.

"I will wear it on a chain about my neck, until you are able," she promised.

He could do nought but kiss her for her words.

"It is not too small a gift," he wondered to her. He had watched how she and her sister had been drawn to the necklace and paired bracelets of gold and coloured gemstones at Oundle. His morgen-gyfu was far more modest, but he hoped she would consider it the more heartfelt.

Dagmar's mother had never received a ring from Guthrum; none of his wives had. A ring as a token had special significance, one they had never been granted.

She smiled at him as she answered. "It is not small at all," she returned, and then looking at it there above her knuckle, was able to laugh, and make him laugh as well, when she said, "You are perhaps right, it is a bit small."

If there was one slight lack in the delight Hrald took in his wife, it was that she had not told him she loved him. He had said it to her that day in the treasure room, using his regard for her as his reason for holding himself back. She had not answered him then with a return of those words, and instead seemed struck he had uttered them. And he had not said them again, though he felt it with all his being. Dagmar's actions in both public and private assured him in all things, and he felt sure she would soon declare her love for him in words as well as deeds. He must not press her. There was about her some slight mystery which served to enhance her attraction, an unknowable quality which he felt he should respect though he did not understand. But then, all women were perhaps the same in possessing this; it was in their nature. He sometimes gave thought to how confounding Ceric found Ashild.

Once when he awakened at night he sensed that she lay awake as well, and was looking at him. They lay side by side, and his eyes were shrouded by his lashes, but he could discern the expression on her face, almost a kind of puzzlement that she should be lying next this man.

He closed his own eyes, pondering this, and fell back into sleep. In the morning when he felt her stir he took her in his arms, began kissing and stroking her, and felt glad in her ready surrender to the act of love.

Two months had passed since Hrald and Dagmar had stood on Oundle's step and wed each other. Trees which had been in full leaf then now held bare branches, reaching up to grey and chilly skies. The shortening of the days and the keenness of the wind heralded Winter soon to come.

One afternoon as the early dusk was falling, three breathless men on winded horses galloped through the gates, whistling alarm as they came. They were three sent to be watch-men along the southern border of one of the roads leading to Four Stones, and their detail was the relief of three who had spent a week there by one of the tall rock cairns marking the keep's property. When they arrived they found the three men dead, their horses and weapons gone, their modest camp plundered. Little remained of their campsite, set back from the road in a thicket of trees. Men on foot had done this, they reported; the number of booted tracks suggested at least two score, and the decay of the bodies told that the hapless dead had lain there for three or more days.

Those gathered to hear this baleful tale included many of Hrald's picked men, and Ashild and Dagmar too. Ashild, alone with Dagmar and her Aunt Eanflad up in the weaving room, had heard the whistled warning and read it correctly. She uttered one word, "Trouble." Then she rose from where she sat at the table, pushing herself up. When she stood long at her weaving her back ached, and she must sit at some other work. Dagmar looked at her, set aside the spindle she held, and followed her down. Ashild felt ungainly on the narrow stairs, awkward and tentative with the weight she had gained. These were steps she was used to fly down. Even her gait was off, and though thankfully the morning retching was behind her, her sense of growing impairment and limitation made her more restless than usual.

The two young women stood there at the outer circle of the men surrounding the returned riders and heard all their report. Hrald's hand had risen to his hair, and he pushed it back from his brow as the men told him the names of the three dead.

"I will ride in the morning," he said. The sky was rapidly darkening; no start could be made tonight.

Jari spoke. "Nej. There is nothing to gain." His look to Hrald said more, told the young Jarl he must stay here and defend his keep.

Hrald paused a moment, then looked to Kjeld. Someone must go, discern what he could of the attackers, and recover the bodies. He did not like risking so trusted an arm, but that same trust forced him to say the next. "Kjeld. You will lead five men, and take pack horses to carry them back. Be ready to ride at dawn."

Jari spoke again. "Hrald. It has been three, four days." His grimace said the rest. Having lain for days, even in the chill of approaching Winter, the corpses would be putrefying. No horse could be asked to bear that. They must either bury them there or bring the bodies back in a waggon. They could not lay a pyre and fire them where they lay; these were Christian men.

"Bury them where they fell," Hrald said at last. The ground was not frozen; it would be a labour, but far less danger to the men than a slow ride back with a waggon in their midst.

"You said two score of men," Hrald asked of those returned. They all three nodded their agreement.

Hrald looked through the still open gates at dusk settling on the village outside the walls. An army was afoot and might even now be overpowering more of his watch-men.

"I will bring the folk in," he said, almost to himself. Ordering the village folk, beasts and all into the yard, would cause fear, perhaps panic. But no panic would be so great as the village overrun by a hungry enemy.

"I will bring the folk in," he said again, louder and with decision. Jari nodded.

Hrald turned to look at the stable door, where he had seen Mul standing, little Bork at his side. Mul had already vanished into the dark interior, gone to fetch the traps of Hrald's bay, standing in the paddock.

Ashild turned too, facing the kitchen yard. "My mother is in her bower; go and tell her," she instructed Dagmar. "I will go to the kitchen yard and warn them."

The night which unfurled was a long one. It began with Hrald riding through the village, telling all they must quit their crofts, bring their beasts and what foodstuffs they had readily at hand, and take shelter behind the palisade walls. Women gasped, children cried, and all who were of an age to bear one took up hoe or scythe as makeshift weapon. The driving of so many cows and pigs into the yard, the capture and carrying of geese and hens was labour enough. The harassed animals filled the cold air with lowing, grunting, and crowing. The sheep, afield in pastures near and far, could not be herded in the dark; that must wait for dawn.

Within the yard there was no way to house so many, and it was too cold for them to sleep beneath the vault of the starry heavens. The second hall must shelter them all, and those younger warriors drew straws to find which half of them would be sleeping on pallets in the great hall, and which would need seek shelter in barn, stables, and outbuildings.

The folk had brought what food they could, but needed means to cook. Their animals need be penned, and fodder found. They themselves must be accommodated within the second hall, and lacking alcoves for all, the young would bunk on the planked floor on anything which could serve as pallet. Ælfwyn and Burginde seemed everywhere at once, ordering kitchen men to dig fire-pits for cooking, entrusting older children to usher the younger to the quieter recesses of the keep where they would not be underfoot, directing fearful crofters to the second hall, whose vastness daunted them. Bork popped up by Ælfwyn's side, and his look of entreaty to be of service was such that she must place him in charge of carrying messages between her and her son, busy with the hasty knocking up of additional animal pens. When at last the evening meal was served in the hall it would be hours past its normal time.

Dagmar and Ashild worked together within the second hall. It was a place Ashild had rarely entered, and Dagmar, never, for it was the preserve of unwed warriors. Now, its rightful inhabitants shooed off, their belongings under their arms, they worked with serving men and women to ready the space for the scores of families who would sleep there.

"Has this before happened," Dagmar asked Ashild in a hushed voice. They were taking bronze cressets from a tray and filling them with oil. The colour had fled from Dagmar's full lips, and it was not only the dimness of the hall which made large her eyes.

"Never," Ashild murmured, keeping her eyes upon the cresset in her hand. "Not in my memory." She paused, remembering what she had been told. "Though by the time my mother came, both hall and village had been almost destroyed. This hall," she went on, "was built by Hrald's father on the foundations of a burnt building."

She did not add that it was during the attack by her father that the fires had raged. No one need hear that now, and she would not remind herself of the fact.

This news, of the rarity of such threats, seemed to add to Dagmar's discomfort rather than allay it.

Ashild too knew fear, but said what she could. She gestured that Dagmar lift the cresset she held nearer the spout of the oil jug she tipped, as it was hard in the low light to see if it were full.

"It is good we are too busy to be frightened," Ashild told her, with as much of a smile as she could muster.

That night Dagmar went to the treasure room long before Hrald did. She had left him at the high table, Jari and Kjeld and his other chief men clustered about him, as they discussed the slaying of the three watch-men. All three men would never be together at one time in their camp, suggesting that one on active watch had been captured and forced to lead his captors to the others, where they were surrounded and killed. How it had truly occurred, and who had done it seemed an endless circle of conjecture, one ending in the death of three men.

Behind the thick walls of the treasure room Dagmar could just discern the muffled voices around that table, low but still urgent. She drew off her clothing, washed, and climbed into bed, pulling the wolfskin spread up high under her neck. There were two brass braziers burning on the floor in the room, but she shivered under the coolness of the linen sheet, and hugged herself for both warmth and comfort. She wished Hrald would come in, though she knew she must work to not show him her fear.

She was safer here behind these stout oak walls than anyplace in the fortress; this was its strong room. She gave thought to Hrald's mother in her bower house, a place undefended save that it lay behind the palisade, and thought too of Ashild, carrying a babe and far from its father. They were fearful too, but she felt their fear of a different quality to her own. This was the hall and folk they loved, and for Ashild, all she had ever known. Their connection to the place was deeply rooted, as it was for Hrald, not only born here but now ruling the domain. Dagmar's attachment was new, both to man and the place. She felt slight kinship to her older brother Agmund, save that fact of their common father, and did not like his choice to break the intent of their father's Peace and side with new invaders. Yet Agmund had been given Headleage, the most well protected of Guthrum's keeps. Perhaps no fortress in the length and breadth of the land could match it for strength, and it was now one of her brother's halls. He might be there now. If she were back at Headleage she could flee to it for shelter.

Was it Agmund's men who had killed these three of Hrald's? Was her brother's hand in the battle ground strewn with dead that Hrald had ridden to inspect? Was Agmund truly joined with the invader Haesten and his vast army, or had they parted ways, and now her brother sought to take over all Anglia – perhaps all Angle-land – himself?

As these thoughts were tumbling in her brain she returned to something Jari had said before she left. The women had risen from the table, each to go to her final tasks of the night. The men stood as well, scraping their benches across the stone floor to crowd about Hrald's chair. Jari at this point had been speaking in a bantering tone about coming war, after the sustained pleasures of peace. The man he addressed was another of the older warriors.

"Men who have been too long from war lose their belly for it," Jari claimed.

The other man tapped the back of his hand to Jari's midsection. "The raven might still emerge to feed," he grinned.

It was all said as a jest; Dagmar knew that was how men often spoke of war. They need laugh at it to mask their own fear. But it unsettled her. If the chief amongst Hrald's body-guard spoke thus, she could not but question their fitness in the conflict now sure to come.

As she lay there, still cold and unable to warm herself, Hrald's key turned in the lock. She had left the cresset burning and she sat up in bed, clutching the wolf spread to her for warmth.

"I – I am so glad you are here," she began. She felt close to tears, and his face made clear he saw it.

Hrald pulled off his belts and clothing and was next her in bed in a few moments. She placed her hand on his shoulder and turned her face toward him, pressing herself against the firmness of his skin. She wanted to bury her head under his strong right arm and shut out the noise of the day, and the confusion of her thoughts. She let herself inhale the scent of his body, that warm mix of leather, horses, and the tang of sweat. His hands and arms wrapped her back and rested on her skin, holding her close.

As he held her, she felt her breathing slow, and within her a welcome calm begin to spread. The broadness of his chest felt a refuge, and the strength of his lean body gave comfort. The memory of another young man's chest and arms arose, a man with golden hair. She bit her lip to drive it away. She was Hrald's wife and was lucky to be so. She had found delight in the embrace of her lover; now she sought succour in the arms of her young husband.

She did not like to think of the difference in their ages, and indeed neither had ever brought it up. But her cousin had told her Hrald was nearly two years from twenty, and she was close to two years past it. Hrald's face, even with its strong brow, dark eyebrows, and shadow of a beard upon his shaved chin, was still boyish. The body she pressed herself against was one of a man. Young as he was it had been shaped by years of training. Yet there was a sweetness about him, a manly sweetness, one easily glimpsed when he looked at her from downcast eyes fringed by his dark lashes. She had seen him flush, as well, the pale blush of colour rising from chin to cheek for a moment, when he touched her in certain ways, or took special delight in looking upon her naked body.

She had made the right choice, she now told herself. This was followed by the rueful truth that her only choice had been to accept him. She had no other offers.

Her hand on his shoulder moved. It touched, and then cupped, the jagged scar there at the top of his upper arm. He was as yet unmarked by battle, save that scar wrapping the top of his right arm. She had not before asked of it, and thought to do so now.

She lifted her head away from his chest, and he stroked her hair.

"This scar," she whispered, pressing her hand more firmly against it.

His hand stilled as he prepared to answer. He would not lie to her. But he could not share the full truth, that he had stabbed himself after unwittingly cutting his best friend. His act seemed too rash, one heedless to the point of utter recklessness. Only Ceric and his sister knew the whole story of the double wounding. All the others had believed them when they said the leathern sheaths covering their blades had failed.

"My friend Ceric and I. We were sparring . . . "

It was all he said, all he need say. Men injured themselves and others in training all the time.

She murmured in consolation, nodding her head, and then lowered it once more against his chest.

He had told no one about the act that had followed, how he had gashed himself by his own knife thrust, how he had told Ceric to stand still while they pressed their streaming upper arms together to become brothers in blood. He had not told Ashild that part, even when she guessed the cause of his wound.

I will tell her that, he thought now. I want Ashild to know this about Ceric and me. If I die soon it might help her go to Kilton . . .

He was so quiet that it made Dagmar lift her head again. "Do not think on it," she whispered.

He made a sound of assent, and kissed the top of her head. "You are right," he answered. "Not when there is so much more to think of."

"You have much to protect," she said next, of the many obligations he must meet.

Hrald wordlessly nodded his head. A deep exhalation of his breath followed. His mind had been so full with the death of his watch-men and the rounding up of the village folk that other pressing concerns had slipped. He lay staring up into the gloom of the roof rafters and named one.

"Oundle," he said. In its way that holy foundation was a greater target than Four Stones, for Oundle held silver and gold. The women it also housed made it a double target. Four Stones held treasure as well, in its weaponry and wealth of horses, and greater treasure in the men beneath its roof, could they be turned to fight for Haesten or Agmund. But the foundation at Oundle and its sacred contents and calling must be preserved at all cost.

Dagmar repeated it, so softly that it sounded an echo to his naming that place.

Her word seemed to rouse him, for he kissed her brow. Of all he was entrusted to protect, his wife, so beautiful and kind, was precious beyond ranking.

"No hand will touch you," he promised.

On the morrow Kjeld and five men set out. They took but two horses for pack, bearing two small tents and four shovels, making for ungainly hide-covered baggage. This was tied to the beasts' saddles, for if one of their own went lame they would abandon this kit in their need to return back to Four Stones at speed. They should be gone three days if all went well, but carried food for twice that. If travelling on the road became impossible they must do so more slowly overland.

Hrald's next act was to send two riders to Asberg at Turcesig, warning him of the deadly incursion. At the same time he sent a score of mounted men to scour the immediate perimeter of the hall precincts, lest any warrior troop be harbouring in the forest beyond the far pasture lands. By midday they returned from their survey with no report of telltale tracks or encampment. This was welcome news, as provisional as it might be. The hall yards could not long support the many folk and animals as were now crowded in, and the folk themselves were eager to return to their crofts, flocks, and vegetable plots. He made decision to open the gates and let them file back to their thatched and waiting roofs. For added caution he doubled the nearest perimeter guard, halving the distance between each set of three men. Every such protection he extended lessened the number of men behind his own palisade, but it could not be helped. Hrald knew he might be stretched far thinner than this before long.

He stood to one side of the opened gates with his mother, wife, and older sister as the village folk streamed through, leading, carrying, and in some cases chasing their beasts back to their respective crofts. Children who had cried in fear last night when they were hustled in now wept anew the leaving of a place they found full of secret hiding places and unexpected tiny cakes handed out by the battery of hall bakers.

The members of the family of the hall who watched their progress did so with faces still grave from the necessity of this general upset. Many of the crofters who were not otherwise occupied with beast or child bobbed their heads at them in thanks, pulled at their woollen caps in respect, or in the case of a few aged women, came to Ælfwyn, and bending their stiff knees, reached out gnarled hands to touch the hem of her gown in reverence. She opened her hands to them in the graceful gesture she often used, and though her face showed the stress of the night, she smiled on them all. She knew the love they bore her, and would shed some of it on the young woman at her side. The cluster of keys Ælfwyn had worn for two decades was now hanging from the waist of Dagmar, and after Ælfwyn made a slight motion to her daughter-in-law, these women, stricken in years but full-hearted, dipped their heads to her as well.

When the last stragglers had been seen out, the heavy gates swung shut. Burginde was already in the kitchen yard, marshalling the same men she had commanded in the digging of cooking pits to the filling of same. Ælfwyn would return to her, while Dagmar and Ashild would go to the second hall and collect the cressets, pouring the costly oil back into the pottery jugs they had filled them from.

As they worked the two young women spoke about the actions Hrald had taken this morning. Dagmar had seen the score of armed men ride out to scan the near boundaries of hall and village. Men in full war-kit were ever impressive to the eye, and seeing their calm determination as they swung themselves up into their saddles and rode out both reassured her and gave her a sense of borrowed pride. She looked over at Ashild, carefully pouring oil from the cresset in her hand back into one of the jugs.

"You rode to battle," Dagmar said. There was more than a tinge of questioning wonder in her voice as she said it.

Ashild did not respond at once. Still holding the cresset, she let her eyes flick up to Dagmar's lovely face.

"I rode to defend Oundle, and its women," was her answer.

This was so simply spoken, and so clear in intent, that Dagmar herself paused before she went on.

"What – what weapons did you carry?"

Ashild set down the cresset.

"A spear. Hrald gave me a Saxon seax from his store to use as knife. Also his boyhood shield."

Dagmar nodded. "And you rode with the war-flag you made," she recounted. "Hrald told me."

Ashild looked down a moment, a wash of pride running through her that Hrald recalled that moment, one when he himself had affixed the raven flag to her cantle.

"Were you frightened?"

Ashild had almost to keep herself from smiling. "At first, not. Here in the stable yard one of Hrald's men spoke in favour of me riding," she said, remembering how her friend Gunnulf had commended her to the other warriors. "He was killed the next day," she added in a quieter tone.

"Riding out from our gates – the hall and yard folk cheering, the crofters looking up at us – it was a kind of glory in itself.

"But as we grew nearer Oundle I began to feel – cold. My breath came fast and I feared ambush. We made it to the abbey, and then came the long wait for the enemy. I was awakened near dawn by one of the sisters; they had come, and were creeping up upon the walls, ready with oil to fire it."

Both their eyes fell upon the jugs they were filling. Fire was the greatest enemy of all.

"From the ramparts Sigewif made parley with the leaders, as bold as any King would, challenging and then threatening them. She drew them near, making it easier for us, mounted and waiting behind the gates, to charge at them.

"Sister Bova – the brewster – was in the church with the rest of the nuns and brothers. She began to ring the church bell. She sought to summon the angels, she told me later, but her surprise clanging of the bell startled the Danes, and at that moment Asberg had the gates flung open. We kicked our horses and raced out.

"Just after that one of the Danes threw his spear at me. It lodged in my shield. I had my own in my hand and made a true throw."

"You killed him," Dagmar guessed.

Ashild nodded. As she had many times before, in her mind's eye she saw the man's knees buckle. She watched his body crumple to the ground, saw his war-cap roll from his head. Most of all she saw the length of her spear shaft as it rose in the air while he fell, protruding from that still-living chest. She would never unsee this, she knew.

Dagmar looked lost in thought, considering this.

"Who – who was Judith?" she asked next.

Ashild told her. "A woman of the Hebrews willing to do anything to save her people, besieged by a huge force of warriors."

There was more to the tale, and Dagmar's face asked her to go on.

"Judith and her serving woman gained access to the camp of the enemy, and she was allowed to visit their war-lord. That night, alone in his tent with him, she killed him. Then she severed his head. The serving woman had a basket ready. They brought the head back to their own folk, so they might fear no longer."

The horror of the endeavour flashed across Dagmar's face as she listened. It made Ashild think anew of it. As well as she knew this tale, Ashild had never given real thought to the performance of the deed itself, and how it need be accomplished. If she had been called to perform such a gruesome act, it was not hard to picture the steadfast Burginde at her side, stealing back to their village with the hideous trophy in their basket. Indeed, she could picture none other than Burginde to aid her.

"That night, in his tent," Dagmar repeated. "So she had to . . . " Her question trailed off.

"Who knows what she had to do," was Ashild's rejoinder. "She set herself a task and she completed it. And she saved her people."

"This is why the Abbess calls you Judith," Dagmar summed. "For your courage."

Ashild snorted. "I was nearly killed. If that Dane had knocked me off my horse another man would have poled me in an instant.

"When it was over and I got off my horse I could barely walk to where Sigewif stood waiting to embrace me. That was how badly I trembled."

Dagmar's next words were spoken with quiet solemnity. "My father told me it is the same for every young warrior." Even Ashild must admit to the admiration in the eyes of her sister-in-law.

They both looked down to the scarred table top. Then Dagmar spoke again. "You are just more honest about it than most men."

At that Ashild had to smile, as did Dagmar.

Kjeld did not return with the five he rode out with. When their approach was whistled, Hrald climbed up to the ramparts so he might see their arrival himself. Five horses and two pack animals met his eyes. Hrald could only swallow, hoping against hope he had not lost so valuable a man as was Kjeld. But he was not riding with them, leading them home.

He scrambled down to hear the reason. His men explained that when they had reached the slain watchmen, Kjeld decided to break from the group and track the assailants. The men were on foot, with their newly gained horses, and their tracks in the still unfrozen earth were clear. The soil had been wet at the attack, and it had not rained since. Kjeld would risk following and see what he could learn. His fellows gave him what provender they could, then set to work on the grisly task of burial. They had been unimpeded on the road back, and every watch camp they passed had known no disturbance.

Kjeld rode back alone, two days hence, hungry and worn. His look to Hrald and Jari as he quitted his horse made Hrald gesture him into the treasure room. There, over a cup of ale, Kjeld told of how he had begun following the tracks, at times leaning low from his horse, at others scanning the undergrowth from a distance to discern the way.

"Yesterday, almost at dusk, I recognized where I was. I trailed them to the gates of Haward's hall."

NEVER
WOULD IT BE ME

HRALD sent riders that hour to tell Asberg to meet him in the morning at the halfway point between Four Stones and Turcesig. Together they would ride to confront Haward. The next day fifty heavily armed men, having made an early start from their respective halls, met at the stream fork which served as marker. Asberg's troop reached there first, their horses nodding and snorting in impatience as they stood. The weather was sharply colder; the breath of both horses and men smoked in the frosty air. A skim of rippling ice sat on the water of the stream, making the fallen leaves resting on the shallow bottom look black.

As they approached Haward's hall the tracks of the men who had marched to his doors were clear. They need not whistle their own approach; Haward's men upon his palisade did it for them, and the gates were speedily opened. This would not be the case if the killers of Hrald's watch-men were still within; that would have occasioned discussion and delay. And in fact the hall yards looked as they always had. Whoever had come here had now left.

Hrald, Asberg, and Jari walked to the hall proper, leaving the body of their men not only within the closed gates but still mounted. If anything went amiss they wanted them to have every advantage.

"Let me speak to him," Hrald said to his uncle as the hall door opened. Asberg nodded.

They stepped within. The long fire-pit cast both light and heat, brightening the hall even in the drabness of the morning. All were breaking their fast, and serving folk moved amongst the crowded trestles. At the women's table Hrald saw the child Siggerith, spooning something into her mouth. Her eyes widened at the sight of Hrald, but she did not seem fearful.

Haward had already risen from the table to welcome the newcomers. He came forth, a smile of greeting on his face, one that shifted when he saw the gravity of his guests' countenances. He turned and led them to the door of the weapons room, and let them in.

"Haward. You have had visitors," were Hrald's first words.

Haward stopped in his motion. His head tilted as if in question, and none of the men from Four Stones showed surprise at the uncertainty of his next words.

"What do you mean?"

"I mean the troop of warriors who my man Kjeld tracked here to your gates. The same warriors who killed three of my watch-men last week."

Haward's mouth opened.

"Where?" he asked.

"At the southern border of my lands, on the north-east road, by the tall cairn."

Haward's eyes looked to the left as he calculated this.

"And then they came here . . . " he conceded.

"Who were they?" Hrald demanded.

The briefest pause before he answered told of Haward's discomfort.

"Men of my cousin, Agmund."

The hands of both Asberg and Jari now flinched, as if reaching for their weapon belts. Hrald stood unmoving, staring at Haward.

"He has thrown in with Haesten," Hrald said. "You are sworn to me, to uphold Guthrum's Peace. Tell me why you let them in."

"They asked for one meal, nothing more."

Hrald kept his eyes on Haward's face. Men on the march would be hungered, but that was not the sole reason why they sought out Haward. Hrald kept his eyes fixed on him.

Haward took a breath in an empty effort to calm himself. He looked at the young Jarl's face, and saw the muscle in Hrald's cheek ripple as he clenched his jaw.

There was no route but forward. Haward must take it.

"They carried a message from Agmund, asking me to join them."

Haward forced his eyes from Hrald's face, to look at both older men.

"Asberg, Jari. Surely you know that a man must have leave to talk, especially with kin."

Neither of their faces provided the slightest encouragement for this supposition.

"What answer did you give," Hrald wished to know next.

"None. I gave none." As soon as Haward spoke thus, he heard how damning it was. "I tried to delay. How could I give answer," he spluttered, "when they were forty men within my gates?"

"You swung wide those very gates," Hrald pointed out. "Why?"

"I told you. Agmund is kin." Haward's eyes darted about the hall for a moment, seeking words. "He is Dagmar's brother," he ended, in needless reminder. "I must at least listen."

"Nej. One does not listen to a broken faith. Agmund broke faith with his own father, then sent men here to tempt you to do the same.

"And I lost three men to them," Hrald ended.

"Your watch-men – I did not know that," Haward said, shaking his head. "I did not know that," he repeated.

Hrald studied his face. "That part, I believe," he said at last.

At Four Stones that night, Hrald spoke before the platters were brought. He was not yet seated, and looked down the length of the high table.

"Kjeld," he summoned. He named rose, and came to Hrald, who held out a neck ring of silver.

"For your service," was what Kjeld's Jarl said. Hrald passed the thick necklet to him.

As was custom, the prize was held up before all, who hooted and whistled their approval. Kjeld then pressed the thing around his neck, at once sporting his reward. His grin said the rest.

When Hrald sat, Dagmar turned and whispered in his ear. "That is a handsome gift. How did he earn it?"

Hrald had not told his bride of Kjeld's report. She knew he had today ridden to see her cousin, but not why.

"Kjeld is faithful in his service," was all he was able to say.

XXXXXXXXXXXX

A few nights later Ashild was lying in bed in the bower house when she awakened. She was not sure why. Then she felt a stirring, almost a fluttering, deep within her belly, the first true sense that her own body now sheltered another. A gasp escaped her lips.

She was alone in her revelation. Her mother slept, and the low and halting snores issuing from Burginde's alcove told that she did as well. Ashild lay there, letting her eyes close. Of a sudden, the grossness of her bodily transformation made sense. Everything was worth it, the breasts grown pendulous, the nagging back ache, her inability to ride or run, her impaired sense of balance, every temporary indignity visited upon her body by her condition, even the sense of awe-ful vulnerability melted away. She wrapped her arms about her belly, holding its distended firmness, awaiting another flutter. It came. With it arose a new knowledge, something akin to a fresh source of power. It was as close to the sacred as she had come.

She was alone in this moment of discovery; Ceric was not there to place his hands on her belly and feel their child quickening. Before she knew it tears had gathered in her eyes. She was not alone. This babe she nurtured was of her, and with her.

That evening, when Ashild and Ælfwyn readied themselves for the hall, the younger woman posed a question.

"My father. I know he died before my birth," she began.
"But did he ever know I was coming?"

Ælfwyn stopped in the combing of her flaxen hair. She
looked at her daughter, and heaved a sigh. "No, he did not.
It would have gladdened him if he had. He was eager to
have children."

Ashild gave a nod, and then must add what she knew
was true. "Especially sons."

Her mother looked at her with a conceding smile. "In
no way would you have disappointed him."

Ashild searched her mother's face. "And you – are you
very disappointed?"

Ælfwyn knew what she meant. Disappointed in her
daughter's choice to remain here; perhaps even disappointed in her. She took a moment before she answered.

"Your happiness, Ashild, is more dear to me than my
own. If you sacrificed that, then I would be disappointed."

Hearing this, so simply stated, forced tears to Ashild's
eyes.

Her mother set down her comb and came to her. She
had not, she thought, been a disappointment to her own
mother, and could not bear for Ashild to think she might
be one, to her. Ælfwyn had now some distance, granted by
the years, and judgement, won by experience, to look upon.
And would share this with her girl.

"My role was decreed by my father and grandsire. I
did not come willingly to Four Stones, yet I have come to
love it, and its folk. And I am not unaware of the good that

my coming has brought to this place. That is satisfaction, indeed.

"The children I have been given are the greatest gifts of my life. You are my firstborn and dearly precious to me. I wish your father had lived, that he might have known you, and you, him. Neither of you were granted that. I wish the Peace had not dissolved. I wish Anglia had still a strong and just ruler, as it had in Guthrum. We have not been granted that. We must make our way as we can without it. And yes, as much as I wish that you could be at Kilton with Ceric, it is enough to know that you bear him such regard to have brought forth a child to bless both houses, and this hall."

Ashild, standing before her and listening, felt a deep harkening to her mother's words. She lifted her arms and embraced her, an embrace paired with a smile at her need to set her body aslant to her mother's slender waist so they might for a moment hold the other.

Ashild felt almost a sense of joy, and of glad expectation. She wanted her mother to know as much of happiness as she could, and her next words suggested where she thought the Lady of Four Stones might find it.

"Will you stay here always, mother, or now that Hrald has wed, perhaps go to Oundle?" she wanted to know.

Ælfwyn did not expect this; but then her eldest had always surprised her. She would answer as calmly and truthfully as was possible.

"I do not know. I may – I may not have the calling for Oundle, as once I thought I might.

"If you had gone to Kilton," she finished, "I would have followed you to Wessex. But we will not speak of that, now that we have a babe to think of."

It was only later that this remark, made in an unguarded moment by her mother, struck Ashild. She wondered why her mother would have forsaken all else here, to follow her to Wessex. But she forgot to ask why.

Winter approached. The hardening weather brought no further incursion nor report of invading force to Four Stones. The borders of Turcesig also lay quiet, like those of Four Stones monitored by doubled teams of watch-men. The mud, sleet, and snow of Winter often assured that the long dark months were those that knew the greatest peace. Bad weather, short days and scarcity of food stores made the movements of men, horses, and supply waggons the more onerous. Attacks were not unknown; the Danes had scored one of their greatest victories in driving Ælfred from his royal hall over the twelve days set aside for the Yuletide observance. Hrald's father had told him of that great action, carried out against many halls in concerted but eventually fruitless effort to overrun Wessex. And from Ceric himself Hrald had heard of the deadly attack on Kilton at the same time, an assault so bloody that small boy as he was, he never forgot it.

The lack of riders bearing news could not of itself bring comfort; Four Stones and Turcesig seemed an island in its support of maintaining the Peace between Anglia and Wessex, and Hrald and Asberg could know little or nothing of the leanings of the war-chiefs whose halls dotted the rest of Guthrum's former Kingdom. Hrald's winning of Turcesig, already an act of great moment, took on enhanced significance in his stand to defend what had been so dearly bought.

Of Haward's hall and its sixty men, Hrald could not be sure. Haward should have a doubled bond with him; Hrald had dealt fairly with him in honouring the pact he had struck with Thorfast before his death, and now Haward's cousin was the Lady of Four Stones. Yet his confidence had been shaken in Haward's admitting of Agmund's men to his hall. He and Asberg and Jari had discussed it at length. Neither of the older men made excuse for Haward, but they allowed that a daunted Haward might feel compelled to receive the men of his powerful cousin, and listen to his arguments. It was a misstep not to be repeated, but to Hrald it felt a disloyalty difficult to overlook.

Given the uncertainties, Yule festivities would be limited. In past years Thorfast and Haward had attended at least one feast at Four Stones, and the family of Four Stones been invited to the brothers' family hall in return. This Winter solstice, no such invitations would be accepted or extended. Even Asberg and Æthelthryth must stay at Turcesig, for none in charge of a hall wished to be away a single night at a time of vulnerability. And the need to conserve food, always uppermost during Winter's scarcity, had taken on additional meaning after the single night the entire village had taken shelter within the palisade. Should the village be denied access to their beasts, their fowl, and their cold-hardy vegetables still in the ground, the hall's stores would quickly be depleted. Such could happen if the enemy appeared with little or no warning and folk barely escaped with their lives to safety behind the planked walls. None welcomed the necessity for a muted Yule, least of all Dagmar, who looked forward to presiding at her first as Lady. But when her mother-in-law privately approached her on this, stressing that it must be her decision, Dagmar readily accepted the suggestion to curtail the feasting to ensure more secure weeks ahead.

"I am sorry I know so little about the running of a hall," she confessed. Indeed, Ælfwyn understood that Dagmar's mother had fulfilled that role for but a brief span of years before being supplanted by another, when Dagmar was yet a small child.

"No one is born into such knowledge; it is gained by watching, and practice," Ælfwyn assured her. "We will make our feasting merry none the less," she promised, then added, "Your judgement in this will make Hrald proud. The men may regret the lack of a whole roast ox, but a boar's head will still grace the high table."

That night when they entered the treasure room Dagmar told Hrald that she and his mother agreed on the wisdom of a subdued celebration. "I will do the best I can, to make sure the hall does not feel too great a lack," she told him. Indeed, she and Ælfwyn had already consulted with the head cooks, who from long experience feeding the hall had many tricks to enhance everyday fare. "We will not roast an ox, but the browis will be thick with it, and it will serve for at least two meals," she repeated.

Hrald smiled at her. It was clear she had given thought to this, another proof of dedication to her role in managing the resources of the hall. He took her in his arms and kissed her, pressing her against his body as he did so. Their bed was just behind them, and soon they would be in it. Of a sudden he remembered his father in this room, looking at the bed, and teasing him with the prediction that one day soon Hrald would bring his wife to it.

"My father told me something when he was here in this room with me," he said. "He hoped that my wife would be as good a woman as my mother." He kissed her again. "And you are."

The wheel of the year turned. The revelry of Yule, even without extended feasting, brought its welcome ease, for just as the dark loam awaited new abundance, folk now paused and rested from their ordinary tasks. Snow fell after Twelfth Night, a dusting on the furrows of the waiting fields, as if awakening all in signal to resume their work. Winter wheat, already long past sprouting, stood undaunted above the rime of white. By Candlemas the lengthening of the days was marked. The watery sunshine of the month was cause for gratitude. Soon the soil would warm. More frost and even heavy snow might come, but the Sun rose higher each day, and stayed longer in its arc across the sky.

Ashild was large with child, and knew that three or four more weeks would bring her to childbed. She had no fear of it, only impatience. She wanted the child here, to be delivered of the burden of bearing it, but most of all, she wanted the child in her arms.

Her mother, freed from most of the needful tasks of the hall by the advent of her daughter-in-law, took pleasure in the production of swaddling bands and tiny shifts for her daughter's coming babe. These were of undyed linen, while Burginde worked up small blankets of the softest wool from thread she insisted spinning and weaving herself. Ashild created a sling from an oblong of lightweight wool, one with which to tie the babe to her side. It was dark blue wool, the hems embellished with coloured woollen thread work in red and yellow. One forenoon when Dagmar sat with them, stitching up a new tunic for Hrald, Ælfwyn could not help from hoping that soon Dagmar would be working on her own babe's swaddling cloths. She must not ask nor hint, to do so brought bad luck; but she hoped and trusted she and her son would sometime this year share news of their own coming joy.

⸎⸎⸎⸎⸎⸎⸎⸎⸎

One afternoon Hrald, Jari at his side, was headed to the valley of horses. Mares pastured there who were ready to foal were by custom led back to the second stable in the hall yard, where the foals would drop under the watchful eyes of Mul and oftentimes Ashild. Mul had pulled more than one breeched foal safely from its mother, and the mares' stable and adjoining paddock was free from the threat of marauding wolves.

This morning one of the men from the long house at the valley had ridden in, to tell Hrald that not one but two mares had dropped foals overnight. Hrald would go look at the newborns, and if the youngsters seemed steady on their feet, lead their mothers, their young trotting alongside, to the stable awaiting them. The day was not bitterly cold, but the dampness in the air and sharp wind blowing across the cloud-scudded sky reminded one it was still Winter. If the foals could not today withstand the distance, Hrald would have one of his men take them into his croft until they could.

After he and Jari rode off, another two horses approached the hall from the village road. One was a pack horse, led by a man clad in a hooded scarlet cloak trimmed with marten fur. He was accompanied by an escort of three of Four Stones' watch-men from the road, who had ridden in turn with the stranger to the next stage and handed him off. They came to the gates, which opened for them.

Dagmar had been out in the kitchen yard conferring with the bakers about their need to build a larger oven. She was now crossing the yard to enter the hall and go to the weaving room. When the gates opened she was not far from where the stranger and his final escort trotted in. One of the watch-men pressed his horse forward to her.

"Your kin, from Headleage, with a marriage gift for you from Helva, Guthrum's widow," was what he said.

Dagmar's lips parted. She looked past the watch-man to the stranger, who sat his horse. He looked across at her and then with one hand pushed back the hood of his cloak. Hair of bright gold lay upon his shoulders.

Dagmar was for a moment struck dumb. The watch-man who had approached her was wheeling his horse, awaiting her approval and his dismissal.

"Já," she told him. "I thank you." It was not only the chill of the day that made it hard to feel her lips move.

The escort nodded, and the three of them rode out.

The golden-haired man in the red cloak was now off his horse. He went to the pack animal and from one of the two saddle bags pulled a leathern bag the length of his forearm.

He walked to her; she could not move. She saw the folk of the yard moving behind him, saw Mul and his son take the horses. Then the golden haired man was before her.

"Dagmar," he said. He was not smiling, but his pleasure in seeing her was clear.

"Vigmund," she breathed.

Dagmar scarce knew how she said the next, for she felt the wind knocked out of her. Yet her words came.

"My husband has just ridden off, to check on some horses. He will return later."

She looked about her. They could not stand here, she must take him within.

She lifted her hand, and he followed her through the side door. It was the closest to the treasure room and that is where she led him. No matter that there were women within the hall, standing by the fire-pit spinning. She led him past the iron hoops holding spears in readiness, past the embroidered raven hanging on the wall, and then past Hrald's split and battered shield hanging next it. They faced the treasure room door. Dagmar's fingers went to her waist and the ring of keys there, and she slipped the needed one into the lock and turned it. She left the door cracked open the slightest amount, telling herself there was no shame attached to an open door.

Vigmund walked in, placed the leathern bag on the table, and at once reached for her. He pulled her to him with the practised draw of one whose arms have often sought their lover. His mouth was upon hers an instant later.

They kissed with the kind of urgent passion only parted lovers know, a thirst for each other's taste, smell, and touch that drove them both. He was almost devouring her, his mouth pressing against her own until she was gasping. She clung to him, unable to believe his return, as it seemed, from the dead. The sense of bodily yearning and possession she had known with him flooded her being. For these first few moments she would not resist, could not resist. Her hands went to his hair, and in a gesture she knew well, she let her fingers comb through it, a webbing of gold. Then she brought her hands to frame the golden beard upon his cheeks. In answer his own hand moved from her back, and he gave himself enough distance from her that he could cup one of her breasts. Even through the wool of her gowns her nipple hardened under his hand.

When she could free her mouth she spoke, full wonder in her voice.

"How are you here?"

"Your brother Agmund lifted the decree of outlaw against me – for a price. I was free to return, to come back. For you."

She stood, still in his arms, shaking her head, and trembling at his words.

"I am wed, it cannot be," she told him. But her mouth, having uttered these words, sought his own. To kiss him again after so many years, to feel the strength with which he held her, to know he still desired her, was like the filling of a well. Yet after another kiss, she placed her hands upon his chest to hold him off. Tears pricked her eyes as she spoke.

"I am wed, to a Jarl," she repeated.

Vigmund would not let her go, and had answer for this.

"He will not be Jarl long. I hear he is yet a boy. He will not hold this fortress. You will be a widow soon, when Haesten sweeps through. What will happen to you then? Haesten will award you to one of his chief men."

The sureness with which he spoke raised terror at this spectre.

"Will it – will it come to that? Will Haesten win?"

She looked about the dimness of the room, frantic with thoughts of Four Stones overrun. It had fallen once, to a force far smaller.

She could not stop her trembling, but must ask of him the next.

"And you – who will you fight for?"

He shook his head, a single, decided action.

"I will not be here to fight," he told her. "I am once again a King's body-guard, in Dane-mark. I have recovered my silver where I hid it; that was what I needed. I will take you with me. That is what I came back for, the silver, and you.

"I have brought you Helva's gift, as I said, my ruse to allow me entry here. And my plan is this. You will ask leave to travel to Headleage, to thank Helva in person, to see Inkera – any excuse he will believe. He will send you with a troop of men, but far less than are here. Once at Headleage it will be easy to slip away."

He began to pull her to him once more, but she resisted.

"I cannot think . . . I have loved only you. But . . . " She hid her face in her hands.

His dismay was voiced in his next words.

"You refuse me now, when you were the cause of my outlawing?"

"Me?" Dagmar's astonishment could not be the greater.

"Your mother then, in her spite."

Again, she was stuck dumb. Her eyes searched his face, looking for his meaning. The reluctance with which he went on made clear his distaste, even disgust, at what he must say.

"She was the jade of the body-guards. Her lust, and the drink, put her beyond shaming. We all knew she would lie with us, and when Guthrum still lived, we feared refusing her, lest she make up some tale of assault and go to him."

Dagmar felt the blood drain from her face. Her mother, a slattern. And with men half her age, men whom she could harm.

She felt near to swooning, he must see this, but he would finish.

"I had long heard of her appetites, but she had never before approached me. You and I were already . . . " he shook his head. "I rebuffed her.

"My punishment was my outlawing."

She felt the floor rise, and began to sway. He caught her, and held her the firmer.

"Now you know the truth. In Dane-mark we will be man and wife. As we are now."

He drew her close again, wrapping his arms about her, pressing his palms into the small of her back, holding her to him.

Hrald, having reached the orchard groves and ridden beyond, bethought him that he had promised to bring a spear to present to the son of one of his men at the valley of horses. The boy had just reached weapon-bearing age, and Hrald would give him a spear from the treasure room store. He turned the head of his horse, and he and Jari trotted back.

He would be inside but a moment, and Jari stayed mounted in the stable yard, awaiting his return. Hrald walked though the side door and behind the high table. As he neared the treasure room door he saw it stood ajar. He pressed it open, expecting Dagmar within.

She was there, but she was being held by another man. He was a warrior older than Hrald, kitted out with a bright-hilted sword, and wearing a fur trimmed mantle. They stood at three quarters to him, Dagmar's back nearest to he who looked upon them. Their mouths were locked as they kissed each other. The man's entwined hands were clasped at the small of her back, pressing her to his loins, in the unmistakable hold of those who have been intimate.

It was just the way Hrald himself had held her, as they readied for a night of love.

Hrald could not blink, and could not move, as he studied them. He was crushingly aware that she and this man had been lovers.

The man opened his eyes and saw Hrald. He took a step away from the woman he held. Dagmar gave a gasping call, too low in pitch to a be shriek, but audible still.

"Hrald! I thought . . . " but her words faltered.

For a long moment Hrald could say nothing.

"What did you think?" he asked.

The man with her had already pulled his sword.

Hrald did not. He looked at the naked blade the warrior held.

Is that all you understand, Hrald asked inwardly.

"Who is he?" he demanded of his wife.

She feared to speak his name, and her throat had tightened so that no sound issued from her parted lips.

Hrald would not speak again until she answered. She swallowed to free her voice.

"Vigmund, of my father's body-guard. We knew each other at Headleage."

"I see you knew each other," Hrald repeated.

The hollowness of his tone said as much as his words.

She had been no maid upon the night of their wedding. Her feigning maidenhood on their bridal night was a deceit for her benefit as well as his own. She had concealed her knowledge, and buoyed his own innocence of the act of love. A rush of rippling embarrassment joined the stunned anger churning in his breast. Young as he was, he had been played almost as a cuckold, and the sting of this discovery felt a cold and lethal poison in his veins.

She had no answer, and he went on.

"And you brought him here." To the treasure room, the place where their bed was, where they slept. He thought the room utterly defiled.

The dread in Dagmar's eyes overwhelmed her shame.

"Hrald, hear me," she pleaded. "Vigmund – I thought him dead; he had been outlawed. That decree has been lifted by my brother. Vigmund came to take me to Danemark. It was shock, and fear that made me . . . " she cast about for words to express that which she could hardly explain to herself.

"I felt fear, fear of war . . .

"The danger here . . . " she stammered out.

"There has always been danger," Hrald answered. "The same danger my mother and sister have had to live under. You must be willing to face it, as they do. You are Lady of Four Stones."

He looked up, far above her head, then returned his eyes to her. He studied the face of his recreant wife. His next words, softly spoken, and rooted not in rancour but in pain, sealed her Fate.

"You were Lady of Four Stones."

He said the next as command, one issued from the void of his heart.

"Go," he told her. "Go now. I cast you from my hall. Take your bridal goods, and go."

Vigmund finally spoke, and to Hrald. "She does not love you, but me, and just told me so."

Hrald barely glanced at him.

"Then go. Take her."

Dagmar gasped. She had not told Vigmund she would go; if Hrald had not come upon them she did not know what she would have told him. She had not had time to think, to look beyond the marvel of Vigmund standing before her. If she had had another kiss or two, she might have been able to push him away for good, tell him she would love him always, but that her choice was made. Now Hrald was making that choice for her.

She had resolved to wed Hrald, resolved to work hard to be worthy of the role bestowed upon her. She had shown kindness, even devotion to him. And she knew a growing affection for Hrald; affection, and respect. He could not repudiate her for one mistake.

"Nej! Hrald, do not do this," she cried.

Vigmund stared at her, disbelieving. He had been expecting every moment for Hrald to pull his own weapon. If he did, he knew that after he killed this young Jarl, he himself would be a dead man. He could never escape the hall yard alive. But Hrald was letting them both free. Now the woman he was risking his life for was turning her back on him.

Hrald saw Vigmund's startle give way to growing umbrage. He stared at his wife's lover, and spoke the truth to him.

"Now she has been false to both of us."

Vigmund, pointlessly holding his sword, now lowered his hand and ran it back into its scabbard.

Dagmar, looking from one to the other, fixed her eyes on Hrald. She cried out in supplication.

"If it had been you, Hrald –"

"It would not be me. Never would it be me."

The resoluteness of his words rang in her ears, and the pain she had inflicted was all too clear on his face. Her chin dropped with her lowered eyes, and her hand rose to her brow, as if to hide her shame.

She was used to her father, and his many infidelities with many women. Hrald was not such a man. He was right. It would not be him, found in the arms of another. He had given his heart to her, and she had brutally flung it away.

"Go," Hrald told them both. "You are taking your lives with you. Do not make me regret that I left you with that."

Ælfwyn now came down the stairs from the weaving room, and saw the door to the treasure room. All during her long tenure at Four Stones, the door to that stronghold was never left open. It was open now. She went to it, and came upon them.

Hrald stood just inside. Deep in the recess of the room stood Dagmar, a strange young warrior at her side.

A look at her son's stricken face made Ælfwyn's heart constrict in her breast.

"Dagmar," she murmured. Ælfwyn placed the back of her hand to her mouth, almost as if she had been struck.

Dagmar ran to her, dropping upon her knees. She grasped at Ælfwyn's hem. "My Lady, my Lady . . . " she begged. "Do not let him cast me off . . . "

Ælfwyn looked to her son for the awe-ful confirmation. Hrald's burning eyes told her of the depths of his anguish.

He forced himself to speak.

"She was in his arms. And kissing, as only lovers do."

Ælfwyn closed her eyes. An unbridgeable breach had sundered her son's union. All was spoilt for Hrald and his young wife.

That this marriage should have ended so soon, and thusly, was a calamity for all concerned. Ælfwyn had grown to care for Dagmar, and had never expected this of her. The Abbess of Oundle's estimation of the girl, that she was guarded, had now proved true. Dagmar had something to hide, her past with this man, a past that extended into the present.

Yet Dagmar's plight could not but move the deepest pity in Ælfwyn's breast. The girl crouched with heaving shoulders and strangled sobs at her mother-in-law's feet, grasping the hem of her gown in both hands and wetting it with her tears. It was all Ælfwyn could do not to reach down and lay a consoling hand upon the girl's back, so pitiable was her distress.

To love one man, and yet be wed to another . . . this quiet tragedy had been her own.

She gave unwilling thought to what might have happened if Yrling had ever learnt that she had loved the prisoner who was left to rot under this very floor. It was true she came as maid to Yrling's bed, but also true she wanted to ride off with Gyric, escape with him, and would have tried to do so, if he had been whole. Traces of that fear and horror coursed through her now, as she thought of what might have been.

Ælfwyn could not extend her hand to Dagmar. The injury to her beloved son, to all of them, was vast. This was near to treason. Dagmar was guilty of a kind of heartlessness; she had lost heart. She had proved faithless to Hrald, and to Four Stones. Finding her once in the arms of another man meant she could no longer be trusted. A Jarl must know his children had sprung from his loins, and none other.

There was no repair, no remedy Ælfwyn could offer. The wound to her son was too deep. He had his father's decisiveness, and like his father, was learning to know himself well.

She looked at her son, white-faced, unmoving, and saw his eyes lift from his prostrate wife to the man she had been caught with. There was no one to bring Hrald to penalty should he slay them both. If her son had been of different nature Ælfwyn might have entered this room to find that he had already hacked them both to death. Even the laws of Christian Wessex allowed a man, finding his wife behind a closed door with another man, to kill without fear of consequence. How much worse was it to come upon your wife in passionate embrace with that man. Wilgot the priest would absolve this sin of murder acted out in passion of betrayal. Yet like his father, she could not imagine Hrald doing so.

In a voice trembling with emotion, Ælfwyn spoke. "I will not intercede, Dagmar. I cannot."

Dagmar's choking sobs slowed. She pressed the fistful of wool she held in her hands to her face a moment, then released it. She drew breath, and lifted her tear-stained face to her mother-in-law. She rose, and her fingers went to the ring of keys at her waist. She untied them from her sash, and Lady of the hall no more, handed them back to Ælfwyn.

Next her hands went to the thin golden chain about her throat, from which dangled the ring Hrald had pre-sented her with as his morgen-gyfu. He had not yet been able to send it to Jorvik. As his morning-gift it was hers to keep outright. No matter. She would never wear it.

She drew it off and held it to Hrald, but he would not take it. A fresh sob shook her as she held the ring out to Ælfwyn, who relieved her of it.

As she was doing so Ashild and Burginde appeared in the doorway. Ashild, now great with child, stepped into the room. Her eyes moved about the space, taking all in. She saw the tear-streaked Dagmar, her mother's pained and pitying expression, and a strange warrior, a Dane, seemingly distanced from the rest. She saw the golden chain which held Dagmar's ring swing from her fingers as she passed it to her mother.

Most of all she saw the devastation on her brother's face.

Ashild felt her own face flame, a sudden rage firing her opening words.

She looked from Dagmar to the Dane, and then to her brother. "Has she betrayed you?"

Hrald turned his gaze to his sister. For answer he said only, "They are going now, together."

Ashild took a step towards Dagmar.

"Strumpet!" she named her.

"What have you done to him?" Ashild demanded. Her voice was just above a hiss, so great was her ire. "What have you done to us?"

Ashild could not stop, and her eyes almost bore through Dagmar as she said the next. "I have oftentimes wished I had been born a boy. It is your great good fortune I was not. My blade would be at your throat now."

Hrald raised his hand to stay his sister. He looked once more at Dagmar. She could not be with child; she had just had her Moon-flow. He need not fear sending away his own coming son or daughter with her. Having found her thus with another man, he reflected, how could I ever be certain any child she bore would be my own. Better to have learnt this now about her.

With a flick of his eyes he paired her with her lover. "Go," he told them. "Neither of you are worthy of the stain on my soul, should I kill you."

Burginde, biting her lip to keep her outrage from escaping, had come up behind Ælfwyn, and laid her arm about her waist in support. Ælfwyn turned her head, and spoke as steadily as she could to her nurse.

"Burginde, Dagmar is leaving us, for good. Please to help her pack her bridal goods, and all she came with."

The nurse moved smartly across the floor to those chests which she knew held Dagmar's belongings. She began rolling her clothing and other goods into the leathern packs stored in the room, both into those Dagmar had arrived with, and others. But Dagmar, at Burginde's side, would not allow her to place anything within which had come into her keeping since arriving at Four Stones. She shook her head against the beautiful veil of silk Hrald's mother had presented her with, and every other gift she had received. She felt the white heat of Burginde's anger against her, and recalling the spinning lessons she had given her, fought once more against coming tears. I can return these things you gave me, she thought, but not the kindness you showed; that is gone.

Meanwhile Ashild had been staring at the Danish warrior. She had one thought whirling in her mind: If she were a man he would be dead now, and this false woman as well.

She heard a movement behind her and saw Jari, drawn by both delay and her raised voice, standing in the doorway.

"Take him to his horse," Ashild told Jari.

The Dane began to move towards the door, and Ashild's eyes, following him, fell on the bulky leathern bag on the table.

"What is that," she demanded of the man.

"A marriage gift to Dagmar. From Guthrum's widow."

Ashild scoffed. "Ha! Take it with you. You will need every scrap of silver, on your sorry way."

As Vigmund picked it up and moved to leave, Dagmar turned to him, a mix of panic and grief on her face.

Ashild, watching this, had further command for Jari.

"Make sure he does not leave without his baggage," she ended, with a glance to the weeping Dagmar.

Dagmar, seeing Vigmund pass out of the room under escort by Jari, was now alone with the family of Four Stones.

"Vigmund," she implored. "Do not leave without me."

He turned his head and gave her a look. Then he moved out of sight.

BLOSSOM AND THORN

DAGMAR and her lover were sent off, relayed by three watch-men riding as escort. None but Jari and the yard folk watched as the unknown man with her swung into the saddle, and then pulled her up behind him from one of the mounting blocks. The warrior put his heels to his horse's barrel, and it and the pack horse tied to a saddle ring trotted out the gates.

The door of the treasure room had closed, leaving Hrald, his mother and sister, and Burginde within. Jari, regaining the hall, now stood in the middle near the fire, rubbing his hands, shaking his great head and blowing out breaths of air as he considered it all. Before that door had closed he shared a few words with Hrald. As a result Jari had already dispatched Kjeld to ride to Asberg at Turcesig.

When Kjeld reached there, he found Asberg in one of the joiners' stalls, working at carving the wooden backing of a new sword scabbard with his eldest son Ulf.

"There is trouble at Four Stones," Kjeld began, without even a greeting. The high alert these words ignited in Asberg was not allayed by Kjeld's report, who told him what little he knew. Asberg interrupted only once.

"Was blood shed?"

"Nej. But Hrald cast her out, at once, with the man Vigmund."

The news was stunning. Asberg, who had the most direct dealings with Dagmar's kin, felt more than a twinge of remorse mix with his anger. He had allowed his misgivings about Guthrum's daughter to be overruled by his desire to abet his nephew in winning the woman he desired. Another thought rose, one which luckily he could dismiss. As grave as this all was, if Guthrum still lived, Dagmar's deceit could have had dire consequences.

He would ride to Four Stones on the morrow, but Haward's hall must be first. Ulf wished to accompany his father, but the boy was now nearly sixteen. Far better training for him to stay with Styrbjörn, and to wait and watch with Turcesig's second in command.

Asberg chose five men, with Kjeld as the sixth, for his visit to Dagmar's cousin. After seeing how Haward had reacted under Hrald's questioning, he had no fear more would be needed. As they rode large flakes of snow began drifting through the air, falling from a milky sky. Asberg thought again and again of his conversation with Haward concerning Dagmar, when the man had hesitated when he had asked if there was anything Hrald should know. Asberg had not pressed Haward then, but noted his hesitation in answering. He shook his head to himself, recalling the wedding at Oundle not six months past. He had looked at Dagmar on that day and summed her correctly, it turned out. Her mouth was indeed hard.

When they reached Haward's the snow lay covering the ground. Asberg gave thought to the young woman, thrust out of a hall like Four Stones, who tonight would be camping with her lover in the cold.

When Haward appeared in his hall, Asberg and the six he fronted walked straight to him. With an uncertain face Haward backed up to the door of the weapons room, unlocked it, and let them in. He stepped to the back of the room, as if in retreat.

Asberg kept coming towards him, his bladed weapons still sheathed but with marked aggression. Haward could not hide the fact that he of a sudden feared for his life. Those men who faced him could see he struggled with the instinct to yell for help. He kept himself from doing so, and Asberg stopped just before him.

"Hrald has been forced to put away Dagmar. He found her in the embrace of another man, a strange Dane who had come from Headleage."

"Vigmund," muttered Haward.

"Já." Asberg's voice was close to a snarl. "Then you knew of this."

Haward was quick in his own defence.

"Not much of it, I swear," he answered, shaking his head. "He had been outlawed by Guthrum, went I think to Dane-mark."

"Why was he outlawed?"

"I am not certain. Something to do with one of Guthrum's wives. Dagmar's mother, perhaps."

"I should kill you now, Haward, and spare Hrald's blade from your craven blood."

This threat was all too real to one who had watched Hrald kill Thorfast. Haward was almost choking over his next words.

"I swear, I know nothing more. I thought this connection over, over and done. I could not risk losing the chance for her to wed a Jarl."

"And to bind yourself closer to Four Stones," shot back Asberg.

"Well . . ."

Asberg answered through gritted teeth.

"You have done yourself no favour, Haward.

"We will send back her dowry in the morning," Hrald's uncle went on. He recalled one part of it, the choicest piece, which was beyond reclamation. "Hrald gave the silver chalice to Oundle as his gift. We will send you its weight in hack."

Haward stood staring blankly, and gave another shake of his head.

"Nej. No need," he stammered, in attempt to offer some meaningful concession. His losses were too great to number, the wrath of Hrald and Asberg foremost. He realised he must at once surrender the fine weaponry he had been granted as Dagmar's bride-price. The swords and spear-points were all behind him, locked in chests, the pride of his armoury.

"The swords and points – I will gather them."

Hrald spent a sleepless night in the treasure room. The bed in which he had found such delight with Dagmar was become a tainted place. When beneath her pillow he uncovered the ribband she used to tie her plaited hair before she slept, he held it to his face, and wept.

He lay there for hours in the dark, looking up into the recesses of the roof timbers. This room, filled with the treasure of arms, of silver and even gold, was the heart of Four Stones in more than this. It was where his father would invite him in as a boy, to glimpse the swords, knives, and spears stowed there. Many times he had gone from chest to chest with his father, and had the thrill of holding up a sword his father admired, and passed to his hands so he might feel its weight, or of running his small fingers through gleaming coins of silver housed in iron caskets. And in this broad bed his own life had started, as had those of his sisters.

He pushed himself up from it, went to the table and lit the cresset. The room flickered into view, but brought no relief to the darkness of his heart. He sunk down on a chair, lay his head in his hands, and at last fell into fitful sleep.

When it was dawning he rose, splashed himself awake with the cold water from the basin, and gathered a few items of clothing. He would go to Oundle for a day or two; he could not stay here. His mouth twisted in a wry smile. Oundle was always refuge, yet it too felt now tainted, for it had been the scene of his pledging to a wife who had proven faithless. Yet where else could he go, but there.

As he reached for his comb he saw the footed silver cup his mother had given Dagmar on their bridal night. Like all the table silver, it resided here when not in use. He picked it up, saw again her name inscribed on the rim of it.

He clenched his fist about it, as if he would crush it. He thrust it in his pack. He would give it to the treasury of

Oundle. Unlike the chalice which he had been granted as a portion of his wife's dowry and then given to the abbey, this he would ask to be melted down to serve the poor.

When he opened the door he saw Jari, fast asleep at the high table, his still-ruddy hair tumbled over his hunched shoulders. Jari and his wife had their own small house, but his faithful body-guard had eschewed it to spend the night outside Hrald's door. This show of paired devotion and concern stopped Hrald in his tracks. He went to the older man and spoke his name. When Jari raised his head, blinking and blear-eyed, Hrald spoke.

"I will go to Oundle; two nights at the most."

Jari began to roll his shoulders as he answered. "I will get ready to ride," he said.

"No, Jari," Hrald told him. "With Asberg at Turcesig you must stay here in command." Jari moved his massive head, taking this in. When Kjeld and Ashild had been left in charge, it had been but for a few hours.

"Then I will ride with you, as escort, and return here," Jari decided. "In three days I will come back for you."

Hrald must agree to this, if only to repay his body-guard's act of staying the night near him.

"Wake Kjeld," Hrald said next. "Ask him to tell my mother and Ashild where I am going, and that I will be back after two nights. I will go to the stable and get our horses."

Jari would not press him to take more of an escort. After what Hrald had been through, he counted himself lucky that Hrald had even awakened him, and allowed a single guard to ride with him.

Early as it was, Mul was astir in the stable. All the yard knew that their Jarl had put away his wife, and the fact that she had ridden off behind another warrior gave damning reason. When Hrald appeared with a small pack Mul nodded as he ever did when Hrald asked for his bay. Hrald heard a stall door open, though Mul had yet to move. He heard next the familiar nicker of his stallion, and then Bork was before them both, coming from the dusk of the stable depths. The boy was leading the animal with only his hand upon the bay's broad chest, as he was too small to slip a lead rope over his neck.

Mul took the stallion as Hrald looked down at the boy. The child was now fed and kindly cared for, but in his haunted eyes lay a deep loneliness.

"Would you like to see Oundle," Hrald asked of him. Bork stared, open-mouthed, and nodded his head. "If Mul can spare you a few days," said Hrald, looking to the stable man. Mul bobbed his consent.

Hrald asked for Jari's horse, and began slipping bridle and saddle on his own. Jari appeared. In the kitchen yard the bakers had been long at work, but now the other cooking folk began to emerge, though the hall itself was still quiet. Those upon the rampart of the palisade looked down at their Jarl and his body-guard, and the men at the gate readied to swing it open.

When they were both horsed, Mul lifted Bork up behind Hrald. With the boy's thin arms around his waist, Hrald nudged his horse out of the yard. Folk were afoot in some of the village crofts, whose cooking-ring fires blazed under cauldrons of warming oats.

As they left the gates behind Hrald's eyes fell upon the thick yew tree border of the burial ground. The snow-flecked grassland around the yews was a ghostly base to their darkness. That burial ground was where he had won consent from Dagmar. The trees looked black in the little light. He turned his head away and urged his stallion on. He had won her as wife by a place of death, a realization as bitter as the poison of the yew fruit.

It was mid-morning when they reached Oundle. Hrald had thirty warriors resident there, a handful of whom had met them on the road and escorted them to the gates. Once inside Hrald went to the brothers' hall, and with Jari and Bork were offered food and drink. Hrald had eaten nothing since the morning of the prior day, and had taken but a cup of mead his mother pressed on him in the treasure room. Now, handed a wooden bowl of boiled oats and a small loaf, Hrald took the food gratefully into his mouth. A serving boy brought ale, and lifting the crockery cup Hrald found comfort knowing Bova had brewed it. Bork, at his side, watched all with wide eyes as he spooned his porridge. The brothers' hall was not as large as that of the nuns', but to a child who had never been within the hall proper of Four Stones, it seemed huge. The dark brown surplices of the men who greeted and served them occasioned wondering stares from the boy.

When Jari rose to leave, Bork jumped up as well, uncertain as to what to do. Hrald placed the boy in the care of one of the brothers he knew, telling him of Bork's service in the stable, but offering him for any task of cooking or serving where he might also be useful.

Then Hrald walked with Jari to the paddock where his horse was resting, and saw him off. After the gate closed behind his body-guard Hrald turned back to face the gardens. The snow which had fallen last night was almost all melted away, with only scant ridges of it piled up against the bottom of fences, or whitening the bare soil beneath the stone benches. The wind, even behind the encircling palisade, was sharp, and Hrald pulled the heavy wool of his dark mantle more firmly about him. The brothers' hall had been warm with fire, but he did not wish to be inside. Far less did he wish to visit the church; he felt no call to prayer. He walked instead into the brothers' side of the garden.

The gravel paths there led him through the beds of mostly withered herbs, and dark and sodden furrows from which vegetables had once flourished. The apple and pear trees, laden with ripening fruit on his first visit here with Dagmar, were skeletal. He found himself clutching the mantle even tighter about his shoulders. He looked over the rose bushes, blasted by Winter's cold. Stripped and bare, their thorns were foremost, those thorns which in Summer hid beneath pale and tender blossom and green leaves. He stared at the roses, achingly aware of the duplicity of blossom and thorn. Beads of water hung from the largest thorns, dropping like single tears to the wet gravel path.

He released the hold on his cloak, and let the next gust of wind flap it open to the cold. He wished to rage, to destroy things, and howl out his pain. He could not stay at Four Stones and do so. He had hoped that the calming atmosphere of Oundle would drive such impulses away. In the brothers' hall he would be under a temporary vow of silence for much of the duration of his stay. Silence is what he sought. Anything to still the turbulence churning in his breast was welcome.

He turned his back on the garden. The doors to the barn were open, and he could see his bay stallion within, a double rope tie tethering his halter to opposite walls. Bork was on tiptoe on a stool, comb in hand, smoothing the long black mane from forelock to withers. Hrald watched the boy take a handful at a time as he worked, and the way the boy leant forward to speak to the horse as he did so.

Kolb is dead, he found himself thinking, naming that man of his who this boy's father had killed. And I have Bork in return. As he stood musing on this he became aware of movement from the tail of his eye. A novice was at the border of the garden, her light grey gown covered by a cloak of darker grey. She smiled in a way that let him know she bore a message.

He walked to her. Abbess Sigewif requested his presence after Sext, or mid-day prayer. Hrald nodded he would come.

After the Abbess returned from the church she found Hrald waiting by the door of the nuns' hall. This was only the second visit Hrald had made here unannounced, and both times his distress was clear. Sigewif embraced him as always, and led him in silence to her writing chamber. She closed the door, and before she could invite her guest to sit, Hrald pulled something from under his mantle and set it on the nearest table.

It was a cup of silver, footed, and deeply incised with flowing and graceful design. At first she thought it another gift, just as after Hrald's wedding ceremony he had presented the treasury with a fine silver chalice. Then Sigewif saw the inscription on the lip of the cup. She lifted the cup to read it. Dagmar.

She placed it down again. Hrald's face told much, but she must hear more.

"I have cast her from my hall. She left yesterday, with the man who was her lover before we met."

Sigewif's intake of breath was deep, but quiet. Hrald went on.

"Wilgot . . . Wilgot named the marriage invalid. I returned to her all her bridal goods.

"She was not what I thought she was," he ended.

The Abbess studied him. This strapping young man stood before her, bodily whole. Only the dark and glistening eyes conveyed how deep ran his wound. The pity she felt for him, for his loving mother, and his wild-hearted sister, was immense. As was the pity she felt for Dagmar.

"We humans rarely are," she answered. "In our frailty, we disappoint. God does not. He may puzzle or even confound us, but in his ultimate wisdom and eternal goodness we can trust."

He squeezed his eyes shut.

"Her cup . . . I would have you melt it, and use it for the poor."

Sigewif looked at the beautiful thing. To him only purifying fire would render it fit for this higher use. She nodded assent.

She reached her hand to his and covered it with her own. "Thank you for coming to us, in your need," she told him.

Hrald answered none of many calls to prayer rung out throughout the day. Vespers and Compline came and went, and he did not place his foot on the broad step of the church entrance. He did not even speak to Bova, though she once caught sight of him and flashed her shy smile. It was some balm to be away from the crowded and noisy hall of Four Stones, to need speak to no one, make no decisions. On prior visits to Oundle he had slept in a simple alcove in the hall as the junior brothers did. This time he was shown to a private cell, that of a monk who had recently died. Like all the nuns' and monks' cells, it had its own door, and was built along the back side of their respective halls. Between walking about the garden, a single foray on foot outside the wall, and the hours spent lying on the narrow cot in the cell, he was alone and silent much of the time. Meals, taken twice a day with the priests, monks, and brothers in the men's hall, were eaten to the accompaniment of a reading from Scripture. The sudden spareness of his life and narrow confines of his transit gave comfort. When he returned to his needful responsibilities as Jarl he must feign indifference to the hurt he suffered, something he could not do yet, and need not do here.

Before Jari arrived Hrald went to bid thanks and farewell to the Abbess. He had Bork with him, and Sigewif, regarding the child, gestured him and Hrald into her writing chamber. She had seen Bork about the barn and garden, and been told he spent most of his time grooming Hrald's stallion and the foundation's two cart horses stabled with him. There were children about the place, the sons and daughters of the lay folk who served there, but Bork spent little time with them. He looked a quiet child, by nature, to Sigewif's eyes.

Now she led the boy to the narrow table between the casements, upon which lay several bound volumes. She opened the first, a movement that surprised the child. He had never encountered a book, nor seen its hinged action.

"This is writing," she told him.

Bork had come to Four Stones speaking only Norse, but had readily picked up the tongue of Anglia. He screwed up his eyes, looking at the tiny rounded lines filling the cream-hued leaf. The Abbess saw he knew not what lay before him.

"They are words, fixed here, for as long as this parchment lasts."

He looked up at her. His fingers went to the dark squiggles.

"Words?" he wondered.

His face scrunched in thought. Words were something that came out of your mouth, and went into your ear. They were sound. But these too were words.

After watching this, Sigewif asked Hrald if the boy was of the hall of Four Stones, or its village.

Hrald would not here rehearse how Bork came to be his dependent.

"No," he simply said. "He is new to Four Stones. He is living with our stableman, and his family."

So the boy was alone. The Abbess often took in foundling children, to save them from starvation or slavery. They became useful serving and yard folk to the abbey, and a gifted few who showed inclination and aptitude had even become sisters and monks. She wondered for a moment if Hrald was offering the boy to her.

But the way the child stepped closer to Hrald's leg as she looked down at him made her smile.

"I think you should teach him to read," she said.

Ashild awoke in the bower house. A gush of fluid between her legs made her try to push herself up. The sound escaping her lips was one of surprise. She felt no twinge, just the warmth of the wetness telling her the long wait was nearly at an end. From the bed against the wall she heard her mother stir, pull on a shift and come to her. Ælfwyn held a few twisted straws to the still-glowing charcoals in one of the braziers, and touched it to the linen wick of a taper on the table. As the light hit her face Burginde snorted awake.

By the time the Sun rose much was in readiness. Hrald was absent at Oundle, but Burginde had early awakened Jari. He had sent a rider to Turcesig, so that Æthelthryth might come and lend her aid. When she arrived by waggon at noon, Ashild's birthing pangs were well advanced. Besides her mother and aunt and Burginde, serving women made frequent calls within, carrying broth and food, bringing hot water for washing and ever more towelling. The small house, warmed by the constant replenishing of the charcoal in the braziers, fairly steamed as the women took turns walking with Ashild across the planked flooring. Fired by the heat of her own bodily exertion she felt stifled. She begged for coolness, but clad as she was in only a shift she was over-ruled again and again.

During the months of carrying the child Ashild had worn neither her small golden cross nor the hammer of Thor which had been her father's. Anything hanging about her neck had felt vexingly irksome. Her mother now fetched the golden cross from where it sat at the base of the crucifix on the weaving room wall, and bade Ashild wear it, for protection.

"For your babe's sake, as well as your own," Ælfwyn asked, and indeed, Ashild, looking at her mother's caring face, could not refuse so small a petition.

As the pangs deepened, Ashild stopped in her walking and held on to the upright timber roof support in the centre of the floor. She lifted her head and glared up at the dark underside of the roof, her jaw clenching with every roiling pang.

"Scream. Scream, you must scream," urged Burginde.

"I . . . will . . . not . . . scream . . . " gasped Ashild.

Sweat beaded her face, both from the demands of withstanding the dark waves of her travail, and from the warmth of the room. The cries of a labouring woman had always been one of the hallmarks of helplessness to Ashild. The pain was intense, worse, if she be truthful, than she had imagined, but she had resolved to resist showing it. As her mother daubed her face with cool linen and her aunt held her about the shoulders, she would allow herself no more than panting grunts in rhythm to the spasms wrenching her belly.

"Screaming brings the babe faster," Burginde admonished, rising off her knees with the help of a low stool to push herself up with. She had been peering between Ashild's legs and saw it would not be long now. Ashild gave but another grunt in answer and gritted her teeth.

Then Ashild's legs buckled, so great was the tightening pang contracting her body. Guided by her mother and aunt, her knees touched the floor. Burginde was ready with linen and birthing straw. For a moment Ashild, freeing herself from the arms that held her, seemed to try to lean forward over her heaving belly. She bit her lip; her face was both white and red. Finally she gave as mighty a yell as had ever been sounded, an ear-splitting war-cry to do honour to the loudest of war-riors. Not even Asberg, with his distinctive two-part whoop, could top it. Kitchen folk scouring pots with handfuls of ashes raised their heads to it; the watch-men upon the palisade ramparts whirled towards the sound, and those within the hall, shut up tight against the chill, heard it and came forth into the grey afternoon, some with spears in hand.

Burginde was right; it did free the babe. The nurse was ready. Into her waiting hands slid the weight of new life, warm, wet, and red.

"A boy, a boy," she laughed.

That night Ashild lay in her bed bolstered by cush-ions, her son under her arm. Her body felt a sense of weary use she had rarely known, a kind of aching sore-ness throughout. But her babe was perfect. Strong as she was, she would soon heal, even those deepest parts of her which felt torn and numb. What mattered was this child she had brought forth.

Ælfwyn, sitting next the bed and smiling on both mother and babe, could not stop the prayer of thanks-giving whispering within her breast. A healthy child had been born to the hall, in the midst of sudden sorrow of loss. She wanted Hrald here, that his grief might be allayed by the advent of this child; and even more so did she wish for Ceridwen's son, the tiny one's father. Ceric was not here to cast loving eyes upon Ashild, to take their fine and lusty son upon his knee and proclaim him truly his. He did not even know their night together had yielded such fruit.

The fear that Ceric might die in battle, or from sickness or accident stemming from the rigours of riding with the Prince, clouded Ælfwyn's brow a moment. He must live, so that he might know this child. Ashild had passed from maiden to mother, and no change was as great as this. Now, loving her child as Ælfwyn guessed she would, she might at last choose to be true wife as well, and go with the man who loved her to Kilton and there build a life.

Her thoughts strayed to another of Wessex, that man of Defenas whom she herself loved. She could name it thus, it was love. And she knew Raedwulf loved her, wanted her to wife, hoped even that she might be brought to childbed as her own daughter had, and bring the joy of a son or daughter into their later years.

The babe mewled. Ashild lifted the linen from her breast. Her son's tiny fingers had reached out and closed about the golden cross about her neck. His rosebud mouth was seeking, and she shifted to allow it to find the nipple it sought. She looked upon the downy head, a smile of mixed amazement and content on her lips.

When Jari arrived at Oundle to ride back with Hrald, his first words were of the son Ashild had borne, and that both lived and were well. The welcome news of the safe delivery of the child served as needed distraction for Hrald. His thoughts went to Ceric, who he knew must be again in the field with Eadward. Ceric had once been entrusted to ride to Four Stones on behalf of Ælfred; perhaps he would again be sent, that he might see Ashild and hold his child.

Hrald rode into the hall yard, his whistled return a signal to Ashild. She wished to present her son to his uncle in the treasure room, as doing so would preserve the female sanctuary which was her mother's bower house. Just as important in Ashild's eyes was the significance of her son being admitted to the stronghold of weaponry and treasure which served as much of the basis of Four Stones' power. The babe was not Hrald's, but this child was of the hall, and positive reminder of its continuance. And there was another, more poignant reason. Ashild knew that her brother discovering the falseness of his wife within had sullied that preserve. Seeing this babe there might dispel this, and restore some small part of the joy of which Hrald had been so recently robbed.

The priest of Four Stones was also listening for the whistle telling that Hrald was returned. Wilgot, uncertain as to the exact status of the child's parents, and fearing the worst, wished to baptise the boy as quickly as possible, as if his hastening the ceremony would somehow assure the relationship was one affirmed. To this end he had approached Ælfwyn the very evening of the child's birth, suggesting that the babe be carried to his house so he might administer the sacrament. Ashild, hearing this, demurred. She wanted Hrald to serve as godfather.

"The treasure room, and when Hrald returns," she told her mother in answer. "It is as holy a place as the priest's house, and he can bring his water and oil there." She looked at her little sister Ealhswith, who had been called in to meet her tiny nephew.

"You and Hrald will be his godparents," she told the girl, which wreathed Ealhswith's pretty face in smiles.

By the time Hrald returned Ashild had still not revealed the babe's name. Ælfwyn had pondered this, wondering if Ashild, granted a boy, might choose the name of her own father, Yrling. But she also wondered if she might choose to name her boy Hrald, to honour her brother. Then again, Ælfwyn recalled Ashild as a child being told by Sidroc the name of her own grandsire, Hroft, and the girl saying how much she liked the name. And it sounded well with Hrald.

When Ashild, her mother, and Burginde went to the hall, Wilgot and Ealhswith awaited them, the priest holding a silver tray topped with a linen covering. Hrald was ready. He unlocked the treasure room and they filed in. He kissed his older sister on her brow, just above the golden circlet she had placed there for the occasion, and smiled down on the swaddled babe, asleep in her arms. Ashild, looking up into Hrald's face, was glad for both kiss and smile. But the change wrought in her brother was all too clear. It was there about his mouth and eyes, a subtle alteration inflicted by the pain he knew. He looked almost bruised to her, bruised and older. Something beyond reclaiming was gone out of that boyish face.

Wilgot placed the tray upon the table and revealed the shallow basin of blest water, and the vial of holy chrism. Ashild placed the babe into the arms of a beaming Ealhswith. Wilgot made the sign of the cross above all, and gestured Ealhswith closer, the infant's head above the basin.

"The child's name," Wilgot prompted, looking at the babe's mother.

Ashild did not hesitate.

"Cerd."

Cerd, for his father's grandsire. It was the name of Ceridwen's father.

It was a Mercian name, a name of Angle-land.

Ælfwyn found her eyes filling. Bestowing this name on the child was a most unexpected gift. It was honour to Ceric, and to Ceric's mother Ceridwen, a woman who Ælfwyn knew Ashild must have guarded feeling for, and even resentment of.

Yet Ashild's own better nature had risen. It might be the one thing she could present to Ceric, to acknowledge him and his own mother in this way, but to Ælfwyn it spoke reams of the nobility of her daughter's heart.

TO THE MOUTH OF HELL

The Year 895

CERIC had twice attempted to send a letter from Kilton to Four Stones. Even during the Peace the sending of letters had been rife with hazards, and their arrival always doubtful. Common brigands could seize travellers and goods; weather could delay attaining the destination, causing an abandonment of the effort; sickness or accident could overtake the bearer.

Yet during that lost Peace Ceric could have entrusted a rolled parchment or single flat leaf to a visiting merchant who would be next crossing into Anglia to sell his goods. Or he might have sent his missive to Witanceaster, with the request that it be given to some of the King's couriers carrying revised trade agreements for Guthrum's approval. Now, with the Peace and its protections no longer acknowledged, the travel of merchants or royal couriers to Anglia was no longer possible.

One class of travellers only hazarded such trips. Priests, monks, and even nuns intent on reaching distant religious foundations remained undeterred. These men and women did not travel blindly; they knew the chances of arriving at church, convent, or monastery in Anglia or Northumbria were slight. Yet a few were granted dispensation to leave their home foundations on errands considered pressing enough to warrant the risk. Even within the borders of Wessex and Mercia travel was dangerous. The repeated incursions of Haesten and those Danes both contesting his claims and joining with him made forays in one's own kingdom fraught with peril. To enter Anglia proper, now under no real governance but controlled by Danes, could rightly be compared to seeking martyrdom. Yet those of the cloth who hoped to serve many more years in the service of the Church would go. They rode, and sometimes walked off toward their destinations, in the hope those Danes they came across would respect their persons and scant property.

Many of the Danes within Anglia now professed the Christian faith; at least a number had been baptised into it, though all knew the degree to which they followed its precepts was uneven. In this past twelve-month Ceric had handed his letters to monks, but without any return. He had no way of knowing if the parchments had reached Four Stones, or if the monks he had entrusted them to had been cut down but a few days after leaving Kilton's boundaries.

During that year he had served two more tours of duty in Prince Eadward's fyrd, both of the prescribed length of three months, interspersed with a three months' return home following each campaign. While with the Prince he and Worr and the rest of Ceric's men had ridden west to help secure the borders of Wales following a great action centred in Powys headed by Eadward's brother-in-law Æthelred, Lord of Mercia, and a number of Welsh princes. Since then they had patrolled uncertain enemy boundaries, chased looting Danes from destroyed hamlets, guarded the passage of supply waggons and once, a number of nuns forced to flee from one convent to another. They had fought almost numberless skirmishes.

Little of this had resulted in decisive return. Haesten and his followers still ranged about the countryside heedless of borders, endlessly on the move, harrowing Wessex and Mercia as they went. Other than the massed assault on Exanceaster in Defenas which had laid waste to so much of that place, and the pitched battle at Powys, in which the forces of Æthelred and the Welsh princes won the field, most of the action was a wearying cat and mouse game of pursuit with little reward.

Much of their effort was directed at keeping the Danes from scouring the countryside for food. And in fact, hunger drove both armies. The King and his son were used to stop at any burh for shelter and meat; it was part of that service due the royal family for the protection their warriors provided. But the predations of roving Danes and a long spell of wet weather which left decaying grain stalks pooled in water made for little surplus. Eadward and his men took advantage of every opportunity to hunt, snare birds, and set up overnight weirs in swift flowing streams where fish might be dipped up. It was never enough.

Ceric had ridden off from Kilton on this latest tour fronting forty warriors, twenty mounted and twenty on foot. His ranks had been replenished by the young men trained by Cadmar, aided by his brother Edwin's chief body-guards Eorconbeald and Alwin. Together these

three had readied a mix of thegns' sons of sword-bearing age, and a number of worthy young ceorls from the
village eager to march as foot-men with the mounted
thegns. The thegns, as professed warriors, were fulfill-
ing their pledge to defend Kilton, and would win silver,
arms, horses and even land if they distinguished themselves doing so. The free-born cottars vied for the chance
to join their ranks. More than a few of the better warriors in Kilton's ranks had been ceorls, starting as boys
as sling-throwers hurling river stones at the enemy, or as
youths as archers or spear-throwers. Any boy of village
or hall yard could aspire to win notice of his lord, and be
trained and armed by him. To win a place in the hall as
one of his lord's men meant leaving a life of mere plough-
ing and herding behind, to take up with honour a spear
and become part of the shield-wall of defence and attack.

Kilton now had nearly five score men trained in arms,
the more than fifty always at the hall with his brother
Edwin, and those forty who had set out with Ceric. After
these two latest tours of service with Eadward, the men
remaining with Ceric numbered one and thirty. Men had
been lost in direct action, by poisoned blood after taking
wounds, and sheer misadventure. One had been killed by
the rear hooves of a kicking horse, another by falling from
a tree he had climbed to espy the countryside ahead. The
hazards of service were many and remedies few.

The Prince commanded the leaders and men of five
burhs, Witanceaster, his own home; Wedmore, Meretun,
Englafeld, and Kilton. As the first three months of this
most recent tour with Eadward were drawing to a close,
he called the leaders of the other four burhs together. It
was a misty Spring morning, just after an Easter which

had gone uncelebrated by all before him. Eadward stood outside his tent, the cow hides that acted as fly providing just enough shelter as the men crowded under it.

His message was as unwelcome as it was unusual. Eadward was not himself returning to Witanceaster, but would stay in the field, continuing his drive north and east after Haesten's raiding troops. He had pressing need for men, and asked those of his followers who were unwed to stay on with him. Those with wives and children should return to their home burhs where they were needed, but any who could remain with him would be regarded with special favour.

Eadward then looked at the familiar faces around him, and called out their names. Of the five war-leaders, four were wed, with growing families, and one had even grandchildren awaiting him. Eadward dismissed these, asking that they go to their men and make his offer for him. Then he turned to Ceric.

"Will you stay?" he asked, in simple query.

Thoughts of Kilton weighed heavily in the minds of its men; Ceric knew this. Worn as he felt, he knew the newest of his warriors, those youngest of the thegns and the foot-men, unused to the hardships of short rations and constant travel in all weather were weary indeed. He was being asked to send many of his better, older men home, and continue on with few exceptions with the least seasoned.

Ceric looked back at Eadward, little more than a year older than he, and with a wife and child awaiting him in Witanceaster.

"I will of course remain, my Lord," he answered.

He went at once to Worr. As was his wont as horse-thegn of Kilton, his friend was amongst those animals. Ceric had brought two of his own, his chestnut stallion and a big bay gelding he used for pack. Only the lords of burhs travelled thus, with two animals. The second horse kept their own mount fresher, as it was not burdened with kit as well as rider. Worr was checking an abrasion the second horse had developed from an ill-fitting pack frame when Ceric neared.

"You will take him with you when you go," Ceric said, as way of greeting.

Worr gave the bay's thick neck a pat. "They will all be eager to see Kilton's green pastures," he answered. The horse-thegn gave a laugh. "As will we."

Ceric nodded. "I am staying on with the Prince," he said.

Worr's head swung round from the horse's shoulder. "Staying on?"

"Eadward is not returning to Witanceaster. All unwed men are asked to stay on." Ceric paused a moment. Worr was wed and had three small boys at Kilton. Like Ceric he had been away half the year already.

"You will lead the rest of our men home to Kilton."

Worr's mouth opened. He shook his head. "I am not leaving you."

"You have no choice. Those who are wed, especially those with young at home – you must return to them."

Ceric turned his eyes to the tents dotting Kilton's encampment. Men sat in the mouths of some, savouring the rare day of rest, while others made for the nearby stand of wood, bows in hand, quivers at their hips, hoping for small game to shoot.

"You must lead them home, and this fellow too," Ceric said, nodding toward the bay.

Worr could only protest. He had known Ceric since this eldest son of Kilton had been a babe. Worr had ridden with his father, and then his uncle, Godwin. He had taught Ceric to ride as a boy, helped train him in arms, and been at his right in every engagement since his sword-bearing. Eager as he was for rest, for Wilgyfu and his boys, he was not leaving now.

"Ceric, this is wrong-headed."

Ceric looked at him. Then with a smile, he answered. "Do as I say."

It was something that Worr had told him many times when they entered danger, when the older man insisted on placing himself in the greater peril they faced. It was also as mild a command as any had ever heard. And Worr was forced to oblige.

Eighteen of Kilton's men remained with Ceric, several of them beardless youths. Twelve, headed by Worr, set off next morning on a southwesterly track.

Eadward was left with sixty men. Ceric became second in command simply by the fact of his presence. The eldest son of Kilton made quick reckoning of his remaining men. None of them owned helmets, but all were equipped with war-caps of shaped and hardened leather, strapped over with iron bars for strength. Likewise he alone owned a costly ring shirt. Two of his men were pledged thegns and bore swords, which at Kilton he had presented them with, as well as spears. The rest were spear-men and archers. Of the other men left with the Prince, less than half of them were fully pledged thegns, some owning swords, not all; but good spear-men every one.

"With sixty we will travel faster, and our food needs are the smaller," Eadward told him, as they prepared to saddle up.

They had not moved far along the path they followed when a blast from a horn caused them to rein up. It was the Prince's own call, a summons to him. Soon a few men from the newly-dismissed burh of Wedmore appeared. They rode as escort to two cassock-clad monks, riding grey asses.

Gaining the Prince they explained that as they reached the path to Wedmore, the two brothers had appeared. It was all they could do to try to catch Eadward before he was lost to their efforts.

The older of the monks addressed the Prince. He was of a burly, even stout build, grey-stubbled, and when he pulled back the hood of his brown cassock his carefully shaved tonsure showed a perfect circle of pink bald head. The second monk was young, small and lively-looking, with hair of swarthy hue beneath his own tonsure, and wiry dark hair upon the backs of his quick hands.

"Your presence is indeed Heaven-sent, Prince Eadward. I am Wulgan and my brother monk, Berhtwald. We are come from Ælthelinga, and our goal is the abbey at Oundle."

"Oundle!" This was Ceric, on hearing the name.

Wulgan looked to him. "Indeed, Sir. We carry a leech-book of healing recipes to the Reverend Mother of that place, Sigewif. And God willing, we shall return to Ælthelinga with a copy of her own collection of remedies, which she has long promised to prepare for us."

Eadward could not suppress his sigh. Ælthelinga was one of two monasteries founded by his father, part of the

King's life-long attempt to reestablish holy foundations throughout Wessex. It was in answer to the many convents and monasteries sacked by Danes and left in ruins. The two he had created and endowed were his father's foothold for learning and righteousness. The King must know these monks rode towards almost certain death. Yet so great was the desire for the continual exchange of knowledge the risk was deemed acceptable. His father, so often struggling against his own bleeding illness, took special interest in the healing arts.

"And you need escort to the Anglian border," Eadward posed.

The monk's benign smile did not fully mask the strength of his intent. "We would be grateful to ride with you, as far as you are headed in that way."

Ceric could scarce believe their goal. Here were two monks risking their lives to carry a book to Abbess Sigewif. He would ask them to carry a message that far. Within two or three days they could get these holy men as near to the Anglian border as they dared.

He must wait for the Prince to grant them escort.

Eadward had but little choice. His father had built Ælthelinga, and these monks were under the King's direct protection, and by inference, his own. "We are going as far as Fullanham before turning south. You are welcome to ride with us."

Wulgan and Berhtwald were with them two days. The leech-book they carried was shown to Eadward and Ceric, hanging in a linen pouch from the older monk's neck, safe from detection under his cassock. Its height was no more than a man's hand, and its breadth not much more than a palm's width, but the parchment leaves were wondrously decorated. Every page bore the painting of a plant or root, outlined in dark ink and coloured in by brush in inks of blue, green, and red. The tiny and copious text was in both the speech of Rome and that of Wessex, so that more could make use of the wisdom compiled within. The binding was plain brown cow hide, a modest garment for a work of subtlety and measureless worth.

The monks proved good company, and Ceric was happy for their presence in their own right. Wulgan had travelled to Oundle years before, and from the founding of Ælthelinga well knew the effort demanded in creating an abbey from almost nothing. He had not upon that first visit met the Lady of Four Stones, but knew of that great benefactress. "Ælfwyn of Cirenceaster," the older monk murmured, in acknowledgment of that rich Lady's generosity.

"I will wed her daughter," Ceric told them. He proclaimed this before both monks, and Eadward too, as they sat over their wooden bowls of thin barley browis the first night. They all looked at him. The Prince knew of Ceric's plan, and of his own father's endorsement of it. He also knew almost two years had passed since Ceric had journeyed to wed the girl. Whether his failure to do so then had been a lucky escape for Ceric or a damaging loss to the cause of peace, Eadward could not guess.

Just declaring his intent to others made the goal more attainable to Ceric. The monks both nodded and smiled, and Wulgan commented on Heavenly Providence bringing them into the others' ken.

"Will you carry a letter for me, to give to Abbess Sigewif? She will see it gets to Four Stones."

"Indeed we shall, my son," answered Wulgan. "And may Berhtwald and I have the honour of meeting the maid's mother, Lady Ælfwyn."

Ceric had nothing upon which he could write, but in the Prince's baggage waggon there was a small store of used parchment, one of which Eadward granted him. It was a trimming from a larger leaf, and had a few random lines upon it, delineating a map of some kind, but the blank reverse was just as smooth. Next morning Ceric set the parchment on a slat of wood on his lap, and cut a new nib from a goose quill which was already old and cracking. The pottery vial of ink the Prince offered smelt ill and was close to spoiling, but for his hurried letter all would suffice. Easter was just past. He dated his letter:

Near the Octave Day of Easter

HRALD – MY BROTHER

Would this scrap of parchment be me myself. Know that I am well and at Eadward's side. Hearing you and Four Stones are whole would be my greatest boon. All my effort is for Wessex, Kilton, and Ashild. May we be granted Peace between our halls, forever.
CERIC OF KILTON

That night before he slept Ceric came to Eadward's tent. That of the monks' was pitched nearby, and both were within, and Ceric thought, asleep. The next day they would come as close to the border of Anglia as they might, and they would see the holy brothers off. Since giving Wulgan his letter, Ceric could not stop thinking of the hardship and difficulty the journey to Oundle presented. Mounted on asses, entirely unarmed, carrying no valuables save for their healing recipes and their own souls, they would go forth. When Eadward gestured him within his tent, Ceric tilted his chin towards the tent which held the monks.

"I would go with them."

Eadward looked at him, his expression as blank as the tone of his response. "To your own death. No. You are needed here."

Ceric's head dropped, but he nodded, as he must.

In the morning they parted with the monks at a stream which would lead them north across the border. Wulgan and Berhtwald raised their hands in blessing to their escort, and with cheerful mien turned the shaggy heads of their grey asses along the cress-clad bank. The animals' long and tufted ears swiveled back at the whicker of Eadward's stallion, and then pricked forward to face the journey ahead.

"God go with them," Ceric murmured.

The Prince's response was less hopeful.

"I fear they will see His face long before they see Oundle."

⁂

Then began the most trying four months of Ceric's life. Daily hunger was a constant. Coming across an isolated farm and its several buildings, Eadward would halt his men and approach at a distance with two or three of his body-guard, one carrying the standard of Wessex, that golden dragon banner. A man might appear, spear in hand, terror on his face as the Prince asked if he had grain to spare so they might make browis. At this point the form of a woman and likely children would crowd the door as well, hunger and fear marking all of their countenances. Eadward was well supplied with silver, and could offer this rare commodity to them, but coinage profited little when there was no grain for which to bargain.

While on the march, discovering the eggs of birds, wild berries, apples, lambs' lettuce, watercress, the fat buds of butterbur or any other edible bounty occasioned a brief frenzy of feeding. Unripe nuts made them sick with their bitterness, but little was beyond their trying. One man found a bee hive in a tree, and helmeted, gloved, and his face caked with mud as protection, suffered the stings of outraged bees as he dug out ladleful after ladleful of dripping comb honey.

As the weeks and then months wore on Ceric learnt to almost make friends with his hunger, to learn not to fear it. The shifting quality of his craving for food was a wave ebbing and flowing. It would recede when he acknowledged it and then, having no means to satisfy it, dismissed it. Every spoonful of oats or rye he savoured. Learning just how little he could make do with bestowed a new mastery over his senses. If he sat at the high table at Kilton again, he would feast; but he would never eat thoughtlessly again.

In these months time itself seemed to change for Ceric. He had been away from Kilton so long that the rhythm of the field was all he knew. Ordinary tasks fell away, and ordinary comforts which filled his days at home were far removed from either waking or sleeping hours. His comb broke, and in trying to make one for himself he gained new appreciation for the woman in Kilton's village who carved them. Labouring over it he thought of the dead wood from the pear trees she was allowed to gather, so she might with her fine-toothed saw and skillful hands make something of both utility and beauty, not the gap-toothed and clumsy product of his knife. For a moment he remembered Begu, and the comb he had presented her with long ago, and wondered if she still used it, or if Edwin had brought her one new.

He lost his razor – a costly item, and one not to be replicated, however poorly, on the road – when the bottom seam of one of his saddle bags split, rotted out from having been too long wet from fording rivers, and the near-continual damp of dew and rain. The razor had been a gift from his grandmother, given when the first downy hairs sprouted upon his lip. It was housed in a small box of wood which Modwynn had a woodcarver decorate with chisel and scoring knife, and carve his name upon as well. He felt its loss, then only shook his head and laced the leathern bag up as well he could. He used the small shears he still had after that, to cut short his beard.

Remaining to him was the silver disc, highly polished, which he had used for shaving. When he looked at himself now, he saw his cheeks, so round as a boy, were deeply hollowed. There was no excess flesh anywhere on his body; he was all muscle, sinew, and drive.

His clothing fell apart, sweat-stained and worn from exertion. The three pair of leggings went first, torn and snagged by brambles and reaching undergrowth. He could not trade with his own men or any others for tunics and leggings or boots; they were as thread-bare as he. After any skirmish in which they won the field, he was forced for the first time to strip the bodies of the Danes he had killed for their very clothing. Actions which had once been abhorrent became commonplace, even life-sustaining. At night, wrapped in a tattered wool blanket within his cramped tent of hide, ignoring the gnawing hunger in his belly, flea-bitten, immune to his own stench, the only thing that brought to him any true comfort was the truth of the gold he carried. His sword with its pommel and hilt chased in that bright metal always lay next him, within ready reach. Uttering a brief prayer before he fell into sleep his hand would close about the golden cross with its garnet heart upon his chest. It had been his father's, yes; a man of whom he had almost no memory; but it had been given to Gyric by a young Ælfred, and then presented to him by his grandmother. The line of continuity in this, from his father to him, ran as strongly as did that of his sword, from his grandsire Godwulf to him.

What brought him greatest consolation was the smallest piece of that precious metal, the ring of gold upon the little finger of his left hand. It was that confirmation ring of his grandsire, which would become his wedding ring for Ashild. The ring was a special emblem. Golden-hilted sword and golden cross were legacies, things of the past. The ring held the promise of a happier, and shared, future.

The peak of Summer had passed. A week after the grain harvest time of Hlafmesse, Eadward's small fyrd, emerging from a wood, came upon two shepherds guiding their flock across a road of pounded clay. The sudden appearance of three score heavily armed men was answered by wide-eyed alarm in the shepherds' faces. While in Wessex the Prince always rode with at least one golden dragon pennon flying, so that all might at once see he was of the King. This reassurance notwithstanding, the men stood stock still in their fright, their animals bumping and swirling about them. One of the Prince's body-guards called out his question.

"What are we near?"

"Welingaford," came the answer. Both men pointed up the road.

The Prince and Ceric were riding side by side, surrounded by Eadward's body-guard. Eadward looked to Ceric, who could read in his commander's face the satisfaction this news brought. Welingaford was a burh on the Thames, and true to its name, at a good fording place. It was heavily fortified, as it held one of Ælfred's mints. As such it would be a rich target if the Danes knew of the store of silver kept in such places. Eadward dismissed the shepherds with a wave of his hand, and called to another of his men as they moved forward.

"Signal my approach," ordered the Prince.

The man put a small brass horn to his lips and sounded the Prince's call. As the troop rode forward he repeated it at intervals. The fourth time it was sounded six mounted men appeared, three from either side of the wood they passed through.

"I am Eadward, Prince," he told them. The startle of the watch-men was only slightly less than that of the shepherds. They had no word of a royal approach, and though the horn blast was that of the Prince, the mud-splattered horses and begrimed men upon them were more befitting a large and failed hunting party.

"Yes, my Lord," replied the head of the guards. He left four of his brethren behind and with the fifth took up their role as escort to the Prince, fronting the long columns as they neared Welingaford.

As they gained the settlement Ceric saw a village larger than that of Kilton. It had, it seemed, remained untouched, the crofts trim, the long rows of vegetables untrampled. The common pastures held scores of cows and goats, and the sheep they had passed were proof that their herds and flocks had remained unharassed. All before him promised that soon the Prince and all his men would be sitting down to full bowls of hearty fare.

The palisade of upright timbers surrounding the garrison was nearly as tall as that of Witanceaster, giving the watch-men upon its ramparts a long view over village and countryside. Eadward's signal horn kept sounding, and the approaching troop was near enough to see the heads of more men pop up above that rampart, craning to see the Prince.

The doubled gates were swung wide to admit them. Entering the burh of Welingaford was a military entrance, and Ceric and the other men who owned them put on their helmets and war-caps.

The Lord of Welingaford stood within to meet his guests. He was young enough that his brown hair showed only the first streaks of gray, set off by long drooping moustaches of still-rich auburn. His burh's central location, and its lord's abilities had brought him early to the King's notice. Welingaford was under Ælfred's direct command, but the King would not deprive so vital a burh of its leader, nor require any of its men to join him in the field.

As they rode in Ceric could not but note the deferential interest in the eyes of the men who watched them. Many of the warriors within were young, and guarding the minting works as they must, were of necessity untried by the active warfare those filing in had seen. Here was the King's son, a leader of great repute, fronting a body of warriors who looked as though they followed him to the mouth of Hell and had yet returned. Those youths of Kilton who Ceric had asked to stay on to serve were tempered by combat and the hardships of months of rough living. The same was true of all the warriors Eadward led.

With his clothes in tatters Ceric thought he appeared almost a beggar. His weapons gave the lie to that, not just his sword, but the bright seax of Merewala, spanning his belly. His blackened helmet with its incised designs upon cheek pieces and sides, and the blackened mass of his still-sound ring shirt also gave testament to the wealth of he who bore them. The men in the work yards who studied him missed none of this. As ragged and worn as they all were, those of Welingaford looked on them all with a kind of awe.

As a royal mint Welingaford had a hall set aside for the King's visits, in which Eadward and his men were lodged. For Ceric to again sleep in an alcove and under a sheet of linen rather than in his own clothes on the hard ground gave as much ease to the mind as to the body. It was but another reminder of all he had at Kilton, and what he fought for.

They spent four days there, their weary horses at pasture cropping the long and lush grasses, and Eadward's men at last eating their fill. To drink ale again, to have their browis enriched with shredded pig or cow's meat, to bring to their mouths fresh bread dripping with sweet butter or spread with sheep's cheese – these pleasures, common-place at their home burhs, were savoured as unexcelled luxuries. The use of the bathing shed and its hot water meant that grime never fully removed from immersion in lakes or a hasty wash in cold-flowing streams could now be scrubbed off with soft lye soap. And with scores of war-riors garrisoned there the men could be clothed, and shod in new shoes. All Eadward's men had won silver for which to trade for such things, and Ceric, after re-supplying himself with leggings, tunics, a woollen blanket and linen towelling, was not alone in flinging his torn and filthy togs into one of the rubbish-burning fires. As befit its impor-tance Welingaford had a priest. Ceric availed himself of his presence, for he would not miss the chance to be shriven of his sins, though they be not beyond that common to all fighting men, the taking of life.

During the days of rest Eadward had sent riders ahead to seek out his father, who the Lord of Welingaford knew had been heading north up the Thames, above the populous trading town of Lundenwic. The riders returned with the King's message, summoning Eadward to join him in protecting the reaping of the grain crop which fed Lundenwic.

This was a more than two day ride, almost due east, but the dry Summer weather now blessing the fields combined with the new fullness of the supply waggon made it almost a jaunt. It also sounded the lightest duty Eadward and his men had known in a long time, patrol-ling the borders of the fields so that reapers could safely gather the early crop.

The King had thrown up his headquarters on the banks of the River Lyge north of Lundenwic. The town itself had been built by the Caesars, and was still clad in some of that greatness. It had fallen years ago to the Danes, and Ælfred had won it back again, and rebuilt the walls of stone the Caesars' men had erected. Then he had awarded the town to his son-in-law Æthelred, Ealdorman and Lord of Mercia.

As Eadward's fyrd made their way, they were escorted in turns by men from Welingaford, and then Lundenwic. These last brought them to the field in which stood Ælfred's tent. Hundreds of men had been gathered here; the sheer numbers of tents made it clear. The small oiled-linen and hide structures were pitched in rows over the greensward, fanning out like the rays of the Sun. The eye was led to the tent centred in these rows, that of the King. To one side an expansive field kitchen, almost ringed with supply waggons, was set nearest the river flow, granting all the water needed for cooking and washing up. The horn-man of the Prince signalled Eadward's arrival, and as the body of his men halted, Eadward and Ceric approached.

The King's tent was a large one, topped with a doubled peak, its oiled roof high enough so that the tallest man could enter and stand without stooping. It was flanked by two royal standards, set into the ground on long poles, bearing the golden dragon of Wessex flying upon banners of linen. The front flap of the tent was open to the fine weather, and held up as a fly. Rush matting formed a ground cloth under this, and two small benches were set upon it. They saw the King come forth from within the tent, and Eadward and Ceric swung off their horses.

"Sire," said Eadward, bowing his head.

A father's affection showed on the King's face, but his personal greeting and embrace of his son would need to wait. Ceric touched one knee to the ground in reverence.

As he lifted his eyes he saw a second man come from the tent. It was Raedwulf, the Bailiff of Defenas, so often with the King. His ink stained fingers showed he had been at work with quill, and in the recess of the tent Ceric could see a trestle table set with writing implements.

Ceric had begun to grin with pleasure at seeing Raedwulf. The bailiff too began to smile. His eyes then shifted, looking beyond Ceric to those men who followed him. The older man's brow furrowed. Ceric understood at once and blurted out the answer to relieve Raedwulf's anxiety.

"Worr – he is at Kilton, God willing."

The bailiff nodded in relief to hear his son-in-law lived, and Eadward took up the story. "I ordered all men who were wed to return home. The excellent Worr was one I was sorry to see go," he said to Raedwulf.

"Those without wives and children, I asked to stay on with me." Eadward now looked to his father. "Ceric of Kilton has in the past amply repaid my trust in him, and has done so again." The Prince glanced at Ceric before looking back to the two older men before him.

"He and all of my men have been in the field for nearly seven months."

The King gave his head a shake at this. Since the arrival of Haesten three years ago Ælfred travelled almost ceaselessly from burh to burh, from conflict to conflict. He must; he was King. To ask the scion of a great hall like Kilton, and the thegns and ceorls that followed him to suffer the same privation was proof of the depth of his Kingdom's need. If they could not stand fast now, the steady attrition inflicted by Haesten's hordes would topple all.

Before they turned to enter the tent and take a cup of ale with the King, Ælfred moved forward to address his son's massed men, thanking them in few but heartfelt words for their service. The cheer that went up in response rang out across the encampment: "Ælfred, Wessex!"

It was a mark of special regard that Ceric was invited within. Though he was one of Ælfred's godsons, an invitation to sit with the King, not at a feast at Kilton, but in his military headquarters was an altogether quieter, and higher, honour. Ale was poured into simple bronze cups, the King's alone being of silver. Ceric recalled the young man-servant who had been with the King as they approached Middeltun; this was the same man.

The King looked tired indeed to Ceric. The dark golden hair had wholly paled to silver, and only the king's beard showed traces of its earlier, warmer hue. The pallor of his skin made the dusky circles under his eyes the deeper. The eyes themselves though were still sharply blue, alert, and keenly vigilant.

Distinction though it be, Ceric was glad when the bailiff and he could rise, leaving father and son to the tent. When last he had seen Raedwulf, the bailiff was making hurried flight from Eadward's camp to Ælfred's side, to help repulse a sudden attack in which the Danes had taken the burh of Exanceaster, and ravaged all along the coast of Defenas. Once outside the King's tent Ceric turned to him.

"Defenas – we heard it was a great action. How did your home fare?"

"My hall was spared," Raedwulf said, "held by the men of Exanceaster who had fled there."

Ceric gave brief thought to this. The routed thegns of the burh might have almost stormed the place in their flight. He did not care to think of the damage a large number of warriors may have inflicted on what he guessed must be a hall known for its handsomeness. At any rate, Ceric knew Raedwulf would not be a man to dwell on mishaps, not when he had escaped disaster.

Raedwulf turned now to the subject of Ceric's home. "I have no news of Kilton," he admitted. He gave thought to this and added. "It is always for the best that we have heard nothing. Word would have been brought to the King of any attack."

This was ever true, though silence was scant consolation.

Ceric would hazard another question of the bailiff, though he asked without much hope of return. Raedwulf knew nothing of Kilton. For him to have heard anything from what was now enemy territory was too much to hope for.

Still, if Ceric had ever earned the right to ask, it was now.

"Have you heard news of Hrald, and Four Stones?" he asked. "I myself know nothing of it. I have sent letters with monks, the most recently a few months ago. They were two we met upon the road, journeying from Ælthelinga to Oundle."

The bailiff's face had changed. Mention of Four Stones summoned its women to his mind's eye. Ashild, the daughter of the hall, was loved by Ceric, who had the approval of his King in her pursuit. He himself loved the

Lady of that place, a feeling as sacred as it was secret. Of Oundle he had the warmest memory. A tiny and now crumbling rose bud from that famed garden sat in a small leathern pouch in his belt.

Raedwulf answered without hesitation. "We know that Four Stones stands firm."

How know you this, Ceric once again found his mind asking the bailiff. It went unvoiced, but Raedwulf read Ceric's question in his face, and answered. "The King's riders carry all manner of news to him." Raedwulf paused. "Also, there are Danes who will bring report."

Ceric considered this. "They have been bought."

The bailiff gave a short laugh. "Almost all men can be bought, for the right price. Hungry men, the more so."

"One of Hrald's men told you?"

The bailiff paused once more. "A man formerly of Four Stones."

Just north of Ælfred's camp lay the fields of rippling oats and barley on which the sustenance of Lundenwic depended. Æthelred, Lord of Mercia, had some number of his own men stationed about the fields, but needed many more now that the crop was ripe and reapers ready to scythe. Under the bright and hot Sun was set a double perimeter. Stationed just at the edges of the golden furrows were foot-men ringing the fields. They stood at intervals with their spears, pacing slowly to meet the next man and return to where they had started. Thegns on horseback patrolled further out, some by pasture lands, others at the edge of forest growth, waiting to respond to any threat.

The reaping took a week. The bundled sheaves were even more vulnerable to theft, and after the reapers had left, the guards remained until the sheaves dried and could be collected and brought within the walls of Lundenwic for threshing and winnowing. There was some interest for the foot-men when the reapers had been afield, with the sharpened scythes flashing as the curved blades cut through the yellow stalks, and those holding them sang their repetitive swing-chants to stay in rhythm as they worked their way across the knee-high grain. Now the furrows were silent, empty of any life save the jackdaws and blackbirds who dipped down, seeking shattered heads of barley or plucking worms from the soil now exposed. When the waggons rolled in laden with men to pluck the sheaves and carry them to Lundenwic, even those who had most craved the rest this detail had given them were ready to move on. Eadward told Ceric that within the week he would dismiss them all, riding with his own men back to Witanceaster, and sending all others to their home burhs.

The Prince did not have the chance to make good on his promise. Before the final sheaves had been loaded, two of the King's riders brought word to him and Æthelred of an encampment of the Danes. The scouts had ridden up the banks of the River Lyge. At midday they heard sounds of habitation; hammering, and distant voices. They quit their horses to draw nearer. Up a slight tributary of the Lyge they found a timber fortress being built, far enough from the banks of the Lyge itself not to be readily discovered. The encircling wall was complete, and men laboured within at their building works. The scouts continued a short way up the Lyge. The numbers of drekars pulled bow-first into the banks, or hauled up entirely to list on their sides on the grass, told that these Danes had sailed in stealth up the Thames, then turned up the River Lyge, evading detection by the Lord of Mercia's men.

Ceric was not privy to the council taking place between the King, his son-in-law, and his son. When Eadward returned from his father's tent to where his own men were camped, he called Ceric to him. He told him more of the discovery, and of the decision made.

"We will attack. The King has placed all in Æthelred's hands; it is a Danish incursion on Mercian lands. But we are to aid."

Ceric drew breath. They were but a day or two away from being released. Now they were being asked to fight for Mercia. He could do nothing but nod his head, and re-double his attention to what the Prince next said.

Surprise, as always, would be their greatest ally. They had questioned the scouts carefully, to make the best determination of approach. Sailing up the Lyge, to land just short of the Danes would grant both silence and secrecy. Yet Æthelred could not supply the troops with enough ships from Lundenwic to carry all, which meant a split force working its way up river, some in ships, others coming by foot and horse. The Lord of Mercia then had decision to make. Eschewing any ships and the ungainliness of a divided force, they would travel by foot and horseback. The scouts warned that owing to the narrowness of the banks they must come largely through the trees. The river bank in most places would allow men to ride only single file.

Eadward summed up the urgency of the task in his next words.

"We start tomorrow, at dawn."

EVER DEEPER

Aforce of over two hundred from Mercia and Wessex set out at daybreak. Æthelred and his chief men led the way, themselves mounted and leading nearly four score of Mercian foot-men. It was the first time Ceric had seen more than a glimpse of the Lord of Mercia. He was approaching his fifth decade, and the long hair for which he was known by the Welsh during his wars against them was now largely grey. Ælfred was both father-in-law and overlord to Æthelred, but the Lord of the Mercians was kingly in dress if not in bearing. His ring-tunic was laid over a leathern tunic of deep red, and his helmet with its wild boar crest upon the skull plate had a thick row of that beast's real bristles running down its iron back. Ceric remembered Æthelred's green serpent banner from the siege at the River Colne, when Eadward had held one bank, and the Lord of Mercia's men, the other. Several of Æthelred's body-guard sported these banners now, rising from the cantles of their saddles.

Eadward and Ceric too would ride, along with the Prince's body-guard, with two score foot-men. When they neared the place, Ceric and most others mounted would quit their horses. Only Æthelred and Eadward and their direct body-guard would remain horsed, that they might see and be seen by their men. With rare exceptions fighting was done on foot, and Æthelred, knowing their palisade to be already complete, planned to call the Danes out for pitched battle on their doorstep.

At mid-morning, after walking their horses upon the firm soil of the river bank, and the foot-men making their way as rapidly as they could through the brush and trees to keep time, the scouts signalled they neared the new fort. In plain view ahead was the stream they had followed, and from which they had heard the work of joiners. Silence greeted them now; no sound of work came from behind that timber wall. None at the front of their ranks stopped to puzzle over this. A clear and blue sky was overhead, with only the finest of clouds streaking the distance. Rising about them was that smell of fresh river water they had walked with the whole journey, and the wood to their right was bedded in a mix of yellow lichens and deep green mosses from which tiny white and pink flowers rose. All moved as noiselessly as they could. Ceric swung from his saddle and handed the reins of his stallion to one of Eadward's body-guards, and joined the foot-men of Kilton.

He had ridden, as they all had, in as full a war-kit as all possessed. For Ceric that was his dark steel helmet, ring-shirt, sword in its black baldric over his left shoulder, seax across his belly, and shield of blue and yellow. He left his spear back at camp; all his foot-men carried them. The Danes were bound to have swordsmen, and as Kilton's leader he would engage as many as he could. Standing there, seeing his horse being led away, swinging his shield round from his back and fitting his hand through the grip behind the pointed iron boss, he was struck by Worr's absence. He had fought skirmishes since he had sent Worr home, but never in his life had he stood in any pitched battle without Worr at his right side.

Worr was not with him, and today, instead of starting for home, he fought for Mercia.

He blew out his breath, trying to clear his head of this thought. Wherever he fought was for Kilton. And his first allegiance, after Christ, was to Wessex and Ælfred. These encamped Danes might be those soon heading for Kilton, or Four Stones.

Those mounted, Æthelred and his men foremost, started up the bank. Ceric slipped into the trees, fronting his men, and began to follow. The dimness of the tree cover made but slight contrast to Ceric's blackened ring-shirt and helmet. His sword was still in its baldric, and for ease of walking he would leave it there until needed. When they gained the fort they would quickly form up into ranks. It was a tactic much used by the Danes, creeping quietly through forest trees to emerge at a clearing ready to assume their lines of attack. This morning would see a shield-wall of the thegns of Mercia in front, with Eadward's men, including those of Kilton, just behind.

They did not get the chance to make good on these plans. Ceric had kept close enough to the river bank that through breaks in the trees and shrubby growth he could see the last of Eadward's mounted thegns. Of a sudden a yell rang out, and the thegn he had watched kicked his mount and sped forward. Ceric could see no clearing ahead of him through the trees, had no idea of how much further lay the fort of the Danes. He only knew they had been discovered. Those foot-men of Eadward's in front of his own began to run, as well as they could in the undergrowth, towards an ever-growing mix of war-cries, yells and oaths.

Ceric pulled his sword and cried out, "Kilton!", a rallying call answered by those behind him.

As he moved forward the light was changing; the trees thinning before him. He could see blue morning sky and a glimpse of fresh, nearly white timber walls. Then one of his foot-men, running a few arm lengths alongside him, screamed and fell. Ceric turned his head to see the throwing spear the man had been hit with, protruding from his lower back.

Ceric was now aware of another man, behind him. His own had kept their distance, while this one was coming up with speed. He jolted himself to a stop and whirled, sword foremost. It would be no good against a throwing spear, but taken in ambush as they were, he would rather die facing his enemy than be dropped by a blow from behind.

It was a Danish warrior, holding a sword and shield. The warrior lacked a helmet. Ceric could guess why he had been his target.

He has no helmet. Ceric heard a voice within him, his own, the voice of Cadmar, of Worr, of every skilled warrior who had ever trained him, posing just this situation to him.

Hit at the head.

In turning as quickly as he had, Ceric had brief advantage. The Dane staggered to his own stop, shield lifted, sword ready to engage. Ceric narrowed his eyes at him through the oval openings of the coveted helmet.

His opponent was as tall as he, no taller, and Ceric was standing on higher ground. A sidewise swipe would give Ceric more strength and leverage. Yet that was what the Dane would expect. Ceric saw his opening and took the offensive, jumping to his right. As he struck out with his blade towards the Dane's shield shoulder, the man recoiled and pulled the shield closer in. As he ducked Ceric was able to lunge forward, and bring his blade directly down through the top of the Dane's head, between the eyes.

There was a terrible moment, one almost of suction, as the blade of Ceric's sword cleaved through the skull. The curved plates of bone seemed to close up around the width of sharp steel, even as the white and red brain matter was expressed about it.

Ceric gave a yell and yanked the blade back, just as the Dane was falling away from under it, to sink spread-armed on the mosses of the forest floor.

Behind him he could see some of his foot-men fighting spear-to-spear with Danes. Others were running toward the open river bank, away from the wood and the dangers it held. Eadward was there somewhere on the bank, and Ceric must go to him.

He yelled again, calling his men to follow, but over the clash of metal and war-cries from ahead could not know if he was heard. He ran, jumping and nearly tripping through the underbrush, to stand panting in the brilliant sunlight spilling on the river margin.

Ahead a few riderless horses milled, snorting and tossing their manes. A shield which he knew to be of Æthelred's men floated upon the water, painted face up, drifting downstream toward whence they had come. He could glimpse a portion of the palisade wall. Before it warriors of Wessex and Mercia faced a growing number of Danes, surging from a gate which Ceric could not see but which he guessed had opened. Æthelred had issued no demand to come and fight, shield-wall to shield-wall. The Danes had discerned their arrival and many awaited them in the wood, picking off the foot-men amongst the trees, as was their wont. Now they swarmed upon them before any had chance to form up. The narrow river bank was grown treacherous, as numberless Danes pushed Æthelred's warriors to its brink, and fighting there meant those struck toppled into its cool and dark waters. The effort had not yet begun, and looked utterly lost.

Ceric could not see Eadward, nor Æthelred. Moving closer was to throw his life away. He brought his left hand, that which grasped the grip of his shield, into his chest, and thumped it against the golden cross that lay under ring-shirt and tunic. He did not want to die, and knew that now he very likely would. But words formed in his beating heart: Take me now God, if it be your will.

He thought of nothing but Eadward as he ran along the bank towards the fighting. He would allow no thought of Kilton, or Modwynn, or his brother Edwin who relied upon him. He fixed his mind on Eadward, and nothing beyond. But the face of Ashild flashed into his mind, and the few hours that had comprised his sole night with her. He squeezed his eyes shut for an instant, that the image be imprinted there for as long as he lived. My love, I thank you, he thought.

Before him horses were wheeling and rearing, the warriors upon them yelling as they manoeuvered in a knot of loose horses and men on foot. Then a horn sounded, three times, that call only the desperate wish to hear. It was the retreat signal of Mercia, Æthelred calling all back, abandoning the attack.

Those same mounted thegns now charged along the narrow bank. Ceric leapt back to the trees to keep from being trampled under their hooves. He saw the body-guard of Æthelred come first, the Lord of Mercia one of a long string of riders. Some forced their horses into the muddy regions of the lower banks, just so that two might ride along the narrowness of that river margin, speeding their retreat. Horses which had lost their riders were amongst them, cantering to catch up or overtake those whose riders they still bore. Foot-men streamed behind and clambered from within the tree cover to join the retreat. Some carried no weapon, having lost or broken their spears. Ceric raked his eyes along the line of flee-ing horsemen, searching for the Prince of Wessex. The horn, sounded by one of Æthelred's men, had blown without ceasing, and now, the holder of that brass far ahead, grew fainter.

A gap of agonizing length was next, until Eadward appeared. With none immediately before him, he rode at speed, slowing for a moment when he spotted Ceric standing on the bank. He had breath to yell to Ceric as he shot by, "Stay with my body-guard. Bring up the rear. Protect the foot-men!"

Ceric stood to see the Prince's body-guards come next. He saw the man to whom he had given his horse, and saw with wonderment that he still held his stal-lion. Ceric was about to pull himself up upon his back when the rest of Kilton's foot-men appeared. Some had the dazed look of those who barely took notice of their surroundings, while others had panic fresh in their eyes. Ceric urged them forward. One of them, Sebbe by name, came slower than the others, in a baltering walk which had him almost stumbling in effort to stay upright. Sebbe was a year or two older than Ceric, a cottar and an able man, one with promise. Ceric called his name, and Sebbe made attempt to hasten. As he neared, Ceric saw the broad leathern belt he wore about his middle, sitting over a tunic now bloodied from waist to thigh. Ceric left his horse and ran to him.

"An arrow," Sebbe told him, in a voice not much above a rasp. By the time Ceric got him on his horse, the rest of the foot-men had passed them. Sebbe's eyes were glazed, and his lids dropped over them almost at once. His hands buried themselves in the dark red mane of Ceric's horse. Ceric held the reins, and walking at the animal's shoulder, he urged him to as fast a walk as he could. Eadward's body-guard was almost out of sight, but thankfully no Dane had appeared, running after those who had fled.

Retreat was ever fraught with peril. Those quitting the contest could be pursued and overtaken. Eadward had ordered Ceric and his own body-guards to stay behind, as the straggling foot-men would be the first the Danes would reach, and he wanted his best men there to face them. But retreat had also been used as a feint, notably against Ælfred's men. Several times Danes had appeared to flee the field of battle to have the men of Wessex break ranks and follow them, in hope of killing more to add to their battle-gain. The Danes had then spun around in counterattack, surrounding and slaying their pursuers.

This morning the lack of pursuit seemed one of the few things that had gone right. Still, Ceric lagged far behind. At the next river bend he would lose sight of the final two body-guards. As he strained his eyes looking ahead, Sebbe fell from the saddle. He almost hit Ceric in doing so, and the stallion snorted and danced sideways to clear the body.

Ceric knelt down, placed his hand on Sebbe's neck. The pulse under that still warm skin had stopped. He stood up, and yelped out his call to the body-guards ahead. One of them turned his horse's head and rode back to him.

The man returned at a canter, his eyes taking in the scene. As he neared Ceric he looked down at the body. "There is no time," he said. "Leave him."

"He is one of mine," Ceric answered.

The eyes of Eadward's man met those of Ceric. It was reason enough; he must comply. He jumped down from his horse and together he and Ceric flung the body of Sebbe across the saddle.

They had just left men dead in the trees and before the walls. But this was different. Sebbe had pulled the arrow from his side, and made it part-way to safety, and Ceric would see he was duly buried at their camp.

A tree felled by wind lay not far off, and the body-guard brought his horse to it. It gave a step to Ceric to climb behind the man on his horse. With two laden horses they made haste to the rest of the line.

They rounded the crook in the river to find that others of the foot-men had begun to collapse from exhaustion. Some were wounded. The mounted body-guard picked up those unable to go further.

When they reached their camp Ceric called the men of Kilton to him. In Ælfred's camp as they were, there would be food and drink ahead of them; this was the sole consolation. He stood, his helmet under his arm, looking out on the blank and exhausted faces of the young men he led. He had lost two of them, Sebbe and that man running to his right in the trees, felled by a throwing spear. He gave the ablest bodied amongst them the task of burying Sebbe. Then he strode to one of the water barrels and poured water from its wooden dipper over his head. He went to his tent where he pulled off his ring-shirt, and waited to hear from Eadward.

The report was grim. Eadward had lost five men, but Æthelred, whose troops had borne the brunt of the assault, almost sixty. And there had been no gain. The losses were so great and so immediate that retreat was not only warranted but required. Æthelred had not guessed the strength of the enemy, nor that they would keep pouring from those gates. Eadward, closer to the front, had seen they were vastly outnumbered.

That night, lying in his tent, Ceric dreamt that he was flying. It was not the darting flight of song birds, nor the soaring of a gull, but rather a slow and serene drifting above the surface of his life. He looked down on the events of the morning, saw himself in a silent retelling making his way through the trees of the wood. Hovering just above his own head, he saw that head turn to see his foot-man fall, the spear in his back. He saw himself run forward, then turn to face the Dane who had trailed him. The entire action was played out until his body beneath him scrambled to the bank while he floated without effort above it. He watched himself thump his chest with his closed fist, on the place where that golden cross lay, and saw himself prepare to die.

He awoke then, not with a start, but the sense that he could no longer see the action unfolding beneath him. The picture had faded, and he was left in darkness. He opened his eyes. His tent was brighter. The soft gleam of a Moon, waxing half, spilled across the ground outside. He lay in that owl-light, wondering, Is this omen, that next time, I shall die? Was that my soul? If so, there is little to fear.

The discovery of a new Danish fort so close to Lundenwic was as startling as it was unwelcome. Built upon the River Lyge, it gave ready access to not only the rich trading centre, but granted escape via the Thames to the sea. Hope of immediate dismissal was brushed away by the finding. Eadward's troops must stay, at least until decision was made for next steps.

Scouts were sent next morning to keep watch on the Danish fort. Approaching on foot as near as they might through the wood, they were greeted first by the sight and smell of wafting smoke. From the cover of the trees their eyes confirmed its source. A pyre had been erected before the palisade, upon which the bodies of their slain had been laid. It smoldered still. Its size proclaimed that their own losses had not been slight.

Æthelred had gone to his hall in Lundenwic, and Ælfred had remained at the camp. The remainder of the grain had been gathered in, but now he must retain a strong presence north of Lundenwic until he and his son-in-law determined the best course of action. Lundenwic too housed a royal mint, Ælfred's largest, and so the richest in silver ingots. During the early years of his Kingship when he had need to pay thousands of pounds of silver to buy off the predations of the Danes, his coinage had been grievously debased. He had worked hard to restore its purity and value, and was not about to now surrender his chief minting works.

Two days after the failed action Ceric was invited to join the King and Prince for a ride along the banks of the Lyge. Ceric had not been called into the King's presence since the day he and Eadward had arrived. He could not think it a mark of any special merit; he had done nothing during the attack to distinguish himself, other than return alive. But then, he was Ælfred's godson, and was acting as Eadward's second in command; that might be enough.

When he arrived at the King's tent he was glad to spot Raedwulf on his black mare. The bailiff was always good company, and link as he was to Worr and Kilton, an important reminder of home. And Raedwulf had proven his ally in his suit of Ashild of Four Stones. The grassy sward of the river banks was broad enough for two men to ride side by side, and the King and Prince took up position in front, with Ceric and the bailiff behind. None of them spoke much. Raedwulf had been at the King's side when both Æthelred and Eadward had made their reports. But the bailiff now had interest in the account of Ceric, and of coming through the trees with his footmen. Ceric related what he could of that truncated experience. Raedwulf listened, largely in silence, allowing Ceric to tell what he wanted, and how he wanted it to be heard.

"It was the only battle without Worr by my side," he finished.

Raedwulf felt Ceric lucky to be alive, and could not regret that his son-in-law had missed the ill-Fated attempt.

He wished he could say that Ceric would soon be back at Kilton, enjoying the rest he so richly deserved, but he had foreboding that respite would again be delayed. Raedwulf himself, travelling almost without stopping with the King, had not been back to his hall in Defenas for ten months.

They both turned their attention to the King and Prince, riding just ahead of them. Eadward was on his grey, and the King a fine pale chestnut. Neither spoke, but just walked along in meditative silence. The day encouraged such; dry, warm, and with little breeze even by the river's edge.

Raedwulf, observing how straight was the King's head, gaze forward, knew these thoughtful moods. Fallen into one, Ælfred would forget to speak for long periods of time. The bailiff let his own eyes drop to the water, where dragonflies skimmed. The King stopped, and they all reined up in answer. Ælfred turned slightly in the saddle, gazing over the scarcely rippling water to the opposite bank. Then he turned his horse and rode back a short distance, passing the bailiff and Ceric as he did. He seemed now to scan both banks at once. The three joined him. The King's eyes had renewed sharpness, and his voice a new vigour.

"This is the narrowest point," he told them, gesturing to the Lyge. "A fort on either side will all but close the channel off. Keep them from their ships, and we keep them from Lundenwic. And we close off escape to the sea." He looked back at their faces. "We must start at once, today."

Start they did. Raedwulf and Ceric were given the task of overseeing work on the far bank, and Eadward on the near. The King summoned boats from Lundenwic with which to make the needed crossing, as men and materials both must be ferried across. They began that very day, marking off the land. Any fortified settlement, especially one built in a time of active trouble, always began by the building of the surrounding palisade, protecting those who worked within. Eadward had with his father overseen the building of many a fortified burh. Raedwulf had his own expertise, gleaned as observer of the King's work, and from his own efforts at his hall in Defenas. The King chose one hundred of his ablest men, and combined with the fittest of those of Eadward, two teams were formed. The tasks ahead were numerous and arduous; felling trees, digging out and setting up saw-pits, trenching out the ground to hold the timber uprights, helping the King's smiths to set up forges so they might hammer out rivets, strapping, and hinges.

Six days passed in a whirlwind of such labour. The King kept close watch on the Danes, sending his scouts each dawn to observe their fort. After the burning of their dead, the scouts heard the sounds of normal activity coming from behind the palisade, and even could spy the watch-men themselves at times as they stood upon the parapet. But on the seventh day, gaining their vantage point, the scouts were greeted by silence. They stood a long time before approaching nearer. Nothing. Stranger still, one half of the broad gate was cracked eerily open.

Daring greatly, a scout shot an arrow over the top of the timber wall, to land within. There was no response, no hue nor cry. The Danes were gone. They had abandoned their newly built fort. One of the scouts swam across the water to walk along the other side, shaking his head at what he saw. They had even forfeited their ships.

Nearly a score of their ribbed-hulled drekars sat stranded on the bank, or nodded with the gentle action of the river. Having earlier explored the Lyge the scouts knew why. The narrowness of the flow from its headwaters would not allow them to long follow its source.

The news was almost confounding. When told it, Ælfred called for his son, and for Raedwulf and Ceric. Æthelred had already been summoned, and the five men met in the King's tent, under its double-peaked roof. They sat about the trestle table, Ælfred on the sole chair, the rest on benches.

"Why," asked the King. He scanned the faces around him for answer.

Ceric, having been in the thick of discovery during the assault, would offer his thoughts.

"We saw ourselves how good their own scouts are," he told the King. "They had watchers who spied our coming well before we arrived. They were ready for us, and waiting in the wood." He went on before the scene of his death-dealing amongst the trees took hold in his mind.

"Their scouts have come down the river under cover of night, or at dawn, and seen the two forts being raised."

Raedwulf took up the thread from the skein. "And realized they were trapped. They could not sail out, so they decamped on foot."

As a deterrent the King's idea had worked no slight wonder. The Danes were not only stopped from sailing to Lundenwic and its mint, they had vanished entirely.

"To where, and to what," Ælfred mused.

It was a question without answer, but the Prince would try to learn.

"I am going after them," he said.

He looked to his father, who nodded assent.

Eadward went on. "These Danes, building as near as they did to Lundenwic, must have been well-supplied. Their confidence tells me they are close to Haesten. Find them, and we may find him."

Ceric found words rising to his lips.

"I will come," he told Eadward.

"I want you there," the Prince responded. "I will wager we are headed north, perhaps deep into Anglia. You have been there."

Ceric had a sole request. "But my men – many of them are boys. I would have them sent home."

The Prince looked again to his father.

"I will see they have escort," Ælfred granted.

Eadward went on. "They have served well. I have a portion of silver for each, and for the folk of those you have lost."

Eadward spoke to his father. "I want a small troop only, thirty of us. That will give me riders to send back, as we learn more." He would keep his key body-guards on, but asked for fresh men to fill out his ranks. Eadward had inherited his father's skill of sizing up the fitness of his men, watching particularly when they were at ease to gauge if they had the bodily and mental toughness to continue on.

Æthelred spoke now. There was a hurried, even brusque quality to his speech, an almost rapid-fire report in contrast to the King's thoughtful considerations. The assault had cost Æthelred precious men, yet he was left with a newly-built fort. The Danes had not fired it as their parting act; to do so would have called instant attention to their departure, and increased the chances that they would be at once tracked.

"My men will claim the ships," the Lord of Mercia began. "Any still sound they will sail down to Lundenwic. The unseaworthy will be broken up and sunk. I will garrison the fort they left us."

There had been rare recompense from repelling the Danes; now Mercia would also gain in the ships that made them so dangerous a foe.

The Prince excused himself so that he and Ceric could begin their preparations. Once outside the tent with Ceric, Eadward spoke again.

"If we find Haesten . . . " he posed.

He shook his head, thinking on it. He had captured Haesten's wife and young sons, only to have them returned by his father without demand of ransom. It had been far from the desired result. The rich trophy was no trophy to the King, but a man's wife and young boys, which need be released to their husband and father with speed and dignity. Eadward had expected the King to award him some large sum of silver or even of gold, of which he would keep half and share out the rest amongst his men.

No reward was forthcoming. Now Eadward was asking his best men to again join him on what might not only prove a fruitless mission, but excelled the first in danger, as he felt certain much of their time would be spent in Anglia, held by the Danes.

At least he felt assured the result would be far different, should he capture Haesten.

They could never take such a war-lord with so small a troop. But one could never tell when any commander might be lightly guarded and vulnerable. Eadward himself was now setting off with only thirty men. They might catch Haesten in similar circumstances. To bring home the great prize of the man himself would be to possibly end the entire conflict.

Barring the war-lord's outright death or capture, if they discovered which fortress he had made his head-quarters, it would go a long way to directing further efforts. Even returning with tidings of how it truly fared with Haesten would be worth the having.

Ceric was struck by all these fleeing Danes had abandoned. "These men have no horses. They came by ship, and have been forced to leave them behind. Anglia is rich in horses. They will be stealing all they can."

Saying this, he could not but help think of Four Stones.

ALWAYS
READY TO DIE

ÆLFRED had not been to Kilton for over a year. The eldest son thereof had been kept in the field by Eadward for seven months. The King must go to the sea-girt fortress. He had need to visit the families of all the burhs of Wessex, that they might know their monarch, and the bonds of fealty be renewed. He needed their loyalty as much as they required his protection. With a burh such as Kilton, the bonds were of long duration. Godwulf of Kilton had been the great friend and brother-in-arms of his father, Æthelwulf. The Lady Modwynn, Godwulf's widow, had been almost as a second mother to Ælfred when he and his brothers were boys. Her oldest son, Godwin, had proved a superior warrior, and unshakable in daring. Her younger son, Gyric, had fought alongside Ælfred when he himself had been Prince. Ælfred never forgot that Gyric had served himself up as decoy to the Danes, drawing the heat of battle away from the Prince and his body-guard, and allowing himself to be captured in his stead.

Ælfred, and Kilton, had lost Gyric and then Godwin, the younger brother blinded out of spite, the elder fallen prey to the Dane Sidroc on the distant island of Gotland. The sons of the hall were now Ceric and Edwin. They had both come of age in a time of war, as had Godwin and Gyric. The King, approaching Kilton, considered the undulating rhythm of the conflict with the Danes. It had ruled every aspect of his life, and was likely to do so for that of his son, and the sons of Kilton.

He had left the rest of his fyrd back in Witanceaster, and travelled with just a small detachment comprised of his personal body-guard. Raedwulf, the Bailiff of Defenas, rode at his right side. Ælfred had sent two men ahead to warn Kilton of his near arriving. On an afternoon marked by its calm Summer fairness, the King advanced at a steady walk through the outlying pasturelands. The horn of a ward-corn in a tower perch hidden by trees sounded, letting all know the royal party was nearly upon the burh.

An answering horn rang out from Kilton's ramparts upon the timber palisade. Edwin, in his finest clothes, stood before the opened gates to meet the King and his retinue. He was flanked by his grandmother, Modwynn, and his mother, Edgyth. Standing off to one side was Raedwulf's daughter, Wilgyfu, and her husband, Worr, the horse-thegn of Kilton. At that second horn blast the folk of the village of Kilton left what they were doing, and lined the road to see their King. A cheer went up for him, cries of "Ælfred" and "Wessex," to which Ælfred lifted his hand. The glad faces of the family of the hall were before him as well. Sometimes his own folk looked at him warily; his men needed constant feeding and this is why he must shift that burden from burh to burh with frequent travelling amongst them. This greeting from

Kilton was genuine. His departure might be regarded far more ruefully.

As the day was a fine one, the welcome-cup of brown and frothy ale was taken in the garden. A tall wooden framework had been placed there long ago, and was thickly grown with roses and twining flowers. It lent beauty and fragrance, and gave some shelter from the oft sharp wind that could sheet across the sea waves below. Seated at the pavilion table now were Ælfred and Raedwulf, Edwin, the young Lord of Kilton, and the two ladies of the hall. Modwynn and Edgyth had known some trepidation in anticipating the King, concerning what news he might bear of Ceric. Their fears were largely set aside when first they glimpsed Ælfred's face. His was not the demeanor of a bearer of tragic news. Still, they were more than glad when the King himself began their converse about Kilton's oldest son. He had left Ceric in good health and spirits, and the news that he continued to distinguish himself at the side of Prince Eadward was welcome indeed.

These assurances over, the King fell into that easy silence that those yearning for peace often crave. Both Modwynn and Edgyth could not help but note the great weariness in his face. The dark circles under his eyes told of many a sleepless night, and the once-fair skin was mazed and browned from being out in all weathers. Modwynn lifted the beaker, one of costly glass, and refilled the ale in his cup. He smiled at her.

"There is something about Kilton. It is part of my boyhood, and separate from war. Here on this cliff was always a sense of refuge from strife." Those tired eyes held true affection for the Lady of Kilton. "And you were here."

Modwynn gave a gentle and self-dismissive laugh. Yet she too had strong and fond memories of those early days, when Ælfred and her own sons were boys, and she herself so young.

Ælfred went on. "My father and Godwulf, they were almost as brothers."

She nodded. "Godwulf's friendship with your father was one of the joys of his life, and made service to him no burden." She gave a gentle sigh, and placed her hand on his own. "You are in my prayers at every evening, and every dawn, as well."

The King smiled, then turned his head across the garden to the stone chantry. "I will give greeting to Godwulf now," he told her, and rose to go to the church.

Edgyth too rose, for there was much to oversee for the coming feast. Edwin, remembering that his grandmother had long acquaintance with the bailiff and might now wish a private word with him, also excused himself. He had said almost nothing in the presence of the King, as he felt was fitting. Once they had heard Ceric lived, the greatest reason for the King's visit had vanished. Perhaps he did crave a few days of rest.

As Edwin left, both Raedwulf and Modwynn looked after him.

"He grows well," Raedwulf judged. "He is, I would reckon, taller than Ceric."

"Ceric favours his mother," Modwynn agreed, with a smile of her own. "But I am glad you approve of Edwin. He is all we could hope for."

The bailiff had turned his eyes back to the sweep of sea before him. "I have not seen the King so at ease, for many a week," he admitted.

"I am ever glad to see my King, and to see you, my friend," she told the bailiff. "I know now that Ceric lives, and serves well. Tell me what more you can."

The bailiff smiled. "It is a tale of perpetual wandering," he answered. "Just as Eadward has not returned to Witanceaster, and has kept Ceric from returning here, so has the King been endlessly on the move, riding after the enemy, seeking provisions, shoring up failing defences, or worse, flagging spirits."

Raedwulf himself had returned only once during the past twelve-month to Defenas. He had journeyed there to act in his role of bailiff, passing judgement on a pressing case which could not be resolved by the lord of the local burh. It was a visit so brief Raedwulf was denied the pleasure of sleeping in his own hall before he must return to the King.

The afternoon was advancing. Raedwulf had given his daughter a single embrace and a hurried kiss. Now he would have time to see her, speak with Worr, and hold his little grandsons.

Modwynn stopped him a moment longer by saying the next. "If you had news of Four Stones I know you would share it," she murmured.

He must sigh at these words. She could not know how much he yearned for positive report from that keep.

"Nothing of substance. Hrald continues to resist the considerable pressure he must feel to join with either Haesten or Guthrum's son, Agmund, in their plans to carve up Anglia, or conquer it whole."

She nodded in gratitude. "So Four Stones holds firm," she summed.

The stillness and the beauty of the place, and the thoughtfulness of her tone, opened a door for his own thoughts, to which he gave voice. It was neither question nor statement, rather admission of what lay deep within him.

"The Lady thereof," he told her. "Ælfwyn of Cirenceaster."

He said no more.

Modwynn looked fully at him, the strong chin dimpled with its cleft, the dark and wavy hair, slightly tousled as it curled over his ears. His eyes, blue and deep of expression. For all the softness of his words it was a declaration of love, no less than that.

Modwynn, watching that face, understood his quietness. "Yes," she said in answer.

She knew his hall in Defenas had never known a mistress. His wife Leofgyfu, Wilgyfu's mother, had died long before he had been awarded the land by the King. At last he pictured another woman to share his life there, when peace allowed.

"May God grant you life to win the woman you love," she said. "Such will give you even more reason to live."

He gave a slight shake to his head, as if his desires had overstepped the boundaries of the possible. His answer, firm and warm, grasped both public duty and private dream.

"I am always ready to die. I must be. But I am always eager to live," he said in ending.

〽〽〽〽〽〽〽〽〽

The King was met at the door of the stone chapel by the priest of Kilton, Dunnere. The priest was of Welsh parentage, and spoke and wrote that strange tongue. He had in the past been a help to the King when he need convey written messages to Welsh kings and princes, during both times of peace and conflict with that war-like folk.

They nodded to each other, acknowledgment of the Earthly and heavenly realms to which they were attached. Dunnere pulled open the door for the King, then slipped inside behind him to stand silently by, ready if needed to provide ghostly comfort to the monarch.

Ælfred crossed himself and took the space in. He had never entered this chantry without the scent of incense wafting to his nostrils; the very walls, hard and cold stone as they were, seemed to carry the whiff of sandalwood and copal. It added to the timelessness of the small space, and added to what felt a sense of almost formlessness, as if the thick walls might melt into a mist of precious smoke.

He moved to the altar to stand before the grey slab of flooring under which Godwulf was laid. He looked down at it, and its simple inscription, summing up the life of the man:

> Godwulf
> Ealdorman of Wessex
> Lord of Kilton

Ælfred spoke to the dead lord, not in words, but in thought. It was a kind of communing he practised more and more with his own lost kin, and with friends he had cherished, and the old lord had been one of these. Then he lifted his eyes.

A shaft of sunlight pierced the casement opposite, to rest on the painted statue of St Ninnoc, standing on a stone base projecting from the wall. He recalled another use of this name. Ninnoc had been the name of Gyric's little daughter, she who had died when he did, carried off by the fever. The wide eyes of the statue seemed to call to him. Those bright blue eyes made fine contrast to Ninnoc's wooden gown. It was painted red, its artfully carved folds resembling draped cloth. He went to it. Something about the face stirred his memory. Who rose in his mind was the wife of Gyric, Ceridwen, daughter of Cerd. Save for the eyes, the statue was like her; or she had been like this statue. Perhaps that was why the lost child had been named Ninnoc. He drew even closer. He saw two finger rings of gold laying there on the base, at the statue's feet, in Offering to the saint. Small as they were, he had not noticed them on prior visits. Gazing on them now, he felt assured they were those of Gyric and Ceridwen.

Where was she now, Ceridwen, daughter of Cerd, once Ceridwen of Kilton? He knew she dwelt in the Baltic, with the man who had been Jarl of Four Stones. She had left fine sons behind.

The Sun had just risen, and thin clouds of rosy pink streaked the sky above the sparring ground in Kilton's yard. Edwin had ceded the treasure room to the King, and Raedwulf and the King's two chief body-guards had slept within. Edwin had spent the night in the hall with the rest of his men. He was now out on the training ground, sparring with Eorconbeald and Alwin under the watchful eyes of Cadmar. Despite the lateness of the hour at which Worr had stayed up talking with his father-in-law, he too was there. This morning Worr was facing Eorconbeald, and Edwin, Alwin, as they practised their spear-work.

Cadmar watched both pairs from the bench, calling out words of advice or jeering taunts as warranted. A man now made his way from the hall towards them. So engaged were the warriors that it took a moment to recognize Ælfred's presence. Seeing the King, Eorconbeald froze for a moment, which gave Worr the opportunity to deliver a lesson. It came in the form of a solid touch with his spear-point to that captain's right knee. In battle it would be a crippling blow.

"One instant of distraction will cost you your leg," Worr told him. He was grinning as he said it, but the message was none the less grave for that.

As the King approached, Cadmar too recognized who he was, and rose.

"Sit, sit, old friend," the King told him, coming to join him.

As they lowered themselves to the bench, Ælfred added with a smile, "Our bones deserve it." As he settled on the wooden seat he gave the warrior-monk a pat on the thigh.

Edwin had feared this moment, though it had always awaited him. Here was come the King, to see him spar. He had suffered Worr's chastisements too many times to break his efforts with Alwin. He must bring the action to a satisfying conclusion, preferably by disarming his opponent in front of the King, before he could make reverence to the monarch for whom he would fight. The Lord of Kilton was now eighteen, both taller and broader of shoulder than Alwin, but the older man, nimble and sure-footed, was a shrewd spear-man. Alwin had also something to prove, and was known as a showy fighter. The greatest spectator of all was now before him.

For his part Ælfred wished to discomfort neither young man. He trusted that Edwin had been well trained. He could assume that at this young age he would have raw strength and little finesse. But that he would gain. The King was more interested in the kind of man Edwin would become, and whether he already possessed in some measure those traits of self-sacrifice, courage, humility, and obedience demanded by his role in life.

Cadmar moved his head closer to his bench mate.

"He will, I think," Cadmar judged, "turn a savvy warrior. He has already learnt much in reading his opponent."

"Comes from good blood-stock for that," Ælfred said with approval. He studied the young Lord, noted the supple strength in his wrists and arms as he moved shield to block and spear to thrust. "Quick with his hands, as well."

The King continued to survey all four at their spear-play. "Worr, I know well," he told Cadmar. "The other two?"

"Eorconbeald, facing Worr, is the captain of Edwin's body-guard. Alwin, facing Edwin, is his second."

"Thus his best men," the King summed.

"They are able enough."

At this point Alwin proved it, by a rapid-fire advance with his shield-arm, which allowed him to make it past the tip of Edwin's spear, leaving him defenceless.

Any other day Edwin would have given a howl and a pointed oath at this conclusion. This morning he was forced to simply nod his concession to Alwin, and bow his head to his watching King.

Ælfred stood up at this. He nodded in acknowledgement at the men now facing him, the butts of their spears set upon the ground, the shafts held at arm's length from their bodies in their extended grasp. Then he turned back to their trainer.

"You have done well, Cadmar," he told the old monk. "As I knew you would."

That afternoon Ælfred asked to see Modwynn and Edgyth. The King came to Modwynn's bower house, where she had oftentimes met with Raedwulf. The King was alone, for he had already discussed the matter at hand with the bailiff. Modwynn welcomed him within the bower, one adorned in that simple but rich taste expressive of every work of her hand. Her bed, though narrow, had an understated opulence in its furnishings. A twill-woven spread in subtly harmonizing shades of pale greys lay upon it. The fineness of the thread and density of its weaving gave it a pearl-like lustre when viewed from certain angles. A length of cloth ran down the middle of the table, its long fringed ends spilling down either side. It was of old silk, light green in hue, with a watery variation in its colour which gave life to the fabric, as pattern-welding gives life to steel.

A small silver ewer filled with mead sat upon the table. Edgyth had the honour of pouring out for the King, her mother-in-law, and then herself. Modwynn had several blown glass cups carried from the Rhineland, fashioned by those folk who excelled at making such things, and was glad to bring them out now. Their clarity served to showcase the golden mead swirling behind their clear walls.

Ælfred wished to tell the two women, privately and first, of his decision.

"I would take Edwin with me. I want only him and his two closest men. And Worr."

Edgyth's pale cheek paled the further. This is what her son had been raised for, to protect Kilton and all Wessex in service of their King.

Both women knew Ælfred had lost important men. He had certain need of men of nobility in command, as young as Edwin was. And the King would not deplete Kilton's defensive force. He was leaving every other thegn and ceorl behind.

"Edwin will travel with me," Ælfred went on, a great but momentary assurance. "I may send him on to Eadward with some of my troops, if the Prince calls for reinforcements."

The women took this in and nodded, assured at least that Edwin would be exposed to dangers not much greater than the King and Prince both faced.

Unvoiced was the question of command in Edwin's absence. There was no way of knowing how long the young lord might be gone. Ceric, due back four months ago, still rode at the Prince's side. Edwin too might be called on for extraordinary duty; the times demanded it. Yet Modwynn had guided and guarded Kilton for long years when it was left Lord-less by Godwin's death. They had been years of mainly peace, but the many challenges of protection and management of resources had been hers.

With his next words Ælfred seemed to be thinking just this.

"I am well aware of the powers of a capable woman. My daughter Æthelflaed holds the vastness of the Mercian lands entrusted to her when her husband Æthelred is afield."

He considered them both, sitting across the table from him. "In you, Kilton has two women of wisdom."

Yet he must make offer, lest the task seem too onerous. "I could leave Worr with you; Raedwulf has offered him, knowing his devotion to Kilton."

Modwynn spoke, quietly but in earnest. "Worr has chafed each day, wanting to be at Ceric's side. His going with Edwin will be the next best thing."

"And you will need every man," Edgyth added. "We are well protected here, our men at the ready."

It was true that Kilton enjoyed rare privilege of position. With its back to the steep cliffs rising from the sea, and the knoll upon which it sat giving long views across the countryside, it was one of the most defensible burhs in the Kingdom. In dire need, Modwynn had a cousin in Sceaftesburh, a capable man of fifty years and still robust, whom she could call on. Yet Ælfred, thinking upon her relation, did not think him any more up to the task than she herself.

"Will you have Edwin brought, that I might tell him this," he now asked.

Edwin appeared. When the serving woman conveyed the King had called for him, he feared it might be due to his shortcomings at the sparring session. This thought vanished when he saw she led him to his grandmother's bower house; the King would not chastise him before her. Some graver matter awaited; perhaps the King had need for more silver, or wanted some of Kilton's men. He was thus unprepared for Ælfred's opening words, sounded just after Edwin had completed his bow to him.

"You are riding with me, tomorrow, with Worr and your two chief body-guards. The rest of your forces will remain here, for Kilton's defence." A moment passed before Ælfred went on. "Or until called for."

Calling out Kilton's men would mean an action on a scale Edwin had only heard about, and never lived through.

But it was the first part of the command that Edwin latched upon. The King of Wessex wanted him.

"I thank you, my Lord," he said, trying not to stammer out his surprise. "I hope to repay your confidence in me."

He looked at his mother and grandmother, smiling at him. His mother had clasped her hands as if at prayer, a gesture he knew well, and her lips were pressed together to hold her smile there. Edwin could see her concern, even fear for him. The young Lord of Kilton had been called to watch and learn, at the very side of the King. He realized now this was why Ælfred had come. He had come for him. He felt deeply honoured that the King himself had done so, and not merely sent a courier to summon him.

Edgyth walked to him now, and embraced him. "Come," she told him, in a voice as strong as she could muster, "we must ready you." She turned to Ælfred and curtsied, as Edwin bowed.

Now alone with Modwynn, the King considered how many like partings she had endured. She had experienced this pride and fear every time Godwulf had left to fight alongside his own father, or her sons Godwin and Gyric had taken up their tours in the fyrd of Wessex; then with Ceric her grandson, and now Edwin. Those remaining at the gate must have abundant store of their own courage to withstand it. He knew such from his own partings from Eadward.

He would leave her now to her own thoughts. He took stock of the room once more, and of how well it told of her nature.

The loom against the wall had escaped his eye when he entered, for it had been warped, but stood empty of any weft. Near it upon the floor a kind of frame held a large, partially folded piece of linen, riotously embroidered along the edges with trailing vines and blooming flowers. He went to it. It was marvelously worked. A needle charged with blue thread was stuck into the cloth, waiting to be again taken up.

She smiled. "My shroud. Edgyth drew this all."

She touched her long and graceful fingers to the cloth in near-caress. The affection she had for her daughter-in-law was reflected in the way she regarded their joint work. "I have nearly finished the last of the thread-work."

Ælfred looked back at her. She had named this final garment so lightly, almost as the mildest of jests.

He knew his wife was privately working on his own. The soberness of his answer was token of his own affection for this noble woman.

"I pray it is long before it is needed."

As mother and son were walking to the hall, Eorconbeald and Alwin called out in high spirits to Edwin. Worr had told them of their mission, and they too were headed to the hall to pack their kit.

Beneath her own smile Edgyth, gazing on the beaming faces of these three young men, had to sigh. How eager they were for adventure, to ride into danger and perhaps death.

Edwin's two chief body-guards began rooting through their alcoves, while he and his mother stepped inside the treasure room. They began the task of selecting and laying out clothing and kit. Edgyth was practised in this, having packed many a saddle bag for Godwin, and Edwin went with a kind of glee from chest to chest with her. He would take full weaponry, a healthy store of silver, and two horses with him. He thought of which horses to choose as he stuffed tunics into a leathern bag. His mother stood next him, carefully smoothing layers of a bedroll. Questioning himself about his horses, he was of a sudden struck by a thought.

Begu.

He must ride to her now, and tell her of his leaving.

"I . . . I must go and arrange for my horses," he told his mother. She smiled wistful assent as he hurried from the room.

He told the stablemen he would need his chestnut stallion in the morning, and to ask Worr to choose the best pack animal for him. Then he swung his leg over his sorrel gelding and trotted out the gate. Once free of the sight of the walls, he pressed the animal forward.

He saw Begu two and sometimes three nights a week. Her presence in his life was become an open secret, spoken of by none but privately understood by all. Even Modwynn and Edgyth knew of it, and questioning Worr were glad to hear of her kind nature and constancy. Edwin continued in his delight of her, bringing her an ever-growing stock of silver coinage, small furs, and cloth from the store of Kilton, woven long ago in Frankland and sitting untouched in a chest of the treasure room. At the same time his understanding of her role in his life had deepened. He no longer expected her to appear at the Mid-Summer fire and dance with him, as he had desired the first year of their acquaintance. He understood she served a certain and important role in his life, as she had for Ceric. Once he was wed she must cease to be a part of his life.

He did not give thought to Begu's future; he could not guess what that might be, just as he could guess only imperfectly at his own. They each had their role to play. He knew he had enriched her greatly in material goods and been as kind to her as he knew to be.

Engaged as he would be in warfare, he might not live long. If he died without issue Kilton would likely be forfeit to the King. For this and many other reasons he was keen to meet the maid he would wed. He looked forward to that day, not only for his own sake, but to see what would come of it for Kilton, and his bride's own burh, or kingdom, for it was not out of the question he marry a noblewoman of Mercia or even Wales.

But just now, today, it was Begu to whom he must bid fare-well.

When he arrived at her hamlet he need not even ride to her house. Begu was standing at the common well, lowering a wooden bucket into its depths, another bucket at her feet.

There was an older woman waiting there, and cottars too abroad in their vegetable plots. As Edwin reined up he saw them nod, or cast their eyes downward in respect. The woman standing near the well dipped her skirts, and stepped back. They had rarely seen the Lord of Kilton in daylight, and now fell away from him in deference. He was left in his own light, one shared by she he had come to see.

Her face lit when she saw him, and at the smile on his own. He was off his horse in a moment, and took the first bucket, which she had nearly hauled up, from her hand. He set it down and lowered the second for her. He pulled that up, nearly brimful, and took the bail of each in hand. The reins of his horse were still over the animal's neck, and she made a slight gesture towards it, as if she should lead him. She was a little afraid of horses; he knew this, and he smiled at her the more. "No need," he assured her. "He will follow us."

They walked, the three of them, the short distance to Begu's tiny house, Edwin holding the buckets carefully level, Begu at his side, and the sorrel nosing behind them. He carried the water into her work yard and set the buckets on the stone pavers laid by the cooking ring.

He dried his hands by wiping them on his leggings. He could not tell his news without a grin.

"Ælfred is here," he began, which gave her a slight start. "At Kilton. He came for me."

She took a breath.

"The King . . . came for you?"

"Yes. I will ride with him, tomorrow."

"Tomorrow," she breathed back.

So she was forced to hear this again. He rode on the morrow, into mortal danger. She might not see him again. She steadied herself, and took what comfort she could. She did not love Edwin as she did his brother. Yet it was impossible not to care for him, and care she did.

"I have little time," he was saying now, glancing to where his loose horse was pulling leaves from a shrub. "But I wanted to tell you, of course."

"Of course," she echoed. Her small white hand lifted to her eye. One of the curls of her hair was near it, masking the act of wiping away a tear blearing her vision.

"I have brought you no silver," he confessed. "I wish I had."

Her fair cheek coloured. "There is no need," she murmured.

He thought of this, remembering how Ceric, set to ride out with the Prince, had asked him to give Begu fifty silver pieces if he died. He did not like to think of that now, nor of how he had leapt up at his brother's words, denying that this could befall him. He could not think of himself dying, not on his first tour of duty. If he did, he trusted Ceric would make good the same gift for her, in his name.

"Will you see your brother?" she asked.

"I do not know. Ceric is off with Eadward, where I would like to be, chasing Haesten."

"You will be with the King," she reminded. It was gently voiced, like so much she said.

He had to admit this was best of all. "Yes," he said, and kissed her. "I will be with the King."

❧❧❧❧❧❧❧❧❧❧

The next morning the hall of Kilton was early astir. The meal that broke the night's fast was of extra hardiness, as bulwark to those who would ride, and those who must stay behind. The kitchen yard had as well generously reprovisioned the saddle bags of Ælfred's men.

Modwynn's fare-well to Edwin, given in her bower house, was difficult, but Edgyth's fare-well to her son was wrenching. Edgyth could scarcely speak, so full was her heart. Even the smile upon his young face occasioned more pain, for the innocence she saw there. As Edwin stood before her in his fine war-kit, she was struck by how much like Godwin he was. It felt the opening of a doubled flood-gate, of paired love and loss.

He had nearly forgotten the golden dragon pennon she had made for him after he was named Lord of Kilton. It was entirely the work of her hands, from the spinning of the linen, its weaving, and then the coloured thread-work she lavished upon it, delineating the proud beast, claws extended, flying through the air. She had it ready for him, and he once more exclaimed over it, then rolled it carefully up to place with his kit.

Before the hall the forecourt was crowded with men and horses. Modwynn and Edgyth stood to one side, their eyes filled with images of Edwin, of the King, of stamping horses restless to make a start. Dunnere the priest would give a final blessing to those departing, and was even now walking amongst them, ready with holy oil. Worr was there, standing by his horse, Wilgyfu at his side. She held their youngest son and the second was in Worr's arms, while the eldest boy was at his grandfather's side. Raedwulf said his fare-wells and left Worr and his family the last few moments alone.

Ælfred was not yet horsed. He watched Eorconbeald and Alwin lead their mounts from the paddock rail, where they had finished saddling them. Edwin stood there between his laden pack horse and his chestnut stallion, and was himself tightening his saddle animal's girth. Cadmar was with him, saying little, just watching in that way that bore witness to something that might be momentous. Edwin saw the King gesture to his two body-guards.

The two came before the King and bowed their heads. In their full war-kit they made fine show, steel helmets glinting as the rays of the Sun struck them, ring-shirts gleaming over their tunics of leather. The painted shields on their backs were boldly coloured in red and white and green and blue. They had the free and easy manner of good fighters heading out to win fame, and battle-gain.

Ælfred studied them for a long moment before he spoke, a pause that as it wore on, made the young men more than a trifle uneasy. Then the King lifted his eyes to the Lord of Kilton standing at the paddock, before fixing them again on the body-guards. His voice was unhurried, his tone low, and the gravity of his message unmistakable.

"Edwin and you now become part of my own body-guard, giving Edwin the greatest protection I can afford him. Your duty to him alone is foremost." His eyes had not left their faces, shifting slowly from one to the other.

"Our lives are ever in the hands of God," he went on.

Each of them could guess what the following words might be. The King's eyes settled on Alwin.

"But the Lord of Kilton must not die."

It was not quite reproach, but it was near. There was to be no showing off at Edwin's expense, or for personal gain. It was reminder that they must sacrifice themselves so that the young lord would live. They nodded their heads with lowered eyes. Ælfred left them to go to his horse.

Edwin had watched all, without hearing any of it. He walked to the two, leading his horse.

"What secret did the King give you," he asked, almost teasing them in his tone.

Eorconbeald did not grin back. "No secret. A mere reminder of the danger we go into, and our pledge."

Edwin cocked his head to the side. There must have been more.

Alwin looked at him, and answered. "I will be dead before they get to you." He gave a laugh at his own words.

One must laugh, saying such a thing. At times one needed to both affirm and dismiss the seriousness of a given role. Eorconbeald too was now grinning.

Edwin alone did not laugh. He thought, This is what it means to be Lord. This man Alwin will stand before me, saying my life is worth more than his.

It made him shake his head. Dunnere preached that every soul weighed the same in the eyes of God. Here on Earth the scales were always tipped.

Before the four riding from Kilton climbed into their saddles, Dunnere made the sign of the cross on their brows with holy oil, blessing each and asking that God receive their souls. The men placed their helmets back on their heads, mounted their horses and took their places. All the hall and yard cheered them through the gates, and again the cottars of the village lined the road to see their King and now their Lord ride off. The four blended seamlessly into Ælfred's troops, save that this time Edwin was at the left side of the King.

Cadmar was ready. At dusk he mounted his horse, and with two saddlebags tied firmly behind him, trotted out the gate. The old warrior-monk was known at times to take himself off to Kilton's forests. There he would make sylvan retreat, for a period of silent reflection and prayer. The guards letting him out thought nothing of it.

Instead he made after the King's troop. He was of no high use to Kilton. He was no leader of men; his life whether as thegn or monk had been one of obedient service, not command. His devotion to the Lady of Kilton ran deep, but he would not be of any material help to her. He might, though, be of real aid to Edwin.

He left a message with a serving boy, asking him to on the morrow tell Modwynn, "Forgive me, Lady. I ride in the name of your grandson, that he might live and return to you."

I WILL COME
BACK TO YOU

Anglia

CERD took toddling steps towards his mother, ending in a run. His dimpled face was framed by curls of reddish-gold, and his nose, small as it was, promised the fine shape of his father's. His skin had the same fair tint as did that of Ceric. Only in the child's eyes could Ashild see something of herself. Her boy's were not the golden-green of his father, nor the grey-blue of her own. They were dark blue, flecked generously with green, the iris rimmed with grey. They had the calmness of his father's eye colouration, but the flash and storm of her own.

Cerd had also her temper. He was a laughing and lively child, but should anything frustrate him his small hands would curl into fists, the rosy cheeks redden, and the plump little feet stamp angrily upon the planked floors of Ashild's house, or even the stones of the hall. He would wail, a pitch beginning at a low howl and rising to a shriek. His mother would look down at him and think,

I know what it is to feel that way. Burginde would laugh at him, sweeping him up into her arms and holding him aloft to sail around with him in the air until he began chortling with her. He was active in body, a little slow to talk, though Ælfwyn and Burginde reminded her it was generally so with boys. Cerd's attachment to his mother was as strong as hers to him. His smile for her when he patted her face was one that caused his blue-green eyes to crease shut in pleasure. For Ashild's part she could imagine standing over him like a she-wolf, snapping to ward off any comers attempting to harm her helpless pup.

Today he and Ashild were in the weaving room together, surrounded by her female kin. Ashild caught him up in one arm and praised him for carrying to her the spindle she had asked him for. Cerd placed the round tip of it in his mouth before surrendering it to her outstretched hand with a laugh.

Ashild and Cerd now slept in the small house Asberg had built years ago for her aunt, Æthelthryth. Ashild had lived there for years with her aunt and uncle, and now they were at Turcesig it was become the home of both she and her son. Sleeping there spared her mother and Burginde the child's fretful cries at night, though the way they both doted on him it was clear no sacrifice was too great.

Ashild took Cerd almost everywhere with her around hall and precincts. He had even been atop a horse with her. She had climbed upon her white stallion and had Byrgher, one of her brother's men, hand the child up to her, his little booted feet gleefully drumming upon the saddle pommel. Byrgher laughed. "In two years you will be searching out a pony for him," he predicted. Byrgher was a family man, a favoured companion of Asberg, and had flanked her with Asberg when they charged from the gates of Oundle to defend it.

The boy was the pride of Four Stones. When Ashild felt strong enough after his birth to take her meals with all, her brother invited her to sit at the high table, next their mother. She had her newborn babe in arms when he told her this, and was struck by the offer. She saw that returning to the women's table as a mother would be wrong; it was for unwed maids and young girls. Within the hall married women and widows always sat at the table of male kin. Hrald was tacitly honouring the supposed marriage between her and Ceric which Burginde had been so good at suggesting. She came to the high table that night, her babe tied in a sling at her side, like any other young married woman. For her and her babe to be welcomed this way by her brother, to sit before all next her mother and amongst Hrald's best warriors was more than a sign of her changed estate. It was a marked sign of esteem. It was granted for her status as peace-weaver with one of the most powerful families of Wessex, a recognition of the treaty between Hrald's part of Anglia and the land Ceric of Kilton had been born into. She knew this, but it did not rankle her as it might have in the past. Her child was a child of Wessex, as well as Anglia. Just as meaningful to those who filled Hrald's hall was the fact that she was Yrling's daughter, and here was Yrling's heir, in the hall he had won. Until Hrald had a son of his own, future hope could rest in this tiny babe, under her arm.

Ashild brought Cerd with her to the high table every night. He would suckle heartily beforehand, and often slept throughout the noise of the meal. But he was there, a son of the hall, just as she was a daughter of the hall. After Cerd was weaned and began to feed himself with help, he sat on Burginde's lap at the women's table. There a laughing Ealhswith kept his fists full of bread while he crowed for more.

The Jarl of Four Stones took delight in his nephew. When Cerd attempted to say his uncle's name, it came out like a growl, which made Hrald laugh. It was at times hard for him to look at the child without thinking that he himself might have been made a father by now. The few months with his wife seemed a dream which he was always pushing back, and not wanting to remember. Indeed, after the wounding first days following Hrald's return from Oundle, Dagmar was never spoken of in the hall. Their union had been brief, no child had resulted, and she had been cast out in shame. The advent of Ashild's babe shifted the eyes of all to her, and the fine son she had brought forth. It was needful and even joyous distraction in a troubling time.

Hrald gave no thought to another wife. Such would emerge one day, he hoped, but he was in no eagerness to place himself again in the way of such dire harm.

⁂

Just past Mid Summer one of the serving folk from the foundation of Oundle arrived at the gates of Four Stones. He was mounted on one of Oundle's two cart horses, and rode saddleless, but with much of the animal's harness upon its back. Like all visitors during this time of heightened caution, he had been met and escorted by three of the watch-men along the road. He bore a letter for Hrald.

Two monks lately come from Wessex had carried the missive to the Abbess. Hrald had no idea what it was, pressed flat between thin slats of wood. He untied the leathern cord securing it. The letter was a single sheet of parchment, a scrap really, which had never been folded, and bore no sign of sealing wax. His eyes skipped at once to the bottom.

Ceric. He must have written it in haste, and on the road. He had dated it, Near the Octave Day of Easter. That was eight days following that high holy feast, a full four months ago. Hrald read it standing there in the hall yard, then went looking for his sister.

He found her by the washing shed near the kitchen yard, her son in a shallow bronze tub, splashing his open palms in the sudsy water he sat in.

Ashild looked up at him, laughing at Cerd's play.

"A letter from Ceric," Hrald told her, as he held it out. "Just brought from Oundle, from two monks stopping there."

Ashild's intake of breath signalled her surprise. She wiped her hands on the apron panel of her gown, and took the leaf of parchment. She read it silently, her eyes slowly moving over Ceric's small and rounded words.

Near the Octave Day of Easter

HRALD – MY BROTHER

Would this scrap of parchment be me myself. Know that I am well and at Eadward's side. Hearing you and Four Stones are whole would be my greatest boon. All my effort is for Wessex, Kilton, and

Ashild. May we be granted Peace between our halls, forever.
CERIC OF KILTON

When she finished she lifted her eyes to Hrald. The letter said close to nothing, yet everything.

Her brother looked at her and said, "I know he will come, if he can."

She nodded, unable for the moment to speak. Ceric had held this parchment, inked these words, named his hopes. She was what he worked for.

Cerd had stopped in his splashing and sat looking up at her. Now he reached hands and arms out for the letter she held. Anything he grasped went straight to his mouth, something in this case she could not allow. She smiled and shook her head at him. The boy, denied the prize he sought, began to twist his face. His mother was quicker. She passed the parchment back to Hrald, then took a towel and stood her boy up in the water while she wrapped him.

"It is from your father," she said, and kissed Cerd on his rounded forehead. I pray you meet him soon, she added, silently.

The watchful wariness which had settled over Four Stones for so long had continued over the year and half since Cerd had been born. The needful tasks of running a fortress – meeting the demands of feeding, housing, and training many men – went on unabated month after month, as did the oversight of the village folk, and the vigilant protection of the boundaries of Four Stones' lands. Oundle and its safety was always a concern. As independent as Abbess Sigewif was, the foundation remained a prime target, and demanded a rotating troop of men garrisoned there to protect it. Yet both Summers since Ceric's last visit here had been fruitful ones. The granary stores were not swept of their last kernels before the new crop of oats, barley, and wheat was reaped. The flocks of sheep, always under Ælfwyn's ready care and management, grew steadily in quality of wool, milk, and meat. The upsets Four Stones had suffered receded, whether the ambush by starving renegades Hrald had been present at, the slaying of his three watch-men by Agmund's men, or the dismissal of the young Lady of Four Stones after a few short months of marriage.

The first of these mishaps had left the hall with an orphaned boy. It took a while before Hrald realised it was not the stableman Mul fostering the child Bork, but he himself. The boy lived with Mul's family, and his wife fed, dressed, and cared for Bork as if he were her own. But the boy's attachments were all to the Jarl and his mother. It was these who first struck him as sparing his life, and caring for him.

Since his coming to the hall Bork had shot up, his scrawny frame filling out, but the added flesh was barely able to keep up with his next growth spurt. Hrald had no idea of the boy's age in years. In some ways he seemed young, and in other ways, far older. Mul's wife, comparing him to her own boys, guessed him to be now of eleven or twelve years. Bork was become Hrald's shadow about the hall yards. Mul, understanding the boy's attachment, put him in sole charge of the Jarl's horses, a task that he took with the gravity it warranted. And taking the Abbess' counsel to heart, Hrald himself began to teach Bork to read and write. He gave the boy his old wax tablet and wooden stylus, and showed him first how to write his own name, both in the runes, and in the speech of Anglia as taught to him by his mother, then Wilgot the priest, and finally Sigewif. Bork took to it well enough; he had nimble fingers given to the plaiting of horses' manes, and with leather-working dies could stamp handsome patterns in the bridle leather and reins Hrald held. He remained a reticent child. He rarely smiled; there was a kind of silent urgency about him, but when praised with a word or two the narrow chest would expand with solemn pride.

Hrald remembered Dagmar studying the boy, and telling him Bork would do anything for Hrald, and for his mother. He did not like to recall his wife's time here at Four Stones, but felt she had been right in judging this. It felt a heavy charge.

Just within the Anglian border Edwin, Lord of Kilton, was headed for service under Prince Eadward. He had been sent by Ælfred to join his son in tracking down those Danes who had camped on the Lyge. Worr rode with him, and Edwin had his body-guards Eorconbeald and Alwin to augment his presence. A fourth man from Kilton had also made himself known. Cadmar had trailed behind the small body of men. On the third day out Cadmar announced himself at dawn by appearing on the opposite bank of the shallow stream by which they had camped.

The warrior-monk knelt at the edge of the water, washing himself as first Eorconbeald and then Edwin approached to do the same. The astonishment of the younger men was met by a shrugging lack of concern by the older, who merely looked over, grey hair dripping, and grinned. Ordering his return was out of the question, for at Kilton Cadmar occupied a special role. He was revered by Lady Modwynn, and held in the highest esteem by all. And as their battle trainer he was in fact a superior to all of them. For his part, Worr was happy to have Cadmar along. Worr was old enough to have strong memory of the man's fighting days, and recalled his cool detachment as a battle mate. His would be a steadying presence for the young lord.

As they broke their fast together Alwin had to tease Cadmar. They had all watched Ælfred's easy familiarity with the old man, and how the two had spoken together at the sparring ground.

"Here to be the King's eyes and ears, are you?" Alwin gibed.

Cadmar laughed and looked at Alwin, Eorconbeald, and then Edwin in turn. "No. Only my own, that my long training of you has not been in vain."

Edwin and his companions were escorted to the Prince by one of the men he had sent back to make report to the King. They followed the northerly route of the stream, which grew broad and active. Their days in the saddle were long, pressing their mounts to make up time to overtake the Prince. The many tracks left behind by Eadward's horses grew fresher. At dusk six days out they caught up to them. Late Summer as it was, darkness fell earlier each day, and the Prince and his men were already at their night's camp.

The escort held his brass horn to his lips. He blew the Prince's three-note call, signalling one of his own men had returned. After it sounded, Worr added the black-bird call he had oftentimes used with Ceric. At the signal horn all of Eadward's men had stood, eager to greet the returning messenger lest he carried news. He appeared, with five others, moving forward on their horses out of the gathering gloom. They came closer to where the small cooking fire burned, and quit their beasts.

Edwin scanned the faces as he approached. In the low light some were indistinct. He did not see his brother. Worr too was uneasy. He knew Ceric would have recognized his call and responded in kind. But the call of the blackbird went unanswered.

The Prince came forward. "My Lord," said Edwin, as he and his companions bowed their heads. Eadward's escort told of the King's request, that Edwin serve here on the hunt for Haesten. The Prince welcomed them, and had a special word for Worr. "You have been missed," he said.

This was high praise for Worr's tracking skills, but both he and Edwin could not hide their growing discomfort. Edwin was about to speak of it when Eadward read this in their questioning eyes.

"Ceric," he said. "He is well. He is serving as scout, riding ahead. We are keeping to the stream, and he will find us within a day or two."

They saw to their horses and then took their places round the cook fire. Edwin was grateful for the browis ladled out; he and those he arrived with were nearly out of provisions. The Prince and his troop had been able to keep themselves supplied by procuring what they could from local crofters they found along the way. It mattered not this was Danish Anglia; times were hard for all, and if a farm had a little grain or a few eggs to spare they would part with them for silver from the men of Wessex offering the metal.

The quiet over Four Stones was an uneasy one, but quiet nonetheless. It was shattered one day by the arrival on foot of an exhausted man, one who had been stationed at the landing port of Saltfleet. He had not even strength to enter the hall, but sunk down on a bench outside the stable, heaving great breaths as he gulped down dippersful of water and then the ale that was brought to him. Hrald, Jari, and Kjeld stood before him, with a growing number of others, including the older warrior, Byrgher. Ashild too was there, drawn by the uproar as she walked through the yard. The man's torn clothing and bleeding and scratched hands and face gave witness to the rough terrain he had travelled. He had in turn walked and run to Four Stones, telling that two war-ships of unknown Danes had appeared from around the sea promontory at Saltfleet, carrying two or threescore men to each ship. They were not Danes settled in Anglia; these were, by their speech, come from Dane-mark. They drew up to the wooden pier, and screaming out war-cries, began leaping to the planked surface, weapons in hand.

There was no question of the ten men stationed at the port holding the buildings. They ran for their lives into the woods, unable even to stop to catch their horses. They had been pursued, and the survivor knew some at least had been overtaken by the invaders; he could hear the oaths of his companions as they were caught. For fear of discovery he had forsaken any known road and come overland, through marsh and wood, to reach Four Stones again.

"Have any returned?" he asked. "Am I alone?"

The faces of those listening told him he was.

Saltfleet, the port that Sidroc had built, had fallen. Nine of Four Stones' men were missing, and likely dead. The outrage this sparked was instant and deep.

Hrald turned away from the returning man to face Jari.

"I will find them and fight them," Hrald said. His jaw was clenched and his words rippled with intent.

Jari's declaration was even more clear. "We will find them and kill them!"

Nearly all around them gave up a whoop of acclaim. Ashild alone was silent, watching them all.

Hrald felt a surge of energy coursing through his body. His anger at the destruction of his men and storming of his port was intense, and he fought to push it aside so his resolve was foremost. To lead with anger brought recklessness, and he could not afford to be reckless. His father had taught him this, as had Asberg. He must now ride to fight, not just to look and learn. He would find and battle this foe, as soon as all could be made ready.

Commands flew from his lips. He looked to Kjeld.

"Send two men to Asberg at Turcesig. Tell him to leave Styrbjörn in charge, and bring fifty men to Four Stones by tomorrow. Turcesig must ready for a siege."

They could not know what targets these invaders sought, but every fortified keep was a storehouse of both weaponry and silver, and must expect the attentions of raiders.

"Haward?" posed Jari.

Hrald spent a moment in thought. "Nej," he decided, with a shake of his head. After what he had learnt of Haward in the past, Hrald wanted to see if he would be carried this news separately, and what he would do about it. "Do not send to Haward. Set two men to watch his hall, to wait, and see if he receives message himself. And who brings such to him."

Hrald nodded his head to himself, as he made further decision. "We have thirty men at Oundle," he told Jari. "Send twenty more to the Abbess, fully supplied, taking them from the men at the valley of horses."

This left only thirty to guard the horses, but some of the men Asberg brought could be sent there. Mindful of his offensive needs as he must be, he need be careful in the rationing of his men for defence of all he owned or supported.

"If Asberg brings fifty, we can ride with seventy or eighty men, and still leave the hall defended."

He felt almost light-headed at all he had just ordered, and all which must be achieved before he rode. He stood in the knot of men as Kjeld and Jari sent men off to their tasks. For the first time he saw his sister, standing there amongst them. She had a stack of folded linens in her arms, which she now lay over the paddock rail.

Hrald nodded at her, and when Kjeld turned back he spoke to both of them.

"We have no idea of who we are tracking, but when we find them we will fight.

"Kjeld, you and Ashild will remain here, in command of Four Stones."

This time Ashild had answer for her brother, one he did not expect.

"Nej, Hrald," she told him. She had been watching his face, seeing his calculation of where and how to use his men. Her voice was clear and with a decisiveness of her own. "Let me go with you. I can act as courier."

Hrald's eyes met those of his sister. Hers were not flashing with anger, but were bright nonetheless.

He could not let her go, not now. She was not only a woman, but a mother now.

Yet looking at her he felt the injustice of this ruling. She had ridden to Oundle and made a clean kill there; Asberg and his father had seen it. He had crowned her with gold, a warrior's portion, for her action.

"You need every man," she insisted, "let me go and spare you another for the field."

He hesitated long enough for her to add, "You told me I was the best rider amongst us, before the fight at Oundle. Use me as a messenger, then." She could not help the slight upturn at the corners of her mouth as she said this.

He found himself answering her with a single condition.

"Only if you will swear not to engage in any way."

"I will swear that. I do swear, Hrald."

It was an easy promise to make. She did not want to kill another man, not unless she had to.

He had to concede. "Byrgher will stay at your side," he said, at which the older man nodded.

At this point Burginde, who had been heading to the kitchen yard, appeared. She took in the activity in a single glance and did an about face back to the hall. She returned with Ælfwyn. Hrald stood there, Jari at his side, and Ashild, with Kjeld at hers. Ælfwyn let her face speak for her. Her son related the news he had been brought, and described his response. He would ride to war, and Ashild was going too, only to act as messenger if needed.

The Lady of Four Stones listened, lips parted, and with cheeks drained of colour. This was war. And her two eldest were running after it. Her son must, he was Jarl. But Ashild . . .

Her mother searched her face. "You will be there, on the sidelines only," she repeated.

Ashild nodded. "Only to serve as courier," she promised.

Hrald was allowing it, and Ælfwyn must accept this. And the thought that Ashild, who loved her brother so dearly, would be near him, gave her a sudden flush of comfort, despite the doubled danger they rode to. She took a breath, noticing the stream of men busy at paddock and stable. She now had her own vital tasks of preparation to attend to.

"The provisions," she asked her son. "How long will you be gone?'

Hrald gave a glance to the shed which housed the waggons. "A supply waggon will slow us down. We will take pack horses. Give us enough for four days."

She nodded, but Burginde did more than that.

"I am off," the nurse said, and made for the kitchen yard.

"The village?" Ælfwyn turned slightly toward the opened gates, her hand lifted.

"They must all come in," Hrald told her.

***

Four Stones had known a wakeful and restless night. The needed horses had already been brought from the sheltering valley where so many of them pastured. By mid-morning both mounts and pack animals were saddled, and every man who was riding with Hrald was busy affixing his leathern bags to saddle rings. Every man's war-kit had been carefully laid out on the trestle tables of the main hall, and men had stood over them, arming themselves. All would be mounted; all would carry a spear, any who owned swords would bear those as well. They all had knives at their hips and those who favoured the skeggox or war hammer had them at the ready, the deadly heads secure in their hardened leathern cases. Ten good archers carried bows with them, their quivers bristling with fletched arrows on their backs. One did not like to give thought to the need for it, but most men carried a roll of linen band for binding wounds.

As far as protective gear, every man had his shield. About half of those riding with Hrald owned ring-shirts, and close to the same number of those had a steel helmet. The treasure room housed no additional ring-shirts, but its chests held several helmets captured in battle over the years, and these Hrald handed to the more senior of his men who lacked one. The others, every man of them, had a war-cap of hardened leather, over which bands of steel were strapped.

Ashild too would wear her war-cap, the one her uncle Asberg had selected for her before the fight for Oundle. She had kept all her kit from that day carefully together in her house. She had already donned the dark leggings she had sewn years ago to aid her spear-throwing practice, and the cut-down gown which served as tunic. Now, braiding her hair into one thick braid, she placed her war-cap on her head. Cerd was sitting up on his alcove bed, watching her, and when she dropped it over her hair he began to laugh at her changed visage. She laughed back at him, glad he was not alarmed at the transformation. Then she stood glancing about the small house. A linen pouch hanging on a peg near her bed caught her eye, and she went to it and took it down.

Two amulets of precious metals lay within. At her mother's request she had worn her golden cross for the birth of her son, but not since. She had set the cross away in this pouch with her father's silver hammer of Thor. Now she placed her hand in the pouch, and muttered aloud. "Which ever I touch first, I will wear."

It was her father's hammer her fingers touched, which seemed fitting, as she rode on behalf of the hall he had won. She placed it over her head, and dropped it under her tunic where it could not be seen.

The last things she needed were to buckle on the seax Hrald had given her, and to take up her shield and spear.

The spear. It was the same she had taken to Oundle, the same with which she had taken a man's life. She would carry it, for she might have need to part her way through trouble.

Of all her horses, she had decided to ride the white stallion. He was by far the biggest and strongest of her mounts. He could carry her back to Four Stones at speed, so she could summon help if needed. And his bright coat would make it easy for Hrald to pick her out on the sidelines as she stood there, should he need send a man running to her with his call for aid.

Hrald had made private goodbye to his mother early in the treasure room, with only Burginde there. He had not been able to say much, and indeed Ælfwyn herself was largely silent. Her kiss, her hand clasped in his, and the tears she bit back had given voice to her love, and to her hope.

By late morning Asberg arrived with his sons, Ulf and Abi, two score and ten mounted warriors behind them. He had overseen the sheltering of the village folk behind the palisade of Turcesig before they left, confident in Styrbjörn's ability to hold it. Hrald had thought hard of the danger to Four Stones' horses, and told his uncle of the result. The fact that these invaders had arrived by ship meant they would be searching out every beast they could. He decided to send a full score of Turcesig's men to the valley, to make up the complement of fifty guarding that most portable of his treasure. It was Four Stones that had been injured by this attack, and he wanted the greater body of the men he fronted to be his own, for they shared that affront with him.

The stable yard and forecourt was now a sea of men and horses. The crofters of the village, having spent their own sleepless night within the second hall, stood with open mouths at the edges of the gathering space, eyes roving over the warriors as they readied themselves.

The animals brought with them added to the clangour of bawling calves, bleating sheep and goats, and crowing fowl resounding within the walls.

The excitement felt by Asberg's sons showed on their faces. Ulf, the older boy, had now seventeen Summers, and would be at his father's side in what might prove to be his first encounter with the enemy. As befitting his father's wealth he was kitted out with ring-shirt, helmet with descending cheek-pieces and nose-guard, and a sword Hrald had presented him with. Asberg, helping the boy arm himself at dawn, had considered the result in sober reflection. There was a balance between needed protection and calling undue attention to an untried fighter. A good kit made you more of a target, and he hoped he would not rue the day he had so equipped his eldest. He must trust Ulf would be up to it. Abi was just turned fifteen, good with a spear for his age and size, but had yet to receive a sword. But Abi had a private plan to serve his older cousin, and stepped forward to name it.

"Hrald, let me hold your war-flag."

Hrald gave his head a jerk. The raven banner Ashild had made him was still in the treasure room. He must ride with it. He was eager to proclaim himself of Anglia, and should they find the fight he sought, a man near him would need to hold the war-flag aloft so his warriors might know he lived, and be ready to rally about him. But the role was not without peril. Any battle standard was a prize piece of booty. A captured flag would be paraded and jeered at. Even if the leader whose battle-flag it was still lived, his own men might believe him to be dead, and lose heart.

He looked at Asberg. It was his son Abi who asked for the honour and potential danger of holding the war-flag.

Asberg nodded his approval.

"Já," Hrald allowed. "I will go and get it. But if the fighting gets thick around me, pass it to another man, and go to your father and Ulf. That is an order."

A beaming Abi nodded his head with such vigour his war-cap went askew.

When Hrald returned with the raven banner, Bork was walking towards him, leading his bay stallion, saddled and bridled. He watched Hrald pass the banner to Abi, and his eyes widened as a grinning Abi stood there, both fists closed about the ash staff, waving it from side to side to make the raven fly above them.

Hrald saw Bork's watching, and extended his hand to take the reins of his horse.

"Let me go with you," Bork asked, a near-desperate plea.

"Nej, nej. You are still a boy."

Bork was quick to refute this judgement. "I have been training, with Mul's sons. I can sling a stone a long way."

Hrald placed his hand on his shoulder. He thought of what to say to convince the boy. "Your work here is more important. You care for my horses. I may need one of them. Stay with them in case I do."

Here the bay pushed his downy muzzle up against Bork's back. The smile that crossed Hrald's mouth was real. "He likes you as much as me. Maybe more."

Bork nodded. Mul came forward to lead the boy back to the stable doorway where he and his sons, work complete, had been watching.

Wilgot was moving amongst the crowd, flinging holy water and chanting a blessing. The horsemen began to form up. Ashild and Byrgher would ride in the second to last rank, so that she could quickly bolt if needed if they faced attack while still on the road. She was not yet on the stallion; such was his height she needed the mounting block. As she led him there her mother, Cerd in her arms, made her way towards her from where she had been stationed at the gate. Burginde and Ealhswith were with her. Ashild had spent time with them in the treasure room, but another embrace, another touch of the hand or tender word was not to be resisted, nor refused.

Before she could pull herself into the saddle Ealhswith darted forward to give her sister a kiss. The kiss granted, Ashild put her foot in the stirrup and swung her leg over the animal's saddle. She adjusted the shield on her back, then looked down at the loving faces filled with concern that were lifted to her. She did not trust herself to speak. Then Cerd laughed and reached his arms out to her. She bent low to take him from her mother, and held him a moment on the saddle before her, as she had done in the past.

"Horse," he crowed, one of his favourite words. She ruffled his coppery curls with her hand, then pressed a final kiss on her son's forehead.

"Yes, horse. I will come back to you, on this horse."

She handed Cerd down to her mother.

They were moving now, a wave of men in full war-kit, astride horses eager for the road. Hrald was flanked by Asberg and Jari, and led the way. They would close up around Hrald once they had left the near boundaries of the hall lands, but just now Hrald wanted to look upon the road stretching before them. Asberg was at his right, and Jari, Tyr-hand that he was, rode as always on his left. Just behind them came Asberg's two sons, Abi holding the staff of the raven flag.

A cry of salute followed them as they passed the gates, led by Kjeld standing at the opening, and picked up by the men crowding the palisade ramparts. It faded from hearing as their horses broke into a canter.

They rode through the village, empty of all life.

Southward they drove, aiming for Saltfleet. There was little chance the invaders had remained there; the land about it was devoid of any hamlet or settlement with food or beasts.

At dusk they camped overnight, tentless, wrapped in their blankets and grateful for a dry night. Ashild lay on the ground between her brother and Byrgher. After she closed her eyes, Hrald spoke to her. He had pulled his blanket around him in the dark, and his left hand had touched the knot of tissue that marked one end of the scar on his right shoulder.

"Ashild," he whispered. Her eyelids fluttered open.

"The day Ceric and I sparred, and I cut him . . . " His voice dropped even lower as his words trailed off. "When my own arm was bleeding, we stood side to side, pressing the wounds together."

This was all he said, this simple admission of that long-ago action between the two of them.

She nodded in the dark, as if to herself. Ceric had twice named Hrald as brother in his letters. Men called each other this when they fought side by side, as well. A thought floated up, one she recognized as a truth. The bond forged by Hrald and Ceric was akin to that shared by their mothers. It would be a life-long linkage, which distance or time could not impair. And it included her. She was sister to Hrald and was, if not truly wife to Ceric, willing mother of the child they had together formed.

She remembered Ceric telling her after their night of love that the three of them were together during the stitching of those arm wounds, and would always be thus. She recalled answering him in hushed agreement: And so we shall be . . .

She fell asleep thinking of her son, overtaken by a sense of his curly head nestled between her and his father as they all slept.

She awakened later in the night with an acute feeling of her aloneness, even though she was surrounded by men. She looked up into a darkly clouded sky. The horses were moving about where they had been staked, a sound that brought its own comfort. Soon they all would be up and afield, and none could know what this new day would bring.

Her hand reached for the tunic she wore, and she pressed it against the silver hammer between her breasts. The hammer of Yrling of Four Stones. Her father could not be with her, but neither could Hrald's. Each must play their part, alone yet together, as well as they could. She knew Hrald would.

They rose before dawn and ate a hasty meal of bread, cheese, and the leavings from the browis they had boiled the night before. Saltfleet was reached not long after. Approaching it from the side path along the coast granted them a vantage point. Two drekars, grim and majestic, stood tied at the wooden pier, coiled prows bobbing slightly with the tide. No sound arose from the ships, nor the timber buildings on the shore.

"They will not use those to escape," Hrald decided.

Emerging from the path, they untied the ships, and pulled them free of the pier and about to the shoreline.

It took six men with axes almost no time to scuttle the ships. To stand within a costly ship and hack at its hull until the timbers burst and rivets popped was one of the most wasteful acts of war. Here it was one wholly needful. Landlocked Four Stones could not use these ships, and they had been the vessels carrying death and destruction to its men.

The tracks of the invaders, now five days old, could still be read in the soil near the road fronting the buildings. They showed the booted feet of many men, and the hoof prints of the few horses they had stolen from the paddock here. They told of a northwesterly route.

"Agmund," posed Jari. "They were seeking Agmund."

Guthrum's eldest son ruled a broad sweep of land in the south of Anglia. If these invaders were followers of Haesten they might indeed be looking for that war-chief. Agmund had at first thrown in with Haesten, only to break the alliance. Yet he still held the greatest power keeping Haesten from his goal of total conquest of first Anglia, and then Wessex.

Hrald and his troop did not stop to search out bodies, but moved on. They took to the road, eighty strong.

A grey sky hung over their heads, one that seemed to rise from the soil over which they travelled. The mist of night had thickened to a cool and damp fog. It was as if Summer had abruptly decided it was over, and a chill was coming.

THE FOREST DUEL

HRALD and his troop moved steadily onward. They kept as silent as any multitude of men on horseback can, not wanting to betray their approach. The tracks diverged from the road to a far smaller pathway. The Danes they followed had headed west a while, then turned north and east. Both Oundle and Four Stones lay there.

The path the Danes took went running close to a free-flowing stream. When the path brought them to its banks, fog rolled off the surface of the water as if it were steam rising from a roiling cauldron. All was damp with it, and the cloud-shrouded Sun, while rising in the grey sky, made little headway in warming the cool air. Their horses walked through mists that swirled about their fetlocks.

The footprints left the narrow trackway. It brought them to a much broader road, one of earth pounded hard by use. Both sides showed the same mixed growth they had travelled through, hickory and hornbeam and stands of young beeches. As they moved forward the light changed; a clearing must be near. They reached it, and found those they sought.

On the right was a large field, devoid of trees, from which the mist still rose. Gathered there, arising from the damp grass where they had stopped to rest, were some fourscore warriors on foot. Some were in the act of replacing their helmets upon their heads, others, taking a drink of water from their newly-filled leathern flasks. Ten saddled horses stood to one side, cropping at the grass.

For a moment both groups froze. Then Hrald urged his horse forward, Jari on his left, Asberg on his right. Behind them came Ulf and Abi. In Abi's fist, the butt of the staff resting on his saddle leather, flew the raven flag Ashild had made.

Even in the little wind, one could see the outstretched wing of a raven upon it.

Hrald stopped a few horse lengths in and studied the men. They were Danes, well equipped, and one of them had at once stepped forward at their appearing. He looked to be near forty years, as hardened in his face as he was in body. He had long mud-brown hair, well streaked with grey, fastened in two plaits that reached past his shoulders. He sported a long beard of the same mixed shade, also plaited, which fell down his chest.

Hrald looked across to where the man stood, and announced himself.

"I am Hrald of Four Stones. Tell me who you are."

The Dane's tone matched the sneer on his face. "I will tell you nothing."

Hrald countered with a firmness that kept his simmering anger in check.

"Then I will tell you something," he said. He tilted his head to the horses. "Those are my horses. Where are my men?"

The Dane gave a snort of derision. "Ha! I sent them to Odin," he scoffed. "They were easy enough to send." Their killer had the broad accent of one born in Dane-mark.

His next words were delivered in the same mocking tone.

"I can hear you are no real Dane, but are tainted by the Saxons. If your men are like you, Odin will likely send them back, to languish in the land of shades with Hel and her ugly crones." He laughed.

The Jarl of Four Stones did not. He delivered his next words with chill precision.

"You are on my lands, and have killed my men and stolen my horses."

Hrald was about to issue a formal challenge, when he realized he might learn something more.

"You look to join to your leader, Agmund," he suggested. "You will not find him near."

The Dane jerked his head. "Agmund," he echoed, and spat on the ground. "We will spit on his grave. That is, if his men can find all the parts we will hack him into."

So. This man fought for Haesten, and Haesten was the greater enemy. It gave Hrald a flush of satisfaction to know this. It was Haesten who had sailed in eighty ships to these shores, and then had rallied the crews of two hundred and fifty more, already come from Frankland.

"Thank you for telling me who you fight for, Three Plaits. You will soon be plaiting Hel's hair of writhing snakes."

Three Plaits was angered at falling for the ruse, and showed it.

"You are nothing but a thrall to Wessex," he growled out, "and like Wessex will fall."

At this Jari let loose a torrent of pungent oaths questioning the Dane's parentage, spanning several generations back. The men of Four Stones behind Jari began hooting and jeering in agreement to his insults.

Hrald's eyes had been shifting over the men massed behind Three Plaits. Every one had a helmet, and most wore ring-shirts as well. As his gaze made the circuit he spotted a big man with a broad face and brown hair.

"Onund." Hrald said. "Agmund or Haesten, to you it would be the same. You are true to nothing, and no one."

Onund's response was to spit in Hrald's direction.

It was Hrald's turn to scoff.

"Does Three Plaits know I drove you off?" Hrald turned his eyes back to him named. "But then, you are used to accepting the discards of better men."

Three Plaits had one response, one all were ready for.

"Get off your horse and fight."

Hrald fairly jumped from his horse.

Ashild, watching from the back of the string of Hrald's men, tried to swallow to keep her throat open. Her right hand was gripped about her spear, the butt of which sat upright upon her saddle in echo of the war-flag Abi held. There was a sense of the unreal about all before her. She stood amidst eight or nine score men, all whole and alive. Soon many of them would be maimed and dying. She knew this; it had happened before her eyes at Oundle.

She had heard every word falling from Hrald's lips. He had spoken manfully, and with a cunning that had tricked the Dane into revealing his allegiance. He must seek the sword's justice for the violence done to his men. Yet the thought that she could see him die filled her belly with ice. Jari and Asberg might fall as well.

Do not think of this, she ordered herself. Hrald had killed Thorfast; he or his men would kill this Dane. But this was a huge force they faced. Even if her brother did kill the Dane, many of his captains would seek to slay Hrald. She fought these fears, aware she was almost gasping for breath.

Byrgher spoke to her, gesturing her away. To their left was only a narrow margin before the trees crowded in towards the road. He turned his horse's head left and both he and Ashild slipped into the sheltering trees. They and their animals were mostly concealed by the shrubby undergrowth. The battle would be held here, and now, and this was a safe place of concealment.

The warriors of Four Stones were quitting their horses, walking them to the tree line to tie them. Without speaking they went about testing their leg wrappings, setting their shields, determining which weapon to lead with. Hrald led his bay to a sapling, just as any of them. Jari was at his side, whistling a tuneless song between his teeth as he did the same. Asberg, his two sons with him, gave thought to Æthelthryth, and of how he had sworn both boys would return unscathed.

None spoke to the other in these final moments. It was a time past words.

Hrald, ready to walk upon the field, gave thought of how this battle, facing other Danes, would unfold.

He well knew how the Saxons fought; he had been told in great detail by Ceric. Jari and Asberg knew it from having faced them as foes, and had told him as well. There was order and discipline, and in a meeting on a field like this, a sequence to be followed. Youths spinning leathern slings over their heads let fly round river stones, pelting the massed enemy before them. A sleet of arrows followed, and when the enemy was within range, a hail of light throwing spears. This would break up the ranks and columns of the oncoming foe, so that when the shield-walls with their spears and swords met, fewer remained. Every Saxon war-chief had a battle cry, from the King to the leader of a handful of men. It was not a simple war whoop, but a word or words to remind the men for whom and what they fought.

Here, this morning, the men would form up. Oaths and insults would be flung, and then one side would start for the other. Both leaders would want to fight each other directly and without interference. Their men would try to keep them from being injured or killed before they could do so. His father had told Hrald about the fight for Four Stones, and how he and Jari and Asberg, as well as Yrling's other men, had protected his duel with Merewala. This would likely happen now.

He began walking towards the greensward where he would fight. He looked carefully at Three Plaits, his shield at his feet, who was now lifting his helmet over his head. Hrald was a little taller, but the Dane broader. That his opponent had been a successful warrior there was no doubt. At the age the man was, Hrald knew he had fought and triumphed over many men.

Asberg and Jari paced steadily at Hrald's side. Ulf and Abi came just behind their father. Abi was not waving the staff with the raven banner, just holding it aloft, trying not to gape at what lay before him. These five were joined by a triple rank of Four Stones' warriors, fanning out on either side of their Jarl. A few of his men were still on horseback; Hrald could hear the near jingling of bridle hardware behind him. He gave thought to Ashild, somewhere on the edges. Coming upon the enemy as they had meant that he had no parting word with her. She was in Byrgher's care. She was mounted and safe. He trusted she would have no need to bolt, and ride hard for Four Stones.

One of the men behind Hrald had his own grudge to settle. Hrald's man Askil, an archer with bow in hand, urged his horse forward a few paces, then stopped him. He stood up in his stirrups, and pulled back his bow string. He let fly his arrow, then bellowed.

"Anulf!"

Anulf had been his younger brother, one who had been at Saltfleet.

The arrow, shot above Hrald's head, hit Three Plaits as he was beginning to lift his shield to his left wrist. The man was leaning forward, and the arrow caught him in the top of the chest, pinning, it seemed, the plaited beard to the man's ring-tunic. The impact knocked him back off his feet and to the grass.

Hrald's men were yelling in sudden triumph. The first kill was of the enemy leader.

The shouts raised by Hrald's men rent the still air. They were answered in yawping disbelief by the men backing Three Plaits. Many of the Danes plunged forward, howling for revenge. But others stood back. Some may have been stunned by the sudden loss. Others looked to be making decision whether to fight or run, or gauging which of their dead war-chief's men would try to claim leadership, and if they would follow such a man.

Those who stormed forward did so in an explosion of rancour, a melee without form or order from the start.

Ashild could not see who had fallen, but she had watched Askil rise in his stirrups and release the bow string. An uproar so great must mean his arrow had found home in one of the chief men of the Danes, perhaps even their leader. She could not see her brother, obscured as he was by the men behind him. Her raven flag marked where Hrald stood, and she kept her eyes on it.

The two sides collided. Raised spears were lowered in attack, and shields lifted under the mutual onslaught. Though they moved forward almost in ranks, any attempt to maintain a shield-wall at once collapsed. Warriors broke through in streams, surrounding their foes, and fought back to back. Ashild saw the steel of swords as they swung. She heard Asberg's two-part war-cry, which gave her heart.

The ten archers Hrald had brought abandoned their bows and horses, and ran into the thick of struggling men, led by Askil. War-cries and whoops gave way to screams as men were hit and fell. A confusion of objects arose and fell about the knots of fighting men: spears, helmets, shields which rolled before landing on their pointed iron bosses. Men tripped and fell over this detritus, as they did over the bodies of those who had dropped bleeding to the grass.

As men were downed or broke away to fight by twos and threes Ashild's line of vision opened. She had let her spear down to the forest floor, resting it against the tree she hid behind. The cool damp of the day ran like a chill over her. She was straining forward over her stallion's neck, her fingers entwined in the ghostly white of his thick mane. She sensed rather than saw Byrgher next her. Even their two horses seemed at attention, and stood with furry ears pricked forward, as if awaiting their own orders.

The raven war-flag was off to one side of the field. A few men moved, and she saw the green of Abi's tunic. Before him Asberg and Jari flanked Hrald, as they drove forward, spears in hand, facing four men also brandishing spears. She expected this steadfastness in uncle and body-guard and tried to take comfort in its display. They had sometimes sparred this way, and she could only hope the practice of fighting shield to shield would serve her brother now.

Hrald, the middle of the three men in his shield-wall, must keep his spear in constant motion, whirling it in a large circle before him as cover to himself and the two who flanked him. In any such formation the greatest danger was not from the man directly before you, but those on either side of that opponent. The man across you to the left would try to knock at the rim of your shield, exposing your torso to a spear coming from the right. The man on the right would look for an opening at your head and neck. Hrald was constantly checking from the tail of his eye from whence the next strike might come. He must worry those facing them with his spear-point, giving Asberg and Jari the chance to knock away their opponent's shields or get in a sudden high jab at the head. Hrald's greater height and long reach aided his spear in dominating the space before their opponents.

Asberg, though unflinching at the right side of his nephew, was distracted by the presence of his young sons. Abi, holding the battle-flag, was armed with his everyday knife and had but a war-cap on his head. He feared the more for his older boy, Ulf, who would try to distinguish himself here before his Jarl. This muddled disorder was a far from ideal first engagement for young warriors. As they had stepped upon the field, Asberg had firm words for his older son.

"Do not engage unless you must. Provide cover for Abi."

Ulf had proven good at this, watching the young-ster's back and using his shield with skill to deflect a rock thrown his way.

Hrald, Asberg, and Jari pushed the four spear-men they faced across the field to the far line of trees, steadily backing them toward the uneven footing and under-growth marking the edge of the grass. The four Danes were well-equipped, with ring-shirts and helmets. They were able enough spear-men, and even Asberg, known to be one of the better spear fighters, was taxed by the extra point they faced. Yet Jari's presence, his spear held in his left hand, posed a special challenge to the Danes. The shield in his right gave extra protection to Hrald, while his spear clattered against the shaft of the man across from him, deflecting its every thrust. Jari had prodigious strength, and he did not tire in his spear-play. Even out-numbered as they were, the men of Four Stones steadily repelled the Danes. Every step carried the invaders closer to the trees, where they must either turn and run, tempt-ing a thrown spear in the back, or stand and redouble their efforts.

The Dane on the far left would choose neither. He made a sudden jump to his right, then jabbed at Jari's left leg.

The spear-point made solid contact with Jari's calf. Still clutching his own spear, Jari fell to one knee, then the other, a dire oath upon his lips. Ulf, behind the men and closest to the spear-man, tried to lunge forward with his own weapon, but the man was already outside his range. The Dane ran along the line of trees before vanishing behind one of the larger of them. Downed as he was, Jari was nearly helpless against being poled or hacked at. His rich war-kit was enough to attract such attention.

Hrald and Asberg moved with renewed fervour against the three remaining Danes. No spur was greater than a downed comrade, and they could not expose Jari to another hit. Hrald leapt at the one on the end before him, striking his spear tip to the iron boss of the Dane's shield with ringing force. It knocked the man off balance, and the shield dropped low, allowing Hrald to get in a spear thrust just below the right shoulder. The man reeled back, and as the shield fell from his fist, Hrald made a second, killing thrust to the breast.

This kill was enough for one of the two remaining Danes. He fled, stopped only by Asberg's flung spear.

"Go," Hrald called to Asberg, as he engaged the sole Dane before him.

Asberg turned to his sons, his orders low and urgent. "Help me get him to the side," was his first, to Ulf, and "Stay with Hrald," to Abi.

Jari sat upon the ground, his hands clasped about his bleeding leg. Stunned and in pain he looked up at Hrald, still fighting. It took him back long years, to the day he had lost his fingers. Sidroc had avenged that loss, and the far greater one of Une, Jari's brother. Watching Hrald now he thought, how alike were father and son.

"Old fool, to be still fighting," he muttered to himself, wincing against the throbbing fire of the gash.

Asberg and Ulf got him to his feet, and placed him between them. The foot Jari held up behind him as they made their way to the trees ran with blood. They made for a fallen tree not far within. Jari crumpled onto the forest floor upon reaching it.

"Where is your linen?" Asberg asked his son. Ulf pulled at the pouch at his belt, revealing the narrow roll. His father nodded. "Put his leg up on the trunk. Bind his wound. Stay with him and protect him."

On the field Hrald was still fighting the last spearman. Abi, looking after his father and brother as they disappeared into the trees, saw the spear Jari had relinquished, lying where he had finally opened his fist. Jari was as an uncle to him, and he would want his spear. Even injured, a man could hold it out before him to fend off attackers. He picked it up from the bloodied grass and ran after his father, holding it upright against the staff of the raven banner. He slipped into the wood.

Hrald, alone with the final Dane, found himself matched with a man of no great height, but possessing a speed which made his spear-point dart. He kept short thrusts of his spear aimed squarely at Hrald's face, and kept his feet in motion, circling Hrald to give himself the greatest coverage with his own shield. Asberg too was fast in his wrists and nimble of foot, and he had trained Hrald to face such a foe. Surprise was ever an ally, and Hrald made the Dane's own lower body his target, just as Jari's leg had been. He made three thrusts at his knees, and got the man to lower his shield to better cover them. Then Hrald took a step back, lifted his right arm, and drove for the man's head.

The Dane's helmet had neither eye-pieces nor nose-guard, but stopped at the hairline. Hrald's spear-point struck above the left eye. The Dane's knees did not buckle under the blow. The man fell back, arms opening, spear dropping, almost in a single line upon the torn grass. Hrald stood, panting, over him. The left eye was already obscured with blood, but the right was blue and staring.

Hrald forced his own eyes up and away. He let his spear shaft slide through his hand until the butt hit the ground, and drew breath. Then something moved in the trees before him.

It was Onund. The man was peering out at him from a thicket of rowans. He had no spear, but was otherwise fully armed with sword, knife, and a shield still upon his back. Hrald spent some little time looking at him before he spoke.

"Onund. You ran, and now are back."

Onund had his answer ready.

"Back to kill you."

Hrald scanned the area behind his challenger. The immediate line of trees opened to a small clearing, large enough to pull their swords in. They would not draw notice, fighting there. Onund stepped into the opening, as invitation. As Hrald took his first steps forward through the undergrowth to gain the space, Onund backed further away. He grinned, then turned and began making his way through the trees.

"You run again," Hrald taunted. "Is it me, or yourself you cannot face?"

Onund did not answer this time, but kept slipping forward through the trees.

Hrald would go after him. He looked at the spear in his hand. He would keep hold of it; it would prove useful as walking staff, and gave him a weapon Onund lacked. Hrald knew entering the trees held its own hazards. He had seen some of the Danes run thence, either to escape, or use the wood as a means of hidden movement, allowing them to reemerge closer to the action. Onund could be leading him to where more of the enemy waited, in ambush. But Hrald, catching a glimpse of the furtive look in the man's eye, did not think so.

※※※※※※※※※※

Abi, standing at the tree line, was no longer certain where his father had entered the wood with Jari and Ulf. He walked in a short distance, brambles catching at his leggings and tangling against the two heavy shafts in his hands. He could see no one, and was loath to call out, so left the spear against a tree, where it could be recovered later.

When he came out Hrald was gone. The man he had been fighting was lying on the ground, but there was no sign of Hrald. Abi caught his breath and stood scanning the field. Men stood fighting, one-on-one or in small groups, but none were Hrald. His height made him easy to pick out, and his helmet too, that which Abi's father had given Hrald, with wolf-like creatures incised on its sides.

He tried to look for Hrald's shield of red and black. No man held one. But shields shattered in fighting, and men would take up any at hand. Still looking, Abi began to move uncertainly. He saw some men he thought were of Four Stones, and tried to call out to them, not knowing what he should do. His father was gone and he had

lost sight of Hrald. Men were groaning from wounds, and
a few lying not far from him reached an arm up in supplication. Oaths and war-cries from those still fighting
joined with the shrill whinnying of horses. Some of the
beasts were loose or had never been tied, and were circling fretfully, shaking their heads and flicking their tails
in the confusion.

As Abi stood there, an arrow whizzed by him from
behind. Sheer surprise forced him into a run. Then he
was hit by another, in the back of the thigh. The stinging
force of it made him stumble and then fall. Face down in
the trampled grass he heard his father's voice shouting
his name.

Asberg ran across the field from the tree line. He
pulled the arrow from Abi's thigh, then scooped him up
in his arms. He carried his son to Ulf and Jari in the wood.
The raven flag lay abandoned on the field.

Sheltered within the trees Ashild and Byrgher had
watched Hrald step into the forest. They could see a man
had appeared before him, but could not tell who; the distance was too great. They had seen Abi's confusion, and
watched him fall from the arrow-hit. It had made Ashild
swallow a cry, to see first Jari and now her young cousin
fall. They watched Asberg race to his son, and carry him
off, returning to the wood with him.

Some disturbance now was happening further down
the road, where the trees on the other side began opening
up to the expanse of grassland. It was the portion of the
greensward where the fighting was now thickest. Directly

before them was where the two sides had first engaged, and where the leader of the Danes had fallen. His body lay there still. No man as yet roamed the field plucking his battle-gain; the fighting was in places still hot. As she and Byrgher looked down the road, a troop of horsemen riding in ranks pulled their horses to a stop. She saw them turn to their saddle bags, draw out helmets and drop them on their heads.

She studied the troop. From the saddle cantles of a few of them sprang war-banners.

Their horses were dancing at the sudden halt, and the pennons hard to focus upon. Ashild squinted across the distance.

"Wessex," she breathed, in wonder. The device on the banners looked to be golden dragons.

She did not have time to repeat her discovery to Byrgher, for of a sudden one of the newly arrived men was hit by a flung spear. It had come from the edge of the trees nearest the road, but so far away she could see neither the man who had thrown it nor where his victim's body had toppled. She heard the cry of their war-leader's command though, as they kicked their horses forward onto the field.

A movement from the trees caught her eyes, and she touched Byrgher's arm. Asberg was back, alone and on foot, making his way toward the arriving men. Danes who had ended their contest with the men of Four Stones whirled to them as well. Asberg, caught between them, saw the peril he was in.

Byrgher spoke. "I am going to him," he told Ashild. He reined his horse free of their leafy shelter, and urged it across the field towards Asberg.

She lost sight of both. One of the oncoming horses of Wessex was downed by a spear thrown into the beast's rump. It screamed, and then tumbled, hoofs thrashing, as the man on its back sailed over its neck and hit the ground. Another horse just behind the first reared in protest, causing the man upon it to fall.

The men from Wessex were leaping from their horses as the Danes, spears and swords ready, rushed at them. To Ashild's eyes it looked a swarm of hornets, breaking up and stinging, and then reforming and moving off over the field.

She forced her eyes away, back to where she had last seen her brother. Hrald had not emerged from the wood.

"Hrald," she whispered.

⁂

The first sign of trouble the Prince's troop came upon was a line of saddled horses, some tied to saplings, others wandering free, in the road before them. Eadward and his men had been following a stream north, one bordered by a trackway. They had come upon no settlement, and when they found the broader road determined to take it for the speed so offered. When they saw the horses they stopped at once. Battle cries, not distant, reached their ears. They were of the Danes, no doubt of that.

Eadward gave the command. They placed their helmets on their heads, pulled their shields around to their chests, and made ready their spears. They tightened their ranks and moved forward. Rounding a slight bend in the road they glimpsed the field of action. The trees on the right thinned to an opening, upon which a struggle, still ongoing, had played. The ground was littered with the dead and dying.

The Prince began reining in his horse. He was five-and-twenty men. Perhaps twice that number lay as casualties upon the grass. During the few moments which passed as he considered his response he lost a man. A light throwing spear was flung from within the trees, striking one of them in the back and toppling him from his horse. The action was not just ahead of them. There were men hidden in the near trees, driven there or lying in wait. One had seen a new target, temptingly close, and it had cost one of Eadward's thegns their life. The shock of it sparked the Prince's next order.

"Onward," screamed Eadward.

His men well knew how to respond. When the Prince stopped and quitted his horse, nearly all of them would do so as well, ready to fight. The four who had brought up the rear would take charge of all the horses. Their role was to gather the mounts, lead them to relative safety, and protect the animals from poaching. Only under the most dire of circumstances, or being summoned by the Prince, could they abandon their charges.

Eadward, leading the rush onto the field, gave little thought to Edwin at his side. The young Lord of Kilton had his own body-guard, and now he would need it. He thought instead of the insult of his downed thegn, and that his long search through Anglia had finally yielded fruit.

Edwin was riding with Eorconbeald at his right. When the Prince spurred his horse for the field, their ranks opened, and two of Eadward's own body-guards closed up around him. It gave an opening for Alwin to ride up next Edwin's left. Worr and Cadmar came just behind.

Edwin's heart was pounding in his breast. In the span of a few horse strides they had gone from riding watchfully along a road to a battle in which they would now engage. On the grassy field onto which they had turned men of the enemy were coming to meet them, forming up in ranks, waving their weapons, and shouting out taunts. Much nearer, Edwin could hear the angry oaths uttered by Eadward's men as they galloped forward.

He thought of his brother. Ceric was due to meet up with them, past due, as Eadward had expected his return yesterday from his scouting trip. He should have ridden back to them along much the same route as they took now, following the stream. The sudden fear that Ceric might have been caught up in this, might already be dead upon the field, overtook him. He forced the thought from his mind by fixing his eyes on the line of men brandishing spears ahead.

As his horse ran under him Edwin clung to a single thought: I am Godwin's son. I am Godwin's son. I will prove this now.

The sword held against his chest was gift of Ælfred, King; but the words he muttered to himself were of his father's blood in his veins.

Before the Prince raised his hand to rein in to a stop, Edwin's horse, legs extended in its run, plunged forward, staggering. Its front legs folded under it, and it fell. Edwin never saw the spear which had killed the animal beneath him; it hit the beast from behind. He went flying over the downed animal's neck, tumbling once, to hit the ground sprawling on his chest. He lost both helmet and sword in the fall. His sword baldric slipped over his head, tangled a moment under his arm, and dropped to his left.

The helmet fell off before he landed and rolled away. His spear-point hit the soil and stuck there, vibrating with the force of impact. He knew none of this; the wind had been knocked out of him. He did not know how Eorconbeald and Alwin were of a sudden on either side of him, hauling him up. Alwin grabbed his sword, but the helmet had been kicked by another horse and was out of range. He did not see Cadmar's horse, just behind his own, rear up in protest of his fallen mount's screams, nor the old warrior-monk be tossed to the ground.

Eorconbeald and Alwin ran with the stunned Edwin to the scant shelter of the trees. They could defend him there, but not on an open field of battle. Worr had at once gone after the horses of the two body-guards, and that of Cadmar. They must not lose them. The horse-thegn whistled a stop to the Kilton horses. They knew him well, and he was able to gather them up by overtaking and stopping Eorconbeald's horse. Grabbing the first, he circled with the other two and pulled them back towards the road and the thegns who would receive them.

Cadmar was upon the ground, sword now in hand, trying to raise himself to stand. The old wound to his leg taken at the Twelfth Night attack on Kilton had ever impaired his movement. Worr spurred his horse to go back to him. He was too late. A spear-wielding Dane ran to the struggling figure, and standing over him, ended his efforts with a single thrust. The assailant snatched at the sword which had dropped from Cadmar's hand. The Dane ran with it, pursued by others of the Prince's men.

Edwin, watching this from the tree line, began to rise from where he sat. "Cadmar!" he called.

Eorconbeald pulled him back. The Lord of Kilton could not be the one to avenge the death, and both body-guards knew it. Blood ran from Edwin's broken nose and split lip. A broad scrape on his right cheek where he had landed coloured that side of his face crimson. A man could fight with such, and many did. But they saw Edwin's eyes, glazed enough that when he tried to stand he wobbled as if flown with mead. He had a hurt to the head that only the passage of a few days would resolve.

Those eyes were fixed on the body of the warrior-monk. "Cadmar," he said again, as if to himself. Cadmar had left Kilton to serve at his side, and now he was dead. Edwin had eighteen years, had seen his first action, and lost one revered by all of Kilton. He sat there, shaking his head at all which had happened in the narrow span of time since they had come along that road.

Alwin had pulled linen from his belt, and was now pressing it against Edwin's face. It forced Edwin's thoughts from the body of Cadmar to the men on either side of him. Cadmar's Fate would have been his own, had his body-guards not leapt from their horses to pluck him from the field. He saw Eorconbeald, also staring at Cadmar. To see the old man die so vile a death was a blow to them as well; he had trained all of them.

It was hard for Edwin to compass. He could scarce hold on to any one thought. His body had been slammed to the ground and he felt that his chest might bear the impress of his ring-tunic, even though one of leather be between it and his skin. His inability to draw breath without pain told him that more than one rib was cracked. His head and face throbbed. He held the wad of linen against his upper lip, attempting to staunch a flow of blood from his nose which would not stop. Blood ran down the soaked linen to the wrist holding it.

He kept looking over the field and its dead. His horse was dead, a mass of chestnut-coated flesh lying there, neck extended, head twisted up in a pose no living horse could hold. Ceric had given him that horse; it was one of the last foals born to their mother's bay mare, that she had ridden from Anglia. Was Ceric too here, lying as Cadmar and that horse were?

"You stay with Edwin," Eorconbeald was now telling Alwin. He must return to the field and find the Prince. The troop he rode in with was scattered and broken, and looking across the greensward he could scarce tell who those fighting were. Eadward's men all knew one another's shields, but shields would shatter under prolonged impact, and a man would pick up any he could. For one close enough, the men of Wessex could be picked out by the seax spanning their bellies.

What Eorconbeald could see was that Danes were seemingly also fighting Danes. He watched certain Danes join with Eadward's thegns, while others fought all comers without distinction. It made any progress in the struggle, that point at which the tide turned for the victors, impossible to call. It looked confusion unto chaos, with no small amount of panic.

Eorconbeald stood, and took up his spear. He would run, skirting the trees, to get closer, then join in when he spotted any of Eadward's thegns.

Hrald lifted his head upward to the Sun. It was hard to see. It was obscured not only by the leafy branches rising above, but for the dimness of the orb in the over-clouded sky. Hrald was not only following Onund, he must also not get lost. Any portion of the wood seemed much the same as that he had just come through. Other than a fallen tree or stump, or a large and mossy boulder, it was hard to mark any unique feature to help guide him back. Onund kept just enough ahead of him so that he could catch sight of the red and blue shield on his back. Hrald had not long been trailing him when the growth opened up. They moved through clusters of smooth-bark beech saplings, standing as grey sentinels.

Hrald recoiled. An arrow whizzed by his head. It hit a beech just past him, close enough so that fragments of bark flew up near Hrald's face. He pulled the arrow out, its fletching still trembling. He broke the shaft in two, and took his shield on his arm in protection. He knew Onund had no bow; another was here, hunting him. He must stick closely to the saplings and larger trees, deny-ing the man another chance.

※※※※※※※※※※※

Ceric cantered down the road from his northerly route. Rounding a bend obscured by trees he was con-fronted by the sight of two men locked in battle. They spilled out before him, fighting at one edge of the road, warriors with swords and shields. He had not heard them over the sound of his horse, and jingling bridle metal.

He had seen no human for five days. He reined to an abrupt stop, put his helmet on, and moved towards them, hugging the far side of the road to provide some cover for his approach. The men vanished, seemingly into the trees. As Ceric moved up on his horse, a grassy plain opened before him, on which a battle had been waged.

His heart skipped. The Prince should have been coming this way. He scanned the edges of the field. Along the tree line were men and horses both. One of the horses, bearing no rider, had sprung from his saddle the golden dragon battle pennon of Wessex. Eadward was here.

He swept his eyes across the field. A horse with at least one broken foreleg was struggling to rise, thrashing and kicking out its back legs as it did so. Another horse lay dead, the spear that had downed it rising at a shallow angle from its rump.

The bodies of men were harder to count. They lay alone, on their backs or faces, and together, arms and legs entangled in a death embrace. A few men ran furtively from body to body, snatching at weaponry. Some still fought, small knots of them. Further up the road a long train of horses stood. A few mounted men rode amongst them, cutting off any who wandered. Ceric could not know who they were. His duty was to Eadward, and he must find him. He moved his horse back to the margin of the road, jumped down, and tied him. He threaded his arm through the loop and boss grip of his shield, took spear in hand, and set off.

He was not the only man making his way either along the trees or seemingly from them. His transit brought him close to several of the dead and dying. A Dane. Another Dane. A third. One of Eadward's men, Felgild. His eyes fastened a moment on Felgild, who lay there with a dark red bloom by his extended right arm. He had beaten

Ceric, and badly too, at dice before he left on this scouting trip. The hand that Felgild had collected Ceric's silver with now lay a distance from his body. He had bled to death. The hand lay open, palm up, cupping the man's own blood.

The branches of a waist-high shrub to the left of Ceric crackled. A Dane was pushing through it to get to Ceric. The man leapt out before him, teeth bared in a war-cry, shield in place, spear tight in an overhand grip and ready to thrust. Ceric raised his own spear-point, right at the Dane's face.

The man ducked, leapt forward, and made a touch at Ceric's shield. It was not enough to knock it away, but it was proof of the Dane's desire for a quick end to the contest. He wore no helmet, and his eyes flitted more than once to the fine one atop the head of Ceric. The man even licked his lips, as if the taste of victory was near.

While still looking at Ceric's head, he made a jab down at Ceric's right, and forward foot. It might have caught Ceric off guard, but Worr and Cadmar both had played this feint with him.

He moved back, out of range of the Dane's spear-point, to try a lunging strike at the man's own shield rim. The Dane responded with a second jab at his foot. It fell short before him, enough so that Ceric stepped on the top of the spear-point just where it entered the shaft. The shaft snapped, the iron point trapped under the booted foot of Ceric. It left the Dane with a pole of jagged ash. The man gaped, and Ceric had his opening.

The Dane gave an angry cry, and swung the shaft through the air. He must drop it to pull the sword at his side, and Ceric made sure not to give him the chance. He drove right for the open arm holding the shaft, catching the Dane in the armpit. The links of ring-shirt gave way under the force of Ceric's strength propelling the iron forward.

Ceric took just enough time to toss the Dane's sword for safekeeping into the shrub the man had broken through to reach him. He would find the body again marking the place, that was sure.

By the tree line a second riderless horse bearing a pennon appeared. He made his way steadily towards it, keeping to the edge and scanning the trees as he did so. The horses were moving about, tossing their heads, and more than one of them trailing a rein. But as he neared he saw the second pennon to be the war-flag made by Edgyth. The golden dragon she had made for Edwin had a curling tail spiraling back over the beast's head. It was utterly distinct from any other.

He spoke aloud, yet to himself. "Edwin."

His brother was here as well. This was the horse of one of his body-guards.

He would risk crossing the field to reach the horse the faster. He ran, his movement bringing him close to the dead animal which had been speared. He jerked to a stop. It was Edwin's horse.

His blood ran cold in his veins, seeing this. He looked to the nearby bodies, dropping shield and spear to turn two of them over. Neither was his younger brother.

He stood a moment by the dead horse, open-mouthed, panting from exertion and dread.

A man groaned. He picked up his spear, ready to pole any Dane who lived. To the right of Edwin's horse, a large man with grey hair lay on his side. The uppermost shoulder ran with blood; he was lying in it.

It was Cadmar.

Ceric dropped on his knees at his side. He feared trying to turn the old man on his back, and instead took up the free right hand. He grasped it in both his own.

"Cadmar. It is Ceric. I am here with you."

The warrior-monk's hand moved between his own, reaching, the fingers clutching the forearm of Ceric. Cadmar's eyes were closed, but the well-known face contorted in a way which told that his words had been heard. The hand upon Ceric's forearm now relaxed, and he again held it in his own.

"Edwin," the old man rasped out.

Ceric looked to the tree line, where the restless horses moved. Two men now stood there. Though bloodied, Ceric was sure the second was his brother.

"Edwin lives, he lives," he assured the dying man. To have this granted to them both, allaying his fear and Cadmar's final concern, seemed the greatest boon of his life.

The warrior-monk exhaled, a long breath of relief and release. The lips moved. Ceric brought his head closer to receive the gift of his friend's final words. It came as a gasp, followed by a final gentle exhale, almost a sigh of recognition.

"Jesus . . . " breathed the old man.

The roughened fingers relaxed their grasp. Ceric let his head drop. He lifted the calloused and time-weathered hand to his lips, and kissed it.

He must stand now, and he did. No one was fighting, at least no one near, and he could not allow the body to be pillaged. The sword Ceric knew so well had already been taken.

He took up spear and his blue and yellow shield and started toward Edwin. It was his body-guard Alwin at his side, Ceric saw. As he neared Edwin tried to raise his arm, then winced and stopped before the arm was waist high. Blood was smeared over his younger brother's face, but if he was on his feet he could ride.

"Cadmar is dead." Ceric told them. "His last word was Christ's name." He was blinking away the water from his eyes, and saw that both Edwin and Alwin did so as well.

Finding the old man here had driven almost all else from his thoughts. Now another came to mind.

"The Prince – where is he?"

Alwin had answer. "We have seen him. He has won the field, and is down the road where the horses are. Eorconbeald is with him."

Ceric muttered a prayer of thanks. Then his thoughts returned to the warrior-monk.

"Cadmar," he said. "We must get his body. We will bury him here, in the wood."

Edwin made to take a step forward, but his body-guard stopped him. "You are staying here. We will work the faster without you."

"Are you hurt," asked his brother.

"No," Edwin lied.

Alwin snorted. "Broken ribs and nose. Almost broke his head, as well." He led Edwin back within the wood, to rest against a tree trunk.

They carried Cadmar to the trees, Ceric at the shoulders, Alwin at the feet. Cadmar had lost his sword, but Ceric would not leave him weaponless. He left the man his knife, and also the small silver cross about his neck. Ceric ran and brought his horse, and pulled his blanket from his saddle bag. They draped this as shroud over the body. There was no way to dig a grave. They must pile the body with rock.

Hrald had lost Onund in the trees. His quarry had removed his bright shield from his back, leaving his pursuer to follow the glint of metal from his helmet, and the duller gleam of the man's ring-tunic. The thickness of the undergrowth and the tangle of ground vines made for noisy passage forward. Now it was silent. Hrald stopped, listening for the crackle of a branch underfoot betraying movement. Nothing. For a moment he remembered walking with Tindr in the woods of Gotland, and the way Tindr, who could not hear, would scan.

As Hrald waited, eyes shifting, Onund stepped forward from behind an oak tree.

"Have you stopped running, Onund?" Hrald asked. "You ran, fearful of Askil or any others who would make you pay for your part in the killing at Saltfleet. But I will make you pay, now."

Onund grinned. "You cannot kill me, for Gunnulf's sake."

Hrald felt his anger flare. Gunnulf had been his friend since boyhood, his closest friend at Four Stones. Onund would not borrow on that now. This man had threatened him bodily, defamed him before the warriors of Turcesig, and taken up with a force of invaders who had killed nine of his men. He at last had the chance to speak the truth to this renegade from his hall.

"Gunnulf!" was Hrald's retort. "You are not fit to name him. If you had been true friend to Gunnulf you would never have betrayed Four Stones.

"You could not bear that he died for Four Stones, that he placed something above you."

Onund gave howling protest to this charge, and pulled his sword.

Hemmed in by trees they had almost no room in which to fight. Hrald dropped his spear and drew his own blade, for in such close quarters it must be swords. They came at each other with all the heat they both felt, slashing at knees, swinging at the head, lunging forward to attempt a strike at an unguarded shoulder. Save for their grunts of effort they were silent. They circled each other as best they could, mindful of the hooking reach of roots and vines that might ensnare their feet. Blows rained upon their shields, and those that struck the iron boss stung their hands within the grip. The steel of their blades clashed, that angry ringing of lethal metal hungry to bite flesh. Sweat ran from their brows as they moved, eyes fixed on the other, in the warrior's ritual of death.

Hrald stumbled. In a deft move Onund swept his shield up and away from his body. It hit Hrald in the head, knocking off his helmet. The iron rim banding the edge of the disc struck his forehead. It opened a seam in his flesh, and the ensuing blood flooded over Hrald's right eyebrow and into his eye. Onund gave a triumphant laugh. Hrald had to step back, give himself as much cover with his shield as he could, and use the wrist of his sword arm to try to wipe the blood out of his eye.

As Onund moved in to reengage, Hrald abandoned all caution. He had been hit and lost his helmet. Onund had drawn first blood, and the advantage he had won was great. He came at Onund, shield pushing, blade flashing, with all the speed and strength he possessed. Leaves trembling from branches were sliced to ribbands of green. Twigs and chips of tree bark flew from where the steel of his sword touched them. He forced Onund to give ground, pushing him back under his onslaught. Then Onund stumbled, his left shoulder dipping. Hrald was ready, and got in with his sword tip at the guard of Onund's blade. The weapon lifted up and out of his grip, and fell into the ferns by the oak.

Hrald must now finish the deed. Their eyes locked for an instant. The blood dribbling from Hrald's forehead again ran into his eye, and he tried to blink it away, unwilling to move his sword hand.

Onund's right hand was bleeding where the edge of Hrald's sword had caught it. He made no move with it towards the knife at his right hip.

Then Onund lifted both hands, his empty right, and his left, still holding his shield. The right was raised palm forward, in the sign of surrender.

Hrald could not attack a man surrendering.

"Pick up your sword, and fight," he ordered.

Onund shook his head. Hrald could see from the line of blood on the man's raised hand that his sword edge had caught at the base of his thumb, perhaps disabling it.

Hrald could not kill him unless he fought. He took a step back, yet they were no more than two sword's lengths apart. Hrald eased the hold on his shield, considering if he should accept the surrender. To kill a man no longer fighting – he did not think himself capable of that, even one akin to Onund.

Then Onund pulled his knife from his hip, and flung it overhand at Hrald's bare head. Up came Hrald's shield, blocking it. The knife point stuck until Hrald flicked his sword to knock it away.

Onund shook off his shield. He yelled in fury as he charged at Hrald. "I will kill you with my bare hands!"

Onund was a famed wrestler, perhaps the best at Four Stones. Hrald would not allow the man to use that skill on him.

He ducked down into a deep squat, shield foremost. He used his whole body to trip Onund, who crashed into him and flipped over, striking the trunk of the oak tree behind which he had hidden. Hrald had held his sword upright in his fist, and the tip of it caught Onund across the tops of his thighs as he flipped.

Onund lay sprawled at the foot of the oak. As Hrald neared he tried to swing a leg up, to wrap it round him and pull him down, but the slice at the top of the thigh was enough to prevent such action. Hrald stood over him, his sword pointing at Onund's breast.

Down your man, then kill him, was the warrior's prime dictate. Hrald's first hesitation to do so had nearly cost him his own life.

Onund closed his eyes. He said a single word.

"Gunnulf."

Hrald gave a cry. Instead of a deep stab to the heart, he swung his sword and hacked at Onund's throat. The man would speak no more. Blood shot forth, pumping in a forceful spray, colouring all behind them crimson. One swing was not enough; Hrald pulled back the dripping blade and used it almost as a lash against the inert form before him.

As he hacked at the body everything he had suffered since he had been named Jarl arose, rushing up as from a dark well deep within him: his battle with Thorfast, once friend and ally, with its most desperate of stakes; the death of Gunnulf at that same contest; the loss of good men who had been but protecting his own lands; the betrayal by his beloved wife, which had struck him to the core as an iron wedge driven by a shaft of steel splits the strongest heartwood.

Hrald could not stop the swinging of his weapon. When he finally lowered the sword for good over the bloody mass that had been a living man, his gorge rose. The smell of blood choked him. He turned away, unable to look down upon the hacked remains. He retched up bile from a stomach both empty and churning with feverish energy.

He dropped his sword, sickened and disgusted. He lifted his streaming eyes to the grey and obscure heavens above him.

His father's words before his contest with Thorfast sounded in his ears, the assurance that his opponents were but men. *You do not fear them. They fear you.*

Now he feared himself, feared what he would and could do.

He raised both hands to his head. He knew he trembled, though his body ran with sweat. He blew out a breath, mind and heart racing. He must get back to his men.

He looked at the ground before him. The knife Onund had thrown at him lay harmlessly on a torn hillock of moss. The brown leathern wrapping of the grip barely showed against the mounded soil. He was victor;

he must take the weapons of the vanquished. He bent and picked it up. He knew this knife. It was Gunnulf's, and he had been wearing it the day he died. Onund must have taken it from his kit after the washing and wrapping of Gunnulf's body.

Onund had loved Gunnulf, and just tried to kill him with his knife. His head swam, and he gave it a shake to try to clear it.

He went for the dead man's sword, in the ferns by the oak. He left the helmet, and the ring shirt, mashed beyond reclaiming. He tore handfuls of green ferns to wipe blood, his own and Onund's, from his hands and head. The slice on his brow was already crusted with drying blood.

He drank the contents of his water flask, dashing a little on his face, collected his sword, and recovered his helmet and spear. He set out, back through the trees to find the field, and his men.

A PRIZE
OF GREAT PRICE

CERIC worked in mournful silence with Alwin, gathering and piling forest stones over the shrouded body of Cadmar. As Ceric bent to place another rock, he saw a movement from the tail of his eye. He straightened. He had glanced more than once toward Edwin's dead horse, to see if any Dane appeared. Any who did might be the man who killed Cadmar, looking for his body, to recover the rest of what he carried. This figure did not stop. There on the grassy field of death a man had come from somewhere, and was carrying a staff. Upon it was worked that emblem of the Danes, a raven in flight.

Ceric narrowed his eyes. Anger overtook his sorrow; the sheer waste of what lay upon that field. He would get that banner, so that no one else could fly it.

He stood up, pushed through the shrubs, and began to run after the man. The war-flag was immediate target for the wrath Ceric felt.

Past Edwin's fallen horse were lying several spears; he had his pick. He grasped at a light throwing spear, then redoubled his speed, slowing to make perfect his throw.

The man dropped in an instant.

His spear had hit the flag-bearer squarely in the upper back. His body spilt forward, face down, arms crooked at the elbow and reaching. The pole of the war-flag was partly beneath him. Ceric knew it had been a flawless kill, yet practice led him to draw his sword as he approached.

Nearing the body he saw the man must have been yet a youth. He gave his head a shake; it could not be helped. Standard-bearers were oftentimes the minor kin of war-chiefs, and as such wore silver or carried things of value. Anything Ceric took from this one would be given to the poor in Cadmar's name. Indeed, now that he was almost upon the body, a glint of silver shone from around the fallen youth's neck, an amulet which had swung around to the back of his tunic. It was a large hammer of Thor.

Ceric replaced his sword in his baldric. He pulled the spear from the flag-bearer's back and flung it, with its bloody point, aside. Then he turned the dead youth with his hand and his booted foot. As he did the head tipped back, and the war-cap upon it rolled off.

His eyes saw it was Ashild.

Ashild. He had killed the woman he loved.

The scream that pierced the air over that now-still field was one scarcely of human making.

He fell down upon his knees at her side. He wrapped his arms around her back, sliding through her warm blood. He lifted her to his chest. Her head fell back, the single plait of her fallow brown hair caught within his grasp. Her eyes of grey-blue, those eyes which he had often seen storm and laugh, were open.

He kissed those eyes, and all her face, as he held her, rocking her as if his movement would restore her own.

Between his kisses he murmured her name, over and again: Ashild, Ashild, Ashild, to summon her back.

The tears falling from his eyes wet her face. They dropped upon her eyes and lips, and ran from the curves of her cheeks to her jaw.

"Ashild, Ashild," he choked. "Ashild. My one and only love."

He lay her over his lap, and pulled his left hand from underneath her. It was red with her lifeblood. He pressed it against his own heart, sobbing as he had never wept in his life.

Upon his smallest finger was the golden ring his grandmother had given him. He pulled it off, and took Ashild's left hand in his own, and pressed it too against his heart. Then he threaded the golden ring upon the fourth finger of her hand.

"I wed thee, Ashild," he whispered. "I wed thee."

He kissed the ring, and the hand that now wore it. It was limp, and the fingers growing cool.

He brought his mouth close to her ear.

"At Four Stones, I told you I would be back for you, and that when next we met, we would bind our lives together.

"Ashild. Ashild. My wife."

He curled over her, holding her, sheltering her, rocking her, choking on his tears and gasping for breath as he chanted her name.

Across the field a man upon the road spotted Ceric. His eyes swept the margins of the trees, mindful of any of the enemy who readied to come after the figure kneeling there. Then Worr made his way to him.

He dropped down next Ceric. He wrapped his arm across his back.

"Ceric," said Worr.

Ceric turned his face to him, then lowered Ashild's body so he might see who he held.

Worr's intake of breath was followed by his stunned words. "Holy Mother of God," he murmured. A sound came from Worr's throat, almost a yowl of disbelief.

Ceric stared at him. He spoke, his words grief-slurred and halting. "Cadmar is dead. I wanted the raven flag."

He turned his gaze back upon Ashild. "It was – it was Ashild who carried it."

Worr gasped. No other response was imaginable, save that which he next offered, to cross himself. He was in the midst of the sacred, and must do so.

The two men knelt there, one holding the body of she whom he loved.

When Ceric next spoke, it was in a tone low and controlled, as if seeing the next step in a planned journey.

"Will you ride with me, Worr?" he asked. "I must take her home to Four Stones."

"Yes, yes, I will ride with you," Worr answered.

"There is a cairn not far up the road," Ceric went on, in the same low and calm voice. "I think it is one of Four Stones."

Worr nodded, soundlessly. He was reminded of the hushed and deliberate voices in the halls of the bereaved. The shock of death rendered those still living a brief span to glide through the needful duties of death. It must be so, lest they lose their reason with grief.

Worr stood. "I will tell the Prince. I saw your stallion back there, which is why I came looking for you. I will get horses and be back."

Worr found Eadward and his remaining men down the road. In but a few words the horse-thegn of Kilton spoke of their going, and the need for it, and asked for his leave. This granted, he found the great white stallion which was Ashild's, pawing at the ground where it had been tied. A spear was nearby, standing against a tree by the animal's head. A small shield was there, next it. He took these as well.

He got his own horse, and Ceric's too, and made his way to where Ceric knelt. Not far away he saw Cadmar's sword, the naked blade lying in the grass. It had fallen from the hand of a Dane, who lay on his back, an arrow in his chest. One of Eadward's archers had struck home in the man's breast. Worr picked up the sword. He took the dead Dane's scabbard, left the weapon, but slid Cadmar's own within it. He added it to the packs. Worr fastened all needful to their saddle bags. He would lead Ceric's stallion behind his own horse. He could ride with his own spear in hand. Those of Ceric and Ashild he tied, points rearward, to the saddle rings of Ceric's horse.

In dreamlike slowness Ceric laid Ashild upon the grass. He rose and closed his hand about the ash staff of the raven war-flag. A sleeve had been sewn into the edge of the flag, and he pulled it free from the staff. He lifted Ashild's back, and moved her plait to tuck the narrow edge of the banner into her collar. The linen of her tunic was soaked with blood, and it wet the fresh linen through, but it would hide the hideous wound between her shoulder blades.

Ceric pulled himself upon the white stallion. Worr picked up Ashild and handed her up so she sat before Ceric on the saddle, her back to the horse's neck. She lay astride against Ceric's chest, her face against his shoulder, their hearts pressed together.

They made their way onto the road. Edwin and Alwin were there, preparing to mount horses. Edwin called out to his brother, who did not respond. Worr looked down at the Lord of Kilton and shook his head. The Prince had been told the story, and Edwin would soon hear it from him. Right now they must move.

They headed on a northerly route, the way Ceric had arrived. If Ceric had truly seen a cairn of Four Stones, Worr would track his way to the hall. They must go slowly for the burden Ceric bore, and in secret to avoid the remnants of those Danes they had just triumphed over. Worr would get Ceric safely there, or die in the attempt.

Hrald stepped through the last of the trees, shivering as if it were Winter. The line of horses on the far side of the road was not half what it had been when he had entered the wood. That eerie half-silence which followed a battle lay over the field, one broken by the jingle of metal being pulled from belts, and the gladsome call of solitary voices discovering some special item of worth in their battle-gain.

These were his men who bent over the inert bodies they plundered. He stood there, looking over them, grateful for his own life, and for their win. A horse appeared,

Asberg's, and he saw his uncle press the animal towards him.

"Hrald!"

They embraced, then the older man held the younger at arm's distance in question.

"I followed Onund into the wood. I killed him there," was all Hrald said. He lifted the dead man's naked sword in his hand.

"Jari will be glad of that," Asberg granted. He put his hand on Hrald's forehead, flicking away dried blood and studying his wound. "You will have an early brow-furrow, nothing worse," he judged.

"Jari – how is he," Hrald asked.

"He is on his way to Four Stones, with the rest of the wounded. They went ahead, with more than half our men."

"Abi was hit, an arrow in the back of the leg."

Hrald shook his head. "I should not have left him."

The boy's father had answer. "He will boast of this first wound."

Hrald lifted his eyes to the far trees, where he knew Ashild had been hidden.

"Where is Ashild," he asked next.

"Riding with the wounded, I am sure. They may even get there tonight."

"How many did we lose," Hrald asked.

"About a score dead, and half as many wounded. We will know more when we are back."

Asberg recalled the man who had been with Ashild.

"But Byrgher – Byrgher is dead."

Hrald closed his eyes.

Byrgher was a good man, one who had served with Yrling and then Hrald's father. Hrald had entrusted Ashild to him, thinking it a lighter duty, and now he was dead.

"How did he die?"

"We were caught between the Danes of Haesten, and the men of Wessex."

"Wessex?"

His uncle told him of Eadward's arrival. The fighting had by that time cooled, but the arrival of the thegns of Wessex had spared Hrald more losses. His uncle had not seen Ceric amongst his men.

"But Eadward took the Danes we captured," Asberg went on.

It was clear he was not fully reconciled to their loss. "They were ours to kill and I would have, every one. Eadward wanted them for his King, as hostages for ransom. He had been trailing Danes who had built a fort near Lundenwic, and came across ours from Saltfleet instead. Still, he wanted those who lived. Eadward paid us well enough for them. He gave us all their weapons and jewellery, their purses too. And we have the Saltfleet horses back."

Asberg gave thought to what further he could tell. "The Danes he took – they were led behind his men, with ropes around their necks, and hands tied. It will be a long walk for them."

⁂

Aided by moonlight the men of Four Stones made their way back to the hall. They came in shifts, the largest contingent first, those of the wounded and their escorts. Ælfwyn had feared seeing either child amongst their number, yet the fact that none of those returned had seen Hrald since the beginning of the action did not reassure her. She and Burginde and the other women of the hall were occupied enough tending to those who limped in between other men, or whose heads, arms, or legs had been cut by steel or bruised by impact. Jari's wound was washed and dressed in the hall by his wife Inga. The spear tip hit the meatiest part of the calf, sparing the cords of the ankle; he should walk without limping when it healed. After several cups of mead he was ready to hobble between two strong men to his own timber house with Inga.

Young Abi's arrow puncture was washed in betony water and dressed by Burginde. Striking as it did the back of his thigh, the whole leg was painful and stiff, and the boy must lie on his belly to relieve it. He took it well, regretting only his dropping of Hrald's battle-flag.

It was not until Hrald and Asberg arrived after dark with the last of the men that Ælfwyn knew her daughter was missing.

Hrald read it at once. Night had fallen, but small fires in iron pots cast their yellow light about the work yard. His mother ran to him, tears of joy in her eyes to behold him. Her hand rose at once to his brow. Then she mouthed his sister's name.

"Ashild," she told him. "She is not here."

Tired as he was, Hrald straightened as if jolted awake. His eyes turned round the hall yard, to rest on Mul, standing in the dimness of the stable doorway with Bork, solemn and wide-eyed at his side. Mul looked at Hrald, and shook his head. The big white horse had not returned for a rubdown; the paddock, full of returned horses, lacked his ghostly form.

All were questioned. None had seen her in the groups of returning men. Had she left, alone, and somehow got turned around on her way back to the hall?

Byrgher, the last to have seen her, had been killed at Asberg's side. The fear that she had been discovered by the marauding Danes and taken prisoner was foremost. It was also something Hrald could not accept. Ashild was mounted the entire time, and would have bolted if danger drew too near. And he felt sure she would have resisted, even unto death, her capture.

Hrald allowed the villagers to return to their crofts. They streamed out, thankful the immediate threat seemed over, and grateful at the prospect of their own humble hearths and beds.

Few at Four Stones slept that night. Ælfwyn had washed the shield rim cut on Hrald's brow, and wrapped a narrow band of linen about it. Lying on his bed in the treasure room, his eyes returned over and again to the corner of the room where the raven banner his sister made for him had stood. Where are you, Ashild, he asked himself. Where are you.

In the bower house, Ælfwyn and Burginde need comfort little Cerd even as their own fears grew. The first night without his mother passed without event for the toddling boy. Tonight, however, he was fretful, and when they held the child he seemed to be looking over their shoulders, searching for her.

Just after dawn Hrald and Kjeld and a few picked men got ready to ride after her. Asberg would command Four Stones; he had sent word to Æthelthryth and Styrbjörn of his promised return to Turcesig as soon as Abi's leg wound allowed.

They were saddling their horses when the whistle rang out from a watch-man on the palisade. Hrald's hand stopped at the girth strap as he listened. Bork, at his horse's head, kept his eyes on Hrald. It was a single shrill note, a call for Hrald. It was only used as urgent summons. A moment later the wide gates yawned open.

Hrald stepped through the opening into the broader gloom of dawn. His mother and Burginde were at his side; his little sister Ealhswith had charge of Cerd in the bower house. Asberg and Kjeld stood at Hrald's right as they waited. The rest of the men who were to ride crowded behind to see who had occasioned the call to their Jarl. Other men and women of the hall and yard joined them, a throng who had spent a restless night, awaiting answers.

The village was just wakening, and on its road in the distance they saw a white stallion, surely Ashild's; but moving so slowly, ever so slowly. Another rider came next the white horse, leading a riderless third. The crofters already stirring in their wattle-fenced plots stood staring at the horsemen. They were women and children at cooking and egg-collecting, men who held a few sticks of fire-wood, or those readying to take a tool in hand. They all stopped what they were doing. Some left their crofts and began following behind.

Ælfwyn clutched at her son's arm, and Burginde rocked forward on tiptoes as if it might help her discern the truth of what approached.

Ceric and Worr had ridden through the night with Ashild's body. They were guided by moonlight, and the need to bring her back to the home she loved. Now they approached the gates of that home, leading a doleful procession. At every croft they passed, the folk thereof, open-mouthed in awe, joined them.

Their horses paced slowly towards the opened gates. Those awaiting them saw the rider on the white stallion to be Ceric. His helmetless head showed his coppery-gold hair, grown long. It lay upon his shoulders, tangled but bright in the growing daylight.

He had his arm around a smaller figure before him, its arms hanging down with a straightness denying any coursing of blood under that pale skin. As the stallion neared all could see the raven banner, turned now so that it flew, gaping beak upward, upon the figure's back.

A whimper came from Ælfwyn's throat, a strangled sound, as faint and bloodless as looked the hands that hung from the body Ceric embraced.

The horses grew closer, and stopped. Hrald had been rooted to the ground, held by his mother's hand on his arm. He now moved up to the stallion. The two men, one on foot, the other mounted, were close enough to speak. The toll exacted by the past two days was written on their faces. It was weariness beyond bodily exhaustion, a deeper sickening exacted by what they had witnessed, and what they had done. In the face of Ceric was some-thing more, the mark of torment.

Ceric, pressing Ashild's body against his own, looked down at Hrald.

"She was carrying a battle-flag. I threw the spear."

Stunned silence greeted this admission, the shock of the report closing the throats of the hearers. The void in all mouths seemed to vibrate with it. That stillness was followed by a wail of lamentation sweeping over the gath-ering. It swelled the wrenching cry of loss into a howl of rage, storming against a Fate that had cut short this young and vital life.

Hrald moved closer, and lifted his arms to receive the body of his sister. With Ceric guiding, he pulled her from the horse. Hrald took her in his arms as if she were a small and sleeping child, the plait of her hair hanging down, as did her left arm. Her knees were gracefully bent in the crook of Hrald's right elbow.

Ceric slipped from the horse and faced him. Through his sunburn, his face was nearly as white as that of Ashild.

"I killed her, Hrald. I killed her. You must kill me. You must."

Hrald closed his eyes.

Burginde stepped forward. She came to Ceric and placed her arm around his waist, and spoke to him as if soothing an injured child.

"Come," she told Ceric, "come into the treasure room."

There was firmness in her coaxing, and Ceric walked with her. Ælfwyn was at her daughter's head, her hand upon Ashild's cold brow, as Hrald carried her into the hall. They reached the treasure room. Burginde took Ælfwyn's keys from her waist and let them in, with Worr, Asberg and Kjeld. The nurse moved to the table and took up the two cressets upon it. Hrald came forward and laid his sister on the bare wood planking of the trestle.

Ceric at once went to Ashild's left, and took her hand in his own. He looked down on it, then to those he faced. "She is my wife," he told them. He opened his hand enough that they might view hers. There on her ring finger was a broad golden band.

It took all Ælfwyn's resources to keep herself upon her feet. She must give one order, and she gave it now. She looked to Kjeld.

"Please to go to Oundle, with waggon and full escort. Bring Abbess Sigewif."

The hours that passed in that room as they awaited the Abbess slipped by almost unmarked. The first to knock upon the oaken door was Wilgot the priest. Those within found themselves sinking to their knees around the table, as if it were an altar. He brought with him his vial of holy oil, and anointed Ashild's smooth and pale brow, stamping the sign of the cross with his thumb as he uttered the blessing of the final sacrament in the tongue of Rome. He made blessing over all of them, then departed until the Abbess should arrive.

Worr and Asberg left, the first to care for the horses and to clear his head; the second to speak to Jari and to see Abi, also under the care of Jari's wife Inga.

The sole window high on the wall showed the passage of a Sun lifting, pausing, and then beginning to decline. Burginde brought food and drink. The food remained untouched, the drink, broths and ale, was swallowed haltingly.

At times Ælfwyn, Ceric, and Burginde just wept at the sight of the body. Ceric sat on a chair at Ashild's side, holding her hand. Hrald stood, almost unmoving, looking at her, heart bursting though dry-eyed, as of yet unable to give outlet to his grief through tears.

Why had he allowed her to go? He was implicated in her death as surely as if he had placed that spear in the hand of Ceric.

No one else was permitted in. Burginde came and went, including a long spell with Ealhswith in the bower house, when she told her of the loss. Ealhswith wished to come to the treasure room at once, but Burginde promised the girl she could see Ashild once the Abbess had arrived, not before. Until then she must take good care of Ashild's son, for love of her sister, and the boy himself. With that admonition she dried the girl's tears with her apron, and taking up Cerd in her arms, brought the boy and Ealhswith up to the weaving room, where the girl's Aunt Eanflad, her gentle soul as yet unknowing the tragedy beneath her, welcomed her to spin as she stood at her loom.

Within the treasure room Ceric did not move from Ashild's side. Burginde had urged him to drink, yet though his mouth was dry, he felt unable to swallow. Something was happening to his bodily senses. At times he felt he could scarce hear what was being said around him, but perhaps no words were spoken. He would close his eyes, which felt as dry as his mouth. When he opened them the room seemed to expand and contract in his line of vision. His hand holding that of Ashild's was reaching on beyond its natural length across some ever-growing chasm of dim and diffuse light.

SSSSSSSSSSS

Sigewif arrived in late afternoon. She was ushered into the treasure room by Wilgot, who entered with her.

She paused to take in the dreadful scene, and let her eyes rest, one to the next, on those clustered about the table. Tapers had been brought, two by Ashild's shoulders and two by her feet, their linen wicks wavering a soft golden light over the room. Burginde had carried in long branches of rosemary, and this herb of remembrance lay surrounding the body. As the Abbess entered, Ælfwyn and Burginde rose, as did Asberg and Worr, who had returned. Hrald had never sat, as if on watch over Ashild. Ceric alone did not seem aware of her presence. He sat by Ashild's side as he had for hours, and would not let go of her cold hand. Burginde went for Ealhswith and returned with her, keeping her hands crossed over her shoulders as the girl quietly wept.

The Abbess moved to one end of the table, by Ashild's head. Wilgot was at Ashild's feet.

Sigewif looked down upon the body before her. The unadorned tunic Ashild wore was of mid blue, her leggings simple, and of a darker blue. The plain leathern belt she wore was hung with a long seax in its hardened sheath, spanning her entire waist. Her everyday low boots of brown were on her feet. Her hair was set in one thick plait, now resting to one side of her head. Signs of soil and grass stains marked her clothing, but her face was as clean and composed as if she slept. Only the pallor of it spoke of death. The Abbess, looking down at her, must smile to see that active face so composed. She made the sign of the cross over her. Then she bent to kiss Ashild's brow. She smelled the scent of the holy chrism the priest had crossed her forehead with, as he gave her final absolution.

Sigewif inhaled that scent. She straightened up, and for the last time placed her hands upon Ashild's shoulders. She addressed the room, and some higher power as well.

"I claim the body of Ashild," she told them, "to rest within the church of Oundle, which she ably defended."

No one had yet been laid beneath the stone floor of the new church Ælfwyn had endowed. Oundle had its own burial ground, outside its palisade. All had thought that burial within the small edifice would be reserved for the most august of Oundle's community, for its priests, and for the Abbess herself. Now Ashild of Four Stones would become the first to lie there. The Abbess of Oundle proclaiming thus made it an order.

Sigewif looked over the stunned and sorrowing faces. Again, she smiled.

"She is beyond our Earthly concerns," she reminded. "Rejoice for her. Take strength in her strength."

Ceric lifted his face from where it was lying upon Ashild's hand, and looked up at the Abbess.

"You must relinquish her now, Ceric of Kilton," she told him, the gentlest of commands.

He found voice, though it be little more than a croak. "She is my wife."

"Live to her standard, and you may meet in Heaven," she returned.

Sigewif looked to Ælfwyn. "We will prepare her for removal to Oundle now."

At this Ceric broke down, sobbing; he was being told to quit the room, quit the woman he loved, and whose life he had ended.

The Abbess had comfort for him in her next words.

"You were perhaps a needed portal to eternal life for her. None can judge, in our Earthly frailty, what any of this means. Rejoice in what you knew together, and for her Heavenly abode. Take strength in her strength," she repeated.

The Abbess looked to Hrald. He came to Ceric with Worr. Ceric gave the hand he held a final, desperate kiss. Then the two men led him away.

Ealhswith ran to her mother, who embraced her, kissing her face in almost desperate need. Then Burginde took her back to the weaving room.

When the three women were alone, Sigewif took Ælfwyn's hands in her own. "Burginde and I shall wash her body."

Though Ælfwyn looked glazed from shock, she contested this claim. "No, I must do it," she murmured. Every particle of her body seemed to rebel over the fact that Ashild lay there upon the table, dead. The raw anguish of the loss was still mixed with disbelief, giving it a potency striking deep into her core.

"You may be present," the Abbess conceded. "Sit there as we prepare what we need."

A glance at Burginde had the nurse moving toward the door. When both Abbess and Burginde were without, Sigewif drew from the pack awaiting her on the high table a small pouch. She brought her head close to Burginde's. "Here is a Simple to make her sleep. Crumble the leaves in this packet into warm broth, and give it to your mistress, making sure she drinks it all."

Burginde carried it off, to bring it back steaming. Sigewif was now sitting next Ælfwyn, and took the pottery cup from the nurse. She placed it in Ælfwyn's hands, which were shaking as the slender fingers wrapped round it.

"Drink this, my child," the Abbess crooned. "Drink this, and when you are done, you may lie here as we work."

The Abbess rose, and Burginde took her place next Ælfwyn, chiding her with loving words, prompting her to drink all.

The Lady of Four Stones did, and after found ease in lying down. Burginde stayed with her for awhile, sitting on the stool she ever sat upon when in the room. Ælfwyn was aware of Sigewif moving about, of the door sometimes opening, but did not feel she must lift her head. The wolfskin throw was thick beneath her, the pillow soft and smooth under her head. She became aware she lay on the bed in which Ashild was conceived. It now gave a strange but real comfort for her to be lying there as her daughter's body was being readied for eternal rest. She let her eyelids flutter shut.

Sigewif found the raven flag as soon as she and Burginde began to undress Ashild. It was stuck to the back of her tunic, but they lifted it without it tearing. The dark body of the bird had absorbed Ashild's blood when it still flowed, but some had seeped onto other areas, staining crimson the light blue of the woven background.

The Abbess spent a silent moment considering it, then folded the stiffened linen in thirds. It had absorbed Ashild's lifeblood, and she would take it to Oundle with her body.

They unbuckled the seax and drew it off. The silver hammer Sigewif removed and set aside. Boots and clothing they removed, and then using the basins of warm water carried to them from the kitchen, began, with tender and loving hands, the washing of the body. Burginde's eyes ran the whole time, and she bit her lip to steady herself, grateful only that Ashild's mother had been spared the act she and the Abbess performed.

⚇⚇⚇⚇⚇⚇⚇⚇⚇

Hrald sat with Ceric and Worr at the high table. The hall had been emptied of women and children, though two serving women stood in the recesses of the kitchen passageway, waiting and watching. Seeing the men settle there, the elder of them, unprompted, returned with cups and a ewer of not ale, but mead. The woman poured out for them, and they took up their cups.

The fullness of its savour, strong, lush, and slightly sweet, filled their mouths and warmed their empty bellies.

After the first long draught Ceric looked down into his cup, and began to speak. His voice was strained and halting, as if he spoke from the distance of events lived long ago.

"I was scouting for Eadward, on the trail of Danes we chased from Lundenwic. I did not know we were close to Four Stones until I saw one of your cairns." He shifted his eyes to Hrald. "It seemed a sign of good fortune; I recall laughing when I spotted it. It would give me a chance to come here, see you. See Ashild."

Hrald took up his side of their recent actions.

"Two drekars landed at Saltfleet and killed most of my men there. One made it back to tell us of this. We set out after them. They were the men we fought."

He looked up at the rafters of the roof, high above his head. He did not want to say the rest.

"I needed every man, sending more to Oundle, and to protect the horses. Ashild wanted to come, to act as courier only, should we need her."

Hearing this, tears began running from the eyes of Ceric. He could hardly bear to revisit the last moments of Ashild's life.

"She had a war-flag . . . I saw a raven of the Danes. It was all I saw."

Ceric sat there, shaking his head against his deed.

Hrald's voice too was raw. "It was the raven flag she made for me. But she was the first to ride under it, when she went to Oundle and killed the Dane there."

Saying this, Hrald was finally able to release his tears. He put his face in his hands and wept.

Worr, sitting across from the friends, was moved to think of his own life. Hardened by battle and years as he was, no man could be inured to such suffering as that visited upon Ceric and Hrald. Losing his wife or boys in such a mishap would be disaster too great to grasp. It was akin to Cadmar, many years ago, going to battle with his sons, and watching them both be hacked down before him.

Worr took another draught of the mead in his cup, letting it drive his thoughts onward. He gestured to the two that they do the same.

Hrald took up his cup. He told of Onund, a man Ceric well remembered, and of how Onund had lured him into the wood. Ceric recounted riding into the dwindling action and how he had stepped on the Dane's spear to sever its point.

For a moment the corners of Hrald's mouth lifted in a brief smile. "Asberg would like that," he said in praise.

Ceric went on, telling of seeing a second dragon banner of Wessex, that of Edwin his brother, and then finding Cadmar dying upon the field. Hrald had heard from Ceric of the warrior-monk, and nodded his head in consolation.

"Did you see your brother," Hrald asked.

"I did, a moment only."

Worr spoke now. "And again, as we were riding out." He looked to Ceric, glad to be able to relate this. "He was on a horse, with his body-guard, Alwin."

The horse-thegn took breath before going on in lowered voice. "The Prince knows what happened, and will tell him."

A silence fell over the men, one broken by Hrald.

"She was looking for me," he said, his voice shaking with this truth. "She was looking for me."

"Yes." This was Ceric, with an answer so deadly he could barely let it drop from his lips. "And I found her."

The cry of a small child rent the ensuing silence. Hrald lifted his head across the hall to the wooden stair near the main door. He looked at his friend.

"You have a son."

Ceric's lips parted.

"Ashild named him Cerd."

Hrald gestured the serving woman over, bid her bring Ealhswith and the child down.

The girl came down, her lovely face tear-streaked, holding a curly headed boy in her arms. Ealhswith tried to smile as she stood before them. The boy was restless and squirming in her arms.

Ceric looked without speaking at the boy. The hair was similar to his own, the eyes closer to those of Ashild. The boy was beautiful. Ceric had never dreamt their few hours together had brought forth new life.

"Cerd," he said.

Ealhswith nodded, and smiled through eyes that still glistened. "It is the name of your grandfather. Ashild told me."

"Yes, it is a name from my mother's family."

She brought the boy closer. The child reached naturally for Hrald, who took him first. Then the boy's eyes were caught by the bright hair of Ceric. He reached for the nearest strand and closed his small hand around it.

Ceric lifted his hands. "Come, come," he whispered to the boy. Cerd gurgled, and let himself be passed from the arms of his uncle to those of his father.

When Ælfwyn awoke, the Abbess and Burginde were at her side. The shrouded body of Ashild lay before them. The binding linen Burginde had carried in was from the linen store, one of the small spaces by the weaving room. It had been destined for tunics, or shifts, or sheets and towelling, the thread spun by Burginde and woven by Ælfwyn, Eanflad, and perhaps even Ashild herself. They used two lengths to wrap the body.

A third linen covering had been placed as pall over Ashild, falling in snowy folds around the edge of the table. Sigewif had gathered up the long wands of rosemary and laid them as a cross on Ashild's breast. The air of the treasure room was scented by the sharp and clean aroma of their spiky leaves.

That night the Abbess slept in the bower house with Ælfwyn, Burginde, Ealhswith, and little Cerd. Hrald, Ceric, and Worr passed the night with Asberg in his house, that which Ashild had been living in. In the treasure room Wilgot the priest took a chair and kept vigil at Ashild's side the night long, chanting the psalms and giving praise to God the Father.

In the morning three waggons were prepared. One would carry Ashild; the second, the Abbess, Burginde, and the women of the family of Four Stones. The third would bear Wilgot, Jari, Inga, and Abi.

All who would be making the journey to Oundle filed in to view the shrouded body. Once it was lifted, Ashild would be carried away from Four Stones, never to return.

A pallet was made ready on which to place her into the waggon. Hrald and Asberg lifted her body, and placed it upon the pallet. With Kjeld and Asberg's older son Ulf they hoisted it shoulder high out to the waiting waggon.

As they left the room Sigewif looked to the two men from Kilton. She had seen three spears set against the wall, not restrained in any holder, and guessed they were theirs.

"Bring me her spear," she asked, to Worr.

He moved to the three weapons and closed his hand about that which she had carried. The Abbess nodded her thanks.

They set off, into a morning which carried more than a breath of coming chill. The troop riding as escort on this sorrowful errand was fronted by Kjeld and others of Hrald's body-guard. Then came the Jarl himself, flanked by his Uncle Asberg, and Ceric, and Worr. Forty men rode with them. As they rolled forward some of the cottars who had followed Ashild's white stallion to the gates of the hall began walking behind the last of the horsemen. They were women and girls mostly, leaving their daily tasks, willing to walk hours to dedicate the day in honour of the daughter of the hall. Once away from Four Stones the mourners passed folk in carts, and shepherds driving their flocks. These asked, with wondering eyes, of their journey, and were told by those trailing behind.

When they reached Oundle, all paused in the hall to wash hands, and to drink the welcome-cup, that symbol of life which was never neglected even in the face of death. All received it, the warriors and family of Four Stones in the hall of the Abbess, the village folk amongst the serving men and women thereof, where they were welcomed by Prioress Mildgyth with the generous hospitality due all guests.

Then the waggon bearing Ashild was driven close to the oak portal of the church. The same men who had carried Ashild from the treasure room now carried her into the church, the first shrouded figure to be sanctified before the presence of the Holy Tabernacle there upon the altar. A table covered in white linen stood before the altar to receive her body.

Every inmate of the foundation stood within the church, nuns, lay sisters and serving women on the left, monks, brothers and laymen on the right. All who travelled from Four Stones crowded in, the door remaining open so that some crofters might stand upon the broad stone step and hear the chanting of the prayers and ringing of the chimes. Ælfwyn's mother, Sister Ælfleda, stood upfront with the elder nuns, and smiled her tender blessing as she saw her daughter. Bova stood in the back of the church with the youngest nuns, her hands clasped, face wet with tears. Wilgot joined the two priests ready at the altar.

The Mass was held, benedictions given, tears shed. A blessing upon the heads of all was made. All filed out, save family, Ceric, and Worr. Sigewif stood before them. In the corner of the church, to the right of the altar, lay one of the largest slabs of limestone which made up the flooring. It was of a whiteness and purity of grain that brightened the corner. The Abbess led them to this.

"Under this stone is where Ashild shall lie."

Through a window on the side, a beam of brilliant sunlight fell upon it.

A meal was shared, no funeral feast, and of necessity simple. With warm embraces and many a kiss the Abbess saw the grieving family off.

Then Sigewif returned to the church. The stone-worker and his men were already prying up the slab of limestone designated to lie over Ashild. They grunted and strained at their work, positioning the small log rollers they would use to push the stone aside so the soil underneath could be dug. For a moment the attention of the Abbess was taken up solely by them. Then she saw a slender figure kneeling on the far side of the trestle which held Ashild's shrouded body. It was a nun in prayer: Bova.

⁂⁂⁂⁂⁂⁂⁂⁂

Ceric and Worr remained at Four Stones two more days. To be amongst the family of the hall and grieve with them as they spoke of Ashild was the greatest solace for Ceric. To learn to know his little son, to see the boy smile and play, to have Cerd run to him, crowing with laughter, gave both a supreme joy and pain. In the boy's presence he could almost forget the act that had denied him his wife, and their son his mother.

"You have nothing of Ashild's," her mother said to him as he prepared to leave. "I have a keepsake." She held out the small golden cross he recalled Ashild wearing, both as girl and later as woman. Ælfwyn's next words imbued the gift with even greater meaning.

"She wore it when your son was born."

He closed his hand about it, uttering his thanks. Before her he dropped it over his head. Then his hand returned to his collar. He pulled from under his tunic the large golden cross with its heart of garnet, and entrusted it to Ælfwyn.

"Ælfred gave this to my father, when he came home blinded. I told Ashild one day our son would wear it."

Tears, always so near, welled in Ælfwyn's eyes. She kissed the cross for its sacred import, and for who had worn it, father and son, and for who would wear it next. She kissed Ceric, a kiss of benediction on his brow.

Cerd in her arms reached for the shining chain, and pulled at it. She let him take it, a cross almost as large as his grasping hand.

Ceric looked at his son. The boy was smiling as he held the gold, then laughing as he placed one arm of the cross into his mouth. This was his child, born of his beloved wife. Their union, however brief, united two great halls, two Kingdoms. Kilton needed an heir, for what if Edwin died without issue? The fear was real, the need urgent. Yet he could not wrench this babe from the bosom of his mother's family. Cerd was all they had left of Ashild. To take him was a doubled cruelty. He could not raise his son, but must try to find comfort in knowing the boy had been granted. If Cerd was needed at Kilton, Hrald, if he lived, would allow him to come.

Another amulet of Ashild's remained at Four Stones. Her father's hammer of Thor was left by the Abbess on a shelf by Hrald's bed. When he found it, Hrald closed his hand about it. As emblem of the Old Gods, it was memory not only of Yrling, but of his own father, Sidroc.

He must go to Gotland, and see his father. Ashild had been in his keeping, and Ceric, widowed of her, was his best friend. None but he could stand before his father and Ceridwen and bring this news. He could not sail until the Spring, but sail he would.

ASHILD OF
FOUR STONES

ASHILD was lowered into the soil beneath the church of Oundle the day of her funeral mass. The stone-worker returned to the sanctuary next day with his chisel, and began pounding at the rock, working the lines of the inscription the Abbess had drawn for him: Ashild of Four Stones.

The morning after Ashild had come to Oundle, Bova arrived early to the church. She laid a single blossom on the slab of white stone beneath which Ashild lay. She did so again the next day, replacing that which she had offered the day before with a fresh flower. Now she placed the bloom upon the name carved there. It gave Bova pleasure to see the tall, sharp-edged letters, as bold as Ashild had herself been. Sometimes it was an herbal sprig the nun bent down and offered. Whatever she laid there, she did so with a prayer for the soul of Ashild.

A month after the daughter of Four Stones had been laid to rest, a woman and her daughter appeared at Oundle's gate. They were finely dressed and accompanied by an escort of five warriors. The girl, of perhaps sixteen or seventeen Summers, bore a large sheaf of flowers in her arms.

"We would visit the resting place of Ashild," her mother told Prioress Mildgyth. The prioress tilted her head to one side in unspoken question, but nodded.

She led them to the church. The single flower Bova had placed upon the stone slab in the corner caught their eye. They went to it even before the prioress gestured toward it, pausing only to genuflect before the altar.

The girl knelt down and placed her flowers at the foot of the slab. The sheaf she had brought to Ashild's tomb was of late-blooming flowers, Michaelmas daisies, leaves of striking colour, boughs with nuts upon them for fruitfulness, dried and feathery grasses, an armful of gathered beauty.

Her mother stood with bowed head at the edge of the slab, and crossed herself.

Mildgyth, seeing the reverence in which they addressed themselves to the tomb, went to Sigewif.

The Abbess, not wishing to disturb their devotion, greeted them as they left the church. They were of an old Anglian family to the west, and the elder daughter thereof had wed a wealthy Dane more than ten years ago. The mother gestured to her younger daughter.

"We had heard of Ashild's courage, and her death. My daughter had been sickly, weak in body and fearful at night. Then she dreamt of Ashild. She began to ask her for advice and counsel, as if Ashild were a friend to her. She grew strong and less frightened. This is why we have come."

The woman wore a costly necklace of strung pearls about her neck. She drew it off and placed it in Sigewif's hand.

"A gift to Oundle," she told her. "In honour of Ashild."

Theirs was but the first visit to Oundle. Other women and girls journeyed to offer their respects, even as the cold hardened and the weather grew harsh. Some had heard of Ashild from monks and priests who had visited the foundation. Others had been read the letters of one of Oundle's nuns, who had described in detail the life and death of the young woman as she knew it. All who came to stand before the gates had some token to give, even if it be a humble branch of evergreen to lay near that which Bova replaced each morning. Rich women pressed purses of silver into the hand of the prioress, or inspired perhaps by the golden necklace and bracelets on the painted statue, removed their own jewels then and there and presented them as gift in honour of Ashild.

Just before Yule the Abbess sent message to Four Stones, asking if the Lady thereof might come for a visit. A stay would be restorative, and with Winter's darkness at its height, she might take comfort there.

Ælfwyn and Burginde arrived in a waggon, little Cerd upon Burginde's lap. Thirty of Hrald's men surrounded them. A strong fire warmed the nuns' hall, which was full of both sisters and lay women at handwork. After their welcome, Burginde took the boy out to run in the gardens. The day was cold but dry, and Cerd was drawn by the tall shapes of twisted vines and gnarled fruit trees before him. Sigewif invited Ælfwyn into her writing chamber, kept warm by the brass braziers set upon the floor.

They had not beheld each other since the day of Ashild's burial. After she closed the door behind them, the Abbess spent some time looking at her. The grey eyes were searching, yet never unkind. Ælfwyn recalled Ashild's complaints of the Abbess' piercing gaze, and smiled to herself at the memory.

The Lady of Four Stones had not suffered the grave after-effects of most bereaved mothers. Many women, losing a child in such a brutal way, would have been hollowed out by grief. Indeed, the Lady's countenance had scarcely changed. She was if anything softer in her loveliness. As they sat down at the table which served as writing desk to the Abbess, she remarked on this.

Ælfwyn was forced to smile.

"It is Cerd," she answered. "I cry every day for Ashild. And for Ceric. Yet there is their child. Cerd is my great joy. He is so like Ashild. I feel her presence every day, through him."

It was Sigewif's turn to smile. "And it is of Ashild I wish to speak."

Ælfwyn's widening eyes showed her interest. The Abbess took a breath, and began.

"Her tomb has become almost a shrine."

Sigewif was studying the gently parted lips of her guest, and went on.

"Women and girls arrive, having heard of Ashild's death on the field of battle. It is her courage that attracts them." She cast her eyes down a moment, and added with lowered voice, "A quality that attracted us all.

"Some say they dream of her, that she gives them heart to do their own duty. A few claim to have known healing, bodily or in their minds, from thinking of her.

"Such claims are serious ones," the Abbess went on. "I have recorded each one, as I must. But I have ordered all under my keeping to hold their silence, to prevent the spread of rumour and speculation.

"Still, women keep coming. At first they were only the rich. Now cottar girls and their mothers and grandmothers come, as well." She looked about. "It is as if . . . they were on pilgrimage."

Ælfwyn's surprise, confusion even, showed clearly in her face. She could almost hear the ring of Ashild's laughter.

"But Ashild . . . " She hardly knew where to begin in her objections. "She was not . . . devout."

The Abbess gave a nod of her firm chin. "And Augustine of Hippo comported with whores, and fathered a child out of wedlock," she returned, naming the great and sainted teacher and philosopher.

"And what has Ashild to do with Augustine?" she further posed. The Abbess went on to answer her own question. "Both can yet be bearers of light for others. Even bearers of grace. Augustine lived long enough to see the error of his ways. Ashild was taken early, and we cannot guess where her particular sense of discernment and force of character might have brought her.

"At any rate we must look beyond their Earthly failings, as indeed I hope others shall look beyond mine own."

The Abbess pondered this a moment. She had given great thought to what she might say to Ashild's mother, knowing her news was much to encompass.

"They come to Oundle with not only prayers, but with gifts," she went on. "Flowers mostly, or some trinket dear to them. But also this."

There was a plain wooden box upon the table, newly made from the freshness of its hue. She opened the lid.

Within lay jewellery of silver and of gold, a necklace of pearls, and several small purses which Ælfwyn could guess were filled with coins. She looked at the treasure, shaking her head in wonder.

"It is benefaction, indeed," the Abbess concluded. "If hearts which may have been closed now open to grace Oundle and our work here, it is proof of God's blessing."

Ælfwyn was nearly too stunned to respond. That her own headstrong Ashild, seemingly undecided in her faith, should become an object of devotion and source of comfort to others almost beggared belief. Yet there was a queer and welcome beauty to it all. These were fearful times. If some found strength in thinking of her daughter, she must strive to understand it. She did the same herself.

Sigewif, reading Ælfwyn's face and sensing what might be her next objection, was ready with assurance.

"We must tread carefully," she told Ælfwyn, "or rather I must. Soon these accounts may reach the ears of our Bishop.

"A claim of heresy, of apostasy, is a grave concern. Yet who could argue that these women have not been touched and inspired by Ashild's example? If they find benefit and solace from their devotion, who am I – or any cleric – to gainsay it, as long as they keep foremost to God the Father, Christ His beloved son, and Mary, the Holy Mother of God?"

Ælfwyn gave thought to who sat before her, aiding her in her bewilderment. Sigewif was perhaps uniquely suited to comprehend such mysteries. Her own brother had been declared a saint, and his murder a martyrdom, within a few short years after his death. Edmund, killed ignobly in battle, had gone from man to King, to martyr and saint. Still, Ælfwyn placed her hands to her face, considering that Ashild's story was being repeated to those who had never known her, and her tomb become a place of visitation.

"Come to her resting place," the Abbess now invited. They rose and wrapped themselves in their mantles, and stepped out into the grey afternoon.

The first thing Ælfwyn saw upon entering the church were the boughs of evergreen. They lay on the stone floor in the corner, to the right of the altar. Abbess and Ælfwyn genuflected before that altar, and went to the stone slab marking Ashild's tomb. Ælfwyn had not seen the handsome carving of her daughter's name, and looked long at it now. Upon it was a sprig of fresh rosemary, tied with a coloured thread.

"From Bova," the Abbess told her. "She comes each morning to place something fresh upon the stone." Ælfwyn looked now to the evergreen boughs at the foot of the slab, seeing that a scrap of birch bark which bore writing was there, tied by a long twisted piece of dried grass.

"The name of the young woman who came yesterday," Sigewif said. "She was of cottar stock, heavy with child. She could not write, but asked Mildgyth to inscribe her name as petition, to ensure the safe delivery of her babe."

Ælfwyn could scarce speak. She stood above the Earthly remains of her daughter, not knowing whether to laugh or cry. Her eye moved from the slab to the wall. A spear had been attached, almost in the corner, held upright in a double iron hanger. She lifted her hand towards it, and looked back to the Abbess.

"Yes," confirmed Sigewif. She smiled now, as she went on. "It is her spear. I had it in my writing chamber, then decided to bring it here. Pilgrims need something to touch. Some bend down and kiss the stone. But Ashild's spear, with which she defended Oundle, and which she carried with her on the day of her death, has special meaning. They can place their hand where her own once touched."

They moved next to the Mary altar at the left of the high altar, where the women of the foundation stood during devotions. It housed the large painted statue of St Mary, from which Ælfwyn's gold and multi-gemmed bracelets and necklace given her by Yrling had hung for many years.

Ælfwyn saw something new had been placed at the base of the statue, a box of carved silver not unknown to her, as she had also given it to Oundle.

The Abbess put her hand on Ælfwyn's own to say the next.

"Within is the banner which Ashild wove and embroidered. When I watched her approach our gates, it was the first thing I saw – she on her great horse, with the banner flying behind her. I wanted it here, as memento of that day when she came, as Judith did, to slay the tyrant oppressing her people."

Ælfwyn's heart was stilled within her breast. The war-flag, soaked with her daughter's blood, had become almost as a relic, sheltered in a box of precious metal, and laid in a place of veneration to the Mother of us all.

※※※※※※※※※

The two nights spent at Oundle did indeed bring comfort. Cerd became the pet of all the sisters, and the

Abbess delighted him with the gift of a handful of goose wing feathers, their quills no longer useful for ink, but made to delight a small boy who loved to tickle Burginde. On the second day his grandmother took him into the church, alone and in her arms. She almost could not speak, but tried to keep her voice light as she carried him about so that he might see the treasure it held. The spear affixed to the wall snared his eye, and his hand and arm reached for it. Ælfwyn caught her breath. She turned away, to distract him with the bronze censer by the altar curb. He would not allow it, but began to cry, pulling for what he wanted. She walked with him to the spear. His hand wrapped over the smooth wood of it at once, and he gurgled and laughed in pleasure. How alike you are, she murmured, kissing the top of his head. How alike you are.

The morning of their leave-taking, the Abbess asked, "How fares Hrald?'

She must tell the truth. "He goes about his daily concerns manfully, with no neglect of duty to hall or village. But he is shattered, within. I know he blames himself for her death. The only time he smiles is in the presence of Cerd. I think that he sees Ashild in him, just as I do."

Ælfwyn had more to say of her son. "The day after Ashild was brought here, he told me he must go to Gotland. He will sail in Spring, as soon as the seas calm. I fear his going, yet I feel his father could help him, more than any of us can. And he must take on the heart-breaking task of telling Ceridwen how Ashild died."

The Abbess could only nod her head at this. "The courage in your line is far greater than only of the body," Sigewif ended.

As the waggon rolled off, it passed another heading to the gates. It was an ox-cart, guided by a male drover who walked at the patient beast's head. Within sat two young women, and a man who might be their father. They looked of a prosperous farm family, all dressed in the best finery they owned, and well wrapped against the cold. One of the girls had a basket of apples on her lap, the handle tied with a brightly woven ribband, clearly meant as a gift. They smiled as they reached Ælfwyn and Burginde, and their open and expectant faces made it impossible not to smile back.

Their words reached Ælfwyn's ears as their cart passed.

"They have seen Ashild," was what one said.

CERIC OF KILTON

Kilton in Wessex

WORR felt that no burden so great had ever been placed upon his shoulders than the safe return of Ceric to Kilton.

They were well supplied; Hrald had given them two pack horses, loaded with food. While journeying across Anglia they might stop at random crofts to try and procure provisions, but it exposed them to greater danger. Worr was leading them in stealth on minor roads and tracks back to Wessex.

Despite the provender Ceric would hardly eat. He seemed dazed much of the time, quietly agreeing to all Worr proposed.

Hrald had also given them a tent, needed now that cold rains fell at night. Despite the wet Ceric would sometimes leave the scant shelter it provided. Worr might awaken alone, but hear Ceric, weeping, without. Something had broken within him, his heart, certainly, but Worr feared for his mind. It was like travelling with one badly injured, yet with no bodily wound giving testament from whence the hurt emanated. Every step away from Four Stones and Oundle took something more out of him.

They had left Eadward's men in such haste that Worr had no real idea of the Prince's response to the calamity. Eadward had listened gravely to Worr's news, and granted his petition that they be dismissed to carry Ashild's body back to her hall. He had told Worr to return with Ceric to Kilton afterward; Ceric had been too long in the field. It would be left to the Prince to tell his father that the hope of binding the halls of Kilton and Four Stones had been sundered in unthinkable violence. In most circumstances this would have occasioned the bloodiest of reprisals.

In Worr's eyes, a further tragedy was that with the advent of Ceric's son, the union of the halls had been almost fully accomplished. Eadward and Ælfred had no way to know of this child; that news must wait, and only Ceric could tell it.

Once they reached Wessex they rode openly upon the roads, and gained speed. Still, it had taken them fifteen days to enter Kilton's lands. The first they came across was that owned by Ceric, for they crossed into Iglea, the holding Prince Eadward had granted Ceric as reward. This property was what he had planned to give Ashild as her morgen-gyfu. Now he rode through it, staring, his head turning from side to side, as he took in the landscape of yellowing trees and ripened grasses. The horse-thegn at his side could not guess his thoughts, and Ceric could not share them.

The road onward was well-hardened soil, little rutted. As they neared Kilton proper they began to meet watchmen and ward-corns along the way. They left these men at their posts, and only when they reached the final watch did Worr allow the men to ride ahead and signal their coming. He wanted Ceric to arrive in as quiet a manner as possible, yet must give some warning to those in the hall, all unknowing his approach was nigh.

As they rode through the village they saw ahead a cluster of folk awaiting them. Worr spotted his wife Wilgyfu, with all three of their sons. Modwynn and Edgyth stood at the opened gate, the steward of the hall waiting by the doorway. They passed within the palisade. Stablemen came to take their weary horses. Worr took time to draw something wrapped in cloth from one of his saddle bags, the shape and length of a sheathed sword.

Ceric walked to the two women, his haunted face telling of tragedy. Worr joined him, pained by the anxiety marking the faces of the two ladies of Kilton. Worr spoke to relieve the worst of their fears.

"In Anglia Prince Eadward came across a battle, well advanced. They were Danes, fighting other Danes. The men of Four Stones were part of it.

"We left Edwin with the Prince. He suffered minor hurt, only."

The gratitude with which these tidings were received lightened the women's faces for only a moment.

More news was coming, they both knew it. Modwynn gave thought where best to receive it. They could go into the hall and empty it of women and children; unlock the treasure room, as Edwin's mother had the second key; or go to her own bower house. She made decision for the last.

"We shall go to my bower," she told them. It would be the most private of all these spaces, and might lend solace in the sharing of a newly revealed grief.

Within the round bower house Modwynn's serving women carried in basins so the men might wash face and hands. They brought both ale and mead to slake their thirst. Then, left alone, the four sat at Modwynn's table, with its covering of watered green silk. Worr placed the shrouded sword upon the table.

During the silence that followed, Modwynn saw that Ceric no longer wore Godwulf's confirmation ring on the small finger of his left hand. The import of its absence grew in her mind. She placed her own hands on the table, slender and long fingered, like those of her grandson.

Ceric seemed ready to speak, his mouth moving in that way that sought words. But he shook his head. Tears began welling in the corners of his eyes.

Worr leant forward in his chair and began. With such news as they bore, there was little way to soften the doubled loss he must report. He could but try.

"Kilton has been struck with two great losses. I will speak of them as they occurred.

"Cadmar is dead, in service to Kilton. His horse reared when the one Edwin was riding was killed beneath him. Cadmar fell to the ground, and was speared by a Dane."

The sudden intake of breath from Modwynn was akin to a gasp. Murmured prayers arose from the lips of both women. When they had learnt the old warrior-monk had ridden away, they need accept the danger that he might not return. Hearing of his death was nonetheless a harsh blow.

Worr went on with the tale.

"He lived long enough for Ceric to be with him at the moment of death. Ceric told him that Edwin, whom Cadmar had ridden to protect, was safe. He died in that knowledge. His body was carried to the forest, and covered with rock."

Edgyth wiped her eyes and spoke. "And he died in the love of God, Him he faithfully served, as well as Kilton."

Worr could not tell the next. No one could but Ceric. Worr turned his head to him.

Ceric began, slowly. His voice, tight with grief, was raw, but he would tell all as it happened.

"I was stacking stones over the body of Cadmar. I saw a man still on the battlefield, walking with a raven warflag. I was angered over Cadmar's death. I ran after the man, picked up a spear."

The hesitation after these first words ended in his eyelids falling closed. His head drooped. Then he drew breath, and looked at Modwynn and Edgyth with burning eyes.

"It was Ashild."

A cry came from the throats of the women.

"I killed her." The declaration was heart-rending in the baldness of its horror. "I killed her."

He must go on, and excuse Ashild her presence there.

"She was not fighting, but there to serve as messenger, should they need it. She was looking for Hrald."

His eyes dropped again, to his hands. He raised them to his grandmother.

"Godwulf's ring . . . she wears it now. I slipped it on her finger as I held her still-warm body."

Modwynn and Edgyth had taken each other's hands, and both took hold of one hand of Ceric. This calamity defied all their hopes. Few disasters visited upon the family of Kilton approached it. They wept together in their pain and loss.

When Modwynn could again speak her first question was of Four Stones.

"Does Hrald live?"

He nodded. "He . . . forgives me."

Modwynn gave silent thanks. The bond between the two had ever been strong. And in the confusion of battle one's men got hacked, trampled, struck by errant weapons which maimed and killed their own. It was more than clear Ceric had not known Hrald's men were on the field.

For all that had been snatched away, one thing had been granted. Ceric told them of it now.

"Ashild had a child. My child, a boy. His name is Cerd. Before I left he learnt to run to me, and laugh in my arms."

Shock gave way to wonderment. Modwynn voiced it.

"You have a son, an heir for Kilton."

Ceric was shaking his head at her hopes.

"I could not take him, grandmother. I could not. I took his mother, forever, from that hall." His voice rose in pitch and urgency. "He is what is left of Ashild. I could not take him."

She must accept this dictum from the boy's father. There would be time for the child to grow, to come here to see his father and know Kilton. Right now she must care for her grieving grandson.

Edgyth, also fearing for Ceric, was of the same mind. He needed rest and care before he could begin to heal, and this was best accomplished while withdrawn from public view.

Edgyth's gentle voice was yet backed with purpose.

"Ceric," she invited. "Let me make ready for you the bower house, where your parents lived."

Ceric nodded, and Modwynn seconded the idea with swift assent. "All know of your return," she told him. "You need not appear in the hall until you are ready."

Modwynn turned to the horse-thegn of Kilton. Her worn and tear-streaked face yet showed her gratitude. "Wilgyfu and your boys await you. We all of us welcome you home."

Worr had a final task. He placed his hand on the wrapped bundle before him. "This is Cadmar's sword, restored to the treasury from whence it came."

Modwynn placed her hands on the sword and pulled back the cloth, revealing the hilt of Cadmar's blade.

Cadmar had been far more than a warrior. But this weapon was the emblem of his service to Kilton, and she was grateful for its return.

"I know the value of Cadmar's sword. My own father gave it to him, when he was old and Cadmar, young. I present it to you, Worr, for your faithful service."

Worr bowed his head in fervent thanks. The legacy of this weapon imbued it with value far beyond the rippling steel of its pattern-welded blade.

Alone in her bower, Modwynn left the doorway where she had seen the three out. She turned in the small space, and walked to her loom. By it was the frame which held a folded length of linen, brightly embroidered at the edges. There was a small cushioned chair there, on which she had sat by the hour, needle in hand. She paused by it now, looking, and seeing nothing. This doubled grief was almost beyond compassing. Cadmar, trusted friend and advisor, was dead, his body lying in an Anglian forest. She was given no chance to bid fare-well to her old friend. None could know when he slipped away that he rode to his death, but he must have suspected it, and wished to spare them both the pain of a final parting.

Her own husband Godwulf had died in a moment, with no chance to bid fare-well. But he had done so in the pleasure garden, and she could drop on her knees and kiss his still-warm face. If she had been near Cadmar she would have lifted his hands in her own, and kissed those.

But Ashild of Four Stones – what tragedy was this? How did one recover? How could Ceric forgive himself his unknowing act of war? Kilton's hope for union with the great hall of Anglia had been piteously dashed. The shock and sorrow of the family of Four Stones staggered her. She lifted her hand to her face as these thoughts came near to overwhelming her. The gladsome news of the child of those halls almost added to her grief. Like Ceric in his shock, like Ashild, this boy, little Cerd, seemed beyond recovery as well. She sank down upon the chair, and wept.

※※※※※※※※※

Ceric walked with Edgyth to the bower house. He took the key from his belt and unlocked the door. He stepped over the spot, deeply sanded, where a serving man had long ago died; saw the alcove where he slept as a small boy. There, by the casement on the other side of the bed, lay the empty cradle. He unbuckled his weapon belts and hung both blades on the pegs by the bed, where his father had hung the same seax. He sat down at the small table. Edgyth and a serving woman moved about, opening chests, making up the bed. His saddle bags were carried in, and more clothing brought from his own alcove in the hall. Edgyth gave him a parting kiss, and left.

There was a tap at the door. Worr came in, Ceric's spear in hand. He placed it by the hanging weapons. It had been the spear of his father, and was thus a family heirloom. It must be kept. Ceric had not touched it since dropping it by Cadmar's body. He had not closed his hand around a spear since he had picked up the throwing spear with which he had killed Ashild. He knew he never would.

Worr came to where he sat. He had brought Ceric home, which Worr knew would be only the start of his reclamation. Right now the horse-thegn would say what he could.

"Ceric. Any man would have done the same, seeing that war-flag. I would have done it."

Ceric listened, and nodded his head.

Later Ceric walked alone through the hall yards, seeing all as they went about the needful duties of their day. He felt as if he saw them for the first time. The stable and kitchen folk looked at him, and his own men, unwilling to intrude, gave him a wary but respectful nod when their eyes met. He moved deeper into the precincts, nearer the bower house, to those places frequented by the family of Kilton. The day was a fine one, the sky the cool blue of shorter days and coming frosts. The sea was active; he heard it pounding against the base of Kilton's cliffs before he saw its curling white wave tips. The pleasure garden was before him, the leaves of its fruit trees withering and falling away, the table and benches in the open pavilion bleached and bare in the strong sunlight. He walked to the edge of the cliff, and looked down at the foaming water. The landing stage had been long pulled up against the threat of raiding ships. But he thought that he wanted to take one of Kilton's small boats, and set out on the tossing sea in it, the way he and Worr used to when he was younger.

Modwynn spent time with him, and Worr too. He went to the hall at night and took his place at the high table, by Edwin's empty chair. The place where Cadmar had sat also lay empty, and would be so at least until his prayer service was held. Ceric lifted his cup to his lips, and tried to eat. Garrulf the scop bowed to him, and began to sing that night a favourite tale of his when a boy, that of sling-throwing David and his triumph over the giant, Goliath. Ceric tried without success to attend while Garrulf struck the strings of his harp and chanted of the adventure. He could not hear of death tonight, nor remain in this crowded hall. He must be alone in his torment. He went early to the bower house, lit the cressets, and sat at the table until they guttered and burnt out.

In the morning as he took clothing where it had been laid, he saw something of wood in the corner of the deep chest. He drew out the wooden bird his father had carved for him as a toy, and ran his finger over his own teething marks on it. He could barely recall his father. The toy made him think of his uncle, calling him Chirp. He placed the bird on the sill of the casement. He may have been Cerd's age when his father made this for him.

⚜⚜⚜⚜⚜⚜⚜⚜

Two days later Edwin arrived home. The Prince had returned to Witanceaster with the captured Danes and to seek his own needed rest. Edwin was thanked and sent west to Kilton. He travelled with Eorconbeald and Alwin, and the full complement of men with whom he had ridden to Eadward; save for the signal loss of Cadmar, he had lost none. It was his sole consolation.

His journey home had been marked by discomfort of both body and mind. Being flung from his horse rendered him almost blinded by searing headaches. At times he had not been able to open his eyes for the pain. His broken nose had been set aright by Eorconbeald, who had given it a stinging wrench to straighten it, then packed his nostrils with thin strips of linen to absorb the new bleeding. The headaches had abated, but his cracked ribs took longer. They made him feel fragile and even flawed. He was unable to draw a full breath without a gasping wince. The broad scrape on the right side of his face had gone from scab to fresh pink skin beneath, but the skin beneath his eyes, which had been blacked from his fall, was still slightly darkened. Far worse than any of these bodily ailments was the sorrow he felt for his brother.

He was aggrieved on his own account, as well. Cadmar's loss felt overwhelming. The man had been respected, even beloved, by all. He was one of the few who recalled his grandmother as a young woman, and had knowledge of her own parents. Cadmar had trained every warrior at Kilton for the past two decades, and overseen the training of the village ceorls. He had been Edwin's special counsel and mentor. Edwin had hoped to return to Kilton with Cadmar at his side, with the big man telling of the young Lord's prowess in arms. Instead Cadmar was dead, and he had not even had the chance to raise spear or sword against a single enemy. The shame he felt at this he was unable to express to anyone. As his horse galloped onto the field he told himself he was Godwin's son. A moment later he was sent sprawling, at once rendered unfit. Rather than winning repute on the field, he had needed rescue. He could not help being disheartened at his own performance. He faulted himself even for the loss of his chestnut stallion.

Ceric went to greet him as they rode in. It was late in the day, and soon they must gather in the hall. First Edgyth, eager to hold her son in the quietude of the treasure room, would bathe his face in the dried flowerheads of the herb ironhard to speed the healing of his skin. Ceric had no time alone with his brother, for before the meal Edwin would be presented with the battle-gain his men had won.

For Ceric to sit there and watch the needful taking up and display of knives and swords and silver necklets and armbands was a form of torture to him. These were carried off from the field upon which he had killed Ashild. As soon as he could he slipped from the table and withdrew.

In the morning Edwin came to him in the bower house. The slight embrace they shared reflected both brothers' tender states. They spoke of Cadmar, and Ceric recounted in as much detail as he could summon the old man's final moments, and concern for Edwin. The silence that followed was marked by a sorrow-shot regard, as the brothers looked at each other.

Ceric did not say more, and Edwin would not ask. Worr had told him privately of coming upon his older brother as he rocked Ashild in his arms, calling her name.

Edwin had been told something else, of lasting import. "My Lady-mother Edgyth told me you have a son," he offered.

Ceric nodded. "Yes. I did not know. We had one night together." He had to pause here, and with a voice near to breaking found need to recount the paucity of what he had been granted. "We had but one night together."

Kilton had so long need of heirs that any son of the hall was cause for rejoicing. The boy Cerd was not only the child of the eldest of Godwulf's grandsons, but the boy's mother was of one of the richest halls in the Dane-law. Edwin was Lord of Kilton, but his brother had already a direct heir, and Edwin did not. Even in his dulled state Ceric knew he must address this.

"Cerd . . . he will stay at Four Stones, to be raised by Hrald and the Lady Ælfwyn. Only if he is needed would he come here."

If he was needed. If Edwin died without issue, Kilton would be ruled by Ceric, if Ælfred approved. And Cerd, as first born, would be next in line. If Edwin died, Ceric would surely call for his son Cerd to come here.

All Edwin could do was nod. He had eighteen years and should wed soon, but could not think of this now.

At length Edwin got up to leave. He could not invite his brother to ride out with him; he himself could not pull his weight up on the back of a horse without pain. In fine weather they had swam or sailed. Right now he could not do either. Even if he were sound, the water was grown rough, and none were to risk making a target of them-selves to passing raiders. There was nothing he could offer Ceric, save his presence.

As he stood in the middle of the floor Edwin's eyes were drawn to the dragon bed. It so dominated the small house that any who entered were forced to regard it. The red-painted tongues of the four dragons' mouths cast their wooden flames up towards the timber roof. Edwin saw the scar on the bedpost nearest the door. Once again he went to it, and placed his finger on the gash.

A thought came to him, for the first time, one that charged him with an icy thrill. He shared a mother with Ceric. Perhaps his father Godwin had come here, to this bed.

Ceric watched him touch the dragon's throat. They had once wondered together about that knife wound. He remembered that he was going to smooth the gash away, before he brought his wife Ashild to bed here.

※※※※※※※※※

That afternoon Edwin went to see Begu. It was broad day, but he felt need of her company, and greater need to tell her Kilton's news. He wanted her softness, and to hear her gentle murmuring in response to things he told her. Though he used the mounting block, he suppressed a groan as he gained his saddle. But once up, he kept his thoughts focused on she he rode to visit. As he passed the limits of the village he was grateful to be away from the hall, and to be riding alone. He took time to look about him. Tracing the road to Begu's hamlet, it felt the last of Summer had fled. Even the birds were fewer. Most fields were laying idle after the final harvest, and the sheep had grown heavy in their wool.

He walked his horse into her small work yard. She was not there, but her door was open. His horse nickered, and a moment later she appeared in the doorway.

She began to smile, but her face changed, seeing his. It was not the slight hurt to his own face, but the distress so clear upon it. Sudden dread clutched at her heart. He was whole. She feared he had come bearing news of Ceric.

She ran the few steps to him, forcing herself to name him first. "Edwin," she said.

The stiffness with which he lifted his arms to her betrayed his healing ribcage. She held him, lightly as one would enfold a dove.

They kissed, then she looked him full in the face. The trouble there drove her next words.

"Ceric, Ceric. Is he . . . ?"

"He is home, he is home," Edwin answered. "But . . ." he faltered.

"Come in," she said, her arm about him. "Come in."

Begu wept, hearing of Ceric. It was the first time she had heard Ashild's name. Ceric had always called her, "the maid I shall wed," or "my bride." Now Begu had a name, a lovely one, to put with the image of she who had so captured Ceric's heart. The tragedy was vast, and she wept for the pity of it.

They huddled together, sitting on her bed. Edwin did not speak of his own fears and blighted hopes. Beset and harried by them though he was, they seemed trivial in light of what had befallen his brother. She sensed this, that he withheld his own concerns in the face of so great a calamity. She was struck, too, by the knowledge that her tears were all for Ceric, but she could not silence the truth spoken in her heart. Yet Edwin had come to her, today, and she must give what she could.

She began to kiss Edwin, gently, so as not to cause hurt to his face. Piece by piece she removed his clothing, unbuckling his seax, pulling off his boots, slowly drawing off his tunic as he grimaced from the pain of lifting his arms. His leggings she left for last.

She drew off her gown and shift, stripped off her stockings. Her love for Ceric had been the greatest joy, and greatest sorrow, of her life. She must bear it as she had borne all else. Yet she could summon ample tenderness for the young man now in her arms.

⸎⸎⸎⸎⸎⸎⸎⸎⸎⸎

With no body to mourn over, a simple prayer service was held for Cadmar. Ceric stood next Modwynn's right, with Edgyth flanked by Edwin. The tiny chantry was full of warriors. Incense of sandalwood was burning, lifting in blue-gray curls from the round brass censer on the raised stone altar step. Every prayer and psalm Dunnere chanted applied as well to Ashild. She was the other they mourned, even if her name remained unspoken. These were the prayers for the dead, and she walked amongst them.

Standing in that haze of sandalwood Ceric gave thought to how she would be judged. She had died with the heathen amulet of a forsaken God about her neck. Yet she had been baptised and confirmed, and could have just as easily been wearing the small golden cross now about his own neck. He stood there, swaying slightly, atop the stone underneath which his grandfather lay, and thought of that other stone at Oundle sheltering the mortal remains of his beloved wife.

His grandmother Modwynn looked pale and pinched at his side. She was known for her stately bearing, but today she leant into Ceric, so that he placed his arm about her in support. Dunnere made his final blessing, slicing the air over their heads with his palm in benediction. There would be a funeral feast, but Modwynn asked him to take her to her bower. She would retire early; her serving woman would bring her food. Edwin would conduct the feast, as was his duty and privilege, aided by his mother.

At her door she kissed Ceric in fare-well. "Ashild," she told him. "I saw her once, when you were toddling babes. I yearn now to see your own."

He could do no more than kiss her in answer.

In the morning Ceric had nearly finished dressing when he was jolted by the shrieking of a woman. He fixed the toggles on his boots, and grabbed his sword from the wall. He looked towards the cries. A woman was by the church, waving her arms in distress. Modwynn's bower was just beyond, and this was one of her serving women. He ran to her.

His grandmother Modwynn, long the Lady of Kilton, was dead.

The woman was frenzied. Ceric brushed his way past another serving woman into the bower house. There his grandmother lay in bed, at rest and perfectly composed. Her arms were outside the grey woven coverlet, stretched with easy dignity upon it at her sides. The long-fingered hands of such skill had never been so gracefully presented. Her head was slightly tilted to one side, almost as if she craned her neck to hear something whispered.

Ceric came to her. After his mother's abduction Modwynn had been as mother to him. His greatest advisor and comfort was now dead.

His own body went slack. He felt her noble heart had at last shattered from a surfeit of sorrow. The shock of

Cadmar's death was great; the shock of his killing Ashild the greater. He bore the blame for the final, unbearable blow.

His sword was still in his hand. He placed it at the foot of her bed. It was the sword of her husband, Godwulf. When she was but a girl he had presented her with his troth ring on its hilt. Now it lay as guardian and sentinel at her feet. He knelt down at the bed side, and bowed his head so that it touched the coverlet her hand lay upon. Edgyth came, and Edwin, and many others.

Just past noon a distinctive horn sounded outside Kilton's palisade, signalling a message from the King. All halted in the needful tasks they had taken up following the death of the great Lady of Kilton. It was not message, but special messenger himself who rode through Kilton's gates, in the guise of Raedwulf, Bailiff of Defenas, riding from Witanceaster and the King. He was surrounded by a considerable escort, ten men and five pack horses.

Prince Eadward had returned to Witanceaster with the woeful tale of Ashild's death. He did not know if her brother Hrald had also fallen, for Eadward and his men had quitted the field before he appeared. Whether Hrald lived or not, the King had been forced to give thought to the matter of potential reparations to the family of Four Stones. One of the King's men had killed the daughter of the hall. Under the terms of the Peace forged by Ælfred and Guthrum, all men in Wessex and Anglia shared the same wergild, according to rank. Left unrecorded was the wergild of their women. The King might make a gift, a handsome one, in reparation, yet Raedwulf felt the crude grossness of such. Four Stones was rich. It did not need Ælfred's blood-payment. Yet the fact remained one of his men had killed Ashild. Some gesture of condolence must be made.

Over the past fortnight Raedwulf's thoughts had kept returning to the mother of Ashild, and the grief she dealt with. One night had the bailiff known with Ælfwyn of Cirenceaster. Since that night she had receded almost as far away as she had been in his youth, when he first saw and loved her. Yet she had given herself bodily to him, and wore his ring. He wanted her to wife each and every day. Now, with the grave loss she had suffered, she had slipped further from him. Her daughter Ashild coming here to Kilton to wed Ceric had been her way to him in Defenas. Ashild was now dead.

He would give much to go to Ælfwyn, or at least, send message. But he could not imperil one of the King's riders for a personal missive. If the King himself had message for the Lady or the Jarl, his own could go along with it. He would risk his life to travel to her, but could not do so without leave from his King. He could not ask for such, not in this state of war, when he was needed by Wessex.

The bailiff had ridden hence to Kilton to learn what he could, and to deliver the King's request.

As he approached the walls his eye was caught by a broad square of white fabric hanging down upon one of the closed gates, a sign of deep mourning within. It was for Cadmar, he thought.

Ceric was there within the gates to meet him. The bailiff knew he had been on extended duty with the Prince, and given the disastrous act which had taken Ashild, he fully expected Ceric to be shaken. He did not think to look upon what he judged a shell of his former self.

They embraced; Raedwulf must attempt to lend comfort to so haggard a young face. He must also deliver the formal condolence from the King before he could speak as a friend.

"Ælfred grieves for you. And for the family of Four Stones."

Ceric had not given thought to how Ashild's death had affected the King's hopes for an alliance between the great hall of Anglia and his own. The answer was clear in Raedwulf's face. It had injured it irreparably.

Ceric brushed away the water in his eyes.

"My grandmother is dead. Her burial is tomorrow."

The colour drained from Raedwulf's face.

"Lady Modwynn," he breathed. He looked stunned, an expression rarely found upon the face of the King's advisor.

"I knew of Cadmar's loss," he offered. "But this . . . " The bailiff could not go on.

Cadmar dead, Ashild killed. Now the great Lady of Kilton. At least both her grandsons lived. There was one thing none in Witanceaster had learnt, the Fate of the Jarl of Four Stones. He asked of it now.

"Hrald . . . did he survive?"

Ceric gave a nod. His answer made fresh the horror of that battle. "After I brought her home, he carried Ashild's body into their hall.

"She is buried at Oundle."

Raedwulf lowered his head. "Which her mother had risen from the ashes."

They spoke thus while still standing in the forecourt of the hall, Raedwulf's escort off their horses and waiting, the thirsty beasts eager for water. Others of the hall were coming to greet him. Wilgyfu had appeared, Worr also, waiting patiently and at a distance.

"Go to them," Ceric told the bailiff. "Go to them." They must celebrate their lives.

Later that day Raedwulf sat down with Edwin and Ceric in the treasure room. Edgyth, now fully Lady of Kilton, was late in joining them, but took her place with quiet dignity at the table.

With the preparations for the funeral of Lady Modwynn tomorrow the bailiff could hardly broach the topic he had been sent to discuss. Yet all knew nothing but an urgent message would have brought him from Witanceaster.

"Tell us why you are come," Edwin asked.

Raedwulf responded to this query with equal simplicity.

"The King has need of silver. Wessex will repay the debt as soon as Haesten is expunged from the land."

He must name the amount now, and did so after a pause reflecting its size.

"Three hundred pounds. If it can be spared."

It was a huge sum. Edwin had been with his grandmother when they had buried much of the hall's store of silver for safekeeping. It had been lowered in fifty pound increments, each placed in leathern bags and then a chest of wood for easy retrieval. He knew where each one was. He knew that Modwynn had often loaned or given funds to shore up the defences of Wessex. Now he could supply this. Edwin was Lord, the silver his to loan. He looked to

Ceric and to his mother. Their faces seemed to confirm what he knew. The King would not ask unless the need were dire.

"We will get it for you, now," he told Raedwulf.

That night Edgyth knelt at the side of her bed in her bower house. She had offered her prayers, those for herself, and most heartfully for her mother-in-law. Still she knelt there, thinking of her life and reflecting on its path.

The needful tasks of the day had extended her waking hours far beyond those she usually knew. This near-endless day had begun early. She had come upon a shocked and silent Ceric at Modwynn's bedside, calmed the frantic serving women, summoned the priest Dunnere to the death bed. The elaborate funeral feast had been planned and its execution begun. And there had been a sacred duty to perform. Together she and the two serving women had washed and wrapped the body of Modwynn. To finger the shroud enlivened with vines and blossoms she had drawn and helped her mother-in-law embroider felt a sorrowful fulfilment to much labour. Yet she recalled the many pleasant and even happy hours they had spent, working on it, as they discussed matters of the hall, and their hopes for Ceric and Edwin.

For years both women had lived with the hope that Ceric would bring Ashild of Four Stones to Kilton as his bride. For the sake of Ceric both had great affection for her already, and Raedwulf's high opinion of the girl's energy and intellect lent surety that she would prove a benison to all. Edgyth and Modwynn had spoken at length of how her arrival would not only allow the elder Lady of Kilton to step back from her myriad duties, but infuse the hall with needed freshness and vigour. Edwin must wed, certainly, but Ashild's presence would be warranty against torpor until he brought a capable young wife to the hall upon the cliff.

Ashild was not here and would never be here. Modwynn was dead and Edgyth was alone as Lady. The latter loss, given the generous span of Modwynn's life, was expected; the former most unnatural. No one could know or guess how long it might take Edwin to procure a suitable wife, or when Ceric could once again bethink himself of seeking one.

Tonight at her bedside Edgyth must lower her head the more. After one night of love Ashild had presented Ceric with a son and heir. It added to the incalculable forfeit of Ashild's loss. That the child might never see Kilton was just now beyond dwelling upon.

She gave lingering thought to Ceric, for whom she truly feared. His haunted eyes never knew rest, and the skin around them was shadowed by exhaustion. He needed sleep, badly, and she feared he was stalked by the night-mare. She could compound a potion to help him safely find rest, and as soon as his grandmother was interred she would make offer to him. She closed her eyes, thinking of the day ahead, and its demands upon her. She drew a deep breath.

She would miss Modwynn sorely. The two women had been united in so much. The younger woman had never sought praise, but had taken deep if unspoken pleasure in the fact that Godwulf had singled her out amongst potential brides for his son. It was true Edgyth was rich, but Modwynn had told her after Godwulf's death that it was her unaffected charm and gentle wit which had made her stand out. The fact that she and their son Godwin shared an almost immediate attraction to each other made the decision easy. Modwynn had valued her for the way she seamlessly took up her duties here, always seeking to relieve her mother-in-law of the more onerous tasks, which she attempted to perform with modest and prompt alacrity. From the onset of her years at Kilton, Edgyth had shared Modwynn's skill and interest in the healing arts, a skill which Edgyth had greatly expanded from her extended stays with the sisters at Glastunburh. Most cherished between the women was their love for Kilton's men. She seemed to naturally understand and share the deep appreciation Modwynn held for the distinct qualities of Godwulf, Godwin, and Gyric.

All three men were gone. Modwynn had need to guide Kilton through a long period of being lord-less while they awaited Edwin's majority. Edgyth had done all she could to aid her in this difficult task. In these later years her desire had been a return to Glastunburh. That holy convent awaited her, and was where she had sought refuge during the several uncertain times in her marriage. Once Edwin was wed she would retire there to take the veil. That was her goal, and in many ways what she had felt born for. No calling sounded so loudly as this, to devote herself to the herbal plants in its gardens, and then in the scriptorium, to record and preserve what she knew of healing. She wished also to lose herself in prayer and meditation. It was tonight a goal further away than ever.

She was now truly Lady of Kilton. This was the role cast for her, and while she walked the Earth she would fulfill it to her utmost. Her own health was not strong; there was some weakness to her heart, she could feel it when it raced and then almost seemed to cease beating. Until it ceased entirely she would serve Kilton.

She crossed herself now, too tired for further tears. She trusted Modwynn would be speedily received into the bosom of Christ, and that His Mother would welcome her as Modwynn had offered welcome to her when she came as Godwin's bride to this shining hall.

Ceric had not slept a full night since the death of Ashild. The night before his grandmother's funeral was one wholly without sleep. He had tried to lie down upon the dragon bed, but the painted eyes above the gaping mouths of the dragons rising over his head leered at him. He felt trapped by them, closed in, almost smothered. He rose, lit the cresset on the table, and sat there, studying the shadows the flickering light made as it danced upon the walls, and the dragon posts themselves. He sat watching them until his head dropped in a stupor upon his folded arms. A night-mare came, a fearsome one, and carried him off on her back, while still awake.

He was on the field of battle in Anglia, running after a figure carrying a battle-flag of a flying raven. He saw himself reach down to a ground littered with weapons and snatch at a throwing spear. He heard his horrified scream against his own act as he tried to stop himself. Yet he flung the spear. The figure he aimed for turned to him. It was Ashild, watching with wide grey-blue eyes as the spear sailed towards her, to lodge in her breast and kill her.

He started, jolted upright in his chair, trembling in terror at her terror. She did not know, she did not see, he kept repeating. She was alive, and then she was dead, without awareness of how it happened.

He walked the small confines of the room, repeating this to himself, until dawn crept through the casement.

Without thought, and yet with great care, he dressed himself. He took from the chest his finest clothing, a dark green tunic and brown leggings woven by Edgyth and embroidered by his grandmother. He combed his hair so that it fell with the slightest wave to his shoulders. He wore no jewellery, his hands and wrists were bare of silver or of gold, but his bright-hilted seax spanning his belly proclaimed its deadly worth.

He went with all to the bower house, and there saw the slender shrouded form of Modwynn, gloriously wrapped in the embroidered linen that she and Edgyth had laboured over. She had already been laid upon a carrying board, and Edgyth, with eyes still flowing, gave her nod to the men who would carry her to the chantry. They were Edwin and Ceric and Worr; and as special tribute to his long service, Garrulf the scop, who had filled the great hall with his song for three decades. The Bailiff of Defenas, as emissary of the King, and friend to Modwynn, came next, escorting Edgyth, Lady of Kilton.

The folk of hall and village had massed outside the stone church. The thegns of Kilton formed a doubled row, and stood with spears in hand, arms extended, spear-butts resting on Kilton's soil, to form a passage-way for the dead and her grieving kin. The gathered women, whether thegns' wives or goose-girls, wailed. Children snuffled in fear. Men who ploughed the great Lady's fields and sheared her sheep clawed off their caps and wiped their eyes. All looked upon the final transit of Modwynn, Lady of Kilton, as she journeyed to her resting place. She was carried to the trestle table awaiting her before the altar.

The men of the family of Kilton took their place. In the front row, just behind Modwynn's body, Edwin stood by the side of his mother Edgyth. Ceric on his right was flanked by the bailiff. Garrulf stepped to one side, needing to see all, hear all, so he might try to shape a fitting song for this doleful loss.

Dunnere moved about the altar, praying, chanting. The air was filled with the blue smoke of incense. Ceric could not lift his eyes from the twining leaves and flowers on his grandmother's shroud. He recalled praising her for her skill, and how she had so lightly shrugged off its purpose. Now she was still and cold, wrapped within that long binding sheet of linen.

Soon the Mass would end, and she would be buried next his grandfather, the great Lord of Kilton. She had told him many times what delight he had taken in him as a babe. They had never had the chance to truly know each other.

He thought of who else lay under these slabs of grey stone. The seax spanning his belly was that of his dead father, first cruelly maimed, and then taken by the fever. He knew without raising his eyes that the golden rings his mother and father had worn were there by the statue of St Ninnoc. That name had been given to his little sister, who died of the fever with their father. She too lay beneath his feet. He had no remembrance of her.

The golden rings at the base of the statue made him think of that which his grandfather had worn as a youth, and which Modwynn had given him as protection. It was now upon Ashild's finger, under that slab far away in Oundle's stone church.

Ashild. He lived, and she did not. He lived; his grandmother did not. Cadmar was dead, left under a carapace of rock he had helped build. It was all death. Yet he lived.

The shrill brass chimes were being rung by the priest. Ceric stepped back from the front line of mourners, and slipped out of the church. Some thought him overcome by the service; he could wait by the door until it ended.

He was not there when they all filed out. Edwin went to the bower house. The door was unlocked and he pushed it open. Ceric was not within. His gold-hilted sword hung in its scabbard from a peg on the wall. Edwin glanced about; all looked as if nothing had been disturbed. He returned to the chantry. Before the Mass had ended, a pall of plain linen had been lowered over his grandmother's shrouded body, and its folds draping the table was the first thing he saw. His entry startled the workmen, beginning to lift the stone. Their picks and shovels were ready, set against the wall. It horrified him, and he hurried out.

Edwin went back, to the pleasure garden, turning his head and scanning the breadth of its rows of browning herbs and climbing vines. He stared at all before him in fear and wonderment. His heart was beating hard in his breast, a palpable pounding echoing the angry surf. The sea was rolling pitilessly on, white-capped, uncaring, and shrill seabirds floating overhead made mockery of his distress. He forced himself forward, to look over the edge of the cliff to see if Ceric had flung himself from its height. He could not voice this even to himself; Ceric would not do this, not commit so great a sin as to cast his own life away. Yet he must look. No body lay there amongst the rough and tufted rock growth.

The men at the gates were questioned. All that could be learnt was that Ceric was seen walking through them; to what destination was unclear. The upset and tumult of Modwynn's death had distracted all. Edwin tried to calm his racing heart. He need trust his brother would soon appear. Ceric would clear his head and return to raise a loving cup to his grandmother. For now Modwynn's funeral feast must be held, and Edwin returned to the hall, filled to overflowing. He sat there next Lady Edgyth, the gap left by both Ceric and Cadmar almost unbridgeable.

Edwin looked down the table. Worr had proved his worth to Kilton over many years. The void left by Cadmar must be filled. Of the new and frightening chasm caused by Ceric's absence he could this moment do nothing.

"Worr. Come sit at my right," he invited.

The horse-thegn rose at this honour, all eyes upon him, and took the seat which Cadmar had occupied. Amendments, great and small, were made within the ranks of a hall following the death of any lord or Lady. It was the first Edwin made.

Edgyth, Lady of Kilton, took up the ewer to pour out wine at that funeral feast. Tears welled in her eyes. She moved around the high table, pouring out for her son, for Dunnere, for Worr and Wilgyfu and every other man and woman seated there. She had always done this task together with Modwynn. Now she must do it alone. The vacant space where Ceric should be sitting yawned far wider than the salver lying there.

Worr, greatly troubled, spent the night in the bower house, awaiting the return of Ceric. He did not come. At dawn he took his horse and went out. A fog had rolled in overnight, and settling on the tops of the grasses formed the lightest covering of early frost.

Worr hardly knew where to start. A lone man on foot was the hardest track to find and follow. Out Kilton's gates, where so many trod day in, day out, with numberless horses and beasts, no single track could be discerned. He rode, skirting the margins of the forest beyond the village, asking himself, if Ceric came here, where would he go? Worr whistled, with no real hope of answering response. Finally in the afternoon he spotted a man returning with his cows from the wood. The man looked up at him in surprise. "I am seeking Ceric," Worr told him. "Have you seen him?"

"Not today. Yesterday. He went into the forest, before noon. About – there." The man pointed.

Worr looked at the spot and marked it.

"Did he carry anything?"

The cowherd thought, then shook his head. "He had no pack."

Ceric had walked into the forest with nothing more than what he wore inside the chantry. No cloak, no weapon save his seax.

"I thank you," Worr said.

He rode to the place the man had pointed out and stood gazing at the thicket before him. A light track could be discerned, the size of that made by a trotting fox. He turned and looked back at the now distant hall. It was almost a direct line, as if Ceric had walked out from the gates and kept going, leaving the road where it bent around the orchards of apple and pear trees to pass through them into the greenwood.

Worr tied his horse and entered the forest. He pressed forward through the thick undergrowth, branches and leaves clutching at him, hitting his face. His eyes scanned both up and down, looking for the results of footfall, for broken twigs at shoulder height, those few signs bearing witness of the passage of a man. A day had passed, but Ceric may have walked through here.

He lost the track when it crossed several, slightly larger trails, those made by deer. He stood for a while looking about him. The ferns at his feet were still bright green, their curling fronds just growing rigid at their tips. Rocks nestling in moss lay wet from the rising ground water; at dawn they would have been mantled with frost. Some of the trees above him were shedding the first of their yellowed leaves. The wheel of the year, a law unto itself, would turn, pulling the rest of those leaves onto the ferns which would themselves crisp and die. Surrounded by this mellowing verdancy Worr could see and hear nothing of the realm of man. The hall of Kilton and its pleasures and sorrows felt far away. He heard himself inhale and exhale, and the distant call of a bird.

Worr made utterance into that stillness.

Ceric, Worr breathed. Gone to the forest, to live as a wild man.

TO GOTLAND

HRALD had planned to sail at the break of Spring. With fair winds and no trouble the voyage to Gotland might be made in a fortnight. Necessity urged him to make the trip, and circumstances allowed it. Haesten and his men had seemingly withdrawn from Anglia, to perhaps shelter in Mercia or Wales; none at Four Stones could know. Haesten had swept through both Anglia and Wessex, harassing and despoiling, but never building enough of a coalition amongst other war-chiefs to conquer either. Guthrum's son Agmund, contesting his claims, had retreated to his own halls, awaiting the passing of Winter. It was not peace which settled over Lindisse, rather an uneasy silence, but it allowed Hrald to absent himself for his needed journey.

The ships to carry him to that island bourn posed a problem. Hrald had destroyed without regret the two fine war-ships of the men of Haesten who had invaded Saltfleet. Now he had need of such, and sailing in two ships granted greater safety. A single war-ship on the prowl would not attempt an attack, not when with canny manoeuvering it could itself be entrapped. It would need to be two or more ships under a single command that they need fear, and Hrald was willing to risk they would not come upon such this early in the raiding season.

Four Stones was land-locked, and now its Jarl needed ships. He had none amongst his men who were ship-wrights, and those of Jari's age who had sailed with Yrling and Hrald's father were now older. Styrbjörn, second in command of Turcesig, had answer. He would go to Jorvik, there to hire ships. His cousin was a shipwright long established there, and would know good ships and the better captains. Hrald would need a partial crew for each, a steering oars-man and star-reader, and as few men as it took to sail the craft down to Saltfleet, where Hrald would meet them.

One of his first acts was to forbid Jari the trip. The spear-wound to his calf had healed, leaving nothing but a puckered scar, and the body-guard protested this charge. "I need no protecting, Jari," Hrald told him. "You are needed here, for the sake of my mother and sister. And my nephew. If you would serve me, stay and serve them."

Jari grumbled, but must agree that leaving Kjeld in sole command was too heavy a burden. Though it denied Jari the adventure and the chance to see Sidroc, he would share command with the younger man.

Styrbjörn would procure ships and essential crew for the voyage. The rest of his crew Hrald would choose from those eager to join him. The journey was laden with danger, from waves, winds, and raiders, yet the tack his father had taken, of leaving early in the season, would spare him the worst attentions of the latter. Storms they might meet in abundance, and the soundness of the ships and skill of their steering oars-men was paramount. Those men of Four Stones who joined him would have as reward the adventure to boast of, and the chance to trade anything they brought with them to Gotland. The island was known for the richness of its goods flowing from the East, from Samarkand and beyond. All Hrald's men had praise-worthy weaponry and silver. These they could trade for rare stuffs such as silk and precious oils, spices too. When Hrald announced his intention in the hall, many men rose to their feet, vying to be taken on the journey. Those who wished to go would hazard all. There was no use repeating to any the dangers they would face, not to men who could be killed here on his lands, keeping watch.

Jari warned him that the tight quarters of a ship could make enemies of friends, and to allow only those men slow to anger to sail. Hrald chose able warriors of even temperament, keen to return with their lives and the goods they had received in trade. He wanted archers with him, and selected six skilled with the bow, including Askil. A well-timed arrow could kill from a far greater distance than any thrown spear, as Askil had proved at the battle in which he killed Three Plaits.

Despite the forethought with which he planned, Hrald made ready to leave almost as if it were a last parting. There was in all of his preparations a sense of final fare-well, as if he would not return. There must be.

Over the Winter Hrald had spent much time with Cerd. The boy was coming two, prattling away, and happy in all things. When he spoke Hrald's name it still came out a growl, which brought a smile to his uncle's lips. Cerd loved to be taken up in Hrald's arms and be held like a soaring bird over his head, where the child could see things he could not from the ground or even from

the arms of Ælfwyn or Burginde. He learnt the dusty
mysteries of the tops of the cross beams in the kitchen
passageway this way, his little hand swiping across them,
pulling back fingers black with years of soot. Cerd hooted
in laughter, until Burginde saw him thrust his fingers in
his mouth, at which point she plucked the boy from his
uncle's arms with a tut. The child had just enough time to
lay his hand upon the nurse's cheek, anointing her with
the grime he had discovered.

Cerd's hair was that bright coppery hue of his father's,
but his eyes were that of his mother, settling into a deep
grey-blue. And Hrald thought the boy saw the world
through Ashild's eyes. Certainly they flashed stormily
when denied anything he wanted. And, like his mother,
the child would often find a way to gain what he wanted,
regardless of cost to himself. Also like Ashild, he had a
bold winsomeness in how he accepted reprimand, which
often times made his grandmother's eyes mist in remembrance of Cerd's mother at his age.

Styrbjörn had been dispatched north to Jorvik, and
returned with the tidings that two drekars would arrive at
Saltfleet, crewed with six men each. They should sail in at
the first full Moon after the Feast of St Cuthbert, that day
of equal day and equal night. Those who recalled the Old
Gods also knew it as the day on which Idun, the keeper of
the Gods' golden apples of youth, was celebrated. Hrald
and his men would meet them there.

During the last few days before he set out, Hrald
went to Oundle, riding with only Jari at his side. He left
the older man in the monk's hall with a pot of ale before
him, and betook himself alone to the church. He wanted
to spend time at the tomb of his sister.

Afterwards the Abbess welcomed him into her writing chamber. Before he left he must see the gift which had been received.

"Ælfred, King, has just sent a rich offering to us here, to honour the memory of Ashild," she began.

First she took from her table top a small flat object, not much larger than the palm of his hand, encased by two thin pieces of wood laced into a leathern sleeve to protect what lay within.

"This missive came with it, a message from Witanceaster. It is for the Lady Ælfwyn."

He uttered his thanks, and slipped it into his belt.

Then Sigewif took from a wall recess something of dazzling white. It was a small casket of walrus ivory, pieced together from the precious stuff, and held in place by a framework of bronze. It was no work of antiquity, Hrald could see this. The ivory was perfect, uncracked, newly carved. The ivory panels were incised with winged celestial beings on the front, flanking the key latch. Sigewif turned the box in her hand that he might see the larger panel in back. It showed a gowned figure kneeling, and a man standing over the figure with a raised sword. The long hair of the kneeling figure touched the ground; it looked a woman. Tears were falling from the man's face as he gripped the blade, tiny raised beads of ivory raining down upon the one who knelt. Hrald touched the carving. His eyes asked the question.

"Jephthah's daughter," the Abbess said, her voice almost a whisper. "He made a vow to God on the battle field. In exchange for victory, he would sacrifice the first creature he met when he returned home. It was, alas, his daughter."

She went on, considering this tragic turn.

"Unlike the sacrifice involving Abraham and Isaac, God does not always stay the hand that holds the sword."

Hrald had need to close his eyes a moment.

"The King sees meaning in all things," she observed. "And the casket was crafted by the monks at Ælthelinga expressly for his gift."

The casket alone, worked of rare material and carved with great skill, was a rich gift. Then the Abbess lifted the domed lid.

It held a giant nugget of gold. It sat within, gleaming dully in ruddy splendour, an uneven orb with its hollows and fissures adding to its wonder. Hrald's lips parted in amaze. It was as large as the largest plum, or a small apple.

The gift struck him, not only for its value, but for its raw state. The gold was unworked, natural, ready to be transformed.

The Abbess read this in his face, and agreed. "Yes," she said, "it is ready for a higher form, just as Ashild was."

Then the Abbess laid her hands upon his head, blest him, and kissed his brow.

On his return to the hall Hrald told his mother of the gift the King had sent. Ælfwyn was full amazed at the tale of the golden nugget, and the priceless casket that housed it. Then he presented her with the letter.

"This came with it. The King's note for you," her son said. In fact the Abbess had not called it such; had named it merely a missive from Witanceaster, but Hrald had linked gift and letter nonetheless.

"Thank you, Hrald, I will read it in my bower. The King's gift, and now his letter . . . I must think about all that is happening around our Ashild." She smiled at him, a smile of wonder.

She had meant to save the letter for the end of her day, when she might read it by cresset light, with no demands of the hall awaiting her attention until she again awoke. But carrying it there, feeling its slight weight in her hand, she felt a strong desire, even unto an urge, to open it at once. The letter had travelled many a day to reach her, but if it concerned Ashild and Oundle, it would bring needed pleasure to her this moment. She snipped open the lacing at one end and pulled off the leathern casing. The thin slats of wood opened to reveal a slip of parchment, with but a short message inked upon it.

Her eyes fell first to the bottom of the few lines. It was not from the King. It was not from Ælfred.

MY LADY ÆLFWYN

I live still, in service to our King, and in hope of again standing before you. No words of mine can assuage the loss of so striking and noble-hearted a woman as Ashild. Yet were I in truth before you, I could hope my arms would lend their strength and support. If God grants me continued life, you shall know those arms.

Press this to your breast, that I may feel your warmth.

RAEDWULF OF DEFENAS

She stood, holding the letter to her heart with the palm of her hand, as tears of loving release streamed from her eyes.

※※※※※※※※※※※※

Hrald stood at the paddock rail at Four Stones, his gaze fixed on the white stallion of Ashild. It was the day before he and his men were to set off for Saltfleet, and he was filling his eyes with things he wished to remember. The horse was across the paddock, at the far rail, standing stock-still, just as he was. Hrald thought himself alone, until a hand was slipped in his. He looked down into the solemn eyes of Bork.

"Take me with you," the boy said.

Hrald regarded him. It was the first sign of affection the boy had shown, and one of the few requests he had ever made. Hrald never forgot the first, made when Bork feared Hrald would slay him, and asked that he be buried with his father. But Hrald knew his answer, as surely as he had known his first.

"Nej. We sail into a sea of raiders. Even this early we may have trouble."

Bork's face showed no fear of such challenges. Hrald went on. "And you – you have a duty here, a considerable one. You care for my horses. It is a grave charge, and one given to you. You will check their hooves, every day. You must wipe them down, comb their manes and tails. You will ride each one in turn with Mul, to keep them in shape. I am trusting you to do this in my absence."

Bork's eyes had grown the larger, listening. His Jarl was telling him of the importance of the tasks he was bound to fulfill. It gave them new meaning to the boy.

"I will," he promised.

"You must also keep on with your writing practice, in your wax tablet. My mother, the Lady of the hall, will work with you. That is important to me."

Bork was less excited about this command, but nodded just the same. But Hrald was not done.

"I will tell Jari to begin to train you with weapons, as well. One day you will serve as my man."

Bork's head jerked back in wonder. The smile which spread from his mouth almost swallowed his face, it was so wide.

Hrald's parting was more wrenching than he imagined. His mother kept herself from open tears, but Ealhswith sobbed, and hung about his neck. He knew his leaving was hard, almost cruel, after the loss of their sister, yet go he must. Cerd had been in his grandmother's arms but the boy had grown restless and eager to be on his own feet. He went running between Hrald and Ealhswith, who was now standing, wiping her eyes, by her mother's side. Ælfwyn placed her arm around the girl's shoulders, and Hrald regarded them both. His sister this year would have Sixteen summers, and was become a young woman. She shared her mother's looks. He smiled inwardly, recalling Ceric telling him Ealhswith would be pretty, and being also of more tractable nature, would be easier to marry off than Ashild.

Hrald might not be here to do so; he saw this now. If he did not come back, his mother would find suitable husband for her.

Burginde, having caught up Cerd to keep the boy out of the way of the horses, sniffed mightily. It was when Cerd reached his arms to him and shrieked out his name that Hrald must steel himself. He was already on his horse, and he tried to smile at the boy. He gave signal to move out, and the two score and ten men sailing with him touched their heels to their horses' flanks. Three waggons laden with supplies rolled forward.

They reached Saltfleet next day. From the road they spotted the two drekars awaiting them, tied to the wooden uprights of the pier, bobbing in the tide. A few men waited on the ships, and more upon the planking of the pier. The ships were close in size, one of twenty-eight oars, the larger of thirty-two, and they would have men enough so that every oar might be manned when needed. The sails of undyed linen and wool were neatly furled against the spars. There was no flash about either of the vessels, no dragons nor sea beasts rising from the prow stems, just a simple curling in of the tips. Yet they were new, stoutly built, well-caulked, and came with a ship-master of repute. As Hrald and his followers eyed the drekars, those stationed at Saltfleet came out to greet them.

Aszur was the name of the ship-master and captain, a salt-toughened, bandy-legged man not much larger than a dwarf. He had a barrel chest, though, and a voice which boomed from it. He nodded respectfully to Hrald, and looked over the men the young Jarl had brought with him to crew the ships, armed with bows, spears, and swords. Aszur's own men looked them over as well. They might be green at sailing, but they were practised warriors, skills which might be called upon, headed where they were. The ship-master did not seem displeased, and in a few days he could make of almost any man a good rower.

He grinned at Hrald, showing long teeth, one of which was wrapped in gold. "When the wind fails us I will make them put their backs into it."

The lading began, provisions first in casks and sacks and chests. Next came the men's clothing and belongings stored in low wooden chests which would serve as their rowing seats, and then goods they had selected to bring to trade in Gotland, protected in bags of leather or oiled linen, to guard against rain and sea-spray. Their weaponry was carried on last so it was nearest at hand, the spears caught and held upon the decking against the mast lock, their shields slid into place by the oar slots beneath the gunwale.

While this was going on, Aszur led Hrald to the sandy banks where sat the ships Hrald had scuttled. The drekars sat on their keels at a leeward angle, just their curled prows and sterns visible above the high water mark. They had sat thus for half a year, and had not yet begun to break apart.

The captain lifted his hand to them. "I took their anchors, two good ones, and groping about, found their chests of tools. Rubbed with sand, the rust will come off, and auger bits and chisels be good as new." Hrald found satisfaction in this, that the ships had yielded something of value.

The tide was turning in their favour; it was time to cast off. Hrald returned to the now-empty waggons to bid fare-well to the men who would drive them and their horses back. He gave a pat to the glossy neck of his bay stallion, which made him remember Bork into whose care he passed the animal. Then he turned to the ships, and climbed aboard that larger one captained by Aszur.

Hrald had not sailed since he and Ceric as boys had returned from Gotland. To feel the vessel moving beneath him, the limber stretch and swell of her as she ploughed the waves, reawakened sensations unfelt for half his lifetime. The weather was Spring-cold but bright, the wind brisk, and they hoisted sail at once after pushing off.

Hrald did not turn his face back to Saltfleet. He must give himself wholly to this voyage, and the goal of seeing his father. As they moved steadily out he stood with Aszur in the stern, his back to Lindisse and all it held. The wind buffeted his face and his hair blew over his shoulders and around his eyes. After what felt a great passage of time he could hold himself back no longer. He turned his head. His homeland was a greenish smudge against the chilly blue sky. He felt a hollowness, seeing it, as if there was no more to what he had known and loved than this jagged and random patchwork of leafy growth.

He had chosen a journey which would bring hazards and hardship. He might die attempting it, but the deep sense of betrayal Hrald felt was so great that standing there on the pitching ship he did not care if he did. So much had broken his heart. He had fallen in love with a beautiful woman, then found her in the arms of another man. Her cousin Haward, whom he trusted and had dealt justly with, had abetted her deceit. Ceric, his best friend, a man he loved as a brother, had slain Ashild, whom they both adored. Everything was out of his control; a cascade of events witting and unwitting that brought disaster upon two halls, and devastation to true hearts. He felt himself harrowed and riven, and only the hope of seeing his father and Gotland again could keep him going forward.

That night when he unfurled his bedroll and lay down upon it, he placed his sword at his side. The ship was creaking and heaving beneath him as he closed his eyes. He thought of the day he chose this sword to be his own from the deep chest of blades in the treasure room. Ashild had taken it from him, and seemed to both bless and challenge him with it. Over the noise of the ship her words sounded again in his ears. "This is the sword with which you will defend our home. May you never fail it."

He had been fifteen when she had told him this. Her voice was low and cool in his ears, just as if she lived and spoke to him tonight. He fell asleep, awakening at a vision rising up like a spectre before his eyes. It was himself, holding this sword, its blade dripping with dark liquid from the hacking slashes he had given Onund's corpse.

Their first crossing was of the North Sea. With the wind at their backs as it was, they might make it to Danemark in four days. A cold rain fell for two of them, so that all were wet through, but the sodden sails, though heavy, sprang in deeper billows when the drying Sun again struck them. Of the twelve men from Jorvik, two were steering oars-men, Aszur as one in the head ship, and two star-readers to keep their course, one per ship lest they get separated. The other ten were solid rowers, manning the oars when needed in slackening winds, and, with no little chaffing, coaching the men of Four Stones in their own efforts. Even Hrald took a turn at the oar, remembering his father telling him of how they had propelled Yrling's ship Dauðadagr when winds were light. Aszur let him stand at the steering-oar as well, his hands wrapped around the beam, feeling the thrust of the foaming water against its rudder end. When Hrald relinquished its oaken mass he looked with respect at Aszur. To hold the oar against the swells and turn it to greatest advantage took both skill and considerable strength. This small man with his golden tooth possessed both.

Dane-mark came into view. Hrald scanned the coastline as they skimmed by: green, but flat. Again, he thought of his father, and how he had spoken of his first glimpses of Angle-land, its cliffs and crags, the towering woodland crowding down to deep coves, and when they passed inland, its verdant dales and valleys. His father's homeland lacked much of this, and for men craving not only silver but fruitful land on which to settle it must have filled the eye.

Their goal was the river town of Ribe on the western coast, where they would stop for fresh water and food. It was a royal trading town, and the protection of the King of the Danes extended to all visitors. Even in times of upheaval when bloody King succeeded bloody King, the tax-collectors thereof kept order in the trading towns. Merchants depended on trade and must continue to sell their goods, allowing tax to be collected to fill the coffers of the next who deemed himself King.

Though the sailing season was just beginning, folk lived at Ribe year round, and those who came overland from the countryside to barter their goods kept it a lively place. They tied up near several coasters, the crews of which looked up at the two war-ships as they oared into position to throw a line to the men tarrying on the pier. It was mid-day, a good time to land, and they spent the time re-provisioning, resting, and drinking good ale at the several brew-houses. They hauled out their cooking kit and built a fire on shore, so that they might at last enjoy hot food, which four days of cold rations made a welcome treat.

Night came on. After they had eaten Hrald sat cross-legged, staring into the crumbling logs of their cookfire. It had burnt to amber gleeds, glowing hotly in the black ash. His eyes narrowed, fixed upon the charred wood as it flared and flaked, shattering to pieces. His thoughts, unbidden, flit to Dagmar. She is here somewhere, he thought, here in Dane-mark. It was so bitter a belief that he jumped up to put it out of his head.

They cast off at dawn, heading on their northerly tack. They would stop again at Aros when they rounded the tip of Jutland, but not before. Aszur had a cousin there, one who had before sailed to Gotland, who could, if the ship-master reckoned properly, be persuaded to come along for the remainder of the voyage.

Thorvi joined them at Aros. Aszur found his cousin where he had expected, asleep in broad day in a brew-house, but once he flung a jug of sea water in his face, a sputtering Thorvi stretched his eyes open and welcomed Aszur with a hug. Thorvi was a slight man of some forty years, his Sun-browned skin making contrast with his hair of almost silver brightness, which he wore in a single long plait down his back. He was oft hired as star-reader and pilot, well-kenned in the peculiarities of the headlands they must pass.

The most treacherous part of the journey lay ahead, the narrow crossing between the many east-lying islands of Dane-mark and Skania, and the land of the Svear. Thorvi had sailed all through this passage, and knew the greatest points of hazard. Sandy shoals lurked under the shallow waters, and the likelihood of meeting raiders was great.

For the first time they were hemmed in by land on both sides. It was one of the parts of his boyhood voyage that Hrald remembered best. The nearness of the banks had made Ceric's uncle more wary than usual, and he still recalled the alertness with which Godwin and Worr had scanned every cove and river outlet, and how he and Ceric had mimicked that watchfulness in their own watching.

They saw small ships out for early fishing, casting nets where perch and pike were flowing in the channel, but no dragon ships pursued them. Still, Thorvi had not left his post in the prow of the lead ship, that helmed by his cousin. The winds were strong and steady, funneled through the channel as they were, and the square sail billowing out under its force was as brilliant as a rush of snow cascading down a mountain. There was ahead a narrowing between islands which opened up to freer waters. It was a particular point of ambush for ships making the southernly route, as raiders lying in wait could shelter out of sight in side coves.

Thorvi was correct about the danger there. The larger ship carrying Hrald passed through a channel much like the narrow neck of a jug. It proved a blind curve to sail around, and when they emerged they were not alone. Two war-ships awaited them, on either side, one to starboard, one to port. In a moment their sails were fully unfurled and their steers-men drove straight at them.

Both were mid-size drekars, of less than thirty oars, but each carried fewer than that number of men, relying on working in tandem to squeeze their prey between them.

Thorvi's yell of warning sounded across the channel. The men behind him scrambled to pull on ring-shirts and put on helmets. Hrald, standing at the steering-oar next Aszur, watched the man bare his teeth in disdain, the gold-covered one glinting behind the sneering of his lip.

Hrald thought, I could die now, and my father never know I was on my way to see him.

It was a thought he must speedily dismiss. His kit was there in the stern recess. He pulled on his ring shirt and dropped his helmet on his head. Then he took up his spear; its long reach was best to resist boarding. He threaded his left arm behind his shield and took up position by Aszur.

The attackers came at them first with arrows, which hit their shields and stuck there, pinged off the hull, and skittered across the deck.

But Hrald had not included Askil and his brother archers for nought. They chose their single target, then let fly at the stern of the closer pursuer. Two of their arrows struck home in the form of the steers-man. He was a large man, and toppled forward across the steering oar. The laden oar skipped, then lifted free of the water. Powered by the wind that drove its own sail, the attacking drekar veered so that unchecked it would ram Hrald's ship.

Aszur gave a howl from behind Hrald. With all his bodily strength and with his sail-men shifting the lines, the captain brought his ship to heel, sending their own prow foremost. The two ships hit, almost prow to prow, absorbing the worst of the impact along the stout oak of the keelson. Each craft suffered an impact that knocked men of both off their feet. The ships recoiled, but the men of Aszur were ready with grappling hooks. In a storm of hurled oaths and war-yells the sharp claws of the hooks took hold in the enemy hull, and pulled it closer. This crippling action was backed by a steady hail of flown arrows released by Hrald's archers, pelting the attackers and dropping many of them before the lines holding the hooks were pulled taut.

Aszur's second ship, captained by one Öpir, had now emerged from the passage into the fray. It headed directly for the starboard side of his first, there to pin the attacking drekar helplessly between them. The enemy ship which had been at the port side of the passage fled. Its sister vessel was caught by hooks, and men from Hrald's ship were leaping aboard, spear first. Some men on the caught ship howled and shook their fists at their abandonment. Others leapt overboard, swimming toward the retreating vessel for rescue. The few that stayed and fought were speedily downed by Hrald's warriors.

It was over so quickly that later the men jested that Thorvi's outraged call was still echoing through the passage when they took possession of the raiding ship. The second ship of the sea brigands had slowed but slightly to extend oars to the men who raised desperate arms from the cold water in entreaty to be picked up.

"Let us run them down," Aszur urged Hrald. Hrald had no need to move from the stern, where he had kept his shield in play, protecting the captain from any errant missiles.

"Nej," Hrald answered. They had watched some of the raiders struggle in the water and slip beneath its dark blue depths, and even now his own men were stripping the bodies of the men they had killed aboard the enemy ship.

They lowered sail, and took stock. The ship captained by Öpir had suffered no losses; its mere appearance had turned the tide for the victors. Three of Hrald's men on the lead ship had taken arrow-hits, none grievous, thanks to the buffering action of leathern tunics beneath their ring-shirts. And they had captured a drekar of twenty-six oars.

Aszur and Hrald joined the rest of the victors aboard the captured ship, a tricky action for the short legs of the ship-master. But his upper-body strength was great enough that he pulled himself with some agility over the gunwales of both vessels, to walk the decking of that they had taken.

These had been local Danes, not far from their homes, and had little with them save their weapons to fight with, and a day or two's supply of food. The weaponry of the men must be forfeit to Hrald, but the ship itself, fully equipped as she was, was well worth the having.

Aszur walked up and down, considering all, then returned to Hrald. "Give me this ship in payment, and keep your silver," he told him. Hrald was to have paid Aszur on the return to Saltfleet a large sum of silver for the use of his ships, his men, and his piloting skills. Instead the golden-toothed man asked for the ship. Hrald was more than willing to comply.

While in the captured ship Aszur took time to inspect the prow of his own. A gash in the new wood and rivets partially popped above and below it gave testimony to the force of the blow.

He clicked his teeth and shook his head, then turned to address the men behind him. The collision had only happened because of the dead steers-man's weight upon the oar. Aszur had saved his own hull from rupture by coming about as smartly as they did, allowing the quick end of the battle. Still, he did not want to repeat the manoeuver, and with a grin let them know it. "When next you kill a captain, knock him clear of the steering-oar, to save me the trouble of setting rivets."

THE WELCOMING

THEY manned the captive ship with fifteen men, three of whom were those of Aszur, the rest from Four Stones. Hrald's men had learnt to be capable enough seamen, and for greater safety they sailed with the new ship tagging along that of the lead vessel. Another day was spent on their southerly course, after which they cleared the end of Skania. Rounding the tip they were met with crosswise winds which vexed all three captains and slowed their progress. The weather remained fair, and the water their prows ploughed through took on a new quality. This was the Baltic, shallow and the more treacherous for it, but blue and wondrously clear.

Finally out into it they ran up the coast past the long island of Öland, close enough to keep it in sight, yet far enough away to give pause to any on land who might spot them with thought of giving chase. They beached that night near the tip of that slender isle, knowing that the morrow would bring them to their goal. Due east lay Gotland. They had only to follow the path of the rising Sun and it would emerge from the blue waters.

None aboard had knowledge of Gotland save Hrald and Thorvi, and Hrald's was a boy's remembrance. Thorvi set the course, for the mid-point of the western coast. "Paviken is the great trading post. We will land there first, as you have goods to trade."

They need stop there, as Paviken was where his men could make the best trades for their silver and weapons. Yet Hrald wished they might go straight on, so eager he felt to be at Tyrsborg. He recalled they would have to round the southern tip of the island and then sail up, half a day or so, to reach that cove above which his father's hall lay.

When Gotland came in sight at mid-day they all strained towards it. The island proclaimed itself with boldness, and to their starboard side stood tall and steep cliffs falling in sheer lines to the water. Vast forests dark with pines topped them. Thorvi's eyes ranged along the expanse of coast open to their view, and chose his target. Like most trading towns Paviken lay up a river, providing both shelter from sea storms, and greater defence in case of attack. His pointing arm served as guide to Aszur, back at the steering-oar.

They drew closer under a steady wind pressing them on. Narrow beaches of almost blinding whiteness spoke of the limestone the island was built from. The water too shifted from deep blue to a pale blue-green, as they neared the underwater rock shelf that skirted so much of the shore.

Seabirds followed them in, gulls and fulmars and teals soaring overhead, and ducks bobbing in the freshwater outlet they sought. A small boat emerged from an almost hidden inlet, and Thorvi whistled back to his cousin. They dropped sail and oared in.

The inlet opened into the lagoon upon which Paviken was set. At once they were amongst the work of men. They passed the domains of shipwrights upon the banks, where men laboured in the bright Sun. They saw frameworks upon which keels were set and ribs attached. Sailmakers were there as well, their vast lengths of woven cloth carried out of doors to be draped upon broad wooden supports so that the men and women who stitched in grommets and reinforced the heavy selvedges could work in the best light. Lines of hemp and leather were pulled, cut, and braided from the shops of those offering this vital furnishing, for a single faulty line could cause a downed sail, and crippled ship.

Paviken was still quiet, for it would be weeks before the trading season was at its peak. A few fishing boats bobbed slightly in the basin of the lagoon, their hauls feeding the long ranks of drying racks lying along one bank, for the flayed white bodies of many herring hung there. Of shops or stalls there were surprisingly few. Much of the trading was done right from the decks of arriving ships, or from the back of carts and waggons driven from the countryside, but a few stalls were in evidence, though with awnings rolled down. Set back on one bank of the lagoon was a small cluster of houses, at which folk were now living, for children played, and laundry hung from prop-held lines from tree to tree. There was at least one brew-house already open to care for the wants of those living and stopping here, and a few men were seated at the benches before it, and looked up from their cups to the new arrivals. Three ships arriving at once was to be remarked upon, the more so as they were drekars. They occasioned no alarm, landing as they did, their weapons stowed, the men at the oars diligently stroking as the steers-man of each ship brought them safely in to nestle aside the long planked pier. They were not quite alone, for a large ship of more than fifty oars was tied up at the second pier. Upon its deck a number of men in gathered, baggy leggings, brightly coloured, or even stitched in stripes, lounged. Some of them stood up in greeting to the three newcomers.

Thorvi turned back to the men on the lead ship. "The Rus," he told them, with real satisfaction. "They have had a long river passage to reach the Baltic, and then across to here. They are bringing furs, I wager, and also precious stones from their mountains."

Thorvi's next words brought grins to his listeners' faces. "Your luck-spirits smile today. They will want your blades, and you can fill your small purses with great treasure from their carnelian stones, jasper, and lapis."

They shipped their oars, tied up, and made ready to quit the ships. Hrald's men retrieved leathern bags and wooden boxes from where they were stowed, and some of the Rus traders, seeing this, had already come forward to meet them upon the planked walkway fronting the piers.

Hrald headed to the brew-house, with Aszur and Thorvi at his side. Off the ship and its ever-present smell of tar, Hrald became aware of something he had forgotten, or perhaps had never noticed when here as a boy.

It was the smell of Gotland, a clean mineral bite, as if the Sun-washed limestone, from which all growth sprang and every building was rooted, lived and exuded its own fresh and stony scent.

They passed through the men sitting at the brew-house benches, who nodded at the tall stranger with the fine weaponry. Within was a man wearing an apron, and wiping a stack of pottery cups. He smiled his greeting, as all in his trade are wont to do.

Hrald gave a nod in return and spoke.

"We are seeking Sidroc, of Tyrsborg."

The brewer regarded him, nodding his head at the name.

"Sidroc the Dane? Já, he trades with us here."

"I am his son."

The man laughed. "I can see that."

At this Hrald too must smile.

"I was here once as a young boy. I have memory of sailing around the tip of the island. It took half a day or more to reach there. Am I right?"

"Já, you are. It is a double cove, one deep, one shallow. There are rauks just north. If you reach those you have passed it. But you will see the landing pier. Also there is a good brew-house there."

Hrald had again to smile. "Já. The brewster is a friend."

Before long the brewer had his reward, and was kept busy carrying jugs of ale to the fifty visitors eager to celebrate their success with the Rus. Hrald lifted his cup with the rest of them, grateful for the safe arrival, but not a little troubled at what tomorrow might bring. Not until he had set his eyes on Gotland had he given thought that all might not be well here. Something amiss could have happened to his father or family since he had seen him, casting them in as great a sorrow as afflicted Four Stones. The brewer's ready naming of his father helped him beat this notion back.

It would have been a simple thing to spend the night at Paviken, and with its ready access to ale his men were eager for it. But Hrald wanted to press on, and Aszur and Thorvi agreed. If they rounded the tip of the island tonight, they could camp just on the eastern side of it, and save the run up the coast for the morning.

They did just that, the quickly lengthening days allowing them light enough to round the vast rauk at Gotland's southern tip. They ran their ships up on a shingle beach that shone in the moonlight, boiled up their browis on shore, and slept on their ships.

Dawn came as early as dusk came late, and they heaved the hulls fully back into the water and splashed through it to clamber aboard. The eastern side of the island slipped by, struck by a brilliant Sun which rose in a sky first pink and then deep blue. A coastline of sand and shingle beaches, wooded coves, towering rauk fields, and watery sea marshes waving with sedge slipped by. The Sun was near to overhead when Hrald, now standing in the prow with Thorvi, spotted their final landfall. He saw the tall and long fish racks first, already partially loaded with drying slabs of fat herring. Then came that solemn place of burial and its pyre-places. His eye skipped onward, and blinked in recognition. Here was the great carved figure of Freyr, with his painted beard of wood, which he and Ceric had gaped at. Just after it came the row of workshops and stalls themselves. It culminated at the far end in the brew-house, looking just as he recalled it, an open-walled building with roll-up awnings, now lowered in the cool weather. Rannveig's brewing shed and many outbuildings stood behind it, and then her snug house, with its gardens running almost to the shingle beach. A road behind the brew-house drove up at a steep angle behind it, where Tyrsborg lay. The leaves of the trees were not yet fully in, and even from the ship

Hrald could see the peak of its sharply-gabled roof. He swallowed.

No ship was tied at the pier, and they oared up to it. As at Paviken, folk came from their stalls to look on the three war-ships. They caused no alarm, peacefully rowing in. Raiders bent on attack would have driven their ships to the beach and leapt out brandishing spears, war-cries straining their throats and distorting their faces. These men looked warriors, but those here to trade, and not to raid.

Rannveig was already out, in her work yard. When she stepped from the brewing shed she saw the ships rowing in. She stood a moment. Warriors often came, just to drink and eat. If they headed for her brew-house she might have a busy and profitable day ahead. They would range along the trading road, bartering from stall to stall what they carried with them for what they needed to continue their journey. The ships tied up. One of the first to jump from the ships was unusually tall, lean, and with dark hair lying on his shoulders. She studied him, and gave a soft gasp.

The man took in the trading road in a glance, as if he knew it, and came straight towards the brew-house, fol-lowed by his men. The brewster stepped from the small garden in which she grew her flavouring herbs for her ale. She took a few steps towards the man. He was young, dressed in a simple dark tunic, leggings and boots, but well armed with sword and knife at either hip. A leath-ern pack hanging from his shoulder was all he carried. A light flickered in his eyes as he saw her.

She was the first to speak.

"Hrald." It was the boy, grown to young manhood, and with a man's cares.

He gave a nod.

She moved, as quickly as her years and girth would allow, to embrace him. "What – what – why . . . "

He gave his head a single shake. She saw a thin white scar on his forehead, one that resolved itself into a furrow on his brow.

"I must see my father, and his wife. Can my men stay here?"

"Já, já, bring them in," she urged.

He could see her concern for him in her face, and he tried to smile at her. He recognised for the first time how old she was; she must have near to sixty years. She jingled as she walked, just as he remembered, the count-less bronze keys at her waist tinkling like the bells of an ox-cart, but far more merrily. Around the plump neck were her bright beads of coloured glass, each different from the next. There were perhaps more strands than ever now, adorning her. She stood before him, studying his face, seeing, he thought, the shadow of the tragedy he must tell.

"I will see you soon," he promised, at which she nodded, biting her lip.

He climbed the hill to Tyrsborg, fastening his eyes on the gabled peak as he started up. The narrow stone face of it came into view, with his father's bind-rune carved above the door. From the stable a thickly-furred and spotted dog with a bent-down ear ran out to greet him. It offered a single yip and a furious wagging of its coiled tail.

The cook Gunnvor and serving woman Helga stood there in the kitchen yard, the first stirring a cauldron, the second wringing out a cloth into a basin. They looked at the stranger, then knew him for who he was. "Mistress, mistress," called Helga, running to the side door of the hall.

At this Sidroc emerged from the stable. At almost the same moment Ceridwen came from the door of the hall. Hrald had stopped just before the stable opening, where his father, confronted so unexpectedly with his son, took a great stride forward. Hrald could not move, seeing him. His eyes were burning, the red heat of the rims brimming with hot tears.

Sidroc threw his arms around him, and a moment later Ceridwen's arms were about them both. A muffled cry came from Hrald, one which dissolved into great shuddering sobs, welling up from the centre of his being.

They stood thus until Hrald's breathing slowed. Neither his father nor Ceridwen let loose their grasp on the boy; and his own grip never lessened, as if he held on for life itself.

Sidroc was facing towards the sea, and the three newly-arrived war-ships down at the wooden pier. They looked ships that would make any war-chief proud to stand at their steering-oars. Ceridwen was aware only of the suffering of a boy she had ever loved. Every possibility of disaster crowded in on both their minds, and each in their way fought to quell them as they led Hrald into the hall.

Both Gunnvor and Helga were looking on, their own distress and eagerness to help manifest in the way they held their hands towards their mistress, awaiting orders.

"Helga," Ceridwen asked. "Please to bring us ale."

They entered the hall proper, passing the two looms set against the side door, a small shuttle dangling from the weft of one where Ceridwen, in her haste, had let it drop. Now finally here, Hrald paused to look and take it in. The Sun was strong, and low enough to pour in through the doorway and cross the breadth of Tyrsborg in a single channel of golden light. The fire-pit rimmed with large stones was there running down the middle of the space, sleeping alcoves on either side. He saw the one he had slept in, and the common wall it shared with that of Ceric's. The door to the treasure room was off to one side, the broad trestle table on which meals were taken before it. Hrald looked to the pegs where as a boy he had claimed one as his own. He moved to them now. He lowered his pack to the floor. He unbuckled his sword belt and hung it from the remembered peg, a gesture which seemed to separate himself from the blade as quickly as he could, now that he was within Tyrsborg's walls.

This ready removal of his weapon was not lost to his father's eyes. Hrald wore the signs of his estate in the sword. It was a blade Sidroc recalled, his own second choice as a fine weapon, which Hrald had wielded at the duel securing Four Stones' future.

They moved to the table, and sat so that Hrald was between them, with Sidroc at the head, Hrald at his right, and Ceridwen next him.

Helga came in with a tray of beaten copper, upon which sat a bronze ewer and deep pottery cups. Ceridwen poured out, placing the foaming ale before them all. They brought it to their mouths, for all had need to ease the stricture in their throats.

Hrald put down the cup and drew breath. "I come to tell you what no one else can," he began.

He looked to his father's wife. In her face was both fear, and loving concern. Knowing what he must tell her, Hrald felt almost unable to speak.

Ceridwen was as well beyond words; the swallow of ale she had taken had come close to choking her, for her throat was too tight to permit real opening. Yet her heart had grown so large in her breast that she could both feel and almost hear it as it throbbed within her.

It was his father's face that spurred Hrald on, the heightening apprehension of the wait marking it with a kind of diffuse anguish.

"There was a battle, last harvest-time," he told them. "Some followers of Haesten landed at Saltfleet, killed nine of our men there. One survived to tell of it. We went after them. Ashild came as well, to serve as courier should we need her to ride back for more men. We caught up to them at a field on the western borders of Four Stones, and fought. After a while I went into the woods to face a single man, one who had been one of my own.

"While I was gone – " his voice broke here, and he took a moment to steady it. "Ashild got off her horse. She had made me a war-flag. Asberg's son Abi had been holding it. He had been hit in the leg by an arrow, and dropped it. She must have come, and picked it up.

"Eadward of Wessex arrived."

Ceridwen's lips had opened in surprise. Hrald went on.

"They had been chasing Danes from Lundenwic. It was all confusion, and my men told me, hard to know who was enemy and who was ally."

He paused, and looked to Ceridwen.

"Your son, Edwin, was there, with the Prince. Edwin's horse was killed from beneath him, and he suffered some slight hurt. But his retainer, Cadmar, was killed."

Ceridwen's hand had flown to her lips.

Hrald had need to draw breath now. "And Ceric . . . Ceric was there. He was with Cadmar when he died."

He must get the next out, and could not without his own eyes again welling.

"Then Ceric saw what he thought was a Dane, carrying a raven banner. He threw a spear."

He turned his head helplessly to those who flanked him.

"It was Ashild. It was Ashild.

"She was looking for me. And he killed her."

A low howl came from Sidroc, an utterance of raw pain. He leapt up.

"Odin!" he cried. "Odin and his spear."

On the day he left Four Stones Ashild had told him she gave herself to Odin. Now Odin had claimed her with a spear. That God of sorcery had indeed demanded the greatest sacrifice of her, as he had warned. It was by the spear that Ashild had distinguished herself, and it was by the spear she died.

Hrald's eyes were locked on Ceridwen's face. Her lips were moving, soundlessly. The tears which had gathered in her eyes were now spilling from them. Her hands rose to frame her face, then closed over it. A choking sob broke at last from within her.

"Ceric lives," Hrald told her. His own voice was hoarse with grief, but say this he must, lest she fear even greater loss. "He lives."

She clung to this, yet to fathom what his act had cost him – what it had cost all who loved Ashild – was beyond her ken. Her son had mistakenly killed the beloved daughter of Ælfwyn. It was disaster beyond her grasp, beyond comprehension. Her thoughts could go no further.

Ceridwen turned on the bench and reached an arm out to Sidroc, who was now standing next to his son. She reached the other arm to Hrald himself. She had no strength to push herself up, but the men took either of her hands, and she was lifted into their embrace.

They wept.

They stood united, clinging to each other in the face of ghastly tidings. Their shared mourning lent solace to each, yet for Ceridwen the unseen suffering of Ceric and Ælfwyn burnt like a flare in her breast. The death of Ashild sundered the hopes of the two halls with the cruellest severing imaginable.

The three sank down again to sit about the table, its broad surface solid and unchanged from the news, as they would never be. They sat a long time, unspeaking, yet as one in their common grief.

Hrald must finish, for any comfort that might be found in the tale's unspooling.

"Ceric brought Ashild home. He stayed with us for several days, and did not leave until after Ashild was laid to rest.

"She was buried in the church of Oundle. Then Worr took Ceric back to Kilton."

Hrald's voice took on new keenness as he told the next.

"Oundle," he said again. "Abbess Sigewif gave the honour of being buried there first to Ashild, for as she said when she claimed her body, Ashild rode to defend it.

"Her stone is a great slab of white, almost like snow, and on it is carved 'Ashild of Four Stones.'

"And – and something began to happen soon after Ashild was laid there. Folk came to visit her grave. Women mostly, and girls, but some men too. They had heard of Ashild's death on a field of battle, and wanted to ask her intercession."

"As if she were a saint," Ceridwen whispered.

Hrald nodded, and must smile. "It makes my mother laugh, and cry too. But Ashild's grave has become a kind of shrine for folk, already.

"I wanted to go there, before I sailed. I saw for myself what my mother had told me. The Abbess opened the chest holding the offerings of silver and gems brought by those who visit. Then I went, alone into the church.

"On the wall by her stone is her spear. Sigewif mounted it there. She told me folk wanted to touch it. I looked at it and thought of how, years ago, I found her one day by the Place of Offering, practising her throwing. The spear she used was huge; it made me laugh. She had a blister on her palm the size of a lady apple, but she would not stop."

Sidroc took a deep breath at this; that was like Ashild, her stubborn persistence.

Hrald looked at his father, and they nodded in agreement. Sidroc had strong memory of Ashild's obduracy as a little girl, a trait that never diminished as she grew to be a young woman.

Hrald went on. "I taught her how to use a spear, along with Asberg."

He said the next with a mixture of awe, and sorrow, yet his eyes shone as he spoke. "To see the spear she had with her that day there on the wall at Oundle – my hand went to it as well. Ashild touched everything at Four Stones. But I too touched it."

Hrald lowered his head at this memory.

Sidroc lifted his hand to his hair and ran it through the dark strands. He sat there, thinking on what power was in the faith of the Christians. To answer this he need only think of Sigewif. She had been named Victory-woman. Warrior blood ran in her veins. She was a princess, sister to a great King, and, Sidroc wagered, the most powerful church woman in all of Angle-land. Sigewif would understand the purport of bringing Ashild's spear into the sanctuary built with her father Yrling's silver.

Hrald spoke again, and to his father. "Her shield – I have it, in the treasure room. It is the same you made for me when I was here with Ceric."

Indeed, Sidroc had memory of her carrying it at Oundle.

Hrald looked again to Ceridwen, recalling something of note he must share.

"Ælfred, your King, sent a rich gift to Oundle, to honour Ashild's memory. Sigewif showed it me. A casket of walrus ivory, holding a huge nugget of raw gold, as large as half my fist."

"The King sent it," Ceridwen echoed in wonder.

Hrald nodded.

At this moment a small child burst through the open doorway and came running in towards her mother. She stopped when she saw Hrald, then placing a finger in her mouth, scampered to Ceridwen.

"This is Rodiaud, our youngest," Ceridwen said, giving her wet eyes a wipe with her fingertips. The child's entrance lightened the mood for all. With the Sun falling on her small back, she seemed almost to glow. The child had bright hair, the same chestnut-gold shade as her mother, and piercing green eyes as well. Ceridwen gave the child a kiss, smoothed the waves of her hair with her fingers, and sent her on her way out to the kitchen yard again.

"Rodiaud," Hrald repeated. "What name is that? It is as pretty as she. I have not heard it before."

"It is known only on Gotland," she answered. "It was the name of Rannveig's mother, she who first owned this hall when Rannveig was small."

"She is beautiful," Hrald told her as the girl ran off. "The same size as Ashild's son, Cerd." As soon as he said it he caught his breath, aware he had failed to convey this vital fact.

Ceridwen's hand rose to her mouth. Tears again sprang into her eyes, but above a mouth which was smiling. "A child . . . Cerd," she gasped.

"Ashild wanted to name him for the babe's grandfather," Hrald answered.

"My own father," Ceridwen murmured, in wonder.

"Ceric did not know about the boy until . . . until he brought Ashild home. But Cerd grew used to him, quickly."

Sidroc had been taking this in. There was joy in the arrival of any child, but this one was an heir of not one but two halls. Urd, the youngest of the Norns, was twisting the thread of life in ways to bind the families ever deeper together. And Ashild had given him a name to honour his shield-maiden's family, and not her own. This struck him. Ashild was of willful, but deliberate nature. There was deep meaning in this, to him at least, almost as if she intended the boy to be raised at Kilton. Certainly with such a name, none would forget he was of Wessex.

Hrald moved his head, as if in remembering. "I have something for you. From my mother."

He went to his pack and drew forth a small and flat wooden box, its two halves tied with a strip of leather. He brought it to Ceridwen at the table, and watched as she opened it. Something wrapped in linen and packed with straw was within, and she shook both from the object. She revealed a piece of fired potter's clay, into which a small child's handprints had been pressed.

"They are Cerd's," Hrald told her. "You and my mother have a grandchild, and she wanted you to have this, until you can meet him yourself."

Ceridwen lifted the piece to her lips and kissed each tiny print. What sweetness was this, to come from so much loss, she marvelled. By some benison of Fate a child had been left, one named after her own father, one now being loved and cared for by Ælfwyn. She could only hope that Ceric could know comfort from his boy.

She sat gazing at the shallow hand prints preserved by the potter. Then she looked up at Hrald, with a question. "Did they hand-fast, or wed in the eyes of the Church?"

Hrald paused a moment. "Their union is seen as such." A wry smile touched his lips for a moment, as he said the next. "And Burginde let it be known as such."

Ceridwen had to smile as well, for her recollection of the resourceful nurse was still strong.

Hrald could say more of this. "Ceric named her as wife many times, to Ashild, to me, and to others. He had a golden ring for her, that of his grandsire, which he placed on her finger after her death. She was buried with it."

Ceridwen gave a nod of gratitude. It signified that Sigewif, Abbess of Oundle, acknowledged the union, and the child as well. No woman would be buried thus with an ornament on her finger; only a ring designating her as wed would be acceptable for such an august interment as that granted Ashild. Cerd would be seen as the true heir of both his parents.

Hrald was aware he had left his men at Rannveig's a long time. He had need to get his other pack, as well. It was then he realised he had carried no gift for the family of Tyrsborg. He had not expected, fully, to survive the journey. It was part of the reason he had forbidden Jari the trip; the sheer danger of it. Yet he had travelled with a full complement of weapons, the act of which assured his innermost self that he did wish to live, or that his life was at least worth defending.

Still he looked at Ceridwen, and his father, and made the simple admission.

"I have brought you no gifts."

She answered with a mild remonstrance, one lit by her smile. "You have brought us the greatest gift. Yourself."

They walked out of Tyrsborg together, into the welcome Sun of a day growing warm with the promise of Summer to come. Little Rodiaud was in the kitchen yard with Gunnvor and Helga, and ran over to them, throwing her hands against her mother's skirts and smiling up at her. Ceridwen picked her up, as she did so thinking of the boy just her size who Ælfwyn was cherishing.

They paused near the stable doors, and Sidroc again looked down the hill to the water, where the fine ships lay tied at the pier.

He looked with admiration at his son. "You come in three ships from Lindisse."

"Two," Hrald corrected. "The third is a capture, from the narrow western straights of Dane-mark."

Sidroc threw back his head. He could not help his glee. "A capture!"

He was about to ask more when Eirian and Yrling emerged from the forest path.

The hound Flekkr raced to them, yipping his greeting. Both children stopped for a moment when they saw the tall man standing next their father. They now had twelve years and had not seen Hrald since they were toddling children not much bigger than Rodiaud. Hrald had been a boy of nine years. Yet they knew him, for Eirian, looking between her father and the tall stranger, discerned who he was.

She ran right to him, shrieking, "Hrald! Hrald!"

Her twin brother was still pulled up short on his heels, and watched his sister run to the arms awaiting her. Hrald caught her up and lifted her in the air. Yrling stood open-mouthed, in awe at this big warrior who looked so much like a younger version of his father.

"Have you come to live with us?" was Eirian's first question of her half-brother.

Hrald had to smile at her. She had unusual come-liness already, with none of the awkwardness marking many girls at the same age. In stature she was like Hrald, or their father, tall and long-legged. Their own leanness was made manifest in her slender form. Her hair too spoke of her father; it was a dark brown, her mother's chestnut tresses adding richness to the hue. She had blue eyes, dark blue, very much those of Hrald or Sidroc.

"Not to stay. For a visit. Until the next full Moon. Then I must take ship again."

The girl had thrust her hand in Hrald's and he kept smiling at her.

"They were at Tindr's home, in the forest," Ceridwen told him. "Tindr is wed, to a beautiful woman of the Sámi, Šeará. Together they have two fine children, a boy and a girl. They live in a forest clearing, in a round house they have built in the way of the Sámi folk. He will be glad to see you again."

Now Yrling came up, grinning. "I am Yrling!" he proclaimed.

It made all laugh. "I recall you," Hrald assured him. Yrling's hair had been a bright ruddy yellow as a toddler, and had darkened to an ambered brown. The boy was more his mother's son in colouring, with fair skin, blue-green eyes, and a nose dotted with freckles. He now rocked forward on tiptoes, spotting the war-ships below.

"Are those your ships?" He was looking in wonder at Hrald.

"I came in them; but two are hired, from the big trading town of Jorvik, in my homeland. The third we captured in Dane-mark, and I have given in payment to Aszur, who owns the other two."

"You captured a ship?" Yrling could scarce contain his excitement at this.

Hrald nodded at Yrling, and then looked to their father. "Two raiding ships of the Danes thought to squeeze us, in one of the western island passages. They did not yet know we had a second ship, ourselves."

Sidroc gave a laugh. "I will walk down with you and offer my praise to your captain," he said. "The story will only get better over the next four weeks, and I want to hear it now."

"I am coming!" Yrling said.

"And I am coming too," Eirian chimed in.

All Ceridwen could do was nod her assent. "Ask Rannveig to come for supper," she instructed Eirian.

At the brew-house Rannveig and Gudfrid, her cook, had indeed been busy, Rannveig with ladling out ale, and Gudfrid with griddling up platters of steaming oat cakes for the men to eat. A score of Hrald's men still lingered within. The others sat resting in the bright Sun, both within the ships themselves, and on the wooden pier.

Hrald's father and siblings were shown the vessels, and after asking leave, Yrling clambered aboard the lead drekar to explore it fully. Sidroc spoke some time with Aszur, Thorvi, and Öpir, glad to learn more of how things lay in Jorvik and in Dane-mark. Eirian, after a look at the ships, passed into the brew-house to convey the invitation, and was rewarded with an oatcake from Rannveig.

Hrald joined his little sister at the brewster's, thanking Rannveig and reaching for the pouch of silver at his belt.

"Nai, nai," she refused. She laid her hand over his to stop him. "Nothing, for this welcome ale. Your father sold a narwhale horn for me, one my husband Dagr won at dice. He sent it with Runulv to Frankland, who sold it in Paris to the King." She smiled. "I may be the richest woman in the Baltic."

They heard a whoop, and saw Yrling at the steering-oar of the lead ship, Aszur at his side. Even if she was tied up, Yrling seemed happiest aboard a ship. Rannveig looked at the boy, and then back to Hrald. "He is like Dagr, more at home on the sea than he is on land. He was born to it, just as Tindr was born to his forests."

When Hrald returned to the pier and his father's side, Yrling came running to them.

"That is my ship," he told Hrald, a declaration made with pride.

The boy pointed down the beach, where beyond the reach of the tide, a ship had been pulled. It lay at steep angle to the pebbles, the open hull shrouded with tarpaulins against the wet of Winter.

"Your ship?" Hrald repeated.

Sidroc gave a laugh. "It is Dauðadagr," he corrected, "the ship of my Uncle Yrling. When I returned from Four Stones three years ago I saw her, tied up at Ribe. Or I should say, the One-eyed God saw me. There is a carving Yrling had made, of Odin, which stands in the stern. The single eye is a chunk of quartz. Odin winked at me. A long dice game later, she was mine."

"And one day she will be mine," Yrling piped. "She is, after all, Yrling's ship."

Hrald had to laugh, as did their father, who also gave warning. "Such reasoning as that will take you far. Far into trouble."

That night, despite her tiredness, Ceridwen lay long awake in bed. A single cresset lay burning on the table, to ward away the greater darkness of her thoughts.

Rannveig and Gudfrid had joined the family of Tyrsborg for supper, and the brewster had been made quietly aware of the news Hrald had brought them. Ceridwen had not yet told her twinned children about this loss; she needed time to consider how best to share it, just as she needed time to absorb it herself. If Eirian or Yrling noticed her eyes glistening at times at the table, or afterwards when they took a walk with Hrald down the trading road, the youngsters might ascribe it merely to her happiness at Hrald's visit.

Now, lying in bed under the arm of Sidroc, she tried to order her thoughts, which seemed to lie like fragments of a shattered bowl upon the ground. She must try to collect the pieces even if the bowl could never be mended. The death of Ashild was as hard to compass as was the birth of her little son. Yet she knew both were real, as real as those gathered fragments which might suggest a bowl, but never again form one.

Ælfwyn had sent no letter with Hrald. There were times when words could not be captured, just as now Ceridwen could not direct her thoughts toward any answer. Yet much was said in the handprints of the little boy who lived on.

Tonight her greatest fear was for her own son, Ceric. Worr was with him, and she felt certain Worr would have taken him swiftly home to Kilton. There he would have his grandmother Modwynn and Edgyth to comfort and care for him. Ceridwen had never thought of Modwynn without her heart moving within her. That great Lady would be old by now, but she must still live; she must. There was no imagining Kilton without her.

She tried now to picture the face of Ceric. She yearned to see him, and wondered if she ever would. And Edwin – Hrald had told them Edwin had suffered some slight hurt, and she squeezed her eyes shut, thinking of him. Edwin had been only a small boy when she last saw him. What kind of a young man was he becoming, she wondered. He had had a taste of the awe-ful reality of war, a combat in which Cadmar, the trusted friend of Kilton, had shed his Earthly garment.

Something she could not fully name was also troubling her, Sidroc's feelings towards this death at her son's hand.

The brutal fact was her son had killed Ælfwyn's daughter. Sidroc had raised the girl as his own for the first decade of her life. The two families were interwoven to a depth that few ever were, in this and many other ways, with secret bindings known only to her, Sidroc, and Ælfwyn. Ashild was the daughter of the hall, a young woman both mothers hoped would become the wife of Ceric. Her loss was a shared tragedy which nonetheless could have riven the two families in a breach that could never be bridged.

The horror of Ashild's death was its own chasm. Yet she must mourn for Ceric in almost equal measure.

She feared naming him, but must.

"Ceric," she breathed. She had been lying on her back in the crook of Sidroc's arm, and now she turned to him.

His exhale was long and slow. "I think of him too," he assured her. He could not but think of him, having seen and done what he had in his own lifetime. He had considered the deed over and again since Hrald's telling of it, and came always back to the same conclusion.

"It was no rash act, done in jealousy or rage towards his wife," he held. "He saw the enemy on the field of battle. He must avenge Cadmar's death. And it was response to all the ugliness upon that field. Battle will blind a man to other actions."

He heaved a sigh, considering this.

"And – she held the war-flag."

The urge to see that flag fall, to snatch it from the ground and carry it back to Kilton as trophy and recompense for the warrior-monk's death would have been profound.

All he could do was repeat these things. War caused unintended casualties as well as those needful for victory.

They were both silent a while, until he spoke his own son's name. "Hrald too," he offered.

Hrald bore the burden of his own culpability in Ashild's death; they had seen that. He had allowed her to come, and was certain she was looking for him. She had died in his service.

Sidroc had further knowledge on this, one he knew Hrald shared. It was burden indeed, to know others died for your sake.

"They are both Christian, your son and mine," he told her. "They will find remedy there."

She put her head down against his chest, and nodded, speechlessly.

He too was silent, considering the two, hoping they would take whatever comfort they could to live with this loss. But he secretly questioned whether Ashild would ascend to their Heaven, or instead be called to the hall of Freyja, or even that of Odin, who took her. Would she be offered a choice, he wondered, and if so, would he see her again in the Goddess' gemmed hall, when he and his shield-maiden were called there? Ashild's father would be in Asgard, that was for certain.

Ceridwen felt an easing within her, listening to him. She wanted his thoughts on another report Hrald had shared with them.

"To learn of Oundle, of something close to veneration happening there at her tomb . . . " she could not complete the thought. "But it gave ease to Hrald to go there, heart-sick as he was."

Sidroc wrapped his arm about her.

"All who knew Ashild may smile at this, but they will also take comfort from it, my shield-maiden. As you must. As you must."

TYRSBORG

BEFORE the Sun had quite risen next morning, Tindr came to the stable at Tyrsborg to tend to the three cows. They had acquired yet another milker, as Ceridwen had begun to make her own cured cheese under the tutelage of Gunnvor the cook, who had blended and pressed it at the farm on which she had once served. As Tindr moved between the animals, the skogkatts, which now numbered four, followed him, opening their pink mouths to receive a squirt of warm milk which Tindr shot them from the teat he pulled. It was something that always made Tindr laugh. It was the first thing Hrald, who was approaching the open doors, heard; the loud mewing of the begging cats, and Tindr's well-remembered laugh, a honking like that of a gosling. He stood in the still-dim doorway, and waited for Tindr to notice him. Tindr rose from his stool and did so, blinking his eyes. He made a gurgling sound of surprise, and recognition. Hrald came to him and they threw their arms about the other.

Hrald was far taller than Tindr now, and Tindr, grinning, lifted his hand up to Hrald's head in acknowledgment of this. Tindr began to sign to him, asking many questions, most of which Hrald could not know or answer, but he thought he was able to make clear that he would be here a full month, until the Moon was at its fullest. He would ask Rannveig to tell her son that he hoped he might be able to walk the woods with him. Perhaps they might set snares for the big blue-tinged hares, or Tindr could just take him on some favoured trackways, or to the caves he had once shown them when he and Ceric were here as boys.

Right now they were just glad to see each other. The third cow lowed, which made Hrald look at her. Tindr then looked as well, to see her shifting her weight in her impatience to be done. Like her sisters she was spotted white and grey, with liquid amber-brown eyes. She lifted her great head toward Tindr and flapped her ears at them both.

Hrald was not alone in being early afoot. Eirian ran out from the hall, basket in hand, and came to the men. With quick hands and a smile on her pretty face she asked Tindr to allow one of the waiting cats another squirt of milk. He did so, and the brown-striped skogkatt, as heavily furred as a fox in its winter coat, opened wide its jaws to receive the treat. She laughed her thanks, then ran off to the fowl houses, where she had care of both hens and geese. These she would free into their pens for the day, and then deftly rob their roosts of eggs so they might break their fast.

Yrling came out as well, and after greeting Hrald and Tindr, went straightway to the paddock where Tyrsborg's four horses stood swishing their tails. They were in the care of Yrling and Tindr, and as the boy began forking hay to them, Hrald thought for a moment of Bork, caring for his own beasts back at Four Stones.

Hrald walked with Eirian to the kitchen yard, where Helga was at work, poking up the fire. The girl held her basket against her narrow front, and looked up at her older brother gravely.

"Hrald," she wanted to know. "Do you know Cymru – Wales? Cymru is its real name. Mother told me. She is half-Welsh."

Hrald shook his head. "The Kingdom of Wales. I know it has had fierce Kings, and many war-like Princes. They are their own people, Eirian, with their own tongue. I do not know them. The Kings of Wessex and Mercia have both made peace, and warred with them."

"I want to go there," she told him, with great seriousness. "Some day. Grandmother is there. She lives by the River Dee."

"I hope you can visit," Hrald said. He knew nothing of the woman, save that she had been of that race. To find her after two decades seemed but a faint hope, but perhaps if she still lived, she could be found. A determined search could be aided by God, and Eirian come face to face with her grandmother, as she wished.

Later that day Ceridwen and Hrald went down to the brew-house to visit Rannveig. Eirian came too, taking charge of Rodiaud, who, screeching with glee, ran ahead down the hill so quickly that the girl had to catch up to her and stop her lest she tumble. Even early as it was in the season, the awnings of the brew-house were rolled up, for with the men of Hrald's ships docked there, the brewster and Gudfrid had constant call for food and ale. Rannveig gestured her visitors out to her own place, and Hrald gave greeting to several of his men as he passed through the brew-house. Once seated at the table in her own snug little house, Hrald delivered his message.

"Sparrow sends you loving greeting," he began, which made both Rannveig's and his mother's face light with pleasure.

"She is known by her name, given in Frankland, Bova. Now she is Sister Bova, for she is a consecrated nun at the foundation of Oundle, near to my hall."

Rannveig was listening with great interest, but it was clear, without real understanding. She could have no notion of what a nun was, but Hrald made it as plain as he could.

"She dedicates herself to her God, the one on the cross she reveres. She lives amongst a large number of other women, and men too, under the keeping of a powerful woman, the Abbess. The men and women live together as brothers and sisters, and pray and work together. Bova is the brewster there, providing ale every day for over one hundred folk. I have heard priests – the men who lead their rituals – jest that Oundle is their favourite spot to visit, for the goodness of her ale."

Rannveig clapped her hands in her delight at hearing this. Hrald had further message to share.

"Bova has warm remembrance of you, Rannveig, and thanks you for the skill of making good ale, with which she serves all who live there, or visit.

"She is still small and brown, like a sparrow, but she smiles every time I see her. She is happy there."

He thought of more to add, now that Rannveig knew the tale of his dead sister.

"Also, she is devoted to my sister. Every morning she goes into the shrine in which Ashild is buried, and places a blossom or branch on the stone under which she sleeps."

Rannveig took this in, nodding solemnly. "It does me good to hear this, about our little Sparrow. She has found her nest, indeed." The brewster craned her neck, looking down at the necklaces she bore. She fingered one. "When you return I will give you the necklace which I had given her, so she might remember me for the rest of her life."

On the way back up the hill, Eirian fell in next to Hrald. She had listened with care to all he said, and now had questions. "Hrald. When you were talking about Sparrow, and where she lives now, what does that mean?"

He looked down at her. Her deep blue eyes were large with interest. He took a breath, and began.

"There is a different God in my land, the big island where your mother is from."

"Only one God?"

"Only one. But he has a Godly son, and there is a Holy Spirit as well."

"Like a ghost?"

He smiled. "Not quite. He is more like a thought that can come to people, when they pray."

The girl was quiet for a few steps. Then she said, "I am sorry about your big sister. Mother told us. She said Ashild was very brave. I am glad Sparrow leaves Offerings at her stone."

Next morning Sidroc told Hrald of his plan for the day.

"Come, let us ride to Ragnfast. We will get you a horse to use while you are here." He grinned as he said the next. "You can ride my wife's mare, she has plenty of spirit, like her mistress, and will take the bit in her teeth if you let her."

Yrling saw them heading to the paddock, and was at once at their heels and wanting to go. Then he remembered he had promised Aszur to help with the rivet setting on the prow of his ship. He had helped his father and Tindr at this with Dauðadagr, and could not fail the ship-master now, not when he had, as offered reward, the chance to take the steering-oar in his own hands later in the day. "I will work on a sea-horse instead," he told them, as he made his way toward the pier.

Father and son saddled Sidroc's black stallion and the dun mare. She was a striking creature, with her mottled reddish coat, dark legs and black stripe from mane to tail, and Hrald said so. The men wore their mantles, for the sky was over-clouded, with no Sun to warm them. They began at the upland path at the end of the kitchen yard, riding single file for the narrowness of the track. The evergreen of pines and spruces looked the darker against the tiny leaves of the white-barked birches, as bright a green as the first peas. The meadowlands were now awash in early flowers, and the birds which flitted, skimming over their heads, were fully intent on nest-building. From their grasping beaks dangled lengths of straw and newly-broken twigs, ready to be woven into the bowls of waiting frameworks. Others were out seeking grubs and seeds, twisting their heads from side to side as they regarded the men on their great beasts. When the horsemen approached a second, well-worn path, Hrald knew it.

"The way to the farm where Ring lives is there," Hrald recalled. It was yet another spark to the memories he carried from his first visit here, with Ceric.

His father turned in the saddle and stopped his horse.

"Já," his father agreed. "I recall how you boys watched Ring at his training of the goshawks."

It brought to mind those at Four Stones, and Hrald spoke of them.

"The goshawks you brought me – they do well."

His father nodded in satisfaction. "I hope they will breed soon, and give you young."

Hrald thought of flying the goshawks with Dagmar. They had come back with nothing. He recalled his pleasure in bringing the female harrier to her, and asking himself, What would my father think, if he knew I pursued a daughter of Guthrum? It had all come to nought, just as their day's hunting had.

Hrald said no more, nor did his father. They looked at each other a moment, and then Sidroc turned his face back to the path and touched his heels to his stallion's flanks. Hrald knew his father was speaking for him as well, that he hoped he would find a mate and have children.

When the trees thinned they entered a clearing, in which fresh grasses were already beginning their climb through the Winter-dried stalks of the old. They rode side by side, a position that eases difficult talk. Sidroc had something he would ask his son.

"The day of the battle," he began. He need not say what battle it was; Hrald knew.

"The man you followed into the forest . . . "

Hrald turned his head and looked at his father's face as he went on. "There was a reason for that."

Hrald nodded.

"It was Onund. He was a friend of Gunnulf's."

Gunnulf was Jari's younger half-brother at Four Stones, and Sidroc had been there when Gunnulf had been killed during Hrald's duel with Thorfast. Onund had not been raised at Four Stones, and Sidroc had never seen him until that day. He had clear memory, though, of the man falling upon the feet of the dead Gunnulf. He did not relinquish his hold on the body until Jari had stooped low to pick up his brother in his arms. Onund had looked up with twisted face as Jari carried Gunnulf away.

Hrald would say nothing of the history of the men; he had not betrayed Gunnulf nor Onund and would not do so, even to his father. Both men were dead, and their story was their own. Yet he could speak one truth, and did.

"Onund always bore a grudge against me for Gunnulf's death. Asberg heard him once at Turcesig telling Thorfast's men that I boasted of killing him. I cast him from the hall for this. I hoped never to see him again. To find him there with Haesten and his renegades – " Hrald shook his head.

Sidroc picked up the thread of the battle. "You killed him there, in the forest."

"Já. He drew me in. We were alone, in a wooded clearing, scarcely large enough for us to draw our weapons."

That desperate struggle needed no power of recall; it was all too near in Hrald's memory.

"I tripped him."

The import of this struck his father. That was how Gunnulf had been killed, a simple trip, then a plunge of the sword into his back. Onund had been a powerful man, older than Hrald, and a more than considerable match for his son. Any means Hrald had used to drop him was meet and right; that was what combat was.

Hrald went on.

"I bloodied him, then killed him with my first blow. Then . . . something happened. I could not stop slashing at him."

Sidroc looked away a moment, then back at his son.

Hrald met his eyes, fully. "It made me . . . fear myself."

Before his son's duel at Four Stones, Sidroc had looked him in the eye and tried to hearten him. Hrald had at last triumphed in that contest, but the older warrior well knew that winning carries its own burdens.

Sidroc was silent a space as they moved steadily forward upon their horses. He would say nothing to deny the boy's fear, so honestly expressed. All he could do was to place it in a larger landscape, to pull away from that single moment which had caught his son and still held him.

"When there have been words between two men," Sidroc told him, "things emerge on the heels of victory. Anger can lift the sword from our hands, and act on its own. Next time your grip will be firmer."

Hrald had looked away, his eyes cast down at his horse's mane.

"Do not reproach yourself," his father went on. "It was not needless savagery. He was dead, a quick kill any man would want." Sidroc's eyes rose for a moment to the cloudy skies. "The Law-giver Tyr sees these things. I know this."

He turned his eyes back to Hrald, and said the next with calm resolve.

"This man betrayed you, and Four Stones. In doing so he was false friend to Gunnulf, who the shield-maidens claimed in an instant for a seat of honour in Freyja's hall.

"You must let this go, as you will much more that will come your way."

They returned from Ragnfast's with the biggest horse the breeder could supply, a pale chestnut gelding with a fine head and cream-coloured mane and tail. On the way back to Tyrsborg Hrald tried leading the dun mare behind him, but true to his father's warning, she was not happy to follow in the footfall of the strange horse. Sidroc took her, and even then she kept coming up alongside his stallion, as if she would take the lead. Both men must laugh at her frowardness, one paired with her quickness, for Sidroc related that of all their horses she alone had learnt to open the door of her stall, by pushing her muzzle against the wooden toggle that secured it shut.

Once back at Tyrsborg they walked down to the pier where the ships were tied. The lead ship was under sail, crossing the bay on which sat the trading road, tacking, and turning back again. As she neared the pier they saw it was Yrling at the steering-oar. Standing next to him, no taller but much stouter, was Aszur, grinning so that his gold tooth glinted in the Sun. Yrling spotted his father and brother on the pier, and lifted one hand to wave at them. Only a few men were aboard, and he needed both hands on the oar to bring her in, with the ship-master's help. They had seen him helming the fine drekar, and Yrling's face beamed at them. He did not run to where they stood, but stayed and withdrew the oar from the water as Aszur instructed, then helped with the tying up with one of the crew.

The men who had made the journey, whether Hrald's warriors or the practised seamen of Aszur, were settling into a routine. They slept aboard the ships, cooked for themselves on shore from foodstuffs they bought from the trading road, and continued to enrich Rannveig's brew-house in their purchase of ale and hot meals. Yrling was much aboard all three drekars, making himself a favourite amongst the men. The boy was willing to take on any task, especially the tarring of the captured ship of the Danes, which had need of it. As Tindr had taught him, he gathered moss and sheep's fleece and stirred it well into the sticky pine tar. Heedless of blackened hands and smeared face, he packed it tightly with a narrow wooden knife into any gaps in the straked planking of the hull. He must rub his hands almost raw with sand and the cold sea water before walking up the hill to the hall, where a laughing Eirian would hold up their mother's polished silver disc to his face so he might see the daubs still on his face and clinging to his hair.

Some nights Tindr and his family joined them at Tyrsborg. The first time Šeará emerged from the forest path Hrald felt himself in the presence of a rare kind of beauty. Everything about her was unlike any woman he had ever seen. The yellow-white of her long hair, the eyes of crystal blue, placed at a slant above high and chiseled cheekbones, the almost milk-like fairness of her skin. She was dressed all in napped deerskin, in a tunic and leggings of that soft but strong covering, with furred boots upon her feet. She came forward with a smile to greet him, in a voice soft and low and with an accent unlike the speech of Gotland. There was a natural directness about her, as well. She knew no sham modesty, no coy dropping of the eyelids or sideways glances when a man looked at her with admiration. Her openness to meet men on their level put him in mind of Ashild.

Her children were dressed as she was, in napped deerskin tunics and leggings, decorated with thread work and ribbands of bright hue. The boy, Juoksa, was a fine little fellow, a few years younger than the twins, and the girl, Jaské, just a bit older than Rodiaud. The two little girls ran off together to Gunnvor as soon as they saw the other, and the ready way the cook produced a honey cake and divided it between them was proof that this hope had been met in the past.

Ceridwen saw how struck Hrald was with the Sámi woman, and smiled at him in agreement. "I thought the same, when I first saw her. One feels the power of all Midgard, and the animal she loves, even in the way she dresses."

Tindr's joy in his family was evident, his ice-blue eyes moving amongst them with quiet pride. Hrald remembered his crude efforts, with Ceric, in making their desires known to the hunter. He now watched with awe the way his wife and Juoksa, and even little Jaské spoke with Tindr, soundlessly, and with their hands and faces.

That night when Hrald lay down in his alcove he thought of Tindr's good fortune. He had been deprived of hearing and speech, but this did not keep from him the love of a faithful woman. Would he find the same, he wondered . . .

Hrald worked with his father and Tindr in cutting and stacking firewood to dry. The long Winter was lately ended, that to come still far distant, but the work of keeping the hall warm was year-round. The trees had been felled by Sidroc and Tindr at the beginning of Winter, and left in the forest until the snow and mud abated, to be pulled out one by one behind the strong backs of the black stallion and Eirian's gelding. The latter horse, though not large, was patient and seemed to derive satisfaction from the task of pulling. They were dragged through the wood, then sawn and chopped in Tyrsborg's work yard.

They took the trip upland to Ring's farm. The whole family came, Sidroc and Hrald on horseback, Ceridwen and Eirian and little Rodiaud in the small horse-cart, with Yrling at the reins, driving his own gelding. They carried food and drink for the outing to share with Ring and Astrid and their young ones. They had need to leave Flekkr at home, not wishing him to disrupt his siblings at their bird-flushing work which Ring had been so carefully training them to.

The ride was a pleasant one, taking the waggon along the trading road, along which all folk raised their hands in greeting to them, then turning up the first of the short lanes leading from it. They rolled over meadows and then along woods roads, noting the signs of an ever-deepening awakening in the warming soil. Great clusters of browned ferns crunched under wheel and hoof. The curled tips of their new growth were beginning to emerge, ready to spring into feathery fronds blanketing the forest floor. The mosses, brilliant green year round, now sported tiny flowers of white, and in every grassland and pasture clusters of yellow or blue ground-hugging blooms winked in the fresh green.

They did not fly the goshawks that day, though Hrald went into the cote with Ring to admire them. But they walked with the hounds and watched Ring as he worked with them, giving Hrald thought to do the same himself back at Four Stones.

About ten days into their stay, some of Hrald's men took the captured ship out, determining to circle the rocky island. Those wishing to see the whole of Gotland crewed it, captained by Öpir, so that they might boast of having seen all the coastline of the fabled isle. Thorvi went with them; he had been to Gotland before and knew farms at which they might buy a number of the large and deeply curved sheep horns which would be much admired for drinking at home. These were abundant here, and cheap as well, for even the ewes bore these formidable weapons.

Yrling, hearing of this, was eager to make the trip. He was not allowed, as Hrald did not want to forgo even a few days away from Tyrsborg, and the boy could not go unless in his older brother's keeping. "Soon – this Summer, maybe – you will take Dauðadagr out, and circle the island yourself," Hrald suggested.

"Já," Yrling admitted. "I will be captain, and Juoksa will be my second and mind the sail. Father and Tindr will need to row!"

Hrald laughed at him, and tousled his shaggy hair. Yrling had never quite cleansed the tar from some of the strands, and had taken the shears to them, leaving him with the ragged look of a thrummy sheep. The two brothers were this day almost alone at Tyrsborg, as Sidroc had ridden to see his captain, Runulv, about the upcoming voyage of goods they planned to send to Paris, and Ceridwen and the two girls were down with Rannveig.

"Let me show you my spear work," Yrling said next. "I practise every day."

Hrald had seen this with his own eyes, and indeed, the many pock marks on the stable wall gave further testament to the boy's diligence. Sidroc had even hammered up another layer of boards to protect the wall itself from their joint practise.

When Sidroc honed his throwing skills, he would draw an oblong shape upon that wall, roughly where the torso of a standing man would be. This was not enough for Yrling. He took a lump of wood charcoal and with sooty hands drew the entire outline of a man, one of his arms up, and holding his own spear at shoulder height.

There was a range of spear-lengths and weights, and Hrald joined him in his practise, throwing from both a standstill and a run. Yrling had good aim, his brother could see that, and also power when hurling the spear from a run. He also took some little pride in his ability, naming the part of the drawing he would aim for, and sometimes crowing in glee when he hit torso, arm, or leg, or came near. Not all the spears lodged deeply enough to stick in the boards. Some hit and then fell, but such a throw would be enough to fracture a shield or puncture an unprotected body. Of those that stuck, they must pull the shafts out after two or three spears hung there, lest the next spear hit those already protruding, quill-like, from the planks.

After a while they let the shafts already in their hands slide through their palms to rest on the ground. They stood there, catching their breath, when Yrling looked up at Hrald.

"Will you spar with me?" he asked.

Hrald gave thought for just a moment. "Já, we can spar."

He was sure his father did the same with Yrling, who in response ran into the stable and returned with two ash poles. They went together into the hall, and got their shields, Hrald's hanging by his sword belt, Yrling's from the wall in his alcove. They slipped them on their left arms and took up the practice poles. The tips were just blunt wood with no iron spear-point, the safest way to learn spear-skills. But it was enough for Hrald to see his younger brother's facility with the weapon.

The boy was of course fast on his feet, given his lightness. Even better, he was canny with his judgement. Their father had taught him well.

"My Uncle Asberg would be proud of you," Hrald told him, after Yrling had made a solid touch to Hrald's right leg.

"What does he do at Four Stones?"

"He was second in command there, under our father. I have won a second fortress, called Turcesig, not far from Four Stones. It was a garrison built by Guthrum, King of the Danes in Anglia. Asberg is now in command there. Father always told me that Asberg is one of the best spear-men he had ever seen. He trained me, and many others there."

Hrald's thoughts leapt for a moment to Asberg's work with Ashild, and he went on in a lowered voice. "All of us benefited from his training."

"I want to train with him," the boy decided.

Hrald had no ready answer. "Father is good with his spear-work as well," he said, tilting his head at the many deep pockmarks on the oblong target. "Else you would not be so good yourself. And Gotland is peaceful. Raiders come here, but to trade."

"Nothing happens here," was Yrling's retort. He picked up one of the tipped spears and threw it, hard, at his target, where it lodged in the head of the charcoaled man.

Ceridwen was laying Hrald's newly-washed clothes on his alcove bed one day when he walked into the hall. She smiled at him. "Your mother sewed this, and I know from the fineness of the linen thread that Burginde spun for it," she said, as she patted one of his tunics. On her wrist was the silver disc bracelet his father had worn at Four Stones when Hrald was young.

He smiled back at her and came to stand by the next, empty alcove, which had been that Ceric had slept in when they lived here.

His mother looked at it too. "I have not seen him since you two left Gotland together." Her face held a wistful sadness.

Ceric had not yet been quite Yrling's age when they left. Looking at the tall young man before her she could only imagine how her son had grown. She wished to speak of him now, and wondered if Hrald had things he wished to tell her. She lifted her hand to the table, and the waiting benches there. They moved to it and sat down.

She was right. Her mention gave Hrald leave to speak of Ceric, something he had been almost hesitant to do, lest it bring more pain. He told her of the two trips to Four Stones Ceric had made, the first in a time of peace, five years past. "Ceric and Ashild saw each other, grown," he remembered. "He brought us all gifts, a ring shirt for me, a golden pin which was yours for my mother, brace-lets and necklaces of silver for my little sister and aunt."

Her face lit at the mention of the pin. "Was it a circle of gold?"

"Yes. That one. It meant so much to her, knowing it was yours. She wears it often."

Ceridwen closed her eyes in pleasure at the thought.

"For Ashild, Ceric brought a gown of pure silk, golden-yellow."

Her lips parted. "It was your mother's," she began.

"Yes, and then yours," Hrald said. "Ashild wore it that night, at the welcome feast."

Ceridwen could almost see Ælfwyn's astonishment at seeing the gown again. Ceric would not have taken such a rich gift out of courtesy; in quality, this was a true betrothal gift.

"He told me then he would wed Ashild. Or try to." He gave a short laugh at the memory.

He went on to tell how news of Guthrum's death reached them near the end of the stay, and of the letter Ceric had left behind telling Ashild he would be back for her.

"He told me that, too," Hrald recounted. "When I was helping him arm in the treasure room. He told me he would be back in two years to wed her.

"But the Peace collapsed, and he could not come. He sent a letter with a priest. Ælfred wanted the marriage, but forbade Ceric to travel. The Bailiff of Defenas had solution, that Ashild should be escorted to the Wessex border, and be met there by Ceric and his men."

"The King endorsed the union," Ceridwen repeated.

"Yes, and later when I saw the bailiff he said the King was adding to the treasure Ceric would offer for her."

They both were quiet after this.

"The Bailiff – that is Raedwulf, Worr's father-in-law," she remembered. She had the warmest affection for Worr, and good memory of the bailiff, a man of high good looks who had come at least twice a year to Kilton.

Hrald nodded.

"Still, Ashild would not agree to leave, at least not then. I knew she had regard for Ceric, and knew he loved her. But she told us she needed to stay at Four Stones.

"The second trip – that was when they were man and wife."

His eyes rose to the rafters. It was a gesture of his father's Ceridwen had seen Hrald do many times, when he was thoughtful. Now Hrald looked at her once more. He could not hide the pain in his next words.

"She stayed for my sake. I know this."

She reached her hand to his arm. "Hrald, you put too much on yourself. I only knew Ashild as a small girl. But from what your father told me, I know she was one who must make her own way, according to the urgings of her own mind and heart."

She had thought the next over, and said it with the firm certainty that only long pondering can bring.

"I believe she had true regard for Ceric, else she would not have given herself to him, nor brought forth their child.

"Our desires, and our bounden duties – they will not always yoke together, and act as a team."

The pull of the heart, and the duty demanded by the mind could easily take a woman in opposing directions. Ceridwen certainly knew this, as did most women.

It brought Ceridwen's thoughts back to Ælfwyn.

"Your mother – how does she fare?"

"She is grateful for Cerd. We all are. If Cerd had not been born – " Hrald shook his head. "He is, as my mother often says, so like Ashild. Willful, clever, also loving and loyal."

The mistress of Tyrsborg had not moved the clay imprint of the child's hands from the table, but had left it there at her place, almost as if the boy was joining them at every meal. Her fingers went to it now and touched one of the tiny prints. "Meeting him will be a joy," she murmured.

"I hope you will find a worthy maid to wed," she finished, a bright hope she held for his future.

He did not answer, only gave a nod. He could not tell her of his brief union; he could not hold two sorrows in his breast at one time, the loss of Ashild, and the faithlessness of Dagmar. All he could do was give a nod of assent.

PAVIKEN

ONE night after supper Sidroc and Hrald arm-wrestled at the table. The days were rapidly growing longer, and it was just dusk. It was still too chilly to eat out of doors, save for some days when it was pleasant to sit in the growing Sun and take a cup of broth or ale in the afternoon, but the fire was always warm within the hall. Helga and Eirian were carrying out platters and bowls to the kitchen yard to be washed, and Ceridwen was there too, going over stores with Gunnvor. Rodiaud was already fast asleep in her alcove, unmindful of the rattling clatter of the men's cups as their entwined fists thumped down upon the table. Yrling sat with them, cheering them on. Each man won some matches, but Sidroc was still able to best his son on most of their tries.

Both men were still grinning when Yrling challenged his brother. Hrald looked at him and laughed, but set his elbow back on the table while Sidroc made way for his younger son. The two clasped hands, and in an unguarded moment Yrling almost flipped his half-brother's fist to the board.

"I was not ready!" Hrald laughed.

Yrling looked at his brother over their still clasped hands. He spoke with perfect coolness. "You must always be ready. That is what father says."

Sidroc gave a low hoot of acknowledgment. "I have trained you too well," he said, with a shake of his head.

"Next time we will play for silver," Yrling decreed. His eyes fell on the long knife Hrald wore at his hip. "Or for your knife."

Hrald considered the boy. He drew the blade from its sheath and placed it upon the table, at which Yrling's eyes grew even wider. Sidroc too regarded it, his own eyes narrowing for a moment before looking at his elder son.

"You have no need to play me for it," Hrald told his brother. "Here," he said, "it is yours." He unbuckled the belt holding the scabbard and slid it off. He placed knife and scabbard on the table before Yrling.

The boy was open-mouthed.

"But you will have no knife."

Hrald shook his head with a smile. "There are many weapons aboard my ship. This one is special, from my own store at the armoury of Four Stones. I want you to have it."

Yrling picked up the knife and studied the hilt. Bands of copper and silver had been beaten into the guard and pommel, and the bluish steel blade rippled where the many layers of metal had been beaten together. Yrling slid the blade into the scabbard, and then on to his own belt, pulling off the small knife he wore. The new was almost too long for him; on the boy's slender body it was like a sword at his hip.

"Thank you," he said, two words full of meaning.

The granting of choice weaponry was something Hrald did often, but this was the first time he had ever taken a weapon from his own person and presented it to another. Yet the doing so felt natural; this was his own brother.

"I recall that knife," their father said.

"It is one you collected, I think," Hrald answered.

"Já. From a ship my Uncle Yrling captured, as we headed to Angle-land."

Yrling looked at his father, awe-struck. Hrald had given him a weapon from a ship captured by the man he was named for. It enhanced the value of the knife ten-fold.

Sidroc looked to his younger son. The knife, and ship, had been won by cunning. He thought young Yrling would show no shortage of this.

"Now it is yours," he told the boy.

The Gods reward boldness, Sidroc knew this; but he knew also his older son's gift was the result of affection, not a prize to a cock-sure youngster.

"Wear it with the same honour your brother has."

<hr />

"I should have a coil of new walrus-hide line waiting for me at Paviken, for Runulv's ship. It will be ready by now, I think. We can ride there, we two, and collect it."

Three weeks had passed in Hrald's stay, and the ride with his father was more than welcome. It would mean camping out overnight, and perhaps a night or two passed in Paviken itself. They would take a third horse for pack, to carry ample provender, and so they might have a tent to keep night rain off their heads.

Yrling wanted to come, but Sidroc shook his head in denial of this hope. "You must stay here with Tindr and watch over the hall." Put like this, it took some of the sting out of being left behind. The boy had taken to keeping his hand on the hilt of his new knife when he stood still, and did so now. "But tomorrow you can help us ready the horses," his father said.

Sidroc chose Eirian's horse to serve as pack animal. Ceridwen's mare was larger, but as Sidroc laughed, "She will not go for pack." And Hrald had seen this himself, on the way back from Ragnfast's when they had chosen the chestnut gelding. The dun must be in the lead, or at least at the head of his father's stallion, on every ride out. Eirian's gelding, though not much bigger than a pony, was placid and far easier led.

Gunnvor baked extra bread in the morning, that they might take ample loaves, and boiled up a score of eggs. They would carry a small bag of barley, to make their own browis at night. She still had cabbages and fat turnips in the root cellar, and gave them one of each. She packed soft cheese into wooden crocks, and had as well a wheel of cured cheese made by the mistress of the hall. As a last touch Gunnvor shaved a mass of smoked deer haunch into a piece of waxed linen. They had a twist of salt, as well.

After the family had broken their fast next morning, father and son prepared to leave. Hrald's pack was already hanging by a post of the paddock fence. Yrling and Tindr were out with the horses, awaiting them. Hrald came back inside the hall and saw his father, carrying his own pack from Tyrsborg's treasure room. He had his sword belt in his hand, as well as the seax he wore every day which spanned his belly from its own belt. Hrald looked at the sword belt. His father just nodded at him.

"Paviken has never been raided," he told Hrald, as he began to buckle it on. "But the Svear and the Rus who come to trade – sometimes, a little show is a good thing."

Hrald understood, and went to his own sword belt, hanging untouched where he had left it the day he arrived.

They would only be gone three or four days, but the parting was a small foretaste of that to come. Ceridwen and Sidroc had known their own leave-taking in the treasure room, but now Rodiaud, held by her mother, reached out to both her father and to Hrald, as if she wished to be taken up in their arms. Eirian had Flekkr on a lead, so he would not follow the horses. Even so the hound was excited, turning in circles, thrashing its furred tail, and giving out with yipping barks as if it were time to play. Yrling stood, feet apart, his right hand upon the bright hilt of his knife, and regarded the two on horseback. His father looked down on him, and spoke with great seriousness.

"Keep all in good order until my return," was his charge.

Yrling pulled himself up to his full height and gave a nod as grave as his father's words.

They set off, with Eirian's horse behind the black stallion Sidroc rode. They must head due west and slightly north, but began by gaining the trading road, which would take them to the inland route they sought. The first portion was that waggon road to Ring's upland farm, but they quickly passed that turning and settled into an easy pace, the ever-lifting Sun warming their backs. The birds were active overhead, calling and darting, some still busy in their nest building, flitting with beaks from which straw or twigs streamed. The white birches held their graceful arms up, as if admiring the fresh green-ery at their tips, and the larches wore a brilliant green as new needles emerged from their outstretched boughs.

Hrald took everything in, remembering those things he had enjoyed as a boy with Ceric, and seeing so much more, as well. The ride itself, alone with his father, was a store of quiet pleasure. He had never travelled thus with his father, save for the overnight trip to Saltfleet, carried out with a troop of men from Four Stones. This time it was the two of them, alone, granting ample time in each other's presence, even if no words were spoken.

They rode all day, stopping just to water the horses and eat some bread and cheese. They pressed on until close to dusk, when they reached a narrow but swift waterway and made their evening's camp. There they unpacked the horses, staking them with long lead ropes where the new grass would keep them busy at their cropping. Hrald built a good fire, with a ready supply of sticks to keep feeding it when either awoke during the night, so that it might not grow entirely cold when they arose. Their supper was bread and smoked deer meat, boiled eggs, and some of the firm cheese made by Ceridwen, wrapped in the early fronds of dill. Unpacking all this, they found a small jug of mead as well. They sat in the fire light, their backs against their saddles, as their horses browsed about them. It was not fully dark, and the sky held a deep blue that foretold a clear and starry night.

After a while of silence Hrald lifted his eyes from the fire and spoke.

"I was wed." he began, in the speech of Angle-land. "To a daughter of Guthrum."

His father had been poking at the fire with a stick. He let it drop from his hand into the flames.

"Her name was Dagmar. She lived at Headleage, but I met her through Thorfast's brother. Her mother was named Bodil."

Sidroc's surprise was great, both at this news and the fact that Hrald had not before mentioned it. The last-named woman struck him, though he said nothing. Bodil had been Guthrum's wife during the term he had served as part of that King's body-guard. She was a tall woman, of unusual allure. He had never seen the daughter, who would have been small then. But if she took after her mother, Sidroc could see why Hrald had succumbed.

"You had wed," his father repeated. Hrald had spoken in the past, and of the clouding of his brow there could be no mistake.

He hazarded a question.

"Did she die," he asked, "bringing forth a child?"

"No." He gave his head a single shake. "I found her being kissed by another man." He paused. "She had brought him to the treasure room. He had been amongst the last of Guthrum's body-guards."

Sidroc raised his eyes to the deepening sky. Any war-chief's body-guards were his most favoured warriors. The danger of their service was great, and their lives corre-spondingly short, but while they served they might live richly indeed. They were rarely wed, but could command a choice woman as wife. And if any woman about the hall had roving eyes, her gaze would fall first upon the body-guards.

Hrald went on. "What there had been between them I do not know, but it was enough to find her in his arms, in my own hall."

"In the treasure room," his father said. His echoing the name of that near-sacred place made Hrald feel he was there again, in the moment of discovery.

"Yes." Sorrow hung on that single word.

The silence which followed was broken by Hrald.

"I cast her from my hall, sending her away with her bridal goods. She took nothing from the hall that she did not bring with her."

"No blood was shed?" his father asked.

"None."

"And the man?"

"I let him go. But he heard her double betrayal, for she begged me to forgive her, in front of him, not wanting me to cast her away."

His father, watching his face, knew that the rending of his heart was bloodshed enough.

Still, Sidroc wished to know the answer to what he must ask.

"Why did you not kill him?"

There was neither challenge nor judgement in his question, just a simple request to know more.

Hrald's eyes shifted up to the darkness above them.

"I know I could have, in law, done so," he said. "But why?

"She was willing in the act. She was no longer mine." He turned his eyes to the fire. "I did not know it, but she had never been mine."

A moment slid by, in which the fire crackled as a log split. Hrald went on. "Ashild would have killed him. And killed Dagmar too, I think.

"That kind of rage – I felt anger, yes, but to kill him . . .

"It would not bring her back to me. It would not undo what was done."

They both studied the flames as it flaked the wood to glowing embers.

"You did right," his father conceded, after thinking on this. The boy's mother, the priest Wilgot, the Abbess – all these had shaped him, and for the better, Sidroc knew.

"Hrald," he told his son. "There are many just and true women in the world. Your mother is one. My wife as well. One will come to you."

Hrald was silent, but his father's thoughts continued on. Both the women he named were of Angle-land. This spurred him to say the next. "A wife from Ælfred's Wessex, or Æthelred's Mercia, would serve you well."

Hrald need respond to this, which he had not before considered. He looked at his father as he answered. "As alliance, yes," he admitted. He thought further, of his mother's long efforts at Four Stones, and their joint commitment to Oundle, which had only grown the stronger now that Ashild was there. "She must be a Christian, or ready to become so," he added, "and any maid of those Kingdoms will be already devout."

Sidroc nodded, glad to see him looking forward like this.

"I think, when you wed again, you will be a good father. My wife tells me this, and on such matters she is rarely wrong."

Sidroc gave a short laugh, as he considered those off-spring he shared with her.

"Eirian has it in her head to go to Wales." He shook his head, but had to smile. "I know nothing of that land, save what I heard from Guthrum, of their fierceness. The women too.

"And Yrling – I named him for my uncle. And the Gods listened.

"Then little Rodiaud came, at last. She was a special granting. An augury was made by an old spice merchant we met on our travelling here, who told my wife she would have two daughters. Eirian was the first, but the second was long in coming. Rodiaud closes that circle."

※※※※※※※※※

They reached Paviken next morning, approaching by the river which formed its lagoon. A cluster of houses appeared first, and then as the current widened, the basin of water upon which the trading post sat. Two fishing boats had landed, the first just tying up, the second actively selling its fish to a group of men and women who stood around with baskets and hand carts to carry the catch home to flay. A third ship also was there, a warship of some thirty oars. The drekar was pulled up to one of the shipwright's yards. Both prow and stern sported carved dragon heads, looking fore and aft, and even dead in the water it was as sleek and sinuous as those fabled serpents. The mast was not up, and none were aboard but the shipwright and his men, bent over some work at the keel.

At one of the brew-houses sat the men who must have come from the drekar. Two score of warriors, with all their war-kit either on their backs or at their feet, sat upon benches, cups in hand. Sidroc and Hrald, shields on their backs, swords at their sides, looked at them from their horses as they rode in. The Norse spoken by the warriors fell on their ears as they neared. Danes.

Sidroc smiled at his son. "Our brothers," he remarked. The massed Danes were a formidable sight. Father and son, armed as they were, and with their three good horses, made their own impress as the Danes looked up at them.

The men were eating and drinking copious amounts, and both onlookers knew their purses were heavy with silver. One of the brew-house cooks was busy roasting fish threaded on metal skewers over an open fire, while another stirred an iron cauldron of browis with a long wooden paddle. A basket of eels, doubtless lately carried from the fishing boat, lay ready for gutting. A baker arrived, come from his own ovens, his floured apron full of still-hot loaves, which he dropped upon one of the cooks' work tables.

The two mounted men nodded a greeting to those nearest the walkway their horses trod upon. The Danes nodded back. Sidroc paused his stallion as they sized each other up.

"Rough going?" posed Sidroc. He inclined his head to the war-ship being worked on.

"Já," returned one of the Danes, a scrappy looking fellow with a balding head of wispy yellow hair. "Bad storm crossing from the Prus. We did not lose the mast, but the mast lock cracked."

Without the mast lock, a drekar was no more than a rowing boat. The fork-shaped block of oak set the mast securely upright in place.

Sidroc nodded in commiseration. "I wish you fair weather ahead."

They moved their horses forward, then Sidroc turned his head to see if any were playing dice. They were not, but he had to laugh at himself for checking. They ambled on, to the line-maker's stall to pick up the walrus-hide line destined for new rigging on Runulv's ship. The line was ready, an entire massive hide of it, cut into one long thin strip of unvarying thickness. The line-maker went over every ell with Sidroc, that he be satisfied it was perfect. Sidroc paid him his silver, and the man recoiled the line. Sidroc did not loop it to one of his saddle rings as he would have common hempen line; it was far too valuable to display before the crew of the drekar. He pulled a linen sack about it, then set it within one of the leathern bags born by their pack horse.

They passed several stalls with arrays of goods, everything from foodstuffs, to empty casks to hold water, to the sellers of sundries such as cooking gear, steel needles, hammered nails, and fishhooks. Sidroc stopped before a woman selling carved combs. They were not of wood, as was common, but shaped from the flattened horns of oxen. He picked up one in swirls of cream and white, smooth and pleasant to the touch. He looked at his son.

"Eirian," he said. The girl had never had her hair cut, merely trimmed, and now, at twelve years of age, it flowed down past her small waist like a dark waterfall. His shield-maiden wanted for nothing, but his daughter always hoped for a gift when he returned from any journey. This put Hrald in mind of Ealhswith, with her long yellow hair. He too selected a comb to take back, one of black and white swirls. Then Hrald laughed and chose a second comb, one swirled black and brown, for Yrling. The boy's hair was jagged from his self-given shearing, long and short at the same time, but a new comb might encourage tidiness as it grew out.

It was time to quench their own thirst. They headed to the second brew-house, the one at which Hrald had inquired about his father. They tied their horses and sat down on a bench under a tented awning. The brewer came forward. "I see you found each other," he said with a grin.

"Já," Hrald said. "Your directions were good ones. I thank you."

"Ale, or mead? I have Frankish wine, as well."

Sidroc laughed. He knew the Danes at the other brew-house had likely gone right to the mead, or even the strong wine, as their ship might not be ready for them until the morrow. "It is early yet," he countered. "Ale for me."

Hrald nodded his agreement, and the man carried out two deep cups of the malty brown stuff.

There was almost no one else at his tables, but a man who sat alone watched Sidroc and Hrald as they entered and took their bench.

They lifted their cups. Sidroc said, "We will see how his Spring ale compares to that of Rannveig," which made Hrald grin. They looked each other in the eye and took a deep swallow. It was good ale, distinct from Rannveig's and less herbal, but of rich savour.

The man sitting alone kept his eyes on them; he was almost staring. He looked a fisherman, from the tall boots he wore to keep his feet from wet, and the short cloak of oiled leather over his shoulders, one made to give ease of movement working aboard a ship. He could not seem to look away. Both Sidroc and Hrald noticed; and each, without speaking, wondered what would come of it. The fisherman finally got up and approached. He stood before them, eyes shifting from one to the next.

"You are Danes," he told them. He looked again to Sidroc, who nodded.

"There is an old Dane, lives up the coast. You . . . you are like him."

Sidroc's sudden alertness was marked by both his son, and the fisherman.

"Both of you," the man went on, looking at Hrald.

Sidroc felt a tightening in his chest. He had not really known where his father had stayed, during his sojourn on this island. But coming as he did from Dane-mark, it made sense that he would have landed on Gotland's western shores.

"What is his name," he found himself asking. His words were slow enough that his son took note.

But the man shook his head. "That I do not know; I stopped at his farm and sold him fish, once, only. But he lives on the sea edge, not a day's ride up the coast."

Sidroc uttered his thanks, and the man left. Hrald sat looking across at his father, his hands circling the thick walls of his pottery cup.

"Your father," he began. "He is dead, lost at sea in a storm."

Sidroc looked back at him. "That was what many thought of my wife and me," he answered. "Taken by slavers, and lost for good."

They sat in shared silence. Each, as young boys, had suffered what they had thought was the death of their fathers. Perhaps loss was the better term; that which was lost could again be found.

Sidroc made decision. "We will ride, now, and find him."

They paid the brewster and set out. Not even the Danes waving to join them at dice could stop Sidroc. They turned their horses' heads north, and followed the coast up.

There were few houses they came across, and no settlements. Fishing huts sometimes appeared, belonging to upland farms, but no farm at the sea edge as the fisherman had described. They rode all afternoon, across sandy beaches, marshland blurring from weeds to sea grass, and cold freshwater streams emptying into the Baltic. The Sun was beginning to lower at their left shoulders when the smell of a cooking fire met their noses, that mix of wood smoke and savoury broth telling of coming supper. Clearing a stand of beach-growing pines, they saw the farmstead.

It was set back from the water far enough to be safe from any Winter-churned surf, yet close enough that the small fishing boat hauled up on the shingle shore clearly was of the place. The sea waves reaching towards it barely crested, but the stones grated on each other with every lapping advance and retreat. Nesting shorebirds scrambled in their horses' path, dancing in the air and scolding loudly at them.

Sidroc slowed his horse as they neared the boat, and just looked at it, recalling that vessel so like this one in which he had fished with his father. A short distance away, wind-fallen branches, anchored upright in the stones, held a fishing net left to dry. A rush of recollection rose like a storm within him, of the day he had become entangled in the net and his father had grasped his raised arm and saved him from drowning.

It was not just the wind picking up which made Sidroc feel chilled. He did not know what he would find ahead in the low timber house. It sat on a swelling rise, and across from it was a barn and a few outbuildings. All was spare and simple, but kept in good repair with that thrift shown by those who have worked with their hands all their lives.

They moved forward, and saw a figure in the work yard spanning house and barn. A plump and elderly woman sat on a stool by the cook fire, singeing the pin feathers off a plucked fowl. Another woman was with her, standing at the edge of the fire, tending something on the coals. A man came into view from the pasture behind the farm, bringing in two cows. The older woman with the fowl saw them first. She set down the bird and eyed them, and did so with growing raptness as they neared. They stopped a distance from her. Sidroc lifted his hand in a gesture which he hoped signified greeting. She rose from her stool and turned towards the barn.

"Hrald," she called.

A man came forth, walking upright but a little haltingly. He was tall and grey of hair. Sidroc got off his horse and took a step to him.

He looked at the old man, and knew.

"I am Sidroc."

The older man was struck dumb. Then his mouth moved, the lips quavering before giving voice.

"I see . . . I see you are."

It felt an endless moment. They regarded each other, face to face, after decades of separation and uncertainty.

The older man began to lift his hands, in a gesture of helplessness or mere wonder. Sidroc bridged the gulf in two strides. He threw his arms about his father, and the old man wept in his arms.

Hrald had quitted his horse, and stood just behind his father. The woman too, had moved closer, wiping her hands on her apron and watching with widened eyes.

When the old man's sobs quieted, Sidroc stood back, and spoke.

"I live with my wife, and younger children, on the eastern coast. Our hall is called Tyrsborg, for the God I have given myself to." He gestured to Hrald, who came closer. "This is my eldest son, come from Angle-land where he was born. The Gods sent him at the right time to meet his grandsire."

"I am Hrald," he told the wondering figure.

Hearing this, that Sidroc had named his own son for him, the old man wept again. Hrald embraced him, trying to give comfort. The man seemed overwhelmed, baffled even, at what was happening. He lifted his arms to Sidroc, in supplication.

The woman now spoke. "Your throats will be dry. We have ale."

There was a good fire going in the cooking ring, and she led them to benches at the table nearby. She went into one of the small outbuildings, and returned with a jug and four cups.

"I am Stenhild, your father's wife. Runa and her husband Ottar live here with us and help with the farm."

The woman Runa gave a nod to the strangers from where she stirred a soapstone pot. Ottar had vanished into the barn after the cows, but it relieved Sidroc to know they had help. Running even a small farm alone would be an arduous task for a young couple, let alone for those advanced in age.

Sidroc did much of the talking, letting his father just look at him as he did so. He told of what happened when his father's boat did not return. "Yrling came for me, took me to Signe and Ful. I was raised with Toki. Yrling began to raid in Summer, to Angle-land. But he always had a plan to build a ship, and he did. The silver that was given me as my portion of what you left went into the ship, as did everything Yrling had ever earned."

"My little brother," the old man mused.

"He captured a great fortress in Anglia," Sidroc went on. "He died a few years later, in battle."

"He died young," came the murmured response.

Sidroc nodded. "He is in Asgard, that is certain. My son at Tyrsborg is named for him."

It brought a flicker of a smile to the elder Hrald's face.

Sidroc thought of something else from his boyhood. He bent down to his left ankle, untied the leg wrapping there, pulled up his legging. He unstrapped something from his bare ankle and laid it on the table before his father. It was the small knife he had given him as a boy.

"I have worn this every day."

The old man almost gasped for breath, seeing this, and hearing what it had meant to his son. Sidroc grinned at him as he said the next.

"That knife helped me win my freedom on a slave ship."

He told of traveling with Yrling and Toki across the North Sea to go a-viking, and of his success there. It was much to take in. The elder Hrald sat shaking his head in amazement.

"To hear how far you went, what you did." He looked about the modest farmstead. "This was all I ever wanted."

Sidroc was forced to nod. "Sometimes it takes decades for a man to learn this – what he truly wants."

"I wanted peace. A woman who cared for me," his father explained. He looked at his wife, sitting to one side, saying nothing yet listening with care to all. "I found her in Stenhild. She has a daughter from her first husband; he was lost to piracy, or the sea. The girl was a toddler when I first met her. She is wed now, living not far with her own family, and is a blessing to us. We had one of our own, carried away by the red-cheeked fever. She would have been about your age," he added, looking at Hrald.

Hrald remembered Rannveig telling him that there had been a terrible fever outbreak, the same that had carried off Tindr's sisters, and rendered him deaf.

They were still sitting at the table, with their ale cups before them, their hands flanking the thick-walled pottery cups that had been refilled again and again with foaming ale.

Sidroc drew a breath, and studied his father's lined face. He asked the question he had always wished to have answered.

"Can you tell me what happened?"

The elder Hrald looked up into the darkening sky over his son's head, then dropped his eyes to the scarred trestle top. No further prompting was needed; the story had been lying there on the surface of his life, unanchored, for over three decades.

"A gale came up."

The silence that followed went on for so long that Sidroc began to wonder if his father, in his despairing unhappiness, had considered not trying to save himself, and instead had determined to allow the wind and waves reveal his Fate.

"I had a hard time with the boat; tried to make a run back instead of dropping sail and riding it out. The mast snapped.

"I got hit by it when it fell. It addled my brain; I could not see straight. The boat was taking on water. I lost an oar, and tried to steer her into the waves with only one, so that I would not be swamped. I was sure I was going to be pulled down to Ran's hall.

"I do not remember much after that. I woke up on a fishing boat, three times the size of mine. They had found me drifting, and plucked me from the boat, which was half-flooded with water. I remember them telling me I could have drowned in my own small boat, it was so full.

"I was beholden; they saved my life. They were from Laaland. They had more nets to drop, but after that they took me to their sea village with them. I had no plan, but I must repay them. I could work my way back to Jutland, and the farm."

And to me, Sidroc thought.

"One of the men had the chance to do some trading in the Baltic." He turned eyes full of entreaty on Sidroc. "I could not say no. I could not say no.

"With each day, each week, my life back in Jutland became more and more distant. It was wrong to forsake you, Sidroc, and it pained me. But when Njord took me, and finally cast me toward Gotland once more, I could not leave.

"I landed again at Paviken. I came looking for Stenhild. I had spent a Summer with her when I had but twenty years. The Gods had driven me back here, where I had known the happiest time of my life. And I thought I could reclaim part of that. I found Stenhild again. She had a small farm. Eight, nine years had passed, but she was still there.

He paused and looked about. "I liked this coastland, here up north. She sold her farm. We bought here, built all you see. We made a life together, a good one."

His father's disappearance caused him so much pain. Just as his own did, to his own son. Hrald.

There was silence. The woman Runa had not stopped in her cooking. The fowl Stenhild had been readying had been pulled into bits, and was now simmering in a browis of wheat kernels and carrots. The air had grown chilly, and Stenhild spoke.

"Go into the house, you three, while we finish making our supper." She looked at her husband. "Hrald, fill the jug as you go in. We will not be long."

These homely needs were a spur to the old man. He looked at his son and grandson. "You will stay, you will stay the night with us," he urged.

Sidroc must consent. "We will stay the night. And soon I will come back for you both, to bring you to my hall for a visit, that you might meet my wife and young children."

The three men walked to the timber house. The door was low, cut so that all three of them must bow their heads as they enter, an old device to make it easy to disable any intruder upon entry. It made Sidroc laugh to see it, but he recalled their farm in Jutland had just such a door; he remembered his father having to duck to enter it.

The inside was snug, a low fire burning in the fire-pit. The man Ottar was at work over it, poking up and adding logs. Within there were no oil cressets nor tapers, but there were rush holders, and Sidroc lit an oiled twist of dried rush which cast good light so they might better find their way around the place. A trestle table stood before the few alcoves, with two benches flanking it. The elder Hrald came back and set the dripping jug on the table. He stood a moment, again just looking at his son.

His hand rose to Sidroc's face. He touched the deep scar there.

"Your face," he whispered.

Sidroc almost smiled, making the scar go crooked as it always had.

"Toki, when we were twelve," he said.

"Toki." The old man shook his head. "Where . . . where is Toki?"

"Lying under the burial mound I carried him to, in Lindisse."

He now stared in wonder. His son gestured him to sit, and he did so. "You have much to tell me," the elder Hrald said.

"You will know all," Sidroc assured him. "Even those things difficult to tell. But tell me one thing first." Stenhild was outside at her cooking, and there might be no better time to broach the topic.

"What is the name of my mother?"

"Jorild," he answered.

Jorild, Sidroc repeated inwardly. How many years had it been since this man had uttered that name, he wondered.

The old man looked thoughtful. "It happened just before I wed Ingirith, a pairing I was bound to. But it was Jorild I always cared for."

"And you sent her away?"

"Já. I sent her away, with all the silver I could give her. I had no choice. Ingirith would not have her there any longer. There was no peace at the farm with both women there. And I feared for your mother, and for you."

Sidroc sat still, considering. "I saw Ingirith," he said. "In Haithabu. It was before I sailed with Yrling for Anglia. She had wed a baker. She hardly knew me. One of my half-sisters was already wed, and had left her."

His father heaved a heavy sigh, hearing this. Then he lifted his eyes and in the flickering light, regarded his son and grandson. "We are much alike," he admitted, with the beginning of a smile on his lips.

Sidroc nodded at this. Looking at his father was almost as if he looked at himself, two decades hence. The younger Hrald, with his far greater handsomeness, was the outlier, but any seeing him would peg him as an acorn dropped from the same oak.

The old man seemed to be thinking the same, for his gaze now fastened on Hrald. "Who is your mother," he asked. He turned to his son to question him. "Who did you wed, that this boy has such looks?"

Sidroc gave a short laugh. "A noble woman from Cirenceaster, a place in Wessex. She was first wed to

Yrling, and she became the Lady of Four Stones, the fortress he captured. Yrling died before the gates of her own family's hall, when other Danes made claim to it. After he was killed I wed her. Hrald is our first born."

The elder Hrald seemed to ponder the exalted circles his son had moved in. He looked again at his grandson, then to Sidroc. "A noble woman of Wessex," he repeated, as if trying out this idea.

"Treasure brings much," Sidroc told him. "Including the chance to wed women of wealth and beauty."

The old man nodded and murmured. "Já, já."

Sidroc looked about at the snug house. The door opened, and a smiling Stenhild came towards them with Runa, bearing trays of food and drink. Ottar took one of the trays and laid it on the table before them.

Sidroc had further words for his father.

"I think you have found treasure enough, here."

A FAVOURED HOME

C ERIDWEN opened the chest in which she kept her prized store of parchment. Sidroc and Hrald were still away, and she would make use of the time to write a letter. She had long ago asked the old leather worker on the trading road to prepare several sheets of white-skinned parchment for her. Now she need only make up fresh ink, and deprive one of the geese of a long wing feather for her quill. She had no need to think of what she would say, but only let her quill speak the words of her heart.

MY DEAREST SISTER ÆLFWYN

When you hold this letter, you hold me. Know that I weep with you for a loss immeasurable. Hrald's coming to us with these tragic tidings has yet been a bridge connecting us in our shared sorrow. To know the brief union of our children brought forth a son is the greatest balm. I touch Cerd's little handprints each day, and marvel that Ashild has left so great a gift to us all.

Of the visitation to her tomb at Oundle, I can say only this. All that brings comfort to those who loved her, and those she is now inspiring – all of

521

this is to me, good. I hope you will find comfort in it.

Hrald has become the young man he always promised to be, the best of both you and his father. May the little one in your keeping prove the same, of Ashild and Ceric.

I fear for my son. It is only knowing that he was in Worr's keeping that brings me solace when I think of him. If they were granted safe return to Kilton, he will be with his grandmother and aunt, two loving and wise women, where he can begin, himself, to heal.

I have no greater wish than to see you, Ceric, and our Cerd. If this is willed, I shall know lasting contentment. May you be guided and guarded in all.

YOUR LOVING CERIDWEN

Thin as it was, the parchment was supple, and after she left it to dry she rolled it and tied it with a bit of yarn. Then she sewed it into a sleeve of linen, waxed with beeswax as proof against any wet.

Eirian was outside with her geese and new goslings when her father and Hrald rode back up the hill. Yrling was riding behind their father; he had been down at the ships and had hollered in joy when he spotted them. She ran to them, and soon the entire family had gathered to welcome them back. Ceridwen had Rodiaud in her arms, and the beaming smiles of both fell upon father and son.

It was late afternoon, and after the horses were unpacked and tended to the men went to the leathern bags the animals had carried. Her father handed Eirian her new comb, with its closely spaced and perfect teeth. It was so smooth to the touch and so pretty to the eye that she gave a little shriek of happiness.

Her mother took full pleasure in her daughter's delight. "Your father has a gift for selecting such things," she said. She looked up at Sidroc, remembering the comb he had bought her on their first full day here.

"And this one is for you," Hrald said with a grin, handing Yrling the black and brown one he had bought for him. Hrald took good care of his own hair, keeping it clean and combed even when travelling. "Every captain of a drekar should have pride in himself."

Yrling spluttered, and then laughed. He put it to use right away, combing through the wind-blown strands. The tar-splotched places he had cut away were beginning to grow out, making him look less like an ill-shorn sheep. Sidroc, watching this, remembered the cousin he had lately been speaking of. Toki took great care of his own long yellow hair, enough so that the other men teased him. He did not think Yrling would share that vanity.

The men gave themselves a wash before coming into the hall. Sidroc gestured Hrald and Ceridwen into the treasure room; he wanted to tell her their news first, and alone with he who had shared the discovery with him. The twins would know soon enough.

Rodiaud, set upon the floor, went at once to her favourite spot, the plush weaving from the Idrisid ship. She plopped down upon it, and sang a little song to herself as her fingers traced the delicate designs woven therein.

Sidroc looked to his wife. There was no way to say it but to get it all out at once, and fill in the story later.

"My father lives. He is here, on the western coast, wed to a woman he met when he was twenty. When the weather warms, I will go and fetch them, bring them for a stay here, that you might meet them, and they know you, and our young."

Ceridwen raised her hand to her mouth. Hrald had been nodding his head to his father's words, and now spoke.

"We look like him," he said, and could not help his grin.

The Moon was climbing again to its fullest orb, and the days Hrald could spend on Gotland dwindling. He tried to wring the most from every hour, and did so in the most tranquil of pursuits. He spent time with Tindr at the workbench in the stable, helping him repair a worn harness, and craft a bridle from tanned leather, with buckles and fittings Tindr had forged himself at the small forge. Together they fletched new arrows Tindr made, using segments of the stiff grey goose feathers from Tyrsborg's gaggle.

He and Tindr took long walks in the forest, sometimes joined by young Juoksa, who could move as stealthily as his father, and be just as alert at picking out the trails of the long-eared hares, trackways of deer, and the best places to set snares for small animals. They did no hunting; it was Spring, and Hrald had, just now, no taste for the taking of life. Tindr's quietness soothed him. It was not the hunter's lack of speech, but his inner stillness that Hrald recognised, and valued. He remembered as a boy telling his father that he wished to stay here, and be like Tindr. He knew then that he could not, and he understood better now why he wanted this.

Meeting his grandsire was the most meaningful part of the trip, that for which he was most grateful. He had seen his father in the presence of his own sire, a man who meant so much that he had named Hrald for him. Both men had left sons behind at young ages. Both had suffered from doing so, as had the sons. Through their actions the three men, now united, shared a bond beyond expression. It restored something to Hrald, the sense of some circle of connection that had felt snapped with his sister's death.

A few days before Hrald was to sail, his father waved him over to the fowl house.

"Choose a cockerel," Sidroc invited. There were several young ones, most bound for the pot sooner or later, and Hrald thought he was being asked to choose one for supper.

"That one," Hrald pointed, "with the speckled breast."

Sidroc gave a nod of satisfaction. He wanted to make Offering for his son's safe passage back to Lindisse.

"I will sacrifice him to Freyr on the morning you sail."

Some nights were already warm enough to take their meal outside. That night was one of them, and they had supped in a gathering dusk, the cooking fire growing brighter as the sky darkened. A single cresset in the middle of the table cast its own cheering yellow light. After Helga and Gunnvor cleared away, Sidroc and Ceridwen remained at table with their children. Rodiaud sat on her mother's lap, gnawing on a crust of bread held tight in her fist, as a shower of damp crumbs fell upon her mother's gown. Hrald's soon departure hung over them, which though none wished to admit, loomed nearer whether spoken of or not. His father broached the subject.

"In three ships," Sidroc judged, "your sailing should be a smooth one. It would take a fleet of raiders to attempt your capture."

Ceridwen and Eirian turned their eyes to him. Hrald had avoided capture on the way out by having two ships, and the third they had won gave him a small fleet with which to sail back to Anglia.

Yrling looked instead to his big brother.

"Hrald," he said, in full earnest. "Take me with you."

His parents' throats opened in a sound of dissent, but Hrald looked back at him with like gravity. It was just what Bork had asked, when he left Four Stones.

"Take me with you, Hrald," Yrling pleaded. "I want to see Four Stones."

"Nai –" began his father. His younger boy turned to him with his challenge.

"You just said there was no danger." Yrling had his right hand on the hilt of his new knife, as if to show how prepared he was.

The boy's father had spoken too soon, and Yrling with his native quickness had seized on his words.

"Less danger. Not none," Sidroc returned.

"Sea storms," his mother said. She could barely get the words out. It was impossible he go; how had he even taken it into his head, she wondered. His father and she would not permit it. Raiders or not, the risks of the sea were always there. Ship-wreck was the Fate of many a voyager.

Yrling would not give up. He looked back at his brother. "How old were you when you came here, with Ceric?"

It was a question that brought a moment of silence to all at the table. Still, Hrald must answer.

"Nine. Ceric had eleven years."

"I have twelve years," Yrling answered. There was triumph in the fact, but not his tone. In his voice and face was only the ardency of his desire.

Ceridwen looked to Sidroc, whose eyes were fixed on their son. She lowered her chin to the curls on Rodiaud's head, and closed her eyes. She recalled travelling so long ago with Gyric, and yearning to go with him to see the hall and seas of Kilton. She was not much older than her son when she held that hope. How could she refuse him, as he pleaded for the chance to see his own birthright.

The boy's next words said as much. Yrling stared his father in the eye.

"It was yours, father. Now it is Hrald's. Let me go with him."

Sidroc drew breath. He looked to the boy's mother. Beyond the concern in her face was something more. She met his gaze in a way that acknowledged the path their son was being called to take.

Sidroc turned to Hrald. Now it must be his decision, his responsibility to take on.

Hrald looked to his brother. "You will miss Gotland," he began. "But you will like Four Stones."

Yrling gave a whoop of joy.

They had not finished sharing their first few words of hope and caution when Eirian jumped up from the bench.

"I will go, too!" she claimed.

Even her father was quick in his refusal.

"Nai," he answered. "It is not safe." It was so decided a tone that Eirian looked up at him, stunned.

"Why is it less safe for me, than Yrling? We are the same age."

"It is less safe," he answered. "You cannot go."

If they were boarded and seized, Yrling risked outright death or thralldom. But Eirian – there was no richer human prize than a young maiden, and one as comely as was his daughter would be highly sought. Young as she was, she would be taken by the war-chief for his own pleasure, or set aside for the better of the slave markets, where an untouched woman would bring the highest possible price. His shield-maiden knew all this; their daughter could not. It was something they would tell her about, but not yet.

"For many reasons," her mother added, none of which she seemed ready to share.

"I want to go!"

Ceridwen took a deep breath. It seemed unjust, she knew it; and left unanswered the question of why she would risk one child, and not the other. All she could do was implore the girl. "Do not leave me, Eirian," she asked, as she fought against the misting of her eyes. "And do not leave Rodiaud." Do not leave Gotland, her heart added.

Rodiaud was looking at her older sister, and screwing up her little face. Her lower lip trembled. It looked like tears might spring into her wide eyes.

"Eww-yan," she lisped, the best she could make of her sister's name. "No go, Eww-yan. No go." She reached her bread-filled hand out to her.

Eirian must concede, but not without securing some future boon.

"When I am older?"

"Perhaps," her mother granted. "But now we need you here, my bright one."

It was the meaning of her name, and whenever her mother called Eirian this, it seemed a special entreaty, hard for the girl to refuse.

Even though she hung her head, she gave a nod.

※※※※※※※※※※

On the morrow Ceridwen took up the letter she had written to Ælfwyn. Using her bird-shaped scissors she snipped out the thread she had used to sew the linen sleeve shut, and unrolled and weighted the parchment. She must add to her text.

Now I burden and entrust you with our son, Yrling. He knows full well that Hrald and Ceric were younger than he when they made the voyage here, and as Hrald sails back well-defended in three ships, we could not forbid the boy his desire to see Four Stones. Yrling needs a firm hand which I hope will not demand too much of either you or Hrald. He has been raised in the ways of the Old Gods, but is quick to question all. Instruct him as you see fit in the faith of the Christians; it may do him good. His father has taught him much of justice, but of mercy there is more to tell.

He is a hard worker, and truthful, but his lust for adventure is great. I think you may see his namesake in him, as I do. Remind him that we will yearn for his return.

YOUR LOVING CERIDWEN

⁂

The three ships were being laden with provisions and water. Ceridwen gathered and re-gathered all that Yrling might find needful, not only for the journey, but for his life ahead at Four Stones. The boy did not wish to take his wax tablet; his mother pressed him to do so, finally laying it in the bottom of one of his packs so he might not find it before he took ship. Both Hrald and Yrling made their fare-wells to Tindr and his family. Yrling had become a good bow-man under the hunter's tutelage, and the embrace he gave the hunter was heartfelt. To Juoksa he promised that when he returned, he could serve as his second on Dauðadagr when they went raiding together. Young Juoksa looked puzzled, but unafraid to let his sadness at his older friend's going show in his warm embrace.

The day before Hrald would sail, he was alone in the hall with his father. The nearer his departure grew, the less they could speak to each other of it. But Sidroc's eye fell upon his son's sword, hanging there by the door. Hrald had worn it only on the journey to Paviken. It was symbol of everything awaiting the young Jarl in Lindisse.

"Are you ready?" he asked him.

Hrald gave a short laugh.

"I will answer that the way I think you would. It does not matter if I feel ready. I am the Jarl of Four Stones. Many depend on me. As they did, for so long, on you."

Sidroc could say nothing to this, just nod his approval. He felt Hrald knew more of duty than many men twice his age.

In the morning, just as the sky began to lighten, Hrald rode with his father down the trading road, out to the wooden statue of Freyr. The cockerel had been dropped in a sack, with only its head sticking out, and was tied to Sidroc's saddle ring. Yrling was with them as well; it was a final ride on his horse, and a chance for him to ask for the God's blessing on his adventure.

No stall or workshop was yet opened, and no one was about. They reached the painted statue, now seeming no hue but brown in the little light. They got off their horses, and Sidroc drew the bird out, powerful wings flapping against his hands. Hrald was Christian, and could take no part in the Offering, yet to honour his father and his beliefs wished to witness. Sidroc drew his seax and crouched down, holding the bird by the legs, and pressing it to the soil.

"Freyr! You and your sister have made this island a favoured home to us. All increase is in your power, and every dealing which profits man and beast. You welcomed my older son twice, brought him safely to us. Now both sons sail from here. We give you this bird that you might smile upon their journey. May their ships be as your own, which knows only favourable winds."

Sidroc looked to Yrling, who came forth and placed his hand over his father's on the hilt. With one stroke the speckled breast was pierced. The wings flapped once, and then were stilled.

Sidroc lifted the body to one of the upright Offering poles behind the God, and placed it on the small platform there.

"A fulmar or gull may eat of it, and its kin a sea away end up guiding you safely to land," he noted.

They rode back. The tide would turn just after full Sun-rise. The early hour mattered not; Rannveig was about, calling the men up to her brew-house that they might roll down her parting gift to them, a cask of ale. A full month of the thirsty crews' custom had fattened her silver store as much as any long Summer of normal trade would.

The few packs of Hrald, and the many of Yrling, were carried on. Hrald would take with him Ceridwen's letter to his mother, and also a length of cobalt blue silk as gift for her. Sidroc had traded for it, but she could think of no higher end for its sumptuous beauty than to adorn Ælfwyn, with her blue eyes. As for Yrling, she sent with him all his clothes, that the hall might not be burdened with outfitting him, Summer or Winter.

The water was changing from near-black to deep blue as the Sun struck it. The dawn rose up, pink and lilac, staining also the ripples of the sea with those hues. Eirian kissed her brothers, and began to cry. She hugged herself, both against the morning chill, and to give herself the embraces they no longer could.

Gunnvor and Helga had come down, and Helga took Rodiaud while Ceridwen made her parting with first Hrald, and then her son. Few words came; these had already been said. She spoke with the kiss of blessing she gave to each.

Aboard the ships the men were making final preparation. All were onboard, awaiting the two that lingered. The men had oars in hand, ready to push away and oar out to hoist their sail in the quickening wind. Aszur whistled out to Hrald. It was time to step from pier to ship, to transit from land to sea. They did so, and took up position next to Aszur at the steering-oar on the lead ship. The captain grinned at them, and at those seeing them off, a glint of gold flashing from his mouth. Yrling had one hand on the hilt of his knife, and the other atop the steering-oar.

The spreading rays of the sun also struck the hull of Dauðadagr hauled up on the pebbles. Yrling narrowed his eyes at it, and looked to his father.

"Take care of my ship for me. I will be back for her, fronting five more!"

Ceridwen spent much of that night weeping. Lying there in Sidroc's arms she could give vent to the numerous sorrows and concerns weighing upon her heart. The past few days had been full ones, preparing Yrling for his journey, and Hrald too. She had attended fully to these tasks. At Hrald's arrival she had wept from the bottom of her soul at his initial telling of the story of his sister and Ceric. She had tried then to put her tears away, so that she might bolster and console Hrald in his own affliction.

Now Hrald, whom she dearly loved, both for his mother's sake and for his own, was gone, taking with him her son by Sidroc. The boundless love she knew for Yrling was matched by growing concern for him. Eirian's sudden insistence that she go as well was a further pang. No loving mother wished her children to flee their home, not when they were so very young.

Above all these piercing griefs was the larger one, of Ashild's death, and at the hand of her son who cherished her. In their final act together he took her truly to wife with his ring and troth. In their brief lives, and through Ashild's grievously wrought death, they were united in ways unfathomable. It was more bitter, and more sublime, than anything she had heard in the Saga tales of tragic heroes. It struck deeply to her core, as it would to any listener. With cruel poignancy had Fate woven the life of Ashild.

Sidroc could say little on this, and knew enough at this point not to stifle a woman's tears. He kept his arm about her while she wept, and let the warmth of his presence lend what comfort it could. She slept at last, and he did as well.

In the morning when they awoke he spoke again of his father. He told of his eagerness to soon bring the elder Hrald and Stenhild to Tyrsborg for a visit. It set her thoughts on a new course, a happier one in the near future, as they planned for this.

The table without Hrald and Yrling felt empty indeed, but Ceridwen tried to meet it with good cheer. Rodiaud, forgetting or not understanding that she had seen the two sail off the morning before, seemed to look for them, as she did at supper last night.

After the table was cleared Sidroc went out, a leathern pack in hand. Ceridwen set about her daily tasks. She stood before her loom, which had been neglected in the past few days. It held a half-woven length of green-tinted wool, destined to become a warm Winter gown for Eirian. The girl was there herself, spindle in hand, working with the same green-tinted wool roving which she and her mother had dyed in the kitchen yard with leaves of dyer's-broom.

Eirian was a better spinner than Ceridwen had been at her age, and her mother knew pleasure in telling her this. Her daughter had patience, and also took a pride in her drawn thread that Ceridwen as a girl never could find. She was always proud when her mother would claim that they had made any garment together. She stood now, drawing the green yarn through her slender fingers as the spindle whirled almost to the floor. Rodiaud squatted at her feet, pulling apart a puff of the fluffy roving her sister had given her.

Sidroc came back to the three of them and looked at his wife. "We will take a ride," he told her.

"A ride?"

He smiled, and nodded. "The two of us. Your mare is already saddled."

They all had tasks to complete; Hrald's visit had taken them away from certain chores which now must be undertaken. But he kept looking at her.

"Come," he invited.

Eirian was looking at them both, and about to ask that she might come too; her mother knew this. Ceridwen spoke first.

"You may go to Šeará, so that Rodiaud may play with Jaské."

Eirian was more than gladdened at this. The Sámi woman was teaching her how to make the coloured trim of folded and shaped ribbands which adorned her skin clothes. Eirian was using this to trim the hem of one of her own gowns, and was so far pleased with the result. She put her spindle back in the roving basket and ran to her alcove to get the gown.

Ceridwen took her lighter mantle from the peg by the door. The Sun was strong enough that she might not need even this, if where they rode was not too windy. She stepped out and watched the two girls as they made their way down the forest path to the round house where Tindr and Šeará lived. Rodiaud was laughing and running ahead of her big sister.

Sidroc was just cinching the girth of his saddle on his black stallion. Her dun mare stood ready for her, shaking her dark mane in eagerness to be off. Sidroc had the leathern bag he had taken earlier, and now tied it to one of his saddle rings. He stepped into the stable and returned with two hempen ropes as well, as if he expected to stake their horses at their destination. More than this she could not know.

They began by taking the forest track the girls had. The trees over their heads were bursting into full leaf, and the birds that darted between them were busy with gathering food for their fledging broods. The warmth was almost Summer-like, and the sky when they glimpsed it through the trees nearly the same blue. It mattered not the nights were still chilly. This morning held every promise of blossom becoming fruit.

They left the track not far after they passed Tindr's memory stone. Their path led them over ground still oozing from the wet of long-melted snow and more recent Spring rains. As the soil dried they climbed a slight rise, to a broad and unfrequented meadow land. Ceridwen had not been here before, and looked at all with interest. Even though they now could ride side by side, she would not ask, as it was clear their goal was a surprise.

They rode some little way, the Sun climbing steadily and warming their backs as it did. They entered a small wood, almost all of birch, its white curling bark shimmering in the strong light. She lifted her chin and looked up, delighting in the verdant green of the fresh leaves over her head.

Then they were there. Passing through the birches her eyes were filled by what lay before them, a lake, its water a deeper blue for the Sun which shone upon it. It was not large, and had the marshy growth about its edges suggesting that if they flourished it one day might become a mere. But now, beyond the thin margin of green spear-like sedge was open and clear water.

Sidroc swung off his horse, and with no mounting block to aid her, moved to help her down off her own. Something about the way he grasped her as he let her down brought to her mind the way he had taken her by the waist the first day they arrived at Four Stones, when he had swung first Ælfwyn and then her from their waggon-board.

She saw they meant to stay, as he took the hempen line from his saddle, and looping neck ties for their horses, walked them to the nearest birches and tied them where they might browse.

She watched him as he did this, and watched as he walked back with the saddle bag in his hand. He took a woollen blanket from the pack. It was one of the old blankets from their bed, the first she had woven for them, and a warm memory of her attempts to make the hall fully their home. He lofted it in the air, and let it spread upon the grass as if they might sit and take refreshment. But she had not seen him with Gunnvor, packing food to enjoy a meal in this pretty place. He had as well a few linen towels, which he let fall upon the blanket.

Finally he spoke. It was hard to read his face; he looked almost grave as he stood before her.

"When you and I first sighted the coast of this island, I made promises. One I felt forced to break, and was forgiven by the Gods, and by you. The rest I think I have kept. One vow only remains unfulfilled. And today I will make good on that promise."

She tried to smile, but knew her puzzlement must show on her face.

Still looking at her he unbuckled the belt that held his seax, and let it drop. Then he pulled off his tunic and stood before her, bare-chested. The outline of the blue dragon on his chest was faint indeed, but she could still trace it with her eyes, as she had done many times with her finger.

He smiled. "I promised to teach you to swim in warm water. I have not done so. All promises are heard by the Gods. I will not miss a day with you in Asgard because I failed to fulfill this one.

"Today I will teach you how to swim."

Her intake of breath was near to a gasp. She too remembered their approach to Gotland in that tiny boat, and the promises he made to her – to keep her warm with furs, that he would earn his silver through trade and not his blade, and that, yes, he would teach her to swim so she might overcome her fear of water. Almost without knowing it she was shaking her head.

"The water is shallow, it will be warm," he assured her. "I will be holding you the whole time. But as you know, water makes clothing heavy."

Here he dropped on one knee before her. He unfastened the toggle on one of her shoes, then on the next, and pulled them off. He reached up her skirts to her knees, untied the strip of cloth tying each of her stockings on, and rolled them down and off.

He stood, and took her in his arms. "I can not –" she began, a protest smothered by his lips. His mouth met her own, gently at first, and then with growing pressure. Her arms rose up about his bare back, she could not help it. He tasted her, nibbling at her lips, and then with the flicking of his tongue. He did not stop, his lips insistent on hers, his tongue demanding more. It had been long since they had kissed thus, and to do so now under the sky and with his bare chest pressed against her – she could not recall such a time.

His hands ran down her back, gathering up fistfuls of gown and shift, pulling them up until his hands met the flesh beneath. He cupped his hands on the bare skin of her rump and pressed her to his loins.

He kissed her again, and smiled down as he loosed her gown. Her skirts fell back again to her ankles. His hands found the knot of her head wrap, untied it and let it fall, freeing her hair of chestnut gold. Once again he dropped to his knee. There at her feet he took the hems of her gowns in both hands, and began to stand, pulling them over her head. "You will swim best if you are naked," he murmured. Now she would wear nothing but the silver disc bracelet upon her wrist.

She stood, as he wanted her, naked in his arms.

He brought his mouth close to her ear and whispered his command. "First I will show you on the blanket how to move your body when you are in the water."

Here Ends Book Eight of
The Circle of Ceridwen Saga

THE WHEEL
OF THE YEAR

Candlemas – 2 February

St Gregory's Day – 12 March

St Cuthbert's Day – The Spring Equinox, about 21 March

St Elgiva's Day – 18 May

High Summer or Mid-Summer Day – 24 June

Sts Peter and Paul – 29 June

Hlafmesse (Lammas) – 1 August

St Mary's Day – 15 August

St Matthews' Day – The Fall Equinox,
about 21 September

All Saints – 1 November

The month of Blót – November; the time of Offering

Martinmas (St Martin's) – 11 November

Yuletide – 25 December to Twelfthnight – 6 January

Winter's Nights – the Norse end of the year rituals,
ruled by women, marked by feasting and ceremony

ANGLO-SAXON PLACE NAMES,
WITH MODERN EQUIVALENTS

Æscesdun = Ashdown

Æthelinga = Athelney

Apulder = Appledore

Basingas = Basing

Beamfleot = Benfleet

Beardan = Bardney

Bearruescir = Berkshire

Bryeg = Bridgenorth

Buttingtun = Buttington

Caeginesham = Keynsham

Cippenham = Chippenham

Cirenceaster = Cirencester

Colneceastre = Colchester

Cruland = Croyland

Defenas = Devon

Englafeld = Englefield

Ethandun = Edington

Exanceaster = Exeter

Fearnhamme = Farnham

Fullanham = Fulham

Geornaham = Irnham

Glastunburh = Glastonbury

Hamtunscir = Hampshire

Headleage = Hadleigh

Hreopedun = Repton

Iglea = Leigh upon Mendip

Jorvik (Danish name for Eoforwic) = York

Legaceaster = Chester

Limenemutha = Lymington in Hampshire

Lindisse = Lindsey

Lundenwic = London

Meredune = Marton

Meresig = Mersea

Middeltun = Milton

Readingas = Reading

River Lyge = River Lea

Sceaftesburh = Shaftesbury

Snotingaham = Nottingham

Sumorsaet = Somerset

Swanawic = Swanage

Turcesig = Torksey

Wedmor = Wedmore

Welingaford = Wallingford

Witanceaster (where the Witan, the
King's advisors, met) = Winchester

Frankland = France

Haithabu = Hedeby

Norse Place Names:

Aros = Aarhus, Denmark

Laaland = the island of Lolland, Denmark

Land of the Svear = Sweden

GLOSSARY OF TERMS

Asgard: Heavenly realm of the Gods.

brewster: the female form of brewer (and, interestingly enough, the female form of baker is baxter . . . so many common names are rooted in professions and trades . . .).

browis: a cereal-based stew, often made with fowl or pork.

chaff: the husks of grain after being separated from the usable kernel.

ceorl: ("churl") a free man ranking directly below a thegn, able to bear arms, own property, and improve his rank.

cottar: free agricultural worker; in later eras, a peasant.

cresset: stone, bronze, or iron lamp fitted with a wick that burnt oil.

drekar: "dragon boat," a war-ship of the Danes.

ealdorman: a nobleman with jurisdiction over given lands; the rank was generally appointed by the King and not necessarily inherited from generation to generation. The modern derivative *alderman* in no way conveys the esteem and power of the Anglo-Saxon term.

fulltrúi: the Norse deity patron that one felt called to dedicate oneself to.

fylgja: a Norse guardian spirit, always female, unique to each family.

fyrd: the massed forces of Wessex, comprising thegns – professional soldiers – and ceorls, trained freemen.

hack silver: broken silver jewellery, coils of unworked silver bars, fragments of cast ingots and other silver parceled out by weight alone during trade.

hamingja: the Norse "luck-spirit" which each person is born with.

leech-book: compilation of healing recipes and practices for the treatment of human and animal illness and injury. Such books were a compendium of healing herbs and spiritual and magical practices. The *Leech Book of Bald*, recorded during Ælfred's reign by a monk named Bald, is a famed, and extant, example.

morgen-gyfu: literally, "morning-gift"; a gift given by a husband to his new wife the first morning they awake together.

rauk: the striking sea- and wind-formed limestone towers on the coast of Gotland.

seax: the angle-bladed dagger which gave its name to the Saxons; all freemen carried one.

scop: ("shope") a poet, saga-teller, or bard, responsible not only for entertainment but seen as a collective cultural historian. A talented scop would be greatly valued by his lord and receive land, gold and silver jewellery, costly clothing and other riches as his reward.

shingle beach: a pebbly, rather than sandy, beach.

skeggox: steel battle-axe favoured by the Danes.

skirrets: a sweet root vegetable similar to carrots, but cream-coloured, and having several fingers on each plant.

skogkatt: "forest cat"; the ancestor of the modern Norwegian Forest Cat, known for its large size, climbing ability, and thick and water-shedding coat.

strakes: overlapping wooden planks, running horizontally, making up a ship's hull.

symbel: a ceremonial high occasion for the Angle-Saxons, marked by the giving of gifts, making of oaths, swearing of fidelity, and (of course) drinking ale.

thegn: ("thane") a freeborn warrior-retainer of a lord; thegns were housed, fed and armed in exchange for complete fidelity to their sworn lord. Booty won in battle by a thegn was generally offered to their lord, and in return the lord was expected to bestow handsome gifts of arms, horses, arm-rings, and so on to his best champions.

Tyr: the God of war, law, and justice. He voluntarily forfeited his sword-hand to allow the Gods to deceive, and bind, the gigantic wolf Fenrir.

Tyr-hand: in this Saga, any left-handed person, named so in honour of Tyr's sacrifice.

Urd: the youngest of the three Norse Norns, determiners of men's destinies. Urd makes decision as to one's calling and station in life.

wadmal: the Norse name for the coarse and durable woven woollen fabric that was a chief export in the Viking age.

wergild: Literally, man-gold; the amount of money each man's life was valued at. The Laws of Æthelbert, a 7th century King of Kent, for example, valued the life of a nobleman at 300 shillings (equivalent to 300 oxen), and a ceorl was valued at 100 shillings. By Ælfred's time (reigned 871–899) a nobleman was held at 1200 shillings and a ceorl at 200.

NOTES

CHAPTER THE FIRST: A KING'S DAUGHTER

St Edmund. Once patron saint of England (later super-seded by St George), he is also patron saint of Kings, and interestingly enough for our times, of pandemics. The King of East Anglia was only twenty-eight years old when he was killed, 20th November in the year 870 (possibly 869). The town of Bury St Edmunds in Suffolk is named for him; and his remains may still reside somewhere on the grounds of the ruined abbey. Shortly after his death his legend began to grow, and eventually coinage was issued in East Anglia with the inscription "O holy king Edmund." The earliest of these may have in fact been struck by Danish King Guthrum, more evidence of Guthrum's own cultural assimilation. The massive Cuerdale Hoard (over 8,600 items, housed at the British Museum) unearthed in Lancashire in 1840 contained 1800 of these coins citing Edmund, evidence of how widespread their minting must have been. Edmund's cult grew following the *Life of St Edmund* compiled by the French monk, Abbo, a distin-guished intellectual who went on to become Abbot of Fleury. Abbo wrote of Edmund's death and subsequent miracles more than one hundred years after the young King's murder, when in residence at the monastery of

Ramsey during 985–987. Abbo was inspired perhaps by his memory of meeting an elderly warrior at the court of King Æthelstan (King Ælfred's grandson). The man had served as personal retainer (possibly even bearer of his war-banner, I like to think) to Edmund, and been with him on the day of his capture. In the Middle Ages the Shrine of St Edmund at Bury St Edmunds became one of the most famous and wealthiest of all pilgrimage places in England, with magnificent gifts presented in honour of the martyr. It was utterly pillaged and destroyed in 1539 during the Protestant Reformation, and the monks driven away. The abbey fell into ruins. Edmund's life continues to inspire, and some believe his holy prayer still protects the town named for him. It is a pity he is no longer regarded as the patron saint of England, for Edmund not only died a kingly death, but is wholly English, unlike the Cappadocian-Palestinian George. Edmund's feast day recalls the day of his death, November 20th.

CHAPTER THE SECOND: THE RICHES OF OUNDLE

Judith. The Old Testament tale of the heroic Judith has been preserved in Old English in a single, precious manuscript, known as Cotton Vitellius A xv. This unique manuscript, housed today in the British Museum, also contains our only copy of the epic *Beowulf.* Thus we find in a single folio a tale of two heroes, one female, one male, risking their lives to protect their people. It makes sense that in an age when physical daring was greatly valued, Judith's courage would be highly appealing to women of all classes.

Chapter the Eleventh: Ever Deeper

Ælfred's doubled forts along the River Lyge – the River Lea – was a good example of his tactical thinking. *The Anglo-Saxon Chronicle* for 895 records " . . . Then the following autumn the king encamped in the neighbourhood of the fortress while the corn was being reaped, so that the Danish men could not keep them back from the reaping. One day the king rode up along the river and looked to see where the river could be blocked, so that they would not be able to bring out their ships. This they proceeded to do: they made two forts on the two sides of the river, but when they had just begun that operation and had encamped thereby, the [Danish] host saw they could not bring out their ships. Thereupon they abandoned them and went across country . . . "

As we saw in Book Seven, *Wildswept*, in the capture of Haesten's wife, the *Chronicle* goes on to once again mention the wives of the invaders: " . . . The Danish men had placed their women in safety in East Anglia before they went out from that fort . . . " (G. N. Garmonsway translation, *The Anglo-Saxon Chronicle*, J. M. Dent & Sons, LTD)

Chapter the Eighteenth: To Gotland

Haesten. This famed Viking leader who wreaked so much havoc in Frankland and Angle-land vanishes from the annals of history after 894. No further mention is made of him in *The Anglo-Saxon Chronicle* nor any other surviving record. He was already old when he landed at Middeltun (Milton in Kent) fronting eighty ships in 892, and it is possible the rigours of his final campaign – in which he harried Wessex and Anglia and yet was ultimately unable to wrest control of either – finally took its toll.

Jephthah's daughter. From the Old Testament *Book Of Judges*. "And Jephthah came to Mizpeh unto his house, and behold, his daughter came out to meet him with timbrels and with dances; and she was his only child; beside her he had neither son nor daughter. And it came to pass that when he saw her, he rent his clothes, and said, Alas my daughter! Thou hast brought me very low, and thou art one of them that trouble me: for I have opened my mouth unto the Lord, and I cannot go back."

ACKNOWLEDGEMENTS

The writing of this novel felt akin to sailing on a ship undertaking a wrenching voyage. I stood in its prow, speechless, but pointing towards its Fated destination. Luckily I was never quite alone. I was companioned by two Wise Women who aided me to shores I could not describe. Beth Altchek was star-reader, encouraging me as to signs ahead. Libby Williams' steady hand on the steering-beam never lifted. Their unflagging interest and support did much to bring this vessel – and its creator – safely to land.

The list of First Readers for this novel was by design extremely small, and each and every one of them exceeded high expectations. For their service to this novel and to me I bear endless gratitude. Judy Boxer, Shani Goode, Krista Gore, Elaine MacDonald, Dianne McDonald, Diane T. Miller, Ellen Rudd, Linda Schultz, and Lorie Witt, my deepest appreciation for your taste, acuity, and passion. You truly embody the reasons *The Circle of Ceridwen Saga* continues, and thrives.

Janine Eitniear and Misi are Founder and Moderator respectively of The Circle of Ceridwen Discussion and Idea Group on Facebook. Their unstinting effort, loyalty, and creativity in that Group, as well as their ongoing service as First Readers, can be matched only by the affection I hope they know I bear for them.

ABOUT THE AUTHOR

Octavia Randolph has long been fascinated with the development, dominance, and decline of the Anglo-Saxon peoples. The path of her research has included disciplines as varied as the study of Anglo-Saxon and Norse runes, and learning to spin with a drop spindle. Her interests have led to extensive on-site research in England, Denmark, Sweden, and Gotland. In addition to the Circle Saga, she is the author of the novella *The Tale of Melkorka*, taken from the Icelandic Sagas; the novella *Ride*, a retelling of the story of Lady Godiva, first published in Narrative Magazine; and *Light, Descending*, a biographical novel about the great John Ruskin. She has been awarded Artistic Fellowships at the Ingmar Bergman Estate on Fårö, Sweden; MacDowell Colony; Ledig House International; and Byrdcliffe.

She answers all fan mail and loves to stay in touch with her readers. Join her mailing list and read more on Anglo-Saxon and Viking life at www.octavia.net. Follow her on Facebook at Octavia Randolph Author, and for exclusive access and content join the spirited members of The Circle of Ceridwen Saga Discussion and Idea Group on Facebook.

Made in the USA
Middletown, DE
23 August 2024

59620368R00338